VOODOO BUTTERFLY

The Voodoo Butterfly Series

Love, purpose, and the paranormal in New Orleans.

CAMILLE FAYE

SOUL MATE PUBLISHING

New York

VOODOO BUTTERFLY

Copyright©2014

CAMILLE FAYE

Cover Design by Niina Cord

This book is a work of fiction. The names, characters, places, and incidents are the products of the author's imagination or are used fictitiously. Any resemblance to actual events, business establishments, locales, or persons, living or dead, is entirely coincidental.

All rights reserved. No part of this publication may be reproduced, stored in a retrieval system, or transmitted in any form or by any means (electronic, mechanical, photocopying, recording, or otherwise) without the prior written permission of both the copyright owner and the publisher. The only exception is brief quotations in printed reviews.

The scanning, uploading, and distribution of this book via the Internet or via any other means without the permission of the publisher is illegal and punishable by law. Please purchase only authorized electronic editions, and do not participate in or encourage electronic piracy of copyrighted materials.

Your support of the author's rights is appreciated.

Published in the United States of America by
Soul Mate Publishing
P.O. Box 24
Macedon, New York, 14502

ISBN: 978-1-61935-839-3

ebook SBN: 978-1-61935-603-0

www.SoulMatePublishing.com

The publisher does not have any control over and does not assume any responsibility for author or third-party websites or their content.

To my Sudhagar.

You inspire me every day.

Acknowledgements

Many people contributed to making this dream come true. Special thanks to:

My husband, Sudhagar, who came all the way from Malaysia, attended my university, worked at the same restaurant with me, lived across the street from me, and then asked me out. God kept lining things up for us and thankfully we finally connected.

My two greatest creations, Xavier and Arianna. Thanks for the daily dance parties, nightly bedtime stories, and an eternal supply of snuggles and kisses.

My mom and dad who kissed every day when Dad got home from work. Mom, you taught me to love reading; thanks for letting me stay up late to finish the chapter. Dad, you have a knack with words; thanks for the little notes scattered across my life.

My siblings, Celeste, Justin, and Miranda. We survived growing up in a haunted house and now I have lots of paranormal stories to tell. Special thanks to Miranda for being the talented, creative, and technologically-advanced sister who built me a website that rocks. I heart you.

My Malaysian family members, Amah, Ayah, Rajesh, Vijay, Nithiya, Seetha, Darshana, and Manoj, whose relationships and customs inspired many parts of this novel. Thanks for the love and support from the other side of the world.

My editor, Deborah Gilbert, for providing insightful feedback that made the story so much better.

My Lit Ladies, Margo Dill, Brandi Schmidt, Grace Malinee, Sarah Whitney, and Tricia Sanders, for your constructive critiques and for being my cheerleaders on this writing journey.

My beta readers, Donna Kelly, Casey Hassell, Sharon Karl, Mary Voss, Barbara Hodges, Stephanie Krueger, and Tracy Bono. I couldn't have done it without you!

My home support team, including Karla Frederick and Elizabeth Booth, who watched over my kiddos when I needed time to write.

My writing groups, Saturday Writers, Joplin Writers Guild, Missouri Writers' Guild, and Ozarks Writers League, where I gained an education about writing and publishing.

My peeps on Facebook, who have cheered me on thus far and those who will keep rooting for me as I walk this crazy, fun, and fulfilling path.

And finally, I'm thankful to all the people who will find and enjoy my book.

Chapter 1
Tale of Two Funerals

When I was twenty, I lost my mother. She'd died in my arms of a heart attack in our tiny bathroom in our tiny house in Saint Louis. Even though I lived with the woman for two decades, I really didn't know her. At. All. But I'd known that for a long time.

When I was a little girl, I had found a cigar box at the back of her closet that contained: a faded photo of a woman in a shawl; a corncob pipe; a blank postcard from New Orleans; one prayer card to Saint Michael; a stack of unsigned love letters addressed to my mother tied in ribbon; a monarch butterfly preserved in a small case; and—the strangest item—a glass eye wrapped in black muslin. When I finally got up the courage to ask her about the box of secrets, she told me, "That's none of your business."

I'd brought the box with me to the funeral home, hoping someone would show up and explain it. Explain to me what the items meant. Explain to me who my mother was and unwrap all of her secrets just as easily as I untied the ribbon around the love letters . . . with one gentle tug. But no one came to the visitation. No one at all. I just sat there with the box on my lap, waiting, and her words pounded like a relentless wave: *That's none of your business.*

Well, actually, I thought, *that's exactly my business.* Since my wonderful mother left me alone, not even giving me a hint about the rest of my family (like who they were, where they were from, what they did, if any were still living), I'd have to figure it out all by myself. Like always.

"Lost," I whispered, afraid of the funeral home's lonely echo. I clung to the box like it was a life preserver as the tidal wave of my emotions hit.

Five Years Later

At twenty-five, I lost my grandmother Seraphina. Mom had never told me that her mother was still living, but according to the last will and testament I received in the mail two days ago, I was the inheritor of the family's voodoo shop. In New Orleans. So I'd packed myself up and boarded my first flight for my very first trip ever outside of my hometown of Saint Louis.

Now that I'd made it to New Orleans, I was searching for—of all places—Saint Louis Cathedral in the French Quarter. Ironic that Saint Louis was where I came from and where I was headed to.

As I picked my way through New Orleans' foreign streets, I checked my watch for the eighty-seventh time, thinking there's probably a special circle of Hell for people late to their grandmother's funeral.

I quickened my pace. Whispers of fear slithered through me as reality settled in. I was lost. I tried the next street. Another dead end. I broke into a run. Tears stung my eyes as I remembered words like "single woman" and "statistic" from the morning paper which covered New Orleans' recent crime wave. I gritted my teeth and stopped, straining to listen. The bells of Saint Louis Cathedral counted down.

There! I hoped my ears weren't playing tricks. *Nope, that's people.* I raced toward their voices. Turning a corner, I finally saw dozens of people one block ahead. A new noise layered itself on top of the crowd's babbling and the bell's tolling, a sound like millions of paper pamphlets falling from the sky.

Several people ran toward me and I slowed my pace, my knees wobbling from the rush of worry and adrenaline.

I wondered what was going on up ahead because, nearing the busy street, I noticed people with hands over mouths and fingers pointed to the sky. Between the row houses that loomed over me, I glimpsed an orange cloud descending upon the city. I squinted.

"Is that . . .?" I asked under my breath.

"Yeah," a tourist with a camera replied. "They just came outta nowhere."

Squinting again, I tried to make sense of something that defied logic. Something . . . not natural.

The man lifted his camera to his eye and the shutter click-clicked to capture the magic.

Millions of monarch butterflies rushed down the street like a tangerine river. A dragonfly alighted on the guy's camera lens before joining the butterflies. The bell's final ring mellowed into silence, the plague of insects growing thicker. That final toll meant the funeral was already starting and I had to get there. Since I never actually got to meet my grandmother, this moment would be my one chance to meet a large number of people who all knew her. It was the best way to get to know her in a quick amount of time. I would not give up. Pulling my waist-length, auburn tresses into a quick ponytail and raising my arm above my glasses like a shield, I jumped into the cloud of insects.

They crawled all over me. On my skin. In my hair. I swatted. Scratched. Ran.

Peeking under my arm so that I didn't trip, I glimpsed a man in a business suit running alongside me before retreating into a nearby building. Then I nearly slammed into a balcony support beam, sidestepping it at the last minute.

"You okay?" a woman shouted down from the balcony. I noticed her teenage kids were armed with cell phone cameras. Giving her a quick wave, I sprinted forward.

My heart thumped. My eyes watered. My breath stopped, then started. The bugs nearly flew into my mouth as I gulped short bursts of air. Drowning in the insects now—they thickened as I got closer to where I needed to be—I jumped into a niche for a moment of relief. My hands shook as I inspected the welts and scratches on my bare arms. People ran by with newspaper helmets and umbrella shields.

Protection. That's what I need. I threw my hands up, air escaping my mouth in a laugh-cry. *Oh my God, I made the worst mistake, and now I'm not even gonna make it to this damn funeral.*

Something flew down my shirt and I did a jig to shake it out.

A woman chuckled from a nearby doorway.

Shielding my eyes with cupped hands, I could barely make out her face.

"Don't you know who died, child?" She shouted with amusement in her tone, as if that explained this whole crazy phenomenon.

Wiping the tears from my eyes, I yelled back, "My grandmother, I think."

A couple of police cars raced toward the cathedral, sirens blaring.

"I'm late," I shouted. "And now this." I waved my hands to indicate the end-of-days scene unfolding before us.

"Here, *ma petite*." She walked over to me and not one bug touched her. Not a single one. "Take this or you'll never make it." She slid her shawl off and wrapped it around me. Then she placed her heavy hands on my shoulders and gazed into my eyes, before glancing across the street.

My eyes followed hers to a shop with bright blue shutters.

"God bless you, honey. Now hurry up," she said before turning her eyes to where the swarm flew.

Draping the shawl over my head, I shouted a thank you over my shoulder, leaving the woman framed in her doorway. Wrapping the long fabric around my arms and torso, I ran through the plague, feeling protected by the soft shawl that smelled, vaguely, of pipe tobacco.

As I entered Jackson Square, a little bird of a girl fell over from the force of the wind. I scooped the toddler up. A woman with wild eyes forced her way through the crowd and the girl shouted, "Mommy!" I handed the tiny girl into the safe arms of her mama and the two retreated into a nearby store.

Raising my eyes to the sky, I saw the winged creatures swirling overhead like a growing hurricane; the mass of them actually churned the air making me feel as if I was inside a swirling cauldron filled with thick, steaming stew. Clouds spun toward this supernatural force, unable to escape the eye of this storm brewing in the heart of the city. Lightning illuminated the freakish scene as the clouds leaked, threatening to rip open.

"What in the hell?" I asked no one in particular.

"You mean Heaven? Because I think an angel has come to save us." Seeming to materialize from thin air, a man with a slick, dark ponytail and a gold watch the size of New Jersey held his hand out to me. "I'm Nico. Nice to meet you, sweetie."

I shook his hand out of courtesy, but he smelled like garlic and smiled like a used car salesman. Nico held my hand for a socially unacceptable amount of time and I literally had to wriggle loose from his grasp.

Just then, the rain clouds burst open, and I turned to run into the shelter of the cathedral and saw that it, too, was swarmed. Monarch butterflies crawled over every square inch of the building's exterior, making the church come alive. The building twisted and turned with the movement of muscles and joints underneath a skin of orange and black iridescent wings.

"Hey!" a burly guy, shouldering a news camera, shouted at me. "You're blocking my shot."

People pushed past me to get out of the storm and it seemed that the butterflies were trying to move within, too. My adrenaline hammered me one more time and I almost decided to run. All the way back to Saint Louis. Instead, I surrendered to the push of the crowd, which forced me into the mouth of the living building.

I hadn't stepped foot in a church since my mother's funeral. Instantly, my hatred for her bubbled to the surface. Immediately followed by guilt. Then sadness pinned my heart to my chest. Taking a deep breath, I searched for a place to sit and saw hundreds of people jammed into pews and standing along the walls. I didn't know a single one.

Why am I here? I thought for the thousandth time. *I didn't even know this woman, even if she was my grandmother.*

As I scanned the room, I saw emotion flow and break like waves across the bereaved faces. Confusion. Shock. Fear. All while the butterflies flitted around us, some even alighting peacefully on the casket.

At least this is better than the ten plagues of Egypt going on outside.

Mass had already started, so an usher led me to some standing room up front, between the casket and rows of lit votives. After drying my glasses on the shawl, I glanced across the hundreds of holy candles flickering in tall clear jars, the wax hovering at different levels depending on when the penitent lit it. Each light represented a person's hope. Each light yearned to shine bright enough to get God's attention. I stared at the dancing flames not knowing if I believed that God could come to the rescue. Not anymore.

Anger choked me. She told me that her mother had died before I was born. Flat. Out. Lie. That was what my mother had always been. A liar.

I shook my head and, with stupid faith and a flicker of hope, grabbed some money from my pocket. Shoving my offering into the candle collection box and using the flame from another person's prayer, I lit the long matchstick, transferring the fire to my candle and my wish. As the wick caught fire, I thought about what I wanted. Answers about my family, a job would be great, and a shot at a decent, loving relationship.

Turning back toward the casket, I pulled the worn picture from my pocket, the one from the cigar box. The only thing identifying the woman in the picture was the name *Mother* scrawled across the back in *my* mother's handwriting. I studied the features of this woman who was a mystery to me and yet had the potential to be a huge part of me. She wore her mahogany hair in short curls framing her heart-shaped face. Now I knew that her glowing caramel skin, the same as my mother's, came from the mixing of cultures here in New Orleans: French, Spanish, African, and Native American. I glanced at the skin on the back of my hand, a shade or two lighter than theirs but with the same olive undertones.

And her violet eyes, the same rare shade as mine, danced with spirit and wanted to tell me about my family. I rubbed my thumb lightly over her face. She stood tall and proud with her hands on her hips and a red and gold shawl draped over her curvy frame. I looked closer at the picture and then down at the fabric wrapped around me.

The same shawl.

Goosebumps skittered up my arms like lightning. My immediate urge was to throw off the wrap, but synthetic fibers and votive candles don't mix. *There's definitely a special circle of Hell for people who set cathedrals on fire.*

Instead, I hugged the shawl and, strangely enough, felt comforted by it. What was the likelihood that this was actually the same exact shawl anyway?

All I knew was that two days ago, I'd received a package addressed to Marie Papillon. My mother's name was Marie Nouveau, but I opened it anyway because my mother never spoke of her past. The envelope contained the copy of a will stating that *Seraphina Papillon bequeaths half of her estate to Marie Papillon or next of kin.*

Skimming to the final page, I discovered the main inheritance.

Seraphina's House of Voodoo
1000 Chartres Street
New Orleans, Louisiana 70116

So if my mother was this "Marie Papillon," did that mean I was "next of kin?" I dug through the envelope, trying to understand, when I found a scrap of paper that read:

Seraphina died.
She left you half of the family business.
The funeral is Nov. 2 at Saint Louis Cathedral.
—P.L.

I'd left the will in my hotel room, but the scrap of paper burned in my pocket. I was determined to find this P.L.

So, as of two days ago, I'd been processing. My mother may have lied to me for my entire life. She may have actually belonged to a voodoo family who owned a voodoo shop and for all I knew, she, herself, was a voodoo priestess. Now, as "next of kin," those responsibilities were mine. She'd even lied about her name, which meant she changed her name from Papillon (French for *butterfly*) to Nouveau (French for *new*). Meaning, my mother wanted a new life, not a life with her family in New Orleans.

Well, at least the Mardi Gras postcard from the cigar box makes sense now.

The priest, a balding man with apricot skin and the trace of an Irish accent in his voice, finished a prayer and his eyes settled on mine for a few seconds. He tilted his head and stared as if he knew me. Finally, his eyes left mine and he surveyed the congregation.

"Seraphina gave us a miracle today," he said.

Miracle's such a strong word. Strange phenomenon? I'll give you that.

The priest paused for a long moment, dabbing his eyes with a handkerchief. He sighed. "To tell you the truth, I had a long eulogy prepared, but look around. God is showing us a miracle right now. You have all been changed by Seraphina Papillon and that's why you're here. Seraphina changed me, too, opening my heart to a world where enchantment and spirituality combine to make a richer, deeper existence. I could not have the understanding of God that I now have if she had not shown me what she knows about Catholicism and about voodoo."

If my grandmother believed in voodoo, why the Catholic funeral?

Father interrupted my wonderings. "And so, brothers and sisters—and we really are family in our communion over the death of this loving matriarch—tell me about Seraphina. Tell me how she changed you."

A murmur arose as people shared stories with each other.

My eyes wandered across the aisle and met the gaze of a man in a sharp, black three-piece suit standing against the far wall. From where I was standing, I sensed a timelessness about him, a la Cary Grant, which matched his perfect features: high cheekbones, strong jaw, intense eyes. Late thirties, early forties, I guessed. I bit my lip, unable to avert my eyes because of some attraction—no, more than that—some strange hold he had on me.

"Yes!" a woman shouted in my ear.

I jumped and clutched my chest. Feeling incredibly stupid, I glanced over to see his reaction to my near heart attack. A twinge at the corner of his mouth. *Was that a—?* *It was.* He was smirking at me.

"Yes, yes, yes," the same woman shouted, raising both hands to testify, "Seraphina helped me to connect with the love of my life. That love potion worked something good, y'all! Mmm!"

A round of hollered "Amen! *Ayibobo, ayibobo*! Amen!" circled the church.

The woman hugged the man next to her. "He's my soul mate."

I never allowed anyone to get close enough to be a soul mate, but, with a spark of wonder, I contemplated the candle I had just lit, where it burned alongside the rows and rows of other votives. All those hopes and dreams. It was strange to wish for my own miracle when I didn't even know if miracles truly existed. As for the man in the black suit, I didn't really know what to think, I just knew I didn't want to take part in another staring contest, so I avoided his general direction for the rest of the service.

As the voices went on, I wondered how my grandmother performed spells. My mother never mentioned magic, so I wondered if she practiced voodoo, too. I wondered why all of these people believed that spells could actually work. The church became quiet for a moment and I thought all the people had spoken, but then one last voice rang out from the back.

"I ran away from home when I was sixteen," the woman said. "I was begging for money. Living on the streets. Trying not to get killed. Seraphina took me in these past ten years. She saved me."

Ten years. That makes her . . . twenty-six. One year older than me. It sounded like she lived with Seraphina so I raised myself on tippy toes, but I just couldn't see her.

When Mass ended, I tried to edge past people to find the mystery woman, but quickly realized it was impossible in the crushing crowd. As I neared the door, a Saint Joan of Arc statue towered above me, shining in silver armor from neck to toe, with her head held high and the white and gold flag in her hand.

A man leaned over and whispered into my ear, "You like her?"

I caught my breath and turned to face the man in black standing very close, so close that I could appreciate every bit of his exquisiteness, like appreciating a Monet from afar and then leaning in to see the painter's individual paint strokes. Black-as-night hair smoothed carefully to the side. A chiseled jaw. Exquisite ivory skin. Even though he was a decade or so older than me, he was easily the best-looking person I'd ever spoken to. Actually, I couldn't speak; I could barely even think. This was my natural response to attention from the opposite sex.

He smiled, waiting for an answer.

Say something! The Joan of Arc statue . . .

"Sorry," I finally said, closing my eyes. *God, I'm pathetic.* "Patron saint," I croaked, opening my eyes again, but avoiding eye contact.

"And as a good Catholic girl . . ." He pursed his lips. *God his lips are perfect, too.* "You take the name Joan."

At least he's leading the conversation. Focus, Sophie. Focus.

"Joan's my confirmation name—yes—but—I'm not really a practicing Catholic anymore." I continued to avoid eye contact, so I could concentrate and say something that made sense.

"Certainly a brave one," he said. "Not afraid of death . . ." The word "death" lingered in the air between us for a moment. "Not afraid of what other people thought about her, even with the voices."

"That's why I liked her." I finally got my bearings and my body relaxed into the conversation a bit. *Don't. Make. Eye contact.* "Back then, I was *naïve* because I actually thought those sorts of things were possible."

"What sorts of things?"

"Miracles, inner voices. Now she'd be on Prozac or Valium."

He laughed, which caught me off guard. I merely glanced at him, but when our eyes met, I immediately felt fuzzy. His gorgeous steely-gray eyes, which were unlike any I'd ever seen, drew me in deeper and deeper. Submission filled my body, making my extremities turn to rubber. Unable to turn away, I said breathlessly, "There had to be some natural explanation for the voices."

"Maybe." His voice so crisp. "But there are some things in this world for which we have no answer." He held out his hand to me. "Miss . . ."

Submitting, I laid my palm on his. "Sophie . . . Sophie Nouveau."

His lips brushed the back of my knuckles and my core tightened.

"Well, Miss Sophie . . . Sophie Nouveau." He sounded amused. Releasing my hand, he turned his head toward the door, breaking his hold over me. "I believe I will take part in this second line."

"What's a second line, Mister . . . ?" I waited for his name.

"Jacques Saint Germain." He bowed slightly. "A second line is a funeral procession, New Orleans style. Most enjoyable."

Jacques walked toward the door, drawing the eyes of every single woman in the room, and when he stepped outside, jazz music blared as if on cue. With a spark of wonder, I turned toward the front of the church, found my offertory candle still burning bright, and rubbed the spot on the back of my hand where his lips had been.

"Well, hell."

Chapter 2
Second Line

On the street, police officers directed vehicles and pedestrians in a traffic symphony, their whistles tweeting and their arms waving in time with the funeral dirges. The butterflies, as subdued as bees by smoke, glided out of the cathedral and floated above the crowd, forming their own second line to the cemetery.

"What's with all the butterflies?" a guy behind me asked with a thick Cajun accent.

"No idea, man," another Cajun replied. "You never know what kind of crazy shit's gonna happen in New Orleans!"

Their laughter faded as I walked forward with the crowd.

Seraphina's coffin bobbed at the very front of the procession while the urban jungle came alive with yowls and whoops that could raise the dead. People shouted Seraphina's name with lifted hands. At times the cries, so guttural and primal, formed a pit in my stomach.

Reporters and cameramen swarmed now and I caught tidbits of their reports: ". . . one of New Orleans' most prominent voodoo queens in history . . . beautiful bugs plague the French Quarter . . . who will replace Papillon in the voodoo community?"

A guy dressed as a boogeyman jumped in front of me with wiggling fingers and I screamed, slapping the white skeleton face and knocking the cigar from his mouth.

"Sorry!" I said. "Reflexes."

He grabbed the cigar from the pavement, brushed the

sleeves of his black jacket, and tilted his top hat to the side before sauntering away.

"Reflexes!" I called after him, raising my hand. The sootiness of the cigar smoke lingered in the air.

"I wanted to kill her!" I overheard a man's voice to my far right.

Kill Seraphina? I shimmied over to eavesdrop.

"I was gonna do it," the man insisted.

"You gotta let that go," a woman replied.

"Renee, I had the gun in my hand. Was going to kill her . . . and him," he said.

"Teddy, just stop," Renee said, obviously exasperated. She acted as if she'd heard this story a million times before.

"Seraphina changed my mind," Teddy said. "I know it was her."

"I understand honey."

Watching the couple out of the corner of my eye, I saw them stop and embrace, so I leaned over and fiddled with my shoelaces, hoping to hear the entire story.

Teddy told her, "Then I met you and I knew it would be all right."

"And it is," she said.

The crowd streamed around them and when he stooped to kiss her, I noticed the glittery wedding ring on her finger. I marveled at how many people my grandmother had affected in such a positive way. Why had my mother kept her from me? Why would my mother run away from such a loving person?

The image of my grandmother's proud portrait entered into my mind and I straightened my posture. I needed to find that final eulogist. I scanned the crowd. Some people wore the traditional mourning black, but many, many more wore brilliant colors, some even wearing a tribal costume with brightly colored feathers from head to toe. I had no idea what this woman even looked like, so I decided to listen for more clues.

Ahead of me were two small elderly women walking arm-in-arm. One wore a royal blue orb of a hat draped in layers of netting and ringed by feathers. The other sported a cherry red straw hat with a big black ribbon tied in an intricate bow at the front. I stepped closer, my ears perked for more information.

"Such a lovely ceremony," the blue hat woman said with a smooth-as-syrup voice. "Don't you think, Yolanda?"

"Showy," barked Yolanda with the command of a drill sergeant.

"Well now, dear. You know Seraphina always liked to employ a bit of showmanship in her magic," the blue hat woman replied gently.

Were these my grandmother's friends? Yolanda sounded like a rival, maybe. Did they all practice voodoo together?

"It's too much, Margaret." Yolanda swatted the air. "All these butterflies. Just too much."

"It's never too much when God gives us a miracle," Margaret affirmed.

Yolanda grunted.

"I wonder who the shop will go to," Margaret said, brushing a speck of dust from her white glove.

Yolanda replied, "I'm assuming Poppy."

I committed the name, Poppy, to my memory, convinced she was the final eulogist. Would this Poppy be a rival of mine? Perhaps. Someone who could help? Hopefully. A sister of sorts? That would be a-mazing. I sighed.

"Poor girl," Margaret said. "Seraphina was like a grandmother to her."

Out of the corner of my eye, I could see Yolanda's huge hat bob as she nodded in agreement.

"Seraphina taught her well," Yolanda admitted. "And Poppy was such a good student compared to Marie."

My ears strained at the mention of my mother's name.

"Marie and Seraphina. Just like oil and water," Margaret commented.

"It's no wonder she ran off," Yolanda said. "It's no wonder she didn't even show up today!"

The two women didn't speak for a few moments and I wondered what had happened between my mother and grandmother. Maybe my mother wasn't a good enough student as these ladies were saying. Maybe Seraphina pushed her too hard. Or maybe my mother never wanted to learn voodoo and she ran away so she didn't have to. Whatever happened between them, it caused my mother to close the door permanently on their relationship. *I* never even did that to my own mother, even though she probably deserved it.

"More importantly . . ." Margaret leaned in, lowering her already soft voice. I strained to hear. "I wonder which mambo will lead the socyete."

Yolanda waved away the question, "Not now, Margaret. Now's not the time."

I checked over my shoulder to be sure they were still nearby. Just then, Yolanda's eyes caught mine. I turned away. *Busted.*

"I need to sit down for a minute, Margaret," Yolanda said, steering them away from me.

I couldn't follow without raising suspicion, plus I really wanted to find this Poppy, so I searched the crowd some more. People waved handkerchiefs high in the air above their heads and swayed to the music. And though it wasn't raining anymore, hundreds of umbrellas dotted the crowd. Black, polka dotted, beige, rainbow striped, even some loaded with fringe and feathers, layered like wedding cakes and processed like homecoming floats.

The crowd moved en masse around the square and onto Bourbon Street, appropriately named because the entire area reeked of hard liquor, cigarette ash, and vomit. Showers of colored beads rained down from the balconies above. *No wonder they need umbrellas.* I lifted the shawl over my head to protect myself from being pelted by beads.

Up ahead, I could see the coffin bobbing even as people crouched underneath and around it. Alternating pallbearers danced with the casket, lifting it up and down in rhythm with the music, moving it closer to me and then—as I tried to get closer to touch it too—retreating. The coffin lurched. Surely it would fall. I opened my mouth to scream for them to stop.

When suddenly, a kaleidoscope of dragonflies descended around me. My breath caught thinking they'd start pelting me along with the beads, but they just swirled around, guiding me a few feet to the left. Then they lifted into the sky as quickly as they had come.

A young Creole woman with warm mocha skin and wild black curls walked alongside of me. Her long silk dress with its bold colors seemed to float just above the pavement.

"Don't worry, sister," she said, laying a hand on my shoulder. "We won't let her fall."

"Mmm," I acknowledged, playing it cool.

The woman nodded to Seraphina's casket, "We don't want Seraphina's ghost to find her way back. She needs to cross over."

"Mmmm," I said, feigning interest, but still having no idea what she was talking about.

The woman continued. "We zigzag and turn circles with the coffin to confuse her spirit. If Seraphina knows how to get back to the familiar places, like her house or the cathedral, then her spirit may never go to the Other Side."

As she spoke, her voice sounded so familiar.

The woman grinned and said, "You never been to one of these before, have you?"

I shook my head.

"Not from around here?"

"From Saint Louis," I replied. *Where do I know you from?*

She nodded. "You knew Seraphina, though?"

"Not exactly," I said.

She asked me point blank, "Why are you here?"

My brain churned out some possible answers. *I'm in quarterlife crisis. I need to learn about my roots. I'm here to run a voodoo shop and live my destiny.*

The woman opened her eyes wide, waiting.

So I explained. "Seraphina was my grandmother—at least I think she was my grandmother—and I was hoping to find other family members . . ."

The woman stopped abruptly, and the second line had to move around us. She studied my face and then looked at the shawl around my shoulders.

"Sophia," she said, testing my name with some new realization. "Sophia."

"How do you know who I am?" I started to back away, but her voice, so familiar, kept me from sprinting right out of this crazy town.

She said urgently, "If you want to know why you're here, meet me by Seraphina's tomb at sunset."

And with that, the mystery woman slipped between the people encircling us. That's when it hit me. *The final eulogy*!

I shouted after her, "What's your name?"

I heard her shout back at me as her umbrella bobbed away, "Poppy Laveau!"

"Wait!" I yelled, but she got lost in the hundreds of other umbrellas. I pulled the note out of my pocket again and looked at the initials at the bottom: P.L. *Poppy Laveau.*

I searched for Poppy for an hour, but she'd vanished. Her words during the eulogy swirled around in my head and excitement at finding her turned to jealousy. Seraphina had treated *her* like a grandchild. I thought about the conversation between Yolanda and Margaret, the two old women in the second line, suggesting Poppy would inherit the shop. The shop willed to my mother then ultimately to me. What would I say to Poppy? And if she knew my name, what else did she know about me?

As I entered the gates to Saint Louis Cemetery Number One, I felt more lost than ever. The white stone vaults drifted past my peripheral vision like silent ships sailing in a dark and infinite ocean. A tear slipped down my cheek. As I laid my last family member to rest in one of those vaults, I knew I couldn't leave until I understood my mother and her past. And if that meant becoming the owner of a voodoo shop, so be it.

Chapter 3
Sitting Up with the Dead

As twilight settled over the cemetery, the funeral attendees departed. The horizon burned tangerine as I made my way to my grandmother's tomb where Poppy lined up clear votive holders along the front of the crypt.

With her back turned to me, so she could concentrate on lighting the candles, she said quietly, "I honestly didn't think you'd show." Then she turned to me and asked sharply, "Marie and Seraphina hadn't spoken in years, but couldn't she at least make the effort to come to the funeral?"

I averted my eyes. My mother had lied to Seraphina, and to me, for decades.

"Mom died," I replied, my voice breaking. The whole situation broke my heart. What a missed opportunity to know my family.

"I'm so sorry." Poppy's brown eyes softened. "Sophie... may I call you Sophie? Or do you prefer Sophia?"

"I go by either one," I said. My mother had always insisted on calling me Sophia because she thought it was a beautiful, old-fashioned name. *It means "wisdom,"* she'd tell me. But at school, kids started calling me Sophie and the name just kind of stuck.

"Seraphina was like family to me," Poppy said. "She was all I had."

I clenched my jaw. I deserved to know my grandmother.

"Maybe I can help you get to know who she was," Poppy offered.

I avoided the comment, because maybe this was chasing ghosts that weren't meant to be disturbed; even if I did find some answers about my family, it didn't guarantee they would be satisfying ones.

Poppy lit the last candle and then stood up. "Now let's see if you can pass the test."

"Test?" I asked.

"It takes a pretty strong person to come sit with the dead at night. But make no mistake . . ." Poppy lifted her finger to emphasize. "This ain't no séance shit."

I cracked a smile, confessing, "But I never really knew her."

"Doesn't matter," Poppy said, putting her hand up to block my objections. "She was your grandmother and, like it or not, you'll do this for her."

Sounded like Poppy could be an immovable force when she wanted to be.

"What do I need to do?" I asked, wanting to start before it got too late, because deep down, I was afraid of the dark.

"Just arrange those flowers around the immortelle there." She pointed to some yellow chrysanthemums and a wire and beaded wreath. "You just have to be with her." Poppy put her index finger on her lip and assessed the decorations. Then she abruptly said, "But first, let me show you where I'll be." She grabbed a candle and started walking away. I followed her through the city-like cemetery with its marked streets and intersections, the tombs going on for blocks and blocks.

"Where are we going?" I asked, wanting to hurry up and be finished with this by nightfall, and at the same time, anxious to have Poppy like me and help me.

"I have a little work to do over here," Poppy said.

Dusk settled around us, but thousands of candles at our feet cut a path through the gloom. I thought about what I had read in my guidebook about the famous New Orleans cemeteries. Oven tombs (the book had called them) bake the bodies so they can be used by families for generations. I shuddered, thinking about my grandmother's body in the Papillon tomb.

"So what do you do in Saint Louis?" Poppy asked.

"I just finished my Master's in the spring," I said. "English."

"A college grad," Poppy said, sounding impressed. "Seraphina would have been very proud."

I smiled widely. Putting myself through college by waiting tables to make ends meet was my biggest accomplishment.

"I'd like to teach," I said. "But the job market's pretty tough right now."

"What made you decide on English?" Poppy asked.

My mother always called me her "smart girl" and I'd always loved books. But another answer popped into my head and I said, "I always wanted to change minds."

Poppy raised an eyebrow. "Well, changing minds is in your blood," she said, as if that explained everything.

"Is that some kind of saying down here?"

Poppy laughed. "Mind changing was part of Seraphina's work." She stopped and turned. "You really don't know anything do you?"

I shrugged and shook my head.

She hurried forward again and a few seconds later slowed in front of a tomb marked on all sides with sets of triple X's.

"Well, here we are." Poppy raised her hand in introduction. "The final resting place of New Orleans' most famous citizen and my ancestor."

She handed me the candle, which I held up to a bronze plaque that read:

Marie Laveau
This Greek revival tomb is reputed burial place of this notorious "voodoo queen." A mystic cult, voodooism, of African origin, was brought to this city from Santo

Domingo and flourished in 19th century. Marie Laveau
was most widely known of practitioners of the cult.

"Wow," I said with equal measures of awe and excitement.

Poppy rearranged yellow, white, and purple mums that admirers had left at the base of the tomb. I reached up to feel a set of X's and looked at Poppy for an explanation.

"Favors granted," she answered. "You ask Marie for a favor and knock three times on her tomb." Poppy demonstrated by making a fist and tapping slowly, one, two, three. She waited for a few seconds to let me try.

What the hell. I knocked three times and imagined the candle I lit this morning at the cathedral with its light burning for my happiness and true love.

Poppy continued. "When she answers your prayer, you come back to make her an offering." She indicated the scattering of coins, Mardi Gras beads, and minibar-sized bottles of Crown Royal and Jack Daniels at the foot of the tomb. "These X's are illegal, not to mention unnecessary. Nothing in voodoo says to make X's and ruin poor Marie's place of rest, but some stupid tour guide told all the people on his tours to do it. And now it can't be stopped." Poppy clicked her tongue, spit on a cloth, rubbed at some crayon X's, and threw the rag over her shoulder. "Even when they restore the surface, the X's reappear because of that dumb ass tour guide. Alls I can say for that guy is, 'karma's only a bitch if you are.'"

Poppy leaned down and picked up some dust, scooping it into a Ziploc bag. She fished a shiny dime from her purse and set it reverently at the foot of the tomb.

I stared at Poppy, completely confused.

She read my face and said nonchalantly, "I need bone dust for certain spells and Marie's my own kin."

"Ashes to ashes, bone dust to bone dust," I remarked, and Poppy giggled.

"Let's get you back over to Seraphina's tomb." We started back to the Papillon tomb and Poppy shot me a mischievous grin. "You got a boyfriend back home?"

"No." My voice faded. Because of problems at home growing up, I never really had any friends, much less boyfriends, and then with college and supporting myself after Mom died, I was just too busy to date.

"How about you?" I asked.

"I've been so busy at the shop that I don't have time for a social life. Someday," she said hopefully. "We have to get your palm read . . . or I know a good love spell," Poppy said in a singsong voice.

I said quietly, "I don't really believe in all that."

"That's got to change," Poppy said under her breath.

We walked in silence for a few moments and I noticed a little girl sweeping along a length of vaults, her mother perched on a ladder, hanging a wreath for someone in the wall.

"What's that?" I tilted my head toward the scene.

"*Fet Gede.* In voodoo, we honor the dead on November first and second.

"All Souls Day," I said, a knee-jerk thought from my days in Catholic school.

"Exact same principle. I'm guessing Marie at least raised you to be a good Catholic girl?"

"She tried. It didn't really take."

"Tell me about your mom," Poppy said.

I struggled with how much to tell her about my mother and then decided to keep it short and simple.

"Oh, you know, she had her problems." *Mean drunk*. "But I loved her. What about you? Are you from New Orleans?"

"Born and raised. Thought about leaving, but then Seraphina gave me a job and I have been her apprentice for almost ten years."

"Apprentice?" I asked, still not fully understanding my grandmother's occupation.

"Seraphina was the voodoo queen of New Orleans," Poppy said with a "duh" tone.

"Voodoo queen." I tested the word, my processor trying to compute.

"She taught me to be a mambo, too," Poppy chimed in. "That's a voodoo priestess."

"So you perform for tourists or something?" I guessed.

"No, I'm the real deal. I cast spells, mix potions, eradicate curses." Poppy said it so matter-of-factly, like performing magic fit right in between brushing your teeth and eating lunch.

"Oh," I said. I didn't believe in praying, much less spell casting or potion mixing.

Poppy looked at me sideways. "You have Seraphina's eyes, you know."

My heart fluttered, the edge of my mouth turning up.

We arrived back at the Papillon tomb, and I noticed the remaining people in the cemetery packing up their painting and cleaning supplies.

Poppy noticed, too, and said, "We don't have a lot of time, so I'll let you pay your respects."

I nodded, uneasy, but the least I could do was say a little something.

Poppy turned to walk away and then spun back around, "Since Marie's passed, I guess you want to know about your inheritance?"

My chest tightened. I had to know about this shop, but Poppy had every right to be skeptical of a woman who just showed up at the funeral of a family member she never met. For all Poppy knew, I just wanted to put my hand in the inheritance pie.

Poppy paused, trying to decide about how to say the next part. She blurted out, "I live upstairs." She handed me a business card with 'Seraphina's House of Voodoo' printed on it and a key. "That's where *we* lived, I mean."

She pointed at the address on the card. "Seraphina wouldn't want you to stay in a hotel."

I was actually flabbergasted—something I'd never been before in my life, but that's exactly what I was at that moment.

Before I could even decide whether to accept the invitation or not, she shoved a lighter into my other hand, "You might need this if the candles blow out. Just shoo away the rats and yell for me if the cats start acting up."

As she walked away, I stared at the lighter. The card. The key.

Finally, I found my voice, "Wait a minute. Rats?" But Poppy had already disappeared around the corner. *And why would the cats start acting up?* On cue, a black cat rubbed up against my shins.

I shoved the lighter and key into my pocket. Then I sat cross-legged, holding the card in one hand and stroking the cat's fur with the other, weighing my options. I thought I would live in Saint Louis for the rest of my life. But if I accepted my inheritance . . . Could I really even consider it *mine*? My mind searched for an excuse to go back home and resume my quiet, albeit boring, life. After all, I already had a plan. Earn degrees in English and Education. Check. Graduate with honors. Check. Get a teaching job, find a husband, live a happy life. But I hadn't planned on two things: A) the economy collapsing and B) this vision quest to New Orleans. Things were changing and I hated it.

If I was honest with myself, I didn't really have anything waiting for me back in Saint Louis. The few friends I made in grad school had moved for jobs or PhD programs. And even though I'd spent months applying for and interviewing for teaching jobs, I still couldn't find work in Saint Louis. With my final student loan payout shrinking every day, I'd have to figure something out. I didn't want to waitress for the rest of my life. Tears formed when I thought of the possibility of being evicted. Such a far cry from the small slice of the American dream I had cut out for myself.

Maybe it was stupid of me to come here. Maybe I was only capable of reliving my mother's failed life. And, with that thought, I could actually feel my heart breaking. I sighed. Maybe that was what my mother died of: a broken heart, not heart failure due to cirrhosis of the liver. I never understood why she hated her life so much. Why she left me with nothing but her funeral bill, her crazy secret box, one absentee father, and one estranged grandmother.

At least now I had a key to the mystery that was my mother. I flipped the business card around in my hands, thinking about the possibility. Could I really move down here and own a business? I frowned and looked up at the darkening sky.

"Well, if you *are* up there and you *do* exist . . ." I spoke up to the emerging stars, ". . . maybe you could tell me what the hell I'm supposed to—"

Before I finished my sentence, a monarch butterfly—the only one I'd seen since the plague of bugs disappeared into the sky after Seraphina's entombment—hovered in front of my face. The preserved monarch encased in glass from my mother's cigar box flitted into my mind momentarily, then the cat yowled and jumped from my lap, scratching me in the process.

"Ow!" I shook my hand and saw blood form in two tiny stripes.

The cat hissed at the Papillon tomb and backed away on its tiptoes, before disappearing behind a tree. My heart did the samba as a wind gust blew the votives out and swept through the tree branches overhead leaving a white haze in its wake. Most of the other candles around the cemetery went out, except for a few that became orbs of light drifting eerily in the fog.

I glanced around the graveyard. Searched for the source of the strange mist. Nothing but trees laden with

Spanish moss. They morphed into giants with heavy beards, their ghostly limbs reaching for me. The fog rolled in. Birds squawked inside the monster trees. Then the birds' calls stopped. Silence. Mice scurried into the shadowy tombs. Didn't matter that the dead were resting. The cemetery squirmed. Restless.

An owl hooted in a nearby tree. My mother always said an owl's hoot in daytime meant death, and superstition's deep roots wrapped around my spine. I searched for the owl, desperate for it to stop. It burst from a tree and I screamed. The bird soared silently above, landing on a limb in front of me. It cocked its head and then looked from side-to-side, its night-vision eyes occasionally glinting red.

I stared at it for a moment.

"Sophia," something whispered in my ear. It tickled. I snatched the lighter from my pocket. Clutching it in my trembling hands, I flicked the thumbwheel. After several attempts I finally struck a flame, and then held it out with both hands still shaking. Another gust of wind blew it out immediately.

"Shit!" I cursed under my breath and stomped my foot.

Where was Poppy? I cupped my hands around my mouth and shouted, "Poppy!" But as soon as the words left my mouth, the wind snatched them away and threw them in the other direction.

"Sophia."

The phantom voice sounded louder in my ear and I swatted at it like a buzzing mosquito.

I plopped down on hands and knees to search for a built-in sound system around the base of the tomb. Of course they would have speakers for playing music or making announcements in such a big cemetery. That had to be the logical explanation for the voice.

As suddenly as the wind started, it stopped and I grabbed one of the candles. As I flicked the lighter, a woman's face flashed in the fog. The votive fell from my fingers. Shattered. Simultaneously, the hundreds of candles around the cemetery flared up. Then burned evenly.

"Sophia." The voice came strongly from the fog directly in front of me. The haze formed into a human figure with hands outstretched and I noticed the pungent, sweet smell of pipe tobacco fill my nostrils. Then the apparition burst toward me as if its hands were trying to shove me out of this place and I could hear the thing whisper sharply, "Run!"

And I did.

I ran through the streets of Saint Louis Cemetery Number One and I could hear heavy footsteps following me. I ran and I didn't look back to see who—or what—those footsteps belonged to.

Chapter 4
Dead Time

Its heavy footfalls echoed off the tombs, but the fog concealed whatever *it* was. *Don't be stupid. It could be Poppy.* But no matter what my logical mind said, my body knew I needed to get away. Away from those footsteps. Away from that fog.

I sprinted past the cemetery's gates and snaked through foreign streets, trying to find my hotel. Even though the darkness frightened me, it made me run harder. No matter where I went, the demon fog kept coming. Something deep inside of me dared it to try and catch me. I cut through the park at Congo Square where, I had read online, voodoo rituals were performed in the past.

No more voodoo.

Darkness settled into the city's bones. I drove my body forward faster. The fog pursued, but I caught my second wind. Thank God I was a good runner and could easily jog five, six miles. Running helped me focus when I was having trouble studying in college and, before that, it helped me escape my hectic home life.

I don't belong here. I wanted to be home. But where was that? Saint Louis didn't feel right either.

I widened the gap between me and the fog. Kept a pace I could handle. Just to be safe. The running cleared my head a little and I wondered if I was just blowing things out of proportion.

Fact: At twenty-five years old, I was still afraid of the dark. Fact: I needed to get a grip and grow up.

Turning sharply, I raced down one street and doubled back on the next block over, scouring the area to find my hotel. After twenty minutes of zigzagging, I noticed a familiar sign. The faint glow of a streetlamp illuminated a sign that read . . . 'Congo Square.'

"Shit!" I slowed a bit and gulped breaths of air, fending off a panic attack. Stopping completely, I folded my body over in half to stretch my calves and hamstrings. I stood up and shook out my arms, determined to get my bearings. The nearest intersection read: North Rampart and Saint Peter Streets.

My body pulsed with fatigue and sweat trickled down my back. I had been running at a pretty good pace for at least thirty minutes.

In my peripheral vision, I saw the vapor slinking toward me. I bolted. My breathing became labored. My muscles turned to pudding. Exhausted from my breakneck pace, I slowed to a jog and stumbled onto Toulouse Street, a block down from my hotel. Upon entering the hotel lobby, I fought the urge to kiss the ground.

"Can I help you, miss?" The front desk clerk asked.

"I'm okay," I said, holding the door closed and pushing my face up against the glass to see where the fog went. It crept down the street and within seconds spread around the hotel's doorstep.

"That's—" the clerk didn't finish his sentence.

The fog swelled into a mushroom cloud and pushed itself against the glass doors, blocking out our view.

I held the door tightly, but it seeped through the cracks.

My heart plummeted because I didn't know where else to go. A voice in my head instructed sharply, "Find Poppy."

"Is there another exit?" I yelped to the clerk.

He pointed a forefinger over his shoulder, without turning or saying a thing, to a door by the elevator.

I grabbed a map off the front desk, ran through the door and down a flight of stairs, exiting the building through an underground parking area. I fished in my purse for my phone and Poppy's card. Adrenaline pumping, I misdialed twice.

Finally I got it right and there was ringing on the other line. *Yes*!

"Thanks for calling Seraphina's House of Voodoo. The shop is now closed," a recorded message informed me.

"Damn!" I shoved the phone back into my purse and opened the map, peering over my shoulder. I found the address on the card. The shop was nearly ten blocks away, but I had nowhere else to run.

Please let Poppy be there.

The fog slid into the parking area and I sprinted. My footfalls echoed off of the row houses rising on either side of me like a parting Red Sea of bricks. The fog moved quicker this time—or maybe I moved slower—and it settled around my ankles, chilling to the bone.

In a last ditch effort, I pushed myself as hard as I could and broke away, emptying myself of energy and fight. At last, my body gave up. The stitch in my side finally stopped me. I leaned on my knees, gasping for air.

My mother always told me to "face my fear" when I woke from a nightmare. We may have had our differences, but she was right about that. I put my hands on my hips and walked in circles to regulate my breathing.

The fog barreled toward me, but I refused to run.

It was within ten feet of me. Now, five. Two. One. Within inches of my face. I closed my eyes. Then . . . Nothing. I opened them.

The fog swirled back and away, ricocheting off of some imaginary barricade in front of my face.

My heart hammered in my chest. The fog blasted the imaginary wall again and again. My body suddenly filled with warmth and an indescribably pure bliss. I spun around looking for a place to go and reached for the nearest door. And there it was: Seraphina's House of Voodoo.

Electricity ran through me.

Then I remembered that the apartment door was in the back, so I peeked around the side of the building. The fog formed a perfect sphere around and over the building, giving me just enough room to slip past it on the sidewalk. I pressed my back up against the brick wall and slid to the back alley, while the fog swirled and pushed against the invisible barrier. My heart skipped again.

What does it want?

Finally, I made it to the back door and rang the bell like a Morse code operator.

"Hello?"

I yelped in fear and spun to face the intercom.

Poppy's voice blared through it. "Is anyone there?"

I pushed the button and shouted, "It's Sophie!"

The door buzzed, and I yanked the metal security door open, slamming it shut behind me. I scrambled up the interior staircase to the second level. The interior door at the top opened.

"What happened to you, girl?" Poppy asked. Then she noticed my crazed, sweaty hair and softened her voice. "Are you okay?"

My body shook. I couldn't catch my breath.

Poppy patted my shoulder.

"I didn't—kn-know—where else—t-to go," I stuttered. I wouldn't cry; I'd hold it together.

"Shh, it's all right." She led me into the kitchen. "Come sit down and I'll make some tea."

Staring at the floor, I mentally ran through a loop of the night's incomprehensible events: the apparition, the voices, the fog . . . those footsteps.

I barely knew Poppy and I didn't want her to think I was crazy, so I just told her I got scared in the cemetery and ended up running all over the city trying to find my hotel.

"Well you are gonna stay with me tonight," Poppy said.

I shook my head, deciding that I needed to go back to my hotel like a big girl.

"No arguments," Poppy said firmly.

"But—" I looked down at my sweaty clothes.

Poppy held a hand up, stopping any further argument.

"You can borrow some PJs. Don't worry, Sophie," Poppy said, resting her hand on mine.

"Thank you," I said, feeling awkward, yet, utterly grateful that I didn't have to be alone.

"Did anything else happen that I should know about?"

I sipped my water and thought, momentarily, about telling her everything. Even if I did sound crazy. But her hand made me feel so safe—this place felt so inviting—and I didn't want her to kick me out. I shook my head again. Poppy's lips formed a tight smile and I knew she didn't believe me, so I examined the nearest wall.

"All right," she said, patting my hand. "Come with me."

I followed her past the entryway and down the hallway. "Bathroom's here, my room's across the way, and this is where you'll stay." She pushed the last door open and flipped on the light switch.

The grass green walls displayed butterfly specimens encased in glass shadowboxes. Everywhere. Just like the monarch in Mom's box.

"Grandma Seraphina loves butterflies," Poppy said. Then she quietly corrected herself, "*Loved* butterflies. She wouldn't allow any to be killed just for display, of course, but all of these came into the shop and died peacefully there. So she felt that framing them honored them."

"They're beautiful," I said, imagining my grandmother giving the monarch to my mother as a birthday present. My mother taking it out of her secret stash, holding it, admiring it.

Poppy sniffed, wiping at her eye with the back of her hand.

"While you clean up, I'll change the sheets," she said. "If you're uncomfortable sleeping in this room, you can take mine."

It *was* weird—completely off the charts strange to stay in the room of a dead woman that I didn't know—but I looked at the room with all of the butterflies and felt that thing which had always eluded me. Home. I took a deep breath and felt safe.

"This will be fine," I decided and faced Poppy. "Thank you."

"Help! Help me!" I tried to scream but the water filled my mouth and drowned out the words. I splashed desperately, in utter darkness, knowing that no one could hear me.

"I can't swim!" I shouted, flailing my arms.

No use. The water swirled over my head.

I sank.

Claws pulled me down. Farther and farther.

Voices growled, "You caused your mother to drink! She wished you'd never been born! She'd have been happier if you didn't exist!" They giggled and tormented me until I wanted to die.

But as I prepared to inhale the water and end my life . . .

I woke.

I clutched the bed sheets to my chest, breathing hard, until I realized I was just having a bad dream. I reached for my rosary. Mom said it would chase the nightmares away.

Where was it?

I felt under my pillow. Not there.

In my pillowcase. Nothing.

The bedside table? *Where was it? Where was I?*

My eyes darted around. Hands shaking, I felt for the lamp and noticed the lingering sweetness of tobacco in the air.

I flipped the light on. Grandma Seraphina's room.

No one's here.

I exhaled and relaxed my shoulders. Then I pulled the sheets up to my chin and continued to take deep breaths. Counting on my fingers, I mumbled Our Fathers and Hail Marys, my Catholic upbringing emerging in my moment of panic.

Since I was a kid, I could never sleep after that nightmare. The demons' words infected my mind with horrible thoughts like: *You're not good enough. You never should have been born. There's no reason you're here.*

Even now, the haunting giggles rang in my ears. Huddling into the fetal position, I decided to keep the light on.

The floor creaked and popped. I grabbed my phone. 3:00. The radiator hissed and clanked. 3:15. Blood pumped in my ears. Every sound a potential threat. I listened for intruders. Those nasty little voices. So real. It probably didn't help that I was in a voodoo house.

If I so much as find a doll with pins in this room . . .

I wrapped my arms around my knees.

Don't be stupid, Sophie. Just go back to sleep. I nuzzled into my pillow and eventually said enough prayers that I grew drowsy. My heart rate slowed. My breathing deepened.

Almost asleep and then . . .

Footsteps.

Someone was in the house! The person from the cemetery found me.

Jumping out of my bed, I searched the dresser drawers for a weapon. Nothing but clothes and potpourri sachets. I picked one up and accidentally spilled an iridescent powder on myself. Setting the sachet back in the drawer, I wiped my hands on my pants.

The footsteps slowly circled the kitchen and made their way down the hall. They knew the house. *Maybe I could gouge their eyes out like I'd seen on TV.* I practiced in the air, my hands like talons. Then I got a hold of myself and tried to be reasonable. *Maybe it's Poppy.* But the shoes clicked like pumps, so why would Poppy be sporting heels at 3 AM? The footfalls approached my bedroom. My neck hairs bristled.

Just. Run. That was my plan if something opened that door. Beat the thing down and run. I nodded at my good plan. *Run.*

The steps passed Poppy's door. Inched toward mine.

My body filled with adrenaline.

The footsteps stopped at my door.

No knock.

The door didn't open and the steps didn't retreat. I waited.

Something wanted to knock.

Nothing.

Something *needed* to knock.

I held my ear up to the door.

The doorknob twisted slowly.

I backed silently away.

Click. The door creaked open.

No one.

I froze.

Heart pounding, a warmth settled around my shoulders.

The demon voices from my dream screamed and disappeared.

The footsteps retreated down the hallway, opened the apartment door, and slammed it shut.

Without touching the crazy door, I peeked into the hallway.

The sliver of light from my little lamp didn't help. At all. So I nudged the door open with my foot and stealthily flipped on the hall light. No one. I jiggled the door handle.

Probably just didn't close it all the way before I went to bed, I thought.

I tried the door again. It snapped closed easily.

Maybe the house settled. That could have explained—

Poppy's doorknob turned. I screamed, doing my scaredy cat dance down the hall.

"Whoa! Whoa! Whoa! What is up, girl? Calm down, calm down," Poppy said.

"Someone's in the house!" I wriggled myself loose from her hug, trying to peek into the living room. "You didn't hear those footsteps?"

"Maybe you're still charged up from your scare in the cemetery. Here." Poppy tenderly guided me to the kitchen and put the teapot on the burner. "What do you mean you heard someone in the apartment?"

I sat at the kitchen table, the events of the night running through my head. "I thought I heard . . ." I trailed off.

Poppy walked over to check the entry door. She confirmed, "It's locked." She took the tea ball out and set it on a saucer. Poppy half-smiled, "Maybe someone's trying to give you a message from the Other Side."

"Like a ghost?" I asked skeptically.

"That is my specialty. And it'll be yours, too, if you take ownership of Seraphina's House of Voodoo. People come in all the time wanting to communicate with the dead. In fact, I had a feeling that Seraphina would try to reach you in the cemetery."

I raised my eyebrows. *She wanted my dead grandmother to talk to me? Wonderful.*

"I had you meet me at dusk because that's when the door opens to the 'In-Between.'"

My chest tightened and my face flushed. Not only had Poppy put me in actual, real life danger by having me go to the cemetery at night, but she also was messing with me with some kind of supernatural shit. Maybe I didn't believe in ghosts, but I did believe in murderers.

I grappled with whether to trust Poppy, now, and firmly said, "I'm sure there's a logical explanation."

Poppy took a sip of her tea and said, "Mmm-hmm." She didn't believe me. "Just like this has a logical explanation," she said, opening the palm of my hand and pointing to the powder from Seraphina's drawer.

I pulled my hand onto my lap. "I was looking for something to defend myself," I admitted, feeling ridiculous.

"Well, we'll talk about that powder more tomorrow. That's Seraphina's most powerful spell."

Shifting in my seat, I admitted, "A nightmare woke me up."

Poppy smiled. "Don't worry about the powder. It won't harm you, but a nightmare can be dangerous. They're a type of spiritual intrusion and a recurring one is a real threat. Tell me about it."

Maybe she could help me. And everyone has bad dreams, so no harm in revealing that part of my crazy experience tonight.

"I've had the same one since childhood, but this time it felt so much more . . . real," I began and told her about the drowning and the dark waters. "What makes it worse is that there's a part of me that is conscious of the fact that I'm in the nightmare. I just can't wake up."

Poppy sat quietly, considering what was going on with me. She finally said, "You know how it feels when someone is next to you, wanting to say something? A friend has a hard time confronting you. A guy—a perfect stranger—wants to buy you a drink and he just can't work up the courage to approach you. Your body understands that the other person wants to communicate." I nodded and she continued. "But no one speaks. And a giant chasm of unfulfilled contact grows between you and them. That's what it's like for spirits trying to communicate with this world. You must open yourself to the message."

I thought about her suggestion and said, "I'll try anything to make these nightmares stop." Even though I had no idea how to "open up" with the living, much less the dead. I studied my empty cup. "Thanks for the tea. I think I'll try to go get some sleep."

"Sophie?"

"Yeah?" I turned around before leaving the kitchen.

"Dreams aren't always bad. Grandma Seraphina came to me in one and told me, 'Sophia's coming. She'll be wearing my shawl.'"

I asked cautiously, "How do you know when she's around you?"

"I can smell her pipe tobacco," Poppy said, and I remembered the corncob pipe in my mother's treasured cigar box stash. She'd taken the pipe so she'd have something of Seraphina to remember her by. Another item explained.

I nodded and returned to my room, my heart bursting with a weird hopefulness. I looked at the powder on my hands and wondered if I should brush it off and then thought of the black crosses on foreheads during Ash Wednesday. *Let it be.*

When I entered the bedroom, the smell of pipe tobacco hit me. And my heart fluttered because both bedside lamps and the overhead light blazed brightly as if to say, "I'm still here."

Chapter 5
The Fortune-Teller and The Prophet

The next morning, I danced around Grandma Seraphina's bedroom, jamming to AC/DC while setting up my new digs. Poppy walked in the door and I stopped mid-air-guitar. She laughed and I hit mute, feeling my cheeks flush candy apple red.

"Get down witcha bad self," she said, handing me a cup of coffee.

"Thanks," I said, grateful for the caffeine but still feeling like a complete idiot.

"You sleep at all?" she asked.

"Finally," I said and took a sip. "But I woke up early, so I decided to go get my stuff from the hotel and get set up here. I hope that's all right."

"Make yourself at home. This *is* your home, after all."

Coming back to my room last night, with all my lights magically turned on and my grandmother's signature calling card of pipe tobacco smoke lingering in the air, should have had me running for the airport, but underneath my initial fight or flight response, I felt my heels dig in. Instead of the haunting details scaring me, I felt watched over, like I had when I was really little. When my mother doted on my every whim and things were still good between us. Last night, I actually slept well for the first time in a long time. So this morning, I decided to hold onto that safe feeling in my heart, even if that meant dealing with the unexplainable.

"I'm glad you've decided to stay," Poppy said, "Seraphina would be very happy."

Wanting to connect with my roommate, I took the plunge and showed her what else I'd been working on this morning. I turned my laptop on the bed toward her.

"I'm starting a to-do list for New Orleans." I minimized a browser about cemetery walking tours to show her the document.

"That . . . efficient. You really know how to let loose, don't ya?"

I raised my eyebrow and explained, "There's a lot to see here, so if I get bored I can cross something off the list. And maybe I'll understand my place here better. Get to know my roots, you know?"

"Let *me* show you," Poppy offered. "Seraphina never worked Sundays, and I'm keeping that tradition in place."

"You don't have to do that," I said.

"I want to."

I smiled, excited I didn't have to go it alone. "Okay."

"So you've decided to stay then?" she asked, setting her coffee mug on the dresser.

"Nothing's keeping me in Saint Louis." I teetered. "And . . . I need a change in—"

Poppy squealed and hugged me.

At first I braced myself against her embrace because I wasn't used to such open shows of affection, but then I rested my head on her shoulder and hugged back.

"I'm so glad," Poppy said. "Relieved, actually. I wasn't sure how I was going to run the shop all by myself."

"I'm glad, too," I said, happy to have someone like Poppy to help me learn the family business. Already I felt a strange, almost familial, closeness to her. "So what will I be doing? What did Seraphina do? I know you said she was voodoo queen, but what's in *my* job description?"

"We, basically, run a business. So we'll be doing paperwork, stocking inventory, customer service," Poppy said.

I lifted one eyebrow. She was holding something back.

"I just don't want to throw too much at you at once," she said. "You don't know anything about voodoo, right?"

"Maybe just start with the basics."

"Well. Seraphina was a specialized type of priestess called a Mind Changer. Did your mother ever use that term?"

I shook my head.

"We believe the Mind Changer has the power to turn evil people good," Poppy said.

"How?" I asked, choosing to go down the rabbit hole.

"There's a potion that we mix in the shop. I can show you," she offered.

Poppy wanted to help me know my grandmother. And I wanted that, too, so I further suspended disbelief.

"So how does the potion work?" I asked.

"Seraphina sprinkled her skin with it—it's that powder you got on your hands last night—and anytime she would touch someone, it released darkness from inside them."

Sounds kinda nuts. How did someone go about "releasing the darkness" for someone else?

She continued. "Your job is to shine the light on the negativity within people. Simple as that."

Well that explains everything, then, I thought sarcastically.

I tried to clarify what she meant. "So am I some kind of therapist or motivational speaker or something?"

"We practice voodoo, so we actually believe in the spell's power."

"So I say something . . ."

"And use the mind-changing powder," Poppy repeated.

"Okay," I said with as much acceptance as I could muster. "So I'll learn how to make this powder?"

Poppy sighed.

I held up my hands in my defense. "I want to learn, but I just don't understand."

"Being the Mind Changer means you can single-handedly change the world. It's total power."

I nodded with wide eyes, still not getting it.

Poppy tried again. "Someone wants to commit murder and you can make that person stop. A guy wants to start a bar fight and you can stop it. Robbery. Rape. Adultery. Lies. All of it can stop with just a simple touch from your hand."

I understood how powerful eradicating evil could be, at least theoretically. No more crime; peace on earth; Kumbaya.

Using her hands, Poppy emphasized, "Changing a person's mind is *the* most significant thing you can do in your life. Lots of people want to make the world a better place and you actually can."

"So Grandma Seraphina was a voodoo superhero?" I asked lightheartedly.

Poppy rolled her eyes.

"I do understand," I acknowledged. I wanted to change minds as a teacher and now maybe I could do it in a different sense. Despite my better judgment, I pressed Poppy again. "So how do you know the powder isn't just a placebo?"

"Not possible," Poppy replied confidently. "Most times, the person didn't even know Seraphina was working magic on them. Didn't matter if they believed in voodoo."

So *I* had to believe in voodoo, but the other people didn't.

"How do you know the people change in the long term?" I asked.

"Didn't you hear all those stories at Seraphina's eulogy?" Poppy asked. "Seraphina did this work her entire life and changed, literally, thousands of lives for the better."

I remembered the man from the second line who nearly killed someone. And I remembered that Seraphina saved Poppy from life as a teen runaway. Maybe Seraphina's gift was persuasion or compassion. She was obviously an excellent listener, trusted counselor, and wonderful human being, but that didn't mean magic actually occurred.

"You don't believe a word of this, do you?" Poppy asked and smiled. "That's okay. You'll see."

We'll see.

"Yeah, I'm excited to get to work," I admitted. And I was. In the past, I'd considered opening a café or a bookstore, but never thought my reality would include owning a voodoo shop.

"I'm not talking about Seraphina's House of Voodoo," Poppy said. "You're gonna train to become the next Mind Changer."

I opened my mouth to say, *Hell No*, but nothing came out.

"Get dressed," Poppy said. "Let me show you New Orleans."

We rambled through the French Quarter as Poppy explained voodoo and its importance in the Papillon family line going back to the beginnings of colonial New Orleans. She reiterated that only the women in my family had the power to change minds. No other voodoo practitioner in the city, perhaps even the world, could do it.

"Poppy," I said, wanting to let her down easy. "I can't replace Grandma Seraphina. I'm willing to learn the business, but I'm no voodoo priestess."

"You will be."

"I don't know what that means," I said, starting to get frustrated by her insistence that I was the next Mind Changer.

Poppy ignored me. "I just have one more thing I want to show you."

I was glad she came with me today, pointing out significant places, even though it meant relinquishing control over my NOLA to-do list. And even though I was losing this battle with her, I was so relieved to have a fast friend in this new place.

We entered Jackson Square and I stopped, awestruck. It looked so different without the crazy scene from the funeral yesterday. Sans monarch butterflies covering the exterior, Saint Louis Cathedral rose up white and gleaming like a fairy tale castle.

"Here we are," Poppy said and then pulled me toward another Jackson Square tourist staple: fortune-tellers.

"Poppy. No," I said.

"C'mon over, ladies," a man called to us from a nearby table, jumping up when I refused to make eye contact.

"Please don't make me do this," I begged. "I don't believe in this stuff."

Poppy giggled.

The man took my hand and I shook it off. "No thanks. Not interested." Then I recognized the fortune-teller with the 'used car salesman' voice. Nico.

"C'mon, sweetie. You're a nurse, are you not?" He held out his hand to me.

Run away! Run away! My mind urged me.

I quickened my step and Nico motioned to his assistant at the table that he would be right back.

"Married?" he asked.

"Nope," I said as Poppy giggled next to me.

"You have pets," he said with absolute certainty.

"None."

"Come on. Sit down, sweetie." He circled his hands around in his "aura" insisting, "There's too much psychic interference with all these people around." He touched his thumbs to his pointer fingers and predicted, "You recently experienced a death in the family."

"How perceptive," I said. "Seeing as how we met at my grandma's funeral. Yesterday."

He shrugged innocently.

"You honestly don't remember me? You hit on me, for Christ's sake!" I folded my arms over my chest. "Poppy, can we please go."

"It's just for fun," Poppy said. "It'll be something to check off of your list." She advised Nico, "Hey, take it easy on her. She's new to New Orleans."

Nico raised his eyebrows and declared, "A virgin."

"Look—" I started.

"It's settled," Nico cut me short. "Your first reading's on the house."

Poppy led me over to his table—through a haze of incense—and plopped me in the chair opposite the assistant. I choked on smoke.

"You're a Scorpio." He gave me the double finger gun.

I gave him the sideways glance. "Gemini."

"You love people and will probably become a politician in this lifetime."

Tempting, but . . . no. I refused to say any more.

"You'll marry a professional athlete."

No thank you. Next.

"Your favorite color is orange."

Purple.

His guesses droned on and on and I tuned in and out, like I was searching for another radio station.

Wrong.

Double wrong.

Were we still talking about me?

When I noticed Poppy was laughing at me, I came back to the present.

"He just said that you were from Malaysia in a past life and you will be returning there in this lifetime. Isn't this fun?" She clapped lightly. "Now it's my turn."

While she got her reading, I got up and wandered into the gated garden at the center of Jackson Square. I weaved through the tropical foliage, which made me feel like I was in the jungles of Malaysia.

"Right, Malaysia," I said under my breath. As I wandered through the flowers and palm trees, the sound of a harmonica drew me to a vacant corner of the park.

I heard a man singing, "Two sisters walk hand-in-hand. Two sisters from the same man."

The world stopped. The park darkened.

The song continued. "Two sisters, one shall die. Two sisters in the night. Sister, sister, listen close. Watch for Seraphina's ghost."

My steps quickened at my grandmother's name. I pushed banana leaves aside and cut through flowerbeds, running to the back corner of the garden.

A glittering spotlight shone down on a man with ebony skin wearing a fedora and classic black sunglasses. I stopped in front of him, unable to look away. He ignored me and sang on.

You'll be raised by angel's wings,
Pay no heed to human things.
Move past this world and into the other,
With special whispers and secret power.
Hold the power of God, Fortitudo dei,
And change the world with the words you say.
Broken souls will want to be cleaned,
Christened by the voodoo queen.
You are of God and the other way around,
You cannot afford to let this world down.

The man riffed on the harmonica, ending with a long, low note. He raised his head and the sun's rays illuminated his black skin, weathered with age. A simple smile, with sparkling white teeth, made him glow from the inside out. His immaculate white T-shirt, shining rainbow suspenders, and lint-free black pants did not match his stubbly beard and shoeless feet.

I leaned down to toss some money in the tin cup next to him.

"Thank you, Sophia," he said, smiling. His head tracked back and forth at the ground by my feet.

"How do you know my name?"

He looked at the air above me, instead of at my eyes, and I understood that he was blind.

"How is it that you do not know *my* name?" He laughed and said, "Child, you are blinder than I."

I averted my eyes.

He kept speaking. "I know much about you. I know you think you lost the last of your family."

"My grandmother just died," I agreed.

He nodded. "Yet you are not alone."

Unlike Nico, the Scam Artist, I wanted to talk to this man. Help him somehow and get help from him.

"Do you have a place to stay?" I asked.

The man started laughing as if I had made a joke. "My name means, 'God is my strength,' and the same goes for you. Don't you ever forget that." He tossed his head from side-to-side and started in on another tune.

How ' bout you take this hand of mine?
Just reach out and grab this hand.
You won't be alone no more.
You won't be alone.
Take your sweet time.
I'll be here.
Right, right here.
Don't run no more sugar.
I'll be here.
Right, right here.
When you're ready, grab this hand.
C'mon, sugar, grab this hand.

The man did one last run on his harmonica and said, "That one was from Seraphina."

The man chuckled, and his infectious laugh grew, making me laugh, too. The warm excitement of truth, joy, peace—all things good—filled me. "Now I think you better go back to your sister, Sophia. Listen to her. Your sister, Poppy, knows."

"She's not—" How did he know I was with Poppy? And how did yet another stranger know my name?

The man chuckled and then grimaced as if Death had whispered a secret into his ear.

He said, "You won't make it, child, unless you reach for the hand that saves. I'll save you. We'll all save you. We'll reach down and hold up the Mind Changer."

My heart jumped, and I looked around to see if anyone else had heard him. Still, the garden was empty.

The man said sharply, "Now go."

He leaned down to play a sad, slow tune on his harmonica and the brim of his hat concealed his face. The wind picked up and storm clouds, like those at the funeral, formed in the sky above us. My heart filled with dread.

After a hasty, "thanks," I jogged back to where Poppy was still talking with the psychic psycho.

Nico shook hands with Poppy and even offered me a handshake.

I rolled my eyes and left him hanging.

"A storm's coming," I told Poppy.

Nico cut in, "Ladies, I normally charge eighty dollars for a reading like what you got, but let's just settle it at eighty for the both of you. Okay?"

"You said mine was free!" I said.

"The first five minutes were free, honey. But I gave you a good, in-depth reading."

"Well, Nico, it's been real," I said. "See you—hopefully—never." I crossed my fingers and started to walk away.

"Just trying to make a living, sweetheart. I'm gonna need that money now." He casually raised his voice, which dripped with the arrogance of someone who knows things will go their way.

"Sophie!" Poppy called after me.

"What?" At this point I felt completely manipulated.

"Can I borrow some cash?" Poppy asked sweetly.

"We are *not* paying him. Mr. . . . What is your last name anyway?"

"Rippemoff."

"Of course it is. A fortune-teller with the last name of Rip-em-off. Really?" I noticed that a crowd was gathering and I didn't want a scene. "Can we just go? Please," I begged Poppy.

"It's bad karma," Poppy said, refusing to leave until we paid him.

"You're lucky, Nico." I dug into my messenger bag and slapped down four twenties on his table. "I can't handle any more bad karma. Thanks for my first 'psychic reading.'" I emphasized the words with air quotes and then turned to go.

"Thank you, ladies," Nico called after us, his schmooze following us across the square.

I flipped him the finger over my shoulder.

Chapter 6
Night Creatures

I was still seething from my encounter with Nico, who escaped the wrath of Hurricane Sophie by *this much*, as we walked across Jackson Square and into the alley alongside Saint Louis Cathedral. Poppy led me into a joint called Night Creatures where she sauntered up to the massive antique mahogany bar and ordered "two Purple Potions" turning to me to explain, "It's a fruity martini. You could use one."

The thirty-something bartender gave us a curt nod, threw a cherry garnish into a drink, and pushed it toward the end of the counter. A waitress wearing a short skirt and fishnet stockings swooped in and grabbed it, hurrying to one of only about ten tables shoved into the tiny dive.

We squeezed by the people huddled around the bar. A handful of fraternity brothers ignored us to slam back some beer, a couple of goth chicks stared us down, and then an Asian-Indian guy, waiting to order, stepped aside to let us pass.

"Excuse me," he said.

Something about his soft brown eyes filled me with pure bliss. For a moment, time stopped. Then Poppy grabbed my hand and broke the spell.

"We should take their spot," she said, nodding to a group of girls sporting matching sorority tank tops. All the sisters stood as a single unit and walked toward the door like a herd of cattle. The last girl stumbled after them slurring about Mardi Gras beads and Bourbon Street.

"What happens in NOLA, stays in NOLA," Poppy said, stacking all their empty cups at the center of the table. Poppy pointed through the open café window by our table to the cobblestone passageway between Night Creatures and the cathedral. "Pirate's Alley, where some of New Orleans' worst—whores, pirates, murderers—did business."

"Whores, huh?" I quipped, raising my chin at the giggling college girls who were now downing shots with the frat boys. My eyes wandered to the other end of the bar and snuck a peek at the Indian guy. With clean-cut black hair and close-shaven cocoa skin, he looked nice in his pullover and jeans.

The fishnet-stockinged waitress slid the purple concoctions in front of us and said, "Sorry 'bout the mess." She bussed the empty drink glasses and beer bottles off our table and then winked. "Let me know if you need anything, okay babies?"

The air, thick and cool as the sun set, settled around my shoulders and I enfolded my sweater tighter around me.

"I'm not sure this place is really me," I admitted.

"We can go someplace else," Poppy said.

"I mean this city," I confessed, "I'm not sure I fit in here." New Orleans scared me and a part of me—the part that overanalyzed everything and played it safe—considered running back to Saint Louis and my boring, safe life there.

Poppy raised her glass and said, "To fitting in to this town full of misfits."

I tipped my glass to hers, unconvinced.

She confided, "It *is* a whole different world down here."

"The psychics . . ." I waved toward the square. "And the voodoo . . . It's just for show, right?" I still couldn't wrap my mind around the harmonica man.

Poppy stared at me over her Purple Potion and replied, "You know my answer for that." She set her martini glass down. "Look. We have to rely on each other. Seraphina would have wanted that."

Poppy was right. I had to trust her, because I had no one else. So I decided, if I wanted to make this new paranormal occupation work, I had to tell her about the experiences I'd been having.

"We're gonna need two more of these," I said to the waitress as she bussed the table behind us.

"Sure thing, baby," she said.

I threw back the rest of the purple liquid courage and shook my head.

Poppy's eyes widened and she laughed. "Something you need to get off of your chest, Sophie?"

Over the next half hour I recounted all the strange experiences I'd had since coming to New Orleans: the mystical shawl lady, Jacques, the fog, the footsteps in the cemetery and in the apartment, and finally, the harmonica man.

"The blind man used the term Mind Changer," I said.

Poppy leaned forward. "Sometimes you think you know everything and then you realize you don't know shit." She swept the rim of her glass with her index finger. "The Choctaw Indians say the land's always been this way. Plus, 'things' supposedly came here on ships."

"Things?" I waited for her to elucidate.

"Creatures attached themselves to humans. Just like the fleas riding on the backs of rats."

She was definitely piquing my interest.

"So they came from Europe during colonization?" I asked.

"Some. Escaping the Inquisition and vampire hunters. Others came from Africa and the Caribbean on the backs of slaves who were infected with black magic."

By this time I was downing my third Purple Potion.

"So Dracula's after me?" I snorted.

"I don't know what it could be. Maybe a diab, a voodoo devil, doing black magic. I'm not sure who or what is after you, but it's not a coincidence that you are having all of these experiences, so let's just keep our eyes open and I'll ask around. Could be that with Seraphina gone, someone's vying for her position as voodoo queen."

"So what exactly is a voodoo queen?" I asked, feeling brave from the booze.

"Well, no one messed with your grandma. She was *that* good. But now that she's gone, I'm not surprised creatures are stirring."

It didn't make sense to me, but it obviously provided an answer in Poppy's world. All I knew was that doors were closing back in Saint Louis and here they were opening, so I refused to be scared away from New Orleans by some hocus-pocus. I would learn all I could about the supernatural to become effective at running Seraphina's House of Voodoo, but that didn't mean I had to believe any of it.

"So there aren't any other Mind Changers in Louisiana?" I asked.

"None in the world," she said definitively. "I believe you can be as great as Seraphina. Maybe even greater."

"Sure." I grinned. With a buzz, anything sounded good.

"Sophie, are you okay?"

"Uh-huh." I nodded, but I hardly ever drank and I had always been a lightweight.

"I think that's enough Purple Potions for one night," Poppy said, flagging down the waitress who hurried over to our table. "Two coffees, please."

"Sure thing," the waitress said.

"But the Purple Potions are so good," I whined.

Moments later, the waitress set down two mugs and filled them. "It's a fresh pot," she said.

When she walked away, Poppy asked me if I liked ghost stories.

"Love hearing them." I ripped open a creamer packet and poured it into my steaming cup. "*Not* living them."

"Well!" Poppy clasped her hands together. "Since you just told me that you met a handsome man named Jacques at the funeral, I'll tell you about our infamous Jacques."

"Before we go any further . . . you don't actually believe I met a character from a ghost story, right?"

"Not sure, but it's a good story either way. So! The Jacques of local lore came to New Orleans in the 1700s."

"That would make him . . ." My brain tabulated, ". . . three hundred years old?"

"People say he's a—"

"Let me guess. A vampire," I said with *dun-dun-DUN* flair.

She continued. "He targets people who are out alone, particularly women. Asks, 'Do you have a light for Jack?' He captivates you with his charm and good looks, his eyes draw you in . . ."

I remembered Jacques' eyes and the heady feeling I got when talking with him.

" . . . and you feel this unexplainable pull toward him. You can't shake it."

"Sounds like an urban legend to me," I explained.

"That's what I thought too, until . . ." Poppy leaned forward. "Someone came into the shop and told us she wanted a protection spell against this guy she'd encountered on her way home after work. He asks for a light and when she hands him some matches, she gets mesmerized by his beautiful eyes. Luckily, someone yells, 'Hey, Jack! That you?' He disappears and she runs home."

"Well if she got away, why would she need protection?" I asked.

"She tells me that a couple of days later, she sees him outside her bedroom window, peeping in, and—get this—her room's on the second floor! He's actually hanging on the screen with claws or something."

"Holy. Shit." I shook my head in disbelief.

"She starts screaming. Her family comes to see what's wrong. Jack jumps off the window. The police check the place and, sure enough, the screen's slashed."

I shook my head. "So stay away from Jacques, especially if he asks for a light." I examined the bottom of my coffee mug. Then, I notice the amazing cologne I'd smelled on the Indian guy at the bar. I subtly turned my head and, not so subtly, nearly rammed my nose into his face. He had been sitting at the table behind us the whole time. My cheeks flushed.

"Sorry for eavesdropping," he said, a mere trace of an accent in his friendly voice. "But I heard Jacques wears black wool suits all year long. Even in August."

I was completely mortified.

He indicated the empty chair at our table, "Mind if I sit?"

"C'mon over," Poppy invited. "What about your friends?"

Two Indian guys, one with curly hair ala Albert Einstein and the other wearing tortoise rimmed glasses, stayed at their table. The curly haired one wrapped his arm around one of the blonde sorority girls while the bespectacled one quietly sipped beer, seemingly awestruck that a pretty girl would even sit with them.

"They are otherwise engaged at the moment," our Indian guy said, a grin crossing his face.

"I think I should go," I told Poppy and stood.

Poppy clicked her tongue at me. "Don't be rude." Poppy pointed at my chair. "Consider this research, Miss To-Do List."

I sat back down and peered at him from under my lashes. He noticed, and my cheeks warmed anew. *God, I'm acting like a tween at a Justin Bieber concert*. I just had zero finesse when dealing with cute members of the opposite sex.

"So what else do you know about Jacques?" Poppy asked.

"Actually, I am more familiar with Count Saint Germain. From Europe?"

Poppy shook her head, but her eyes twinkled and I knew she was bluffing. She was probably a human encyclopedia of the paranormal.

The guy said, "When I went on one of those haunted tours, they talked about Count Saint Germain who lived in the courts of many famous monarchs including Louis XV and Catherine the Great. Historic records prove he wined and dined in the courts of London, Versailles, and Saint Petersburg from the mid-1600s to the late 1800s. He just drops out of the sky, living as a guest of the court, coming from nowhere and disappearing just as quickly. But he enchants royalty with his vast knowledge and charismatic conversation about everything from music to politics to alchemy. The Count hands out diamonds to people as if they're candy. No one knows how he makes his money. And he speaks several languages from both the East and the West."

"Oh, I remember hearing about a Count, now," Poppy said in her singsong voice. "Just like Jacques, the Count is never seen eating food, but there has been reports that the Count would drink red wine out of a crystal goblet at parties and people would whisper about it being blood or a secret, ancient elixir of life."

Our waitress buzzed by. "Y'all need something?"

"Anything for you, ladies?" the Indian guy asked.

I shook my head and Poppy rolled her eyes at me.

"No, thanks," Poppy said.

"I will have another beer," he told the waitress.

Poppy elbowed me in the ribs.

Ow.

"What do you think about this conversation, Sophie?" Poppy asked.

I just wanted to disappear is what I thought. Finally, I said, "Sounds like Cartaphilus, the Wandering Jew."

The Indian guy replied, "I have not heard of him."

More awkward silence.

"Carti who?" Poppy probed, an edge seeping into her voice.

"Cartaphilus. I researched him for a class," I began. "He witnessed Jesus carrying his cross and told him, 'hurry up.' Jesus replied, 'I will go, but you will wait until I return.'

And from that moment, Cartaphilus was destined to walk the earth until Christ's Second Coming. Never aging, but watching his loved ones grow old and die."

"That's so sad," Poppy admitted, but then wrinkled her nose. "He kind of deserved it."

"Hey, let's go!" the wild-haired Indian guy yelled from the bar, downing a shot with the frat boys.

The guy sitting next to us turned and shouted something back in a foreign language. His words held me transfixed and I stared at the exotic, cocoa skin of his face without him seeing me watching him. My cheeks flushed. Again. What was wrong with me? His friends nodded and headed for the door. He threw back the last swig of amber beer from his pint glass.

"Well, ladies, it was nice meeting you. I will keep my ears open for good paranormal stories and report back to you." He stood up.

I nodded and waited for him to leave.

Poppy looked back and forth from me to the guy, the guy to me. No one said a thing.

Then, with an awkward clearing of his throat, he turned and left.

"Really?" Poppy demanded after he was out of earshot.

"What?"

"That guy clearly liked you and you just blew him off. You never even asked for his name."

"Neither did you."

"But he wasn't interested in *me*. I was just sticking around to help keep the conversation going."

"Sorry."

"Well, sorry isn't gonna cut it. You know why?" She didn't let me answer. "Because you are going to have to learn to let people in. It's part of your job description at the shop."

"Look," I said softly. "I just want to get a new start here, but you don't really know me yet. I have things to work on. I know that."

I stood up to leave, not knowing what else to say.

"I'm sorry," Poppy said.

"It's okay." And it was. "I just want to get a good night's sleep so I'm ready to start work in the morning." I smiled to show her there were no hard feelings.

"Well, I have to go pick up a few groceries. Can you make it home by yourself?"

"Yep," I said and grabbed my bag.

The night air made me feel like I could breathe again. I needed to open up to people, I knew that, but the problem was that I had no experience depending on someone else. I hurried through the empty streets; no people because it was low season and a Sunday night, I guessed. The flickering gaslights, romantic yet spooky, transported me to a bygone era.

My heart started to skip as I imagined someone lurking in a dark corner, waiting to jump out and get me. *Almost there*.

Rounding the last corner, I nearly bumped into a couple going at it against the building.

"S-sorry." I backed up to give them some room and noticed the woman's eyes couldn't focus. Her petite frame slumped into the man and her long, blonde curls landed on his shoulder. She moaned lightly, and I wasn't sure if she was completely wasted or enjoying herself. I never saw the man's face, but my body suddenly felt weak. My knees wobbled, which concerned me because I didn't want to pass out, so I hurried the half block to the apartment door. With each step away from the couple, my strength—strangely—returned.

As I reached the door, I glanced back to see the man put his arm around the blonde's shoulder and they walked around the building. My mind tried to make sense of the strangers' interaction. Did the woman want to be with him? Was she safe?

No, something in my gut told me. I took off running back to the place where they'd been seconds before. I peeked around the corner. Gone. My pulse thumped in my ears. I circled the block, trying to find her. She needed my help. Somehow I just knew it.

My mind grappled with raw details like: the man's impeccably styled hair, his black clothing, the mesmerized look in the blonde's eyes, the feelings of surrender in my own body. And then recognition. *Jacques*.

Chapter 7
The Voodoo Shop

The next morning, I saw the blonde again on the front page of the newspaper. The article didn't say much except that the 18-year-old from Lafayette, Louisiana, went missing during a walking tour of the city yesterday.

I put my hand to my head. The Purple Potions from last night had not treated me well and I questioned whether or not I had, in fact, seen the same girl. And I didn't have any real proof that the man I saw was Jacques, either.

"Poor girl," Poppy said, reading over my shoulder as we strolled around our building to the shop front. She slipped the key in the lock, jiggled the handle, and leaned into the stuck door to open it.

My eyes adjusted to the dim light. A smudge of incense hung in the air.

"That never would have happened," Poppy said, pointing to the headline, "if Seraphina was still around." She flipped on the lights and Seraphina's House of Voodoo sprang to life.

Dried monkey heads edged the ceiling. Voodoo candles lined the shelves. I spun a rack of tourist paraphernalia containing kitschy items like voodoo dolls and Bourbon Street magnets that doubled as bottle openers. In the front window a boa constrictor stretched in the sun, all six feet of its iridescent scaly body spread across a branch in its tank. I bent down and gently tapped on its glass house.

"Weird," I said quietly.

"That's Waldo," Poppy informed me.

"He's cute," I said.

Waldo raised his head and seemed to smile.

"She. Not he," Poppy replied.

"Waldo's a weird girl name," I commented.

"She's named after Ayido Wedo, an important female figure in voodoo," Poppy said. "But tourists butchered the name Wedo and it became Waldo."

"Why do you keep a snake in here?" I asked, examining Waldo's beautiful rainbow scales that shone in the sun. Under the shimmering sheen, her body was rust-colored with black ring patterns running down the length of her.

"Snakes are important in voodoo. They symbolize the life cycle," Poppy said. "The shed skin represents the passing of the generations and our overall connection to the entire human race." Poppy wrinkled her nose. "Groovy, huh?"

"Kind of." I pulled out a notebook that I'd started to help me study about the family business.

Snakes=circle of life, I wrote.

I pointed to the monkey skulls. "How do you get something like that through Customs?"

"We just claim that the Customs agents are infringing on our religious freedom and they back off." Poppy winked. She stepped in front of an altar constructed next to Waldo's tank. She lit candles and peppery incense in front of a picture of Marie Laveau, waved out the match, and said a short, silent prayer with her hands pressed delicately together.

Would I ever understand all of this? I ran my hands along the shelves of magic trinkets, which included things like alligator claws and tiny cloth bags with God-knows-what in them.

Poppy held the stick of incense and approached the entryway, tracing a path of incense around the entire doorframe. She bowed her head and mouthed some prayers.

I felt like I was interrupting, so I moved across the room to the designated "Herbal Area." On shelves sat clear canisters labeled red brick powder, anise seed, red clover, witches grass, bloodroot, sea urchin, golden bough.

Taking purposeful strides, Poppy disappeared into a room in the back with the incense and, I assumed, blessed that space as well. Finally, she returned the incense to the front altar and then made her way behind the checkout desk. She dug through a pile of paperwork and the leaning tower fell to the floor.

"Damn," Poppy said.

"I'm good at organizing," I offered, peeking at the disaster area that was the desk. While standing at the counter, I noticed a soft fluttering coming from the back office.

"What's that?" I asked.

"What's what?" Poppy balanced the papers back on the desk and laid a stapler on them to weigh them down.

"It's a strange . . . soft . . ." I stepped toward the French doors to the back room and pushed them open. The space gave the impression of a typical hobby room, but instead of crafting or woodworking supplies, there were shelves and drawers of voodoo paraphernalia.

Poppy's voice brightened. "Good! Sophie, that's really good."

I cocked my head to the side.

"They know the new Mind Changer's here. They haven't come for the past couple of days." Poppy approached the back office's window.

"What hasn't come? Customers?" I asked.

"Butterflies." She opened the window and a large blue and black butterfly sailed across the room. It lit on a chair, revealing round bronze patterns on the tops of its wings. Its incessant fluttering resembled the purr of a cat.

"Why do they come here?" I asked.

"To die." Her voice, like that of a mother telling her child that Grandma's in Heaven now. "Nature's creatures do not fear death, like we do."

I thought of my mom's last days. She told me every day that she was doing "just fine." I think she didn't want me to worry about her, but her body was worn out. In hindsight, I wish I would have been kinder, given her the benefit of the doubt. Maybe she had changed at the end.

"Come here, sweet one," Poppy said, holding her hand out to the butterfly. She turned to me. "As long as the weather's nice, we keep the windows open and they come in and make their tired little bodies comfortable anywhere they like." She smiled another sad smile. The monarch crawled from one hand to the next as she moved her hands from front to back, front to back in a soothing movement.

"Why don't you take her?" Poppy said.

I jotted a few more notes, then placed my notebook on the desk next to the window. Poppy cupped her hands around the powdery wings and entrusted the tiny creature into the palm of my hand. I couldn't believe it didn't fly away. Instead, it crawled around, tickling my hand with each of its infinitesimal steps.

Poppy walked over to the counter opposite the desk and filing cabinet.

"This is our work space," she noted, grabbing a mortar and pestle from a shelf that had quart jars containing powders of every hue. Above those, gallon-sized jars contained amber liquids of substances like 'snake juice' and 'frog eggs.'

Surprisingly, the space smelled fresh and clean, despite having all these bizarre—and probably decomposing—ingredients.

"Everything that we need for our conjures is right here. And this"—she flipped through an oak card catalog circa my grade school library days—"is where we store the spells."

"Wow," I said. "I haven't seen one of these in forever."

Poppy smiled and continued to search for the card she needed. She pulled out a three-by-five card and shut the drawer with her hip. "Seraphina would sing to the butterflies on the breeze. 'Come in my little darlings,' she'd say. 'Let us do God's work together, *ma petites*. Thank you for your sacrifice.'"

"Sacrifice?" I asked. Instinctively, I held the butterfly to my heart. "What do you mean?"

"Your gift, Sophie. Your purpose."

"My purpose," I repeated, not understanding the connection.

"To serve in a way that no one else can. To change the world one mind at a time. To use your power for good."

I nodded, still not understanding what we were going to do.

"Give me that beautiful little one." She indicated to the butterfly in my hands. In such a short time, I already felt a certain attachment to it.

"What for?" I asked.

"So I can teach you what you came to learn . . . the Mind Changer potion."

I hesitated, holding the butterfly defensively to my chest. I didn't think she was going to teach me this on day one. She put one hand on her hip and held the other out. There was no getting around it, so finally I surrendered the butterfly.

"Sweet little one," Poppy cooed, gently placing the butterfly in the mortar. It lay on its side. Completely still.

"What are you doing?" Concern entered my voice. "No, wait, you can't just—"

Poppy pounded the butterfly's body with the pestle, breaking its wings into shimmery dust and grinding the body into mash.

"—crush it," I finished.

She grabbed an ingredient from the shelf, like murdering butterflies was just business as usual, and sprinkled a pinch of gritty dust into the mortar before continuing to mix.

"You *must* powder your skin with this. *Every* day," Poppy stressed the words "must" and "every" with a pound of the pestle. "The conjure's sealed with the Mind Changer's magic, but the powder gets into the person's DNA." She waved the pestle like a wand, searching for the right word. "... or biology."

"Biology?" As if magic had anything to do with real, actual science.

Poppy shrugged. "Something like that." She continued to pulverize the poor thing. "In voodoo, we believe that since we are of the earth, we react to the organic materials within our potions. But the spell's power comes from the mambo herself."

The guilt was getting to me. I just couldn't handle the constant dull thud in the mortar, so I grabbed my notebook and started writing notes to focus.

"You okay?" Poppy asked.

"I just didn't know it would be like this," I said softly.

"This is for a purpose." Poppy indicated the mashed butterfly in her mortar.

I nodded, fighting down . . . what was it? Culture shock? My gag reflex? I whimpered . . . audibly whimpered. What was I getting myself into?

Poppy worked passionately, and her mortar pounded harder and then softer at intervals. She emphasized, "In a person's transformation from evil to good, you will remove the darkness from a person's heart."

"Well," I started, feeling a little ridiculous about my question. "How is this different from black magic? Is there such a thing as black magic?"

"True followers of voodoo forbid it, but there are sorcerers called bokors who dabble in dark magic. The Mind Changer dissolves the evil that bokors unleash on this world."

"Why can't *you* just be the Mind Changer?" I asked, the thought not occurring to me until that moment. "Seraphina already trained you." My heart soared as I thought about the possibility. I would only have to run the shop. I wouldn't have to murder butterflies.

Poppy shook her head. "Mind changing is only passed down through *your* matriarchal line. It's in *your* blood. It's who *you* are."

My heart thumped against my rib cage like the pestle on the mortar.

"Well I don't think I can do that," I said, pointing to the dead butterfly mash with my pen.

Poppy said sternly, "It has to be while they're still alive."

"Why?" I crossed my arms.

Poppy set her work aside and kindly said, "Because the magic formula needs their life force. Butterflies symbolize transformation and we need their transformative nature to attach directly to the other ingredients."

"Have you even tried it after they, you know . . ." I waved my hand in the air and then crossed my arms again, " . . . die?"

"The spell doesn't work unless they're alive and, as I said before, they come here willing to give their lives for this work."

A pit settled into my stomach. This was the only way.

Poppy's voice softened. "It gets easier. With time you'll become more connected to the conjure." She laid a hand on my arm and I eased a bit. "We don't want to ruin this batch so we have to keep working," she said, letting me down easy. She handed me the three-by-five card from the card catalog. I accepted it. Poppy nodded and said, "Go on."

> So I read aloud:
> *Butterfly wings mixed with bone dust*
> *Take these innocent lives we must.*
> *The sacrifice is great to evade harm's way.*
> *God change your mind from night to day.*

After I finished reading the words, it was like a fuse had been lighted, crackling and running its way throughout all the nerves and blood vessels in my body. It didn't hurt. It invigorated me. It felt like the excitement of the countdown on New Year's Eve.

"You okay?" Poppy asked.

"Yep," I said a little too enthusiastically while my body still buzzed.

She instructed, "Now we imprint our intentions onto the next ingredient: water. We believe water takes on anything you say, and with this magic, we want the target to move from negative emotional patterns to positive ones."

"Targets are the people we cast the spell on?" I asked.

"Very good," she commended.

"And so the magic doesn't really change them. It affects their emotions?"

"When people bottle up their emotions, it always leads to a bad result. We're expressive beings and our souls need a release. So, yes, this spell helps people to release all that pent-up energy."

I jotted notes about emotions and the importance of water in magic, which reminded me of a bit of conversation from last night. Poppy had told me that the reason I was having these mystical experiences in New Orleans was because of the water surrounding the place. Lake Pontchartrain and the Mississippi actually acted like a magnifying glass, enhancing spiritual power in the city.

Poppy filled a clear glass decanter with water from a tank in the corner of the room and told me, "Now, flip the spell card over and read the next two lines as I pour."

As I recited, she tipped a few splashes of clean water into our potion.

*'Holy water take on the words we say,
Transform dark to light and night to day.'*

"Good. I'll just add a pinch of cayenne. That will distract the target while the magic takes hold. The last—"

"It doesn't work instantaneously?" I would be confronting a desperate person—possibly a violent person—and I was just supposed to hope this spell would work. And my only line of defense . . . a pinch of pepper.

"It works very fast," Poppy reassured me. "And the pepper doesn't act like a weapon. It acts more like a stunning agent in the spell."

I still didn't like it.

"Let's just take one step at a time," Poppy said and smiled. "We're not going out on a change tonight."

I nodded. There was barely a sliver of a chance that I would actually go on a mind change anyway. In my mind, I simply wanted to be a shopkeeper. But Poppy didn't have to know that. Yet.

"The last two lines require us to light some incense because it helps cleanse the entire potion and seal it. Take these and circulate the incense's smoke over the potion." Poppy handed me a black feather and a white feather.

I held one in each hand and dipped them into the smoke before waving the gray stream toward me and into the mortar doing a cyclical motion over and over several times while I read the remainder of the spell.

Cleansing smoke, a pinch of pepper,
God, clean this person's mind forever.

Poppy took the mortar and set it on the windowsill. "In the next day or two the bone dust will draw the moisture out of the butterfly's body and we can put the powder into the jar on the shelf." Poppy put the lit incense stick into a potted plant on the sill.

I numbered the steps in my notes.

"Do you have some of the finished product?" I asked, trying to be a good student.

She eased a jar off the shelf, balancing it in her hands with the reverence of a pilgrim handling a holy relic, and unscrewed the top. I half expected it to sparkle like Tinker Bell's pixie dust, but it was just a flat gray powder. Almost like concrete. She screwed the lid on and set the jar on the table.

Poppy finished by saying, "The powder will protect you during a mind change, but you'll need another form of daily protection—"

"What if I just decide to run the voodoo shop?" I asked tentatively.

"The things that have been happening to you the past couple of days could be harmless, but we don't know yet. Someone may be vying for the Mind Changer's position."

I guess she was just going to ignore my comment. I repeated, "So what if I can't do it? What if I don't want to become the Mind Changer?"

"You will." And that was that. "This entire building is protected by a conjure," Poppy said, and my mind instantly returned to the night that I ran from the fog. When the strange mist tried to attack me by this building, it just swirled back and away.

"Step one," Poppy said. "Stay near the building when you lock up." I remembered hugging the wall, because the fog stayed just outside the sidewalk. "Step two: *Walk* to the apartment door out back. Do not, I repeat *do not*, run. Understand?"

"Yes," I said.

She grabbed a card from a drawer.

"Dark forces pick up on fear. So do not run."

"Don't run," I repeated.

She gave me the card. It was a Catholic prayer card—just like the one in my mother's cigar box—with artwork on the front portraying an angel spearing a dragon. On the back was printed, 'Prayer to Saint Michael.'

"You will need to say this every day. I bless the shop and the apartment on a regular basis, too. Like bug bombing." She winked. "It keeps the vermin out. See the rooster claws and Saint Benedict medals nailed above each door and window?"

An orange scaly foot with three long toes and a spiky spur sat above the window where the butterfly had come in. Poppy reached up to grab it and a small circular piece of metal.

"Saint Benedict protects you against demons and the rooster foot represents Papa Legba. He's a voodoo guardian that lives at the crossroads of this world and the next."

I madly wrote notes, which was helping me process all this new information.

Poppy continued. "So all three holy objects—Papa Legba's rooster foot, Saint Benedict's medal, and Saint Michael's prayer—will form a trinity of protection and power that will keep you safe. In order for you to take the protection outside, you must wear your powder." She grabbed a makeup brush, reopened the mind-changing dust, and started applying the dull gray powder to my skin.

"This is kind of grossing me out," I said.

Poppy shrugged. "You'll get over it. You won't even think about mashed up butterflies when you do this enough."

After the initial gag reflex, I felt a warmth spread across my skin wherever she painted the stuff on me. It wasn't a burning or allergic response, but more like a deep relaxation in my muscles. The feeling penetrated deep down inside of me and my whole being pulsated—that's the only word for it—with energy. The gray color faded immediately and left my skin luminescent. Glowing like all the makeup advertisements in the skin care industry promised.

Poppy dusted it on my arms and asked, "Do you believe in God?"

My usual knee-jerk reaction to the subject of God was to clam up, but the powder was having such a relaxing effect. I wondered if there was some kind of drug in it that Poppy hadn't told me about.

"As far as religion goes," I said, "let's just say I'm looking for representation."

"How is it that Grandma Seraphina followed *two* religions and you follow none?" She smiled and dusted the powder on my legs. She conceded, "I'm worried about you, because a Mind Changer works with deeply spiritual issues. If you don't develop a strong spirit, you will be vulnerable."

"I do believe in an ordered universe," I said firmly. "And I believe enough in what you're teaching me to stay safe."

She poked me with the makeup brush. "Say your Saint Michael's prayer."

"Okay," I said with exasperation in my voice.

"And get your key ready before going outside because you don't want your back to them for too long."

"Them?"

"Anyone or any*thing* intending you harm. These next few months could get tough. I really think some people in the socyete are going to put up a fight to be the next voodoo queen."

I ticked the different points on my fingers. "Don't run. Stay aware. Move quickly. Say my Saint Michael prayer."

"Exactly."

"How come you never put in an interior access door so that you and Seraphina wouldn't have to worry?" I asked.

"What were we supposed to do? Stay inside forever?" Poppy shook her head. "Seraphina loved being around people and she loved to walk around her city. Went to church every morning at the cathedral. And anyway, these old buildings are a tangle of electric and plumbing. It's impossible, or at least too expensive, to cut into that kind of spider web just for a doorway."

Chapter 8
The Most Valuable Spell

"We have about thirty minutes before the shop opens, so let's learn another spell," Poppy said.

"Right now?"

"Yes, now." Her voice rose. "That's what you're here for, isn't it?"

"I want to learn," I reassured her. "It's just . . . it's my first day."

"Girl, please. I cannot run the entire shop by myself. You have got to step up and start TO-DAY." Poppy emphasized each syllable. "I'm gonna teach you our most popular item, the love spell."

"Do you have any Post-it notes?" I asked.

"Right top drawer." Poppy nodded at the desk and began pulling weirdly fantastic ingredients off the shelves and cubbies above the counter.

I scrambled to grab the sticky notes and labeled the pages in my notebook: Voodoo Basics, Mind Changer Spell, Love Spell.

"So what are the ingredients?" I asked, holding my pen at the ready.

"Two turtle dove feathers because those birds pair up and form strong, lifelong bonds of true love. Oak leaf powder." She held the jar up and set it on the counter. "The oak is a strong, long-living tree whose roots run deep, so the powder gives the relationship stability. Red pepper will keep the love life spicy." Poppy winked.

I smiled and noted, *Red pepper=spicy love life*.

Poppy opened a drawer full of thread spools and selected a cheerful blue. "A piece of blue thread. We use thread to tie in a color's specific qualities." She handed me a color chart.

I read, *Blue repels evil spirits.* I thought about the shop's front door and window boxes and asked, "Is that why you painted the front door blue?"

Poppy nodded. "That's an old, old custom going way back." She turned her attention back to the juju. "But in this spell, blue opens up the lines of communication."

I dreamed of finding a guy who really got me. Someone who allowed me to speak my truth, no matter how angry or sad I felt.

Poppy grabbed one more jar containing black dirt. "Finally, a sprinkling of blessed soil from a hallowed spot, like a graveyard, will sanctify the union." I remembered Poppy scooping up the bone dust at Saint Louis Cemetery Number One after Seraphina's funeral and guessed it was from the Laveau tomb. "It's best if it's collected under the light of a full moon, but the cemeteries are so dangerous at night that they lock them. So I normally go out to the country to get my midnight dust."

I nodded and turned my attention to the ingredients lined up on the counter. Mentally, I ran through the names of each ingredient and noted their size, color, and shape, as well as the containers that they had come from.

"Help yourself," Poppy said, waving her hand at the workspace.

Luckily, the ingredient shelves and drawers were organized alphabetically and by type. I pulled open the tiny drawer marked 'feather' and located 'Turtle Dove' under the 'T' section.

"You ever been in love?" Poppy asked.

"Yeah, right." I was convinced that I couldn't ever have it. Could never feel its deliciousness the way it had been described in movies and in books. My heart bounced, unexpectedly, with some strange sort of hope.

"No," I said quietly and scanned the shelves' ingredients, not really reading them, just trying to avoid the topic of love.

"Use your senses, girl," Poppy said.

At first, I thought she meant in the love department, but then I realized she meant the ingredients.

"Ohhh-kay." I shoved the possibility of a magical love from my thoughts and picked up the turtle dove feathers, smoothing them between my thumb and forefinger. Their lightness impacted me the most. A love that could be light and airy. Effortless. A relationship with a person who is easy to be with.

Replacing the feathers on the counter, I picked up the baby food jar filled with oak leaf powder, twisted the top off, and took a tiny whiff, smelling the earthy goodness.

Goodness: Another quality that anyone would want in a long-lasting love. And how many times had people indicated a desire for someone "down to earth." I took a pinch of the powder and spread it in the palm of my hand, swirling the ashes around.

"Here." Poppy handed me a wet wipe.

Next jar. Red pepper. I twisted the top off and the spice immediately filled the workspace. Hot. Spicy. A lover needs to be passionate, otherwise you just have friendship. I replaced the jar in the lineup on the counter and moved on to the next ingredient. The black dirt disturbed me the most.

How do I handle something of the dead? In a weird way I did understand that hallowed ground made sense in the spell. People would want their God to bless their relationship, but I didn't want to open it, smell it, touch it. *Moving right along.*

The final ingredient: the azure blue thread. Communication had always been difficult with my longest, closest relationship: the one with my mother. In a way, I doubted if I truly loved her, because she ruined my life in so many ways. When you cannot love your own mother, maybe you are not capable of love. I held the nearly imperceptible thread and pulled it with both hands. It was surprisingly strong and would be able to stand tension and could also sew things together.

My mind wandered through images of endless blue sky, faraway sapphire mountains ringed by billowy clouds, tropical waters that sparkled in the sun. The feeling of being completely free and open. Uninhibited expansion. Timelessness.

"Sophie?" Poppy asked, breaking the spell I was under.

"Sorry." I laughed a little, unsure what had come over me.

"Love is by far what people want most," Poppy continued. "Above all things—even money and fame—people want love." She pushed open the French door to the shop and pointed.

I peeked through the doorway and there, behind the checkout counter, were two bulletin boards papered with pictures and invitations. Smiling couples beamed at the camera, their love coming through the lens; certainly, the light in the couples' eyes revealed something special. Perhaps even magic.

"And that's just the past six months," she said.

"This is only six months' worth?" I was astonished at the volume of people who believed that a potion had given them the treasure of love. It was pretty compelling that the work Grandma Seraphina and Poppy did, enriched so many lives.

Poppy beamed. "Couples write the most amazing letters to thank us for the work that we do. I just feel blessed that I can help someone find the right person in a world filled with billions of souls."

"What do you do with all of these?" I asked, fingering through exquisite wedding invitations and perfect engagement photos.

"Once the bulletin board becomes too full, we use them in a thanksgiving ritual," Poppy said. "When it comes time, I'll teach you that, too."

"Six months." I was still dumbfounded.

"Before our clients even begin using the potion, we ask them to— Sophie, you might want to write this down."

"Oh, sorry," I said, grabbing my notebook.

"We tell people to find something that represents the person they want to fall in love with. They can use a picture of the exact person; we don't recommend that method of falling in love, because people are not always what they seem at first. Instead, a more powerful way to get exactly what you want in love is to create your perfect mate from the inside out."

"Sounds very bibbidi-bobbidi-boo."

Poppy shot me a sideways glance. "Most people just clip out a picture from a magazine of a model who contains the desired physical attributes."

"But wouldn't that make that specific model the target of the spell?"

"The client can set the intention for similar physical features, without necessarily involving that specific model. Good question, Sophie." She dug in a drawer for something and then shook her head, closing the drawer without taking anything out. "Regardless of looks, it's most important that clients list—in detail—the character traits they want in a mate."

"Honest, handsome, a good sense of humor," I said, sounding slightly like a pageant contestant.

"Exactly." Poppy nodded to the bulletin board. "Those clients found success because they identified at least twenty traits in their ideal mate. They were specific and universe-God provided for them."

Ask and you shall receive. "So a client finds an image, lists traits . . . then what?" I asked.

"The person burns the image, which sounds harsh, but actually burning seals the lover's identity into the ashes. The person sprinkles the ashes into our *gris-gris* . . ." She held up a tiny, red bag tied with twine containing secret potion. ". . . says the magic words and *voila*."

"What's gree gree?" I said, drawing out the E's to try the new word.

"Literal translation is gray-gray. It's a protection pouch that voodoo practitioners use." Poppy pointed to the sign that said 'gris-gris' above a box of similar cotton pouches.

"Oh . . ." My voice went up as the word registered in my mental dictionary. "I wasn't pronouncing that right in my head. At all. Gree gree sounds much better than griss griss. How long does it take for the magic to work?" I asked, feeling absolutely ridiculous asking about the effectiveness of magic.

"It depends on how badly the person wants love. Passion fuels the conjure. But it never takes longer than a year for someone who has an honest desire to love someone else." She walked quickly back to the office and I jogged to keep up.

I had a feeling that this pace was normal for Poppy when she was working. Over her shoulder, she said, "Some people even find their true love within hours or minutes of conjuring the spell."

I wondered how a coincidence could happen that fast.

Poppy pushed through the French doors. "It's very simple."

"Are there instructions?" I asked, nervous to get everything exactly right.

"Yeah, they're right here on the card. Don't worry so much, Sophie. I'll help you."

She took a three-inch square of red cotton and placed one turtle dove feather to either side of the fabric. Next she sprinkled some oak leaf powder in the middle of the cloth square, followed by a dash of red pepper and a pinch of graveyard dirt.

"Does it matter which order you sprinkle those three ingredients?"

"Yes. Spells must never be altered, or they can have disastrous consequences. Now are you paying attention?"

I held my pen and paper at the ready.

"One inch of blue thread." She snipped the thread and it fell onto the three powdery contents. Finally she held the feathers in the palm of her left hand, positioning her right hand underneath as if she were taking a communion wafer. She stood mouthing a silent incantation. Then she reverently placed the feathers—which remained touching, I noted—into the center of the fabric. Pulling the four corners of the fabric together to make a small sachet, she carefully tied the piece of blue thread around the top to secure the potion inside. The work required nimble fingers and Poppy performed so effortlessly, I wondered if I would ever be as adept at potion making.

"A pouch of love potion," Poppy said, handing it to me, and I balanced the insignificant weight of the most valuable spell in the palm of my hand.

"What if the feathers don't fit?" The feathers she chose were very tiny, but I saw that some of the feathers were too big for the little potion pouch.

"You can always cut them down to size, but it is required that you bring a reverent attitude toward the process. The spirits understand what we're trying to do as long as we pair our magic with the proper intention. Now let me see." Poppy flipped through the card catalog and pulled out a particularly worn card.

"Do you ever invent new ones?" I asked.

Poppy held the card to her heart in mock horror. "These spells are passed down through generations; you cannot alter the ancestors' knowledge, or you dilute its power."

Poppy took my pen and notes and set them to the side and then placed the piece of paper in my hand. "Go on. Let's hear you say the sacred words."

"Are you sure?" I asked, holding the card at bay.

"It's not going to hurt you," Poppy teased and shoved the card into my unwilling hands.

I hesitantly read aloud, "Father, Son, and Holy Ghost: Help me find who loves me most. Virgin Mary, Erzulie: Bless this union, blessed be." I noticed the same walking on clouds feeling I had gotten when I handled the ingredients initially: freedom, optimism, buoyancy. My heart soared.

"And that's it," Poppy said nonchalantly as my breath quickened and my heart fluttered. She pulled open a door, that I thought was a closet, and revealed a half bath where she washed her hands and dried them quickly on a towel. "Now let's go open the front doors and pray to Mama Marie for good cash flow."

I set the spell card down slowly and took a long, deep breath. I prodded the tiny fabric pouch with my pointer finger, afraid it might shock me.

"And that's it," I said to myself. Then I backed away from the worktable and walked through the French doors to help Poppy open up shop.

Chapter 9
Helpless

Poppy continued her lesson as we walked around the store. "The love potion is one of the items we always carry, but custom love spells and personal consultations are available for an additional fee."

"Got it," I replied.

"The love potion we just made is stored next to the Love Potion Number 9." She indicated the row of colorful liquids lined up on the shelves.

The light from the windows behind the shelves illuminated the jars, casting a stained-glass effect across the floor; a prism of rose, teal, honey, and indigo.

"They're so beautiful." I marveled at the brightly hued liquids that promised money, luck, and protection.

"The liquid ones do contain some magic, but are not as authentic, or effective, as the gris-gris."

There were other powders at eye level with labels like: Jinx Remover, Spiritual Power, Steady Work.

Poppy stated, "Some of our items are made by other local mambos and ougans who decided to go corporate with their conjures and, though a lot of us in the socyete do not think that mass production of voodoo is the best thing, Seraphina wanted to support those trying to do good in the world." Poppy shook her head, but didn't say more.

"What do *you* think?" I prodded.

"I want to support Seraphina's legacy, but mass production is . . ." She reached for the right word. ". . . impersonal."

"Most customers are probably just tourists, aren't they?" I pointed out.

"True. But our bags are printed with the store's information and customers can also find us online. I tell every person that comes through to follow up with us if they have questions or concerns."

"Full service voodoo pharmacy," I suggested.

Poppy smiled, but I knew that she took the business of spirituality very seriously. Would I ever believe in voodoo as strongly as she did? Or would I simply see this shop as a business?

"One thing's for sure," she told me. "We need more help. I cannot handle the paperwork, answer phones, fill web orders, help customers, and run the register. And you won't be able to work the morning shifts because you'll be out late with your other occupation."

I knew she was talking about that mind-changing business, but teased, "You make it sound like I'm a streetwalker or something."

"Which means," she said, ignoring me, "you need to hire some help." She held up a 'Help Wanted' sign and put it in the front window by Waldo the snake.

"You mean 'we' need to hire some help?" I asked tentatively.

"No," she said. "You." She took my hand and patted it a couple of times before letting it drop. "You want to own a shop, then you need to hire people."

"But, um . . ." I finally found some words, "I don't know the first thing about hiring anyone."

"Not my problem," Poppy sang the words. "No better way to learn a business than to just jump right in."

"Judging people makes me uncomfortable," I said, desperation choking my vocal cords.

"Not my problem."

"Poppy, please. I don't have any friends and I don't need to start making enemies. I think I'll do enough of that if I become a Mind Changer."

"Actually. The minds you change will have Sophie amnesia. And as for hiring someone, I will say it for the last time . . ." She walked into the back room. "Not my problem." The door clicked shut behind her.

"Grr." I crossed my arms. Then the bell jingled as the front door opened.

"Shit," I whispered and ducked behind a rack.

"Hello?" a man with a subtle accent called.

"Hello," my voice squeaked. I shook off my insecurity and stepped from behind the rack as confidently as I could. Then I realized it was the Indian guy from the night before. My heart leapt because I was excited to see him again, but then I remembered my less than friendly behavior and wondered if he would be happy to see me.

"Can I help you with something?" I asked.

"Nice to see you again," he said and chuckled.

Cute laugh, cute guy. As he came closer with an outstretched hand, I noticed the same intoxicating cologne. "I saw the 'Help Wanted' sign and I thought I could help." He smiled brightly, and I shook his hand.

My head was in the clouds again. Was there some kind of hallucinogenic in that love potion that Poppy hadn't told me about? I smiled back at him. *Was I actually flirting?*

"Let me see here," I said, fumbling under the counter for application-looking materials. *This desk is a wreck. I have GOT to organize this place.* "I know I had some applications here, but there have just been so many people coming in . . ."

"I only noticed the 'Help Wanted' sign this morning."

I popped my head up fumbling for an explanation. "True, but this is very lucrative work, Mister . . .?"

"Jahan," he said. "Taj Jahan."

"Well, Taj, it would seem that we are out of paper applications, so I'll just have to take notes." I grabbed my voodoo notebook and pasted a sticky-note to a clean page labeled *Taj Jahan*.

"Are you the manager then?"

"Owner," I said and smiled like a tween girl at a boy band concert. Seriously, what was wrong with me? "I'm Sophie Nouveau."

"Nice to see you again, Sophie."

His sincerity caught me off guard, but it was the same quality he had maintained during our conversation last night, so I knew he was being, well, sincere.

"Were you named after the Taj Mahal?" I asked.

"It depends if that has bearing on whether I get hired or not," he said.

"Just curious," I said, blushing. Again.

"Actually, yes."

"Did you know it was built for the emperor's *third* wife and that she died giving birth to their *fourteenth* child. Can you believe that?" I asked incredulously.

Taj cleared his throat, or maybe he was laughing at me. "Well, I wouldn't be so hard on the emperor. You know what he had to say about the Taj Mahal?"

I didn't.

"He said, 'Should guilty seek asylum here, Like one pardoned, he becomes free from sin . . .'"

I listened to the lovely cadence of Taj's voice, his subtle accent transporting me to exotic lands that I would probably never see in my lifetime.

"' . . . Should a sinner make his way to this mansion, All his past sins are to be washed away.' So . . ." Taj's soft brown eyes searched mine. "It seems the emperor felt deep remorse in losing his wife. Not only that, he wanted to help others deal with their inner demons."

Taj was a poet. Impressive, I admitted to myself, and kind of romantic.

"But anyway . . ." Taj said to get us back on track. Bonus point for Taj. "I will give you my resume." And another brownie point. "Right now, I work in IT, but since I work from home I'd like a fun part-time job where I could earn some extra money and interact with people. Before that, I earned a bachelor's from Loyola here in New Orleans."

"What country are you from?" I asked, jotting down some notes on the resume.

"Malaysia."

My pen stopped. I remembered that Nico, the psychic psycho, had mentioned something about Malaysia in my reading.

Taj continued. "I wanted a fresh start. Just a guy seeking my American dream."

I looked into his eyes again and could see a quiet determination burning under the pleasant demeanor. This guy had ambition. And that left me pleasingly surprised, too.

"Plus"—Taj put on a thick Indian accent and placed his hands in prayer position, bobbing his head side to side—"this Louisiana humidity is like being in the motherland."

Honest, handsome, a good sense of humor. I recalled the list of attributes I'd thrown out while prepping the love spell. I sifted through his resume materials and noticed his perfect GPA and a list of references, mainly Loyola professors. And deep down, I trusted Taj. I couldn't tell why. I just did.

"So what's your availability?" I asked.

"Since I work from home, I choose my own hours. You could schedule me anytime, no problem," he said. "Really, it's no problem. I like to be busy," he assured me.

"Well, everything sounds good," I said. He was perfect. I was making a good decision. A good *business* decision, I reasoned. Finally I told him, "You're hired." As soon as the words left my mouth, a peace settled over me, letting me know I'd done the right thing.

"Thank you, Miss Nouveau." He shook my hand and a tingle ran through me.

"Just Sophie." I released his hand and blushed. "I want to apologize for being rude to you last night at Night Creatures. I'm going through some . . ." *Crazy shit*. ". . . big life changes."

"Maybe we are meant to help each other in this life; it could be written in our stars."

My heart skipped again, like it had when I handled the love spell, and I instinctively put my hand to my chest.

Taj's eyebrows knitted together.

"Are you okay?" he asked.

The front bell jingled as another customer opened the front door.

"I have to get that," I told Taj. "But could you come in tomorrow morning for training?"

"Perfect," Taj said.

"At nine?"

"See you tomorrow, Sophie." Taj waved and walked outside, sunlight forming a halo around him.

The other customer made his way along the wall of windows on the opposite side of the store, flicking a lighter. The sun shone through the glass jars stacked up along the windows, but the man's dark overcoat—overkill for the nice weather—absorbed all of the light. Each of his footsteps were confident. *Click*. Insistent. *Clack*. Frightening.

"Can I help you with something, sir?" I asked.

He flicked his lighter shut with one last snap and tilted his head down so that I still couldn't see his face.

"Miss Nouveau. How nice to see you again," he said, his voice like cream.

Finally, the man turned to me.

Jacques.

I froze. My eyes scanned the shelves behind him for some sort of weapon, especially after seeing him last night with that missing blonde, who now graced the front-page news. My brain tried to reason that I should calm down, because I didn't know, with one hundred percent certainty, that it had been him with the now missing girl. But my body still tensed.

His beautiful eyes managed to capture me in the same way they did the first time we met. Their steely quality took hold, and I felt as though a chain were attaching him to me, link by link, and I could not stop it. He broke the spell when he abruptly turned to inspect some items on the shelf.

"Do you remember me?" he asked coyly.

"Jacques Saint Germain," I said breathlessly.

"Very good, Miss Nouveau. Most find it hard to remember my name upon hearing it just once."

"Are you looking for something in particular, Mister . . . ?" *Mister Germain? Mister Saint Germain?* I didn't know how to address him.

"How about we become a little more familiar. I will be Jacques and you will be Sophia." Had he just read my thoughts about what to call him? My hands started to shake, so I clasped them in front of me. *Steady*.

In thirty seconds, I had gone from a comfortable conversation—and successful interview, I might add—with Taj, and now Jacques was completely unraveling me.

He scanned my body. Down. Then up. He searched my face.

"Tell me what you are thinking, *ma chérie*," he encouraged and tilted his head to the side.

Maybe I need to get some pepper spray.

"Nothing. I wasn't thinking anything," I said, but he smirked as if I'd made a joke. It had to be nerves. There was no way that a person could read another person's thoughts. Right?

"Is there something you came in for?" I pressed. Psychic abilities or not, I wanted him out of here. Then it dawned on me. Maybe he knew that I saw him last night with that missing girl and he was trying to intimidate me by coming in here. Anger surged inside of me.

He tilted his head and smirked again. He held me with his eyes. Some kind of strange, but artificial calm washed over me.

No! I wanted to stay angry.

"I saw you last night," I accused him. "With *her*."

"Hmm," Jacques said. He turned to the side, but I could still see his non-reaction to my words. He lifted a tiny statue from a shelf, inspected it. Admitting nothing. Denying nothing.

At least Poppy was in the back prep area, so I could—what? Scream?

He smirked again and returned the statue to the shelf. Regardless of how frightened I was, I could not stop noticing his impeccable appearance. It astonished me how he could be so intimidating and seductive at the same time with those gorgeous eyes and that perfect hair.

What are your intentions? I thought.

He remarked, "Intention is the most powerful force in the universe."

My blood chilled. He had responded directly to my thought. Again. *I'm going to go get Poppy.*

As I turned to go, he laid a gentle, yet firm, hand on my shoulder. Then, with violent quickness, he held up his other arm. I flinched, thinking he'd hit me, but instead he opened his gloved hand to reveal an antique lighter.

"Take this lighter, for instance, *ma chérie*. It remains useless until I intend to use it. A simple movement of my thumb, then . . ."

Flick!

I jumped, my heart running a marathon.

"Everything changes," he said. "Then when I finish using it, I can extinguish the light." He snapped the lid closed, and I jumped again. "Just like that. At my whim."

Adrenaline surged through me, fueling my body's alternating emotions of fear and anger. Indignation kicked back in. Who did he think *he* was coming into *my* shop intimidating *me*?

"Is there something I can help you with?" I demanded, wriggling out of his grasp. *Where the hell is Poppy? Can't she hear us up here?*

"You are a persistent salesperson." Jacques smiled. "So quick to take ownership of this place?"

"How do you know I own the shop?" I pushed back against him invading my thoughts, if that's what he could do.

"Oh, people talk. Word gets around." If he was lying he didn't skip a beat. "Anyway, Seraphina and I were very . . . close . . . at the time she died."

Close, how? I wondered.

"She knew a lot of people," I said. "Let me just go and get Seraphina's apprentice. She'll be able to help you."

His hand clamped around mine and he twirled me into his arms, taking hold of me yet again.

"I am entirely helpless when it comes to matters of the heart. Can you help me, *ma chérie*?"

"I—" I didn't know what to say to that. Was he flirting with me?

"With a juju, I mean," he said.

"This is my first day, so let me get Poppy to come help us."

His arm tightened around my waist.

"I am a patient man. We will go through your first time together. How does that sound?" He loosened his grip and laced my arm in his and we strolled through the store arm-in-arm.

There was no way I'd give him the most authentic love spell, I decided. Partly because I didn't want him to use it on me. I remembered how strangely it had affected me when I helped Poppy prepare it. Scanning through the rows of holy candles, I found a pink one in the shape of a curvy woman marked 'Love' and a bright red one with a sexy figure marked 'Seduction.' In the tourist bins I found a miniature "Voodoo Love Kit."

I yanked my arm from his, flashing him the evil eye, then searched the spells on laminated cards at the counter. I spun the rack until I found one for "Love Spell." Finally, I headed over to the glass jars along the window. The pink tinted love potion smelled like lavender and pumpkin pie, when I unscrewed the lid. There were recycle bins, labeled, SMALL, MEDIUM, LARGE, along with a note in Poppy's handwriting saying, *We recycle for our Mother Earth*, which held old jars that had been cleaned. I ladled the mixture into a baby food jar, spilling a bit on my shoe.

"Whoops," I breathed, then searched for a lid from the bin.

Poppy had even put out permanent markers so people could label their jars and I wrote, 'Love Potion' on Jacques' jar. At the counter, I rang up all the items.

"Forty-one dollars and seventy-one cents," I said, feeling better that the counter was between the two of us.

He took off his glove and fished a hundred from a thick bunch of bills in his wallet.

"Keep the change," he said. "Gratuity."

I took the money and shoved the bag into the air between us. He calmly gripped the bag, his hand over mine, and I yanked my hand back like I'd been bitten. It didn't hurt when he touched me. I actually felt an extreme relaxation course through my veins and into my muscles, like morphine.

He pulled his glove back on and nodded to me. "I *intend* to make these work for me. Thank you for your help, *ma chérie*."

"Sophie's fine," I corrected him. "Or Miss Nouveau."

"*Adieu, ma chérie*." Jacques tucked his scarf closely around his neck and strode out of the shop.

I wondered if I would be seeing much more of Jacques and a chill ran through me at the thought. Poppy abruptly opened the back room door and the loud noise made me scream.

Flipping through some paperwork, she glanced at me like I was a crazy person. "Who was that?"

"Nobody. Just a customer."

"Mmm-hmm." She looked me up and down, before dropping her clipboard on the leaning tower of paperwork at the register. "I'm gonna grab lunch for us and we can eat here in the shop. What sounds good?"

"You decide."

"Muffaletta?"

"I have no idea what that is, but sure."

"A deli sandwich with olive tapenade. You can add it to your New Orleans' list." She grabbed a twenty from the cash register then I followed her to the front door and watched as she dug through the mailbox.

"Sophie, there's a letter for you," she said, sounding as surprised as I was, handing the mail to me. "Call my cell if you need anything. My number's on the board in the back."

"Okay," I said. Making my way back to the counter, I sifted through the mail and found the letter addressed to me on elegant ivory stationery. Sliding my finger under the red wax seal, I wondered who used wax seals anymore. Inside was a note written with neat, calligraphic scrolls on handmade ivory paper.

I dropped the card. Even though the ivory paper fell face down, the message was seared into my brain:

Death is coming for you.
You are helpless to resist.

Chapter 10
Hope for the Hopeless

"We talked about this," Poppy reminded me for the umpteenth time. She was watering Grandma Seraphina's hibiscus by the dining room windows in our apartment. The sunny red blossoms were my favorite and it felt good to know they were Grandma's favorite, too.

"You need to meet with Father Malachi. Especially," she emphasized, "since you received that awful message."

I had shown Poppy the death threat and she said Seraphina went through the same type of intimidation when she became the Mind Changer. The socyete has an unspoken hierarchy and those seeking power will do anything to get it. Seraphina never really felt that her life was in danger, but I was a complete outsider. So Poppy said we should tread carefully and get some input from Father Malachi, a Catholic priest who was one of Seraphina's closest allies.

"I don't even go to church anymore," I said, wanting to get out of this meeting. I fluffed the pillows on the couch, paced, rearranged the pillows some more, paced again. "I can't be some 'Chosen One.' It should be someone who is good and—and . . . spiritual."

"Relax, Sophie," Poppy said. "This is not The Inquisition."

I huffed and threw a pillow into the wingback chair.

Poppy set down the watering can and put her hands out toward me like I was a startled horse. "Father was very close with Seraphina. He knew about the mind changing and—like it or not—faith is what makes your spell work. So he can help you cultivate your spiritual side."

The intercom buzzed. Poppy hurried to the door and pushed the button.

"Hello?" she announced into the speaker.

"Good evening, Poppy. Father Malachi here," the strong, calm voice said with the hint of an Irish accent.

"C'mon up," Poppy replied.

When Father Malachi entered, I recognized him as the priest at Seraphina's funeral Mass.

Poppy took his coat and hat and introduced us.

"Very nice to meet you, Sophia," he said warmly and took my hand.

"Nice to meet you, too," I said.

Poppy indicated for him to take a seat. "Please, Father, make yourself comfortable."

He eased into the wingback chair while I forced myself into the furthest corner of the couch.

"You can come closer." Father patted the arm of the couch next to him. I smiled tightly and shimmied to the middle as he reached into his jacket pocket and pulled out a memo pad.

Oh, Jesus. I picked my cuticles.

"Now let's see here, Sophia." He licked his thumb to turn to a blank page. Poppy tried to sit next to me. I huffed loudly at her, and she bounced up like she'd sat on a thumbtack.

"I'll just," Poppy said, pointing to the kitchen, "go make us some tea."

Father turned his attention to me. "Did your mother raise you in the Catholic faith?"

I hadn't practiced in years, so all my Catholic guilt bubbled up. My face burning bright red, I nodded.

"Baptized and confirmed?" he asked.

"Yes," I squeaked. *So far, so good.*

"Good. You have some knowledge of the Catholic faith, so we can build on that," he said.

I relaxed a little.

"But finding God is your own business, not mine."

I stopped picking my cuticles. *Shit. Shit. Shit! I should just tattoo an 'A' on my forehead. Sophie Nouveau: Atheist, agnostic, Type-A control freak!*

Father raised his voice pleasantly. "Poppy?"

Poppy peeked her head through the arch between the kitchen and dining room. "Yes, Father?"

"Tell me. What exactly does Sophia know about Seraphina's work?" The way he said "Seraphina" was as fragile and beautiful as a butterfly's wing.

Poppy answered, "She knows."

He nodded and turned his attention back to me. "When I say that God is your business, I mean that I can teach you the doctrines of this manmade faith called Roman Catholicism. But I cannot teach you to know God. No religion can."

He took his glasses off, set them on the end table, and rubbed his eyes. "And it is a flawed system, because it is run by humans who are inherently flawed. Thus, connecting with the universal spirit will be your own responsibility."

Poppy set the tea tray down and asked, "Milk or sugar?"

"Just a drop of milk, thank you," Father Malachi said. "Sophia, do you believe in God?" He sat quietly and sipped his tea.

I wanted to throw up from nerves.

"You can tell me. I'm not here to judge," he assured me.

"Since my teens, I've been . . . uncertain. But in New Orleans I've had these . . . experiences."

Father hummed and took another sip.

"Now I'm confused, I guess."

He hummed again.

"Because now I have," I put my fingers up in air quotation marks, "'proof.'"

"Proof?" he asked.

"Things I don't fully understand." I couldn't find the words. "These supernatural—or paranormal—phenomenon . . .

whatever." I tried again, "What I am trying to say is now I don't know what to believe."

"Well, if it makes you feel any better," Father said, "in my experience, atheists tend to have some sort of . . . How shall I say it? . . . Emotional baggage."

"Baggage," I repeated. A*nd this week on 'Sophie has Mommy issues . . .'*

"In my experience, there is always a spot of darkness that keeps an atheist detached from God."

I poured some milk into my tea and listened.

"Something as simple as a shadow of doubt can keep a person within an arm's reach of true faith. In most instances, there was a childhood trauma: an abuse situation or a hurt that never fully healed."

Father had hit the nail on the head. My mom's alcoholism hovered like a black rain cloud over most of my childhood. I scooted closer to him, not really wanting to get into my past, but feeling intrigued by his insights.

I chose my words as carefully as I could. "Certain things have been happening." How to explain a ghost to a Catholic priest? I tried again. "These . . . things . . . don't necessarily have a logical, or natural, explanation."

Father Malachi raised his eyebrows and asked, "You are speaking of Seraphina's ghost?"

I spilled tea on my lap.

Poppy jumped up and offered to get a towel, saying over her shoulder, "Father Malachi and Seraphina spent a lot of time together, Sophie. A *lot*. So he knows everything about her."

"Seraphina and I worked together for a number of years. She lent me an ear when I needed someone to talk to," he said. "And I helped her on some of her more difficult mind-changing cases."

At the mention of mind changing I spilled more tea on my lap. Exasperated, I set the cup down and wiped at my jeans.

"Here ya go," Poppy said, handing me a tea towel and wiping up the floor with another. "You know, I think we should all go out on a mind change together."

"Excellent idea, Poppy," Father said.

The way they said it, it was like we were going to dinner or something.

"Can we do that?" I set the tea towel on the table and looked at each of them. "Isn't it dangerous? And won't we draw attention with three of us, you know, casting a spell, or whatever it is?" I still had no idea what a mind change actually entailed.

"Mind changing can be subtle," Poppy said.

Father nodded and added, "There is no waving of wands nor loud incantations, I can assure you."

Poppy added, "Sometimes Seraphina would just pat someone's hand at the supermarket and, if need be, she could rain down apocalypse." She turned to Father and said, "You know, I bet she was responsible for that storm and those butterflies on the day of her funeral."

Father chuckled.

A Catholic priest and a voodoo priestess teaming up to fight evildoers. I couldn't quite wrap my head around it. Father Malachi leaned forward and set his empty cup and saucer on the coffee table and grabbed his memo pad.

"We should start with something simple; I think I know just the person who could use our help."

"Excuse me." I held up my finger. "I don't think I'm really ready for—"

Poppy waved my concerns away. "It'll be fine."

Father winked at me. "Easy case, Sophia. Nothing dangerous," he reassured me. "And, Poppy, why don't you contact Teddy and see if he'd be willing to meet with us, too."

"Sounds good," Poppy replied.

I guess I didn't have a say in this.

Father Malachi snapped his notepad shut and put it in his shirt pocket along with his fountain pen. "Can I tell you a story?"

Poppy took the tea tray and ran some water in the kitchen sink. I turned my attention to Father Malachi's story.

"I once knew a man whose pregnant wife died in an accident with a drunk driver. Terrible thing," he said, shaking his head. "The accident took everything . . . including the man's faith. For years—many, many years—he refused to attend church, because in his mind, God had abandoned him. But God is not of the mind. God is of the heart." Father Malachi tapped a finger to his chest and squinted to see if I understood.

I nodded slowly, but I didn't understand. That was my problem. I just couldn't get a handle on the whole faith thing.

Father spoke again. "The man wore a mask. He wanted everyone to think he had moved on, but deep inside, he was just an abandoned boy."

The little Sophie in me could understand that. I investigated my cuticles and pinched back the beginnings of tears.

He continued. "But those people do not have to stay in the dark. God's light is in many places." Father Malachi sat back in his chair and folded his hands over his belly, "A new love. Or an enchanted moment, whether it is terrifying or wonderful, makes a person realize that there are still unknowable things in this world. That kind of magic . . ." Father held his finger up. ". . . the magic of possibility, draws a person's spirit into the light."

We sat in silence for a moment.

I didn't want to go there, but I cautiously asked, "Did you know my mother?"

"No," he said softly. "But Seraphina spoke of her often—all good, of course."

I confessed, "I want to believe there is some kind of universal order or a benevolent force watching over us. I really do. But my mother made that impossible for me."

I tensed, waiting for a long sermon on how wrong I was. *Traitor!* he would yell. *Heretic!*

Instead, he quietly put his glasses back on and asked, "What is your story, Sophia?"

I sat back and studied my hands in my lap again.

He clarified, "What happened to you to cause the disconnect?"

I shrugged. A voice in my head urged me, *Trust him.*

I closed my eyes and took a deep breath. "My mom drank too much." But what I couldn't tell him was that it killed me, too, every time she opened the bottle. I clenched my teeth to hold back the tears, "Then five years ago she died."

He spoke tenderly. "Your emotions have become a parasite, my dear. Emotions are fine if you can feel them in the moment that they are applicable and then let them go, but you have held onto them for much, much too long and now they won't let you go. The ghosts of your past are making you miserable."

Father placed his hand on mine, and I sat rigid, but didn't pull away.

"You have to forgive your mother and move on," he said. "You know this, don't you?"

Any logically thinking person knows that it's damaging to hold onto past hurts, but I was in the grips of my past demons and couldn't shake them. Tears gathered and I sniffed them back, holding everything in like the tough girl I'd become.

Father paused for a moment and carefully chose his next words.

"We are vessels." He stared at a spot on the floor, but kept his hand on mine. "Life moves through us in beautiful and mysterious ways, if we will only allow it," he whispered and his voice echoed in the stillness. "Sometimes we encounter difficult people or disastrous situations. They make us into something that is not who we truly are. We must allow the flow of life back in, so that we can reclaim our true spiritual power." He looked up from the floor, his words complete.

The eye contact undid me. I shook my head, a frown spreading across my face as the walls came crashing down. And then I couldn't hold them in anymore; the tears dripped down my cheeks. Poppy sat down right next to me and held an arm around me.

Father said softly, "We cannot understand everything in this world, Sophia. Human beings are fallible. We're vulnerable."

I started to cry harder. I pulled my sleeves down to my fingertips and held them to my streaming eyes, embarrassed by my tears. Poppy played with the ends of my hair; something Mom did that always made me feel so much better whenever I was upset.

Father suggested, "Maybe we should talk some other time, Sophia."

Poppy nodded.

He stood up and knelt down on one knee so he could embrace me as I sat. He felt like a father should, humble yet strong, so I leaned into him and cried, finally letting my angry and terrified inner twelve-year-old out.

"It's just so hard," I stuttered, "to see my life as some universal plan." I held my sleeves to my eyes again. "I—I can't trust people."

Poppy rubbed my back, which made me cry harder.

Then I exploded from a deep, dark place. "What sort of God gives a child a negligent mother and an absentee father?"

"Let it out," Father Malachi said, pulling a fresh handkerchief from his pocket. "Just let it all out."

I held my head up and yelled, "Why didn't God help me?" I started getting the heebie jeebies—that's what my mom always called those hiccupping sobs that kids get—and I tried to calm my breathing. "I did pray! No one listened!"

Then I cried so hard I couldn't talk anymore. I thought of all of my prayers. Then the feeling of abandonment.

I was twelve and I knelt on the mulch flowerbed, rosary in hand. I had knelt in front of our Immaculate Heart of Mary statue in the backyard for weeks praying for a miracle. At school we had been learning about the Marian apparitions at Fatima and Lourdes and I really identified with the children who could see these miraculous visions. Wanting to be as devout as possible, I prayed the rosary as perfectly as I could. If I made even a single mistake, even something small like a missed word or an accidental sneeze, I would begin again. I did not want a sneeze to mess up the chance to have something special happen to me. My fingers felt the beads and my mouth whispered "Hail Marys" and "Our Fathers." And I would search the statue's face for miraculous tears of blood or I would scan the skies for Our Lady floating on a cloud, coming to communicate an urgent message for humankind. I was so focused and I just knew that God would speak to me through this wonderful, gentle mother figure. I prayed and prayed, waiting for some special purpose, some special mission, some special moment to show that God cared for me and thought I was special. My miracle never came.

A tidal wave of pain rolled over me, threatening to overtake me. I stayed under its powerful force, wanting to exorcise it all. Wanting to die unless I could get it all out. Right then. When the storm subsided, minutes or even an hour later I didn't know, I placed my hands on my swollen eyes and didn't speak.

Father finally said, "I understand your pain, my child. I do. Because I was that man."

I raised my head.

"The one who lost his pregnant wife in the car accident."

I inhaled and exhaled slowly, the full force of his confession sinking in.

"Eventually, I found peace through the Church. I became a deacon and, over time, answered God's calling to become a priest. After losing my wife, I thought I would never love again." He tilted his head and his eyes softened.

A thought struck me. *Until he met my grandmother.*

I remembered his admiring tone during Seraphina's funeral and noticed the loving way he said her name this evening.

"Give your soul time to heal, my child. Call me when you are ready. Poppy has my number."

Poppy nodded.

Father Malachi put his hand on my head before heading to the door. He donned his worn brown hat and turned to say, "Good night, girls."

I mustered a smile, my cheeks taut with dried tears. And Poppy closed the door, his footsteps echoing down the stairwell. I headed out to the balcony and Poppy joined me. She put her hand on my shoulder, but didn't say a word. Father Malachi stepped into the street below, nodded to a woman and child who walked hand-in-hand, and then disappeared around the corner. I leaned on the iron railing.

"Father Malachi loved Grandma Seraphina, didn't he?" I asked.

"Very much," Poppy replied.

Chapter 11
The Power and the Paranormal

I knew I needed Father Malachi's help. So I called him the next morning and he became another mentor. Poppy taught me the voodoo aspects of mind changing and he taught me the Catholic aspects.

Father began each session with the same Prayer to Saint Michael that Poppy wanted me to be saying:

Saint Michael the Archangel,
defend us in battle.
Be our protection against the wickedness and snares of the devil.
May God rebuke him, we humbly pray;
and do Thou, O Prince of the Heavenly Host —
by the Divine Power of God —
cast into hell, Satan and all the evil spirits,
who roam throughout the world seeking the ruin of souls. Amen.

The words 'evil spirits, who roam throughout the world seeking the ruin of souls' always stuck with me.

During our first lesson, Father told me, "You will be inextricably linked with dark forces as long as you're the Mind Changer." He peered over his spectacles and waited for my reaction.

Hands folded on my lap, my head bobbled like a kindergartner's. Even though I didn't really understand how to apply his abstract teachings about faith, I trusted Father Malachi enough to try to learn.

"Once the Mind Changer accepts her role," he warned, "she automatically attracts souls who are lonely, desperate, violent, even. But you must resist their darkness for it is not yours."

I raised my hand.

"Yes?"

"But I do have bad days. Everyone does, right?" I didn't believe that a little negativity would really cause me any harm.

"When you are having a difficult day, call on God. Those on the Other Side will help, my dear," he reassured me.

"Right," I said, exasperated. If I never heard the words "Other Side" used together again . . .

Father clarified, "The essential thing is not to stay entrenched with people at their darkest moments, even if you feel lonely sometimes. Envision yourself as the rope that guides people from their deep dark holes into the light. You do not have to be a part of the darkness, just because you are lowered into the pit. Instead, be the light that helps others see a way out. A higher possibility."

Finally, Father and Poppy wanted me to try a supervised mind change, in broad daylight and in public. So we met at Café Du Monde for beignets and café au laits.

"She's working today," Father mentioned, sitting down at an open-air table.

"Who is she?" I asked and scanned the outdoor seating area.

"Christy's been having financial problems and is close to being evicted from her home," he said. He could see I was tense, so he added, "No history of violence with this case, Sophia."

Sigh of relief.

"She has three little ones at home." He swallowed. "She needs your help very much, Sophia, and she can help you, too," he pointed out.

"It should be an open-and-shut case," Poppy chirped. "Easy peesy."

Easy peesy for her to say. I pictured myself standing in front of this stranger, Christy. Staring. Waiting. And then—*poof*—nothing happens. I pictured Christy giving me the 'alrighty then, crazy girl' look and I would feel like a complete moron.

Father and Poppy talked while I ran through a stack of note cards that highlighted the Catholicism crash course and my mind changing lessons at the voodoo shop.

The first card stated simply, 'Good and Evil.'

In one of my lessons, Father told me, "The most important piece of knowledge I can share with you is that there are universal forces, for lack of a better term. Catholics label these opposing forces as 'good' and 'evil,' but the ancients accepted both darkness and light as a part of the whole. Think about it. Scientifically, we need the darkness. What would happen if we didn't have day *and* night?"

"All the plants would die," I answered. Too much sunlight and they would burn up. Too much darkness and they would starve. Up until that point, I never really thought about it that way. We need the darkness. A balance of day and night makes life on Earth possible.

Father continued. "These dualistic forces in nature, even within our human nature, continually come into play regardless of how people label them. They're a constant for life to exist."

"Unstoppable," I said, thinking about the force of attraction growing between Taj and I since we'd been working together. Whenever I thought about him, I would get all warm and fuzzy. A smile spread across my face, and Father Malachi observed me curiously over his reading glasses.

"So, Sophia, if we accept this natural interchange between light and dark, then as believers we must also trust that God can help us navigate this dualistic world.

Which leads us to another universal law, which states that we have the power, as sentient beings, to call anything in the universe to us. That's why we pray." He opened his hands. "Or meditate."

My heart surged with hopefulness as I thought about lighting the votive candle for love. Seraphina's funeral had been weeks ago, but that tiny flame burned brightly in my heart. I longed for the kind of love that transcended everything, and when I thought about Taj, my heart filled up.

Father cleared his throat, "You seem a bit sidetracked, my dear."

Busted. What was it with Taj? I'd never felt so distracted by a guy. I actually thought people who fell head over heels were just being overdramatic. Is that what I was doing? Falling head over heels in love with someone I just met?

"Sorry, Father," I said. "I'm listening."

He smiled. "If you have something on your mind, I know how to handle a confession."

I smiled back. "I appreciate that. But I'm good."

He picked up right where he left off. "The Mind Changer's job is to deal with the darkness and lightness of being."

Poppy had told me that one way darkness came into the world was through bokors, voodoo priests who dabbled in black magic. Violence, poverty, hunger . . . all things bad in this world were perpetuated by keeping people in darkness. Bokors and other bad guys—like Enron execs and Darth Vader—employed the dark side. I would use the force. Except, instead of a light saber, I had magic fairy dust made from butterfly mash and cemetery dirt. While working at the shop, I'd tried to get specifics out of Poppy about how the mind-changing powder actually worked.

"Does it stun the person? Will they have some kind of short-term memory loss?" I didn't want to hurt anybody, but I also didn't want to get hurt, or killed, myself.

"It stuns them, so you can get out of harm's way," she assured me. "Especially if they have a weapon."

"A gun. I should probably have a gun," I said anxiously. At the very least I'd be vigilant about bringing my pepper spray wherever I went. How else would I protect myself? Because I just didn't trust an enchanted powder to protect me—not until I saw it work with my own eyes. At times, my mind would whirl with all the negative scenarios I could be faced with. I would stand at the register in the shop and stare, picking at my cuticles.

When she caught me mulling, Poppy would grab me by the shoulders and say something like, "You're a brave, strong woman, Sophie Nouveau." Or, "You can do this, Sophie."

She and Father Malachi always reminded me that my targets needed my help. Some had bad juju from a root doctor or were facing spiritual demons, but when I worked my spell, minds would change. Hearts would change.

When it came down to it, would I be willing to put my life on the line for them? I wouldn't know until I tried it.

"So which one is she?" I asked.

Even though I didn't understand exactly how the spell worked, Seraphina had performed it tens of thousands of times in her life, and I had to trust in her success if nothing else. Doubt tried to settle on my back, so I rolled my shoulders and loosened up my neck like a boxer readying for a fight. I wanted this, right? All of it. To learn more about Grandma Seraphina, to have a life of purpose, to make the world a better place. Here it was all wrapped up in one nice, neat little package. Except for the psycho stalker sending me death threats. And the fact that mind changing was a dangerous career choice.

"I can do this," I proclaimed, either for myself or Poppy and Father. Maybe all of us.

Poppy placed her hand on mine. "It's an easy case."

"We are here for you, Sophia," Father reassured.

I took a deep breath and stood up.

"She's the young lady at the counter," Father pointed to a blonde woman wearing a dark green 'Got Beignets?' T-shirt.

"Try the good ol' Money Changer technique," Poppy suggested.

"Okay." I shook the apprehension from my fingers.

"You can do this, my dear," Father said, putting his hand on my arm. "I have faith in you."

I walked confidently—well, as confidently as I could—to the line. Periodically, I would look over my shoulder at Father and Poppy who would give me a thumbs-up. Wave. Smile encouragingly.

Ugh. I feel completely ridiculous.

What if nothing happened?

No, I can do this!

I would just use the Money Changer, like Poppy said. Along with learning potions and inventory at the shop, I'd been practicing the mind-changing techniques that Grandma Seraphina had perfected.

The Damsel: Seraphina would feign distress and the target would almost always hand her a tissue or hold her hand. *That works better on men.*

The Oops! My Bad!: Spill something on the target and hand them a hankie to clean their shirt. Or bump into the target, causing them to drop their groceries and force a physical touch.

Nope. Definitely do not want to spill hot coffee on this poor lady who is already having a tough time in her life.

The Nice To Meet You: Shake hands with the target. *Nope. It would be stupid to shake her hand when I'm only ordering coffee.* I straightened the hem of my shirt.

The good old Money Changer then.

The line was full of tourists who couldn't decide what to order and, invariably, ordered the same thing, "Beignets and a café au lait, please." The long wait caused fear to creep back into my rib cage at intervals and I breathed deeply to push it back down. Finally, my turn.

"What can I getcha, baby?" Christy asked with a thick Southern accent and a pasted on smile.

"Refill on my café au lait." I handed her a five-dollar bill that I had dusted meticulously with mind-changing powder this morning. Poppy had also rubbed the powder into my skin for what seemed like an eternity before we left. She made sure it covered every square millimeter of my skin and nails. And I had made sure not to wipe it off, even eating my beignet with a fork and knife.

"You have to let go," Christy said, smacking her gum while maintaining her customer service smile.

"Let go?" I asked nervously.

She arched her eyebrows and looked at the bill that I was still clutching in my fist.

"Right. Sorry," I said. *God, this whole thing's so stupid! I can't believe I'm doing this.* Christy took the cup that I had touched for the past hour over breakfast while I wondered what would happen next.

Please let this work. Please let this work. Please let this work.

One night last week Father Malachi had told me, "Mind changing is an exorcism of sorts."

"Exorcism?" I immediately thought of spinning heads and pea soup.

Father held up his hand. "No, no, my dear, we'll leave the Rite of Exorcism to the priests trained in that sort of thing." He chose his words more carefully. "Seraphina described mind changing to me in this way. It's like erasing a person's demons so they can have a clean slate."

"That sounds kind of terrifying," I said.

He assured me that it would be much clearer when I tried a supervised mind change.

So here we were: Christy and I. She smacked her gum, while waiting for the coffee machine to free up to refill my cup. She stared uneasily at the floor and a crease gathered between her brows. I imagined she was thinking about how to pay this month's rent. Food service was such a tough job. I knew because I'd waited tables through college, and servers had to deal with bad tippers and entitled customers all day long.

My heart swelled with compassion for this woman whose real life—hidden by a customer-service smile—was a mystery to me. The skin on my fingers tingled slightly and I investigated my hands. They weren't red and the sensation wasn't a burning, exactly. It was more like static electricity.

"Here you go," Christy said, handing me my cup of coffee. Our fingers touched again, but this time, when we made contact, I felt a subtle zap. Instantaneously, the corners of her mouth eased down and her face went blank. A split second later, she squeezed her eyes shut and shook her head a little. And then she smiled radiantly.

Okay, that was weird, I thought.

"You have a good day, baby," she chirped. Her face literally glowed and I nodded, completely confused.

Was that it? Did I do it?

I remembered what Father Malachi told me. "An exorcism of sorts. A clean slate."

Did that mean people would shine like Christy was doing at this moment? The first time I touched her with the powder—when she took my order—nothing happened. Poppy said it was supposed to happen immediately, so why didn't it? Did I do something different when I took the coffee from her than when I gave the cup to her in the first place?

I looked back at Father Malachi and Poppy and shrugged. They waved me back, so I hurried over to them.

"Wonderful." Father drew out the word when I reached the table. "Simply marvelous, my dear."

Poppy lightly clapped her hands a few times. "Yay, you."
Father pulled my chair out for me.

"Was that it?" I asked, sitting down slightly stunned.

Poppy nodded like a bobblehead doll. "Not bad for a first time. Right?"

I frowned, still confused. "But it didn't work like you said it would. She didn't respond immediately."

"You were nervous," Poppy said, waving away my concern. "The whole time you were up there, you were fidgeting and picking at your nails."

"So it doesn't always work instantly?" I asked again.

"From what Seraphina told me," Father said, resting his hand on my arm, "your inner state of being powers the spell. So if you are feeling weak, spiritually, the magic experiences a lag."

"Lag," I repeated. What happened if there was real danger? Could that cause the spell to work too slowly and cause someone, including me, to get hurt?

Poppy leaned in and stared at me until I made eye contact with her. "You did *really* well, Sophie. You did."

Finally I allowed myself a tiny smile. I was being way too hard on myself. I couldn't be perfect on my very first attempt.

"Poppy!" a man called from the sidewalk and hurried toward our table.

"Hey, Teddy." She stood up and, reaching on tiptoes because he was so big, gave him a giant bear hug.

I recognized him from the second line after Seraphina's funeral, when I'd overheard him recounting to his wife about almost killing someone in the past. I sat up, anxious about his admitted history of violence.

"I'm so sorry about Seraphina," he said.

Poppy nodded and turned to introduce us. "Teddy, you know Father Malachi from church."

"Good to see you, Theodore." They shook hands.

Poppy turned to me. "And this is Sophie. She's actually Seraphina's long lost granddaughter, believe it or not."

"Well praise Jesus!" He laughed from his belly and held out his book-sized hand to me. "Marie's girl?"

"Nice to meet you," I said and his contagiously upbeat personality made me giggle.

"So did Marie come down, too? Seraphina always hoped to see her again," he said.

"She actually passed away," I said. "A while ago."

"Oh, I'm so sorry," he said and looked at his feet. He was every bit of six foot four and easily over three hundred pounds and would have been intimidating if he wasn't such a nice guy.

"Well, I'll stop by the store sometime soon," he said, ready to continue on his way.

"Oh, Teddy, actually Father and I wanted you to tell Sophie your story. If you have a minute," Poppy said.

He checked his watch. "I can spare a few."

Poppy nodded to me, and I had no idea what was about to happen. Like always. "It's voodoo to me" was quick becoming my new M.O.

Poppy said, "Seraphina changed Teddy. One of her proudest moments."

I looked at each of the three trying to understand.

"I nearly killed my wife," he admitted solemnly.

I was floored he would so openly admit it, but managed to use a calm voice to say the only thing I could, "Wow."

Father Malachi pitched in, "Seraphina saw him walking down the street in an absolute rage. She told me she was terrified, and yet, at that moment, she felt absolutely compelled to help him."

Grandma Seraphina frightened? From what I'd heard of her, she'd seemed completely confident in her role as Mind Changer.

Teddy settled into the chair across from mine and waved his finger toward me. "If not for your grandmother, no doubt—no doubt!—I would be in jail." He emphatically tapped his index finger on the table. "Right now. For the rest of my life."

I wondered how much he knew about mind changing. Maybe some targets remained coherent during the change and then remembered everything. Or maybe, to Teddy, Seraphina was a Good Samaritan who was in the right place at the right time.

"Ever since Seraphina intervened, Teddy would come into the shop every now and then and have tea with us." Poppy sounded so proud. I could tell this work really meant a lot to her, and I'm sure my grandma felt the same way. Would I make such strong connections with the people in the community? Connecting with people sounded absolutely a-mazing to me.

"I was crazy," Teddy said, avoiding Father Malachi's general direction. "I don't really remember grabbing the gun. I keep it at my house because I live in a rough neighborhood. I was on the way to his house, the dude's house. Then I heard a voice call to me, 'Fine night.' Seraphina stood at the voodoo shop door, smoking her pipe, like she always did." He fiddled with his watch before staring me square in the face, the posture of full, unabashed confession. "I must have looked a mess, sweating, angry, like an animal or something. But the whole time, she spoke calmly. Kindly." He squinted, making sure I was still with him and I leaned forward, willing him to tell me more.

Teddy began again. "I sat down on the stoop and she sat down next to me. I put my head in my hands. And when she put her hand on my shoulder and told me, 'You don't have to do this, son,' my body, I don't know, changed somehow. It's like"—Teddy put his thumbs and forefingers together to grasp the words—"It's like something good, something light, rushed through me. I should've panicked when I realized she knew." Teddy smiled, his gaze softening. "She always knew, didn't she?"

After a moment of silence, I asked, "So what changed you?"

"She did," he said simply. "It's like her soul or something." He grasped again for the right words. "She was a good person.

Seraphina was peace and joy and you became that, too, when you were with her."

"What happened afterward?" I asked. "That night, I mean."

"I went home and slept a good sleep. Then I made up my mind that I had had enough with my woman. She was no good from the very start."

Poppy agreed emphatically with a drawn out, "Mmm-hmm."

Father Malachi interjected, "And things have been much better for you since you remarried. Let us not forget about that."

Teddy beamed. "She's my true love. I'm so happy. So, so happy." He checked his watch. "Shoot, I'm gonna be late." He turned to me. "It was nice meeting you, Sophie. And thank you," he said emphatically.

"For what?" I asked.

"For carrying Seraphina's torch. She really was a wonderful woman, your grandmother."

I teared up a bit and waved goodbye as he walked away.

When Teddy was a safe distance away I whispered to Father and Poppy, "So how much does he know?"

"About . . .?" Father raised his eyebrows to imply the words mind changing.

I nodded quickly.

"Absolutely nothing," he said.

Poppy added, "None of the targets remember anything out of the ordinary, they just remember Seraphina as a nice, grandmother type who was easy to talk to."

Father said, "Seraphina always entered their lives at the exact moment when they needed her most. People do not forget someone who changes their life for the better."

I wouldn't forget someone like that either.

Poppy needed to run some errands, so Father Malachi and I returned to the apartment together. He held his tired brown hat and we walked in silence, him inspecting the sky at intervals. Abruptly, he stopped and pulled me out of the pedestrian traffic.

"No one knew it, Sophia."

"Knew what?" I asked, completely lost.

"I loved Seraphina. Loved her so much that I wanted to leave the priesthood to marry her."

He waited for my response to his admission.

"I . . . don't know what to say." It's not that I had a problem with it, but it was certainly "out there" for a Catholic priest to fall for a voodoo priestess.

Father began walking again. "I suppose it is disconcerting to hear that a priest was in love with your grandmother."

"Did you have a relationship, a romantic one, I mean?" I asked.

"We were very close," he admitted. "But she did not want me to leave the priesthood. So no. No romantic relationship." Father paused. "Seraphina and I spent the last decade of her life talking and laughing, learning and sharing. I valued her mind and spirit and she led me to the understanding that God wants us to just be happy." He chuckled and fiddled with the brown hat in his hands. "Just."

"How do we 'just' be happy?" I asked.

"Indeed." He studied the sky. "What a large order for the smallness of human minds. I want to reconnect with myself after being a priest for so many years."

"A good goal," I said.

"So I left the priesthood," he said offhandedly.

"You mean you retired?" I asked, trying not to let a look of shock cross my face.

"My last Mass was Seraphina's funeral." He put his hat on and clutched his hands behind him.

We walked in silence.

Father Malachi was a wonderful person and, from what I'd heard, my grandma was a wonderful person. And if they shared such a strong love, it wasn't fair that they couldn't be together. But leaving the church altogether seemed like such a strong action to take.

"Such a beautiful day," he said and smiled at me.

So that was all he was going to say about that. When we got back to the apartment, he told me that I had learned enough to understand mind changing from the Catholic perspective. We spoke candidly, sharing personal stories and reviewing the material he had taught me over the past several weeks. As the conversation flowed, I realized that I felt more and more connected to the people in my life. Father Malachi, Taj, and Poppy were becoming like family to me and I felt more optimistic that, maybe, a greater force was at work in my life here.

Father ended the conversation with a question for me: "Have you decided to become the next Mind Changer, my dear?"

"Yes." My reply had started in my heart and my mouth automatically responded.

"You know, I had a dream about Seraphina the night after she died. She whispered 'Sophia' in my ear and wrapped me in her shawl. During my sermon I noticed you in that shawl and it caught my eye, so when Poppy said a young woman named Sophia needed my help, I was so excited to see if it was you. And now I feel as if I have a granddaughter of my own." He patted my shoulder and turned to go.

At the door, he placed his hand on the knob, then turned. "Sophia, you must be careful. The universe hears your decision and you will be vulnerable to dark forces until you are fully trained. Maintain your anonymity for as long as you can. Be aware of those around you. Be safe, and God bless you, my child."

That night, the nightmares returned and I clutched my rosary in the darkness. I clung to the prayers like they were a life saver, and I waited for the tall, dark waves of fear to swallow me. But the fear would leave, I would sleep, and, eventually, I trusted that my purpose would protect me. With each step in learning the craft of mind changing, I was putting on a piece of armor against the darkness just like the shining suit that Saint Joan of Arc wore. Suddenly, I could understand how Joan could listen with such faith to the voices that were giving her instructions. *Of course* she would feel sure beneath the shield of the holy words and the holy purpose. But Joan of Arc died. And it was a horrible death.

Where had God been then?

Chapter 12
Practicing Love Spells

Each week, I got better and better at helping customers at Seraphina's House of Voodoo. When the store was empty, I would memorize product labels or practice a spell in the back room to get even better at my job.

"So far, I've had to burn all of my attempts," I told Taj one day after tying a blue string around another completed love gris-gris. We had the back room door propped open so we could watch for customers. I tossed my latest gris-gris into a growing reject pile.

"Isn't that kind of wasteful?" Taj asked. His eyes sparkled and he added, "Especially for Poppy, the recycling queen."

I laughed because he was right.

"Be good to Mother Earth and she'll be good to us," I mimicked Poppy's motto.

We recycled, we composted, we reused glass jars for customers to use in our potions area, we bought recycled printer paper and merchandise bags. When I thought of all the careless ways that I had lived before knowing Poppy—and I was just one person—I was sure our planet was doomed. I pulled out another small, cloth square to try the love spell again.

"Poppy says that practice is important because we don't want to be screwing with peoples' lives," I explained. "Especially their love lives."

"Do you believe that?" Taj asked.

I shrugged. "Lately, I don't know what I believe."

"How so?" He was so attentive during our conversations.

He really listened, understood me. I liked opening up to him, even about subjects that made me uncomfortable.

"I feel like every day that I spend here, my world is slowly tipping upside down. And now I have to process the world from a new perspective. You know, readjust."

"How are you sleeping?" He asked because I had mentioned my drowning nightmare to him.

"The same." I pursed my lips.

He nodded. "Did Poppy give you a voodoo concoction to help?"

"Incense works. She thinks the dream may be some sort of spiritual intrusion . . . or some kind of psychic effect because New Orleans is surrounded by water." I rolled my eyes, forever the skeptic.

"New Orleans is an odd place," he agreed. "But unexplainable things happen in Malaysia, too."

"What sorts of things?"

Taj straightened some jars on the shelf then looked at me with doubtful eyes. "And frighten you more? Do you never want to sleep again, woman?"

"Fair enough. Tell me about your family, then. What was life like growing up in Malaysia?"

"We lived on an oil palm and rubber plantation where my father was a supervisor."

"Sounds exotic."

"When you fly into Malaysia, you see thousands of acres of palm trees planted in never-ending rows," he said, extending his arms wide.

"So you lived in the jungle?" I quipped.

"It takes thirty minutes on dirt roads to get to town and the rainy season washes out the road."

In America, we had so many ways to get what we needed: supermarkets, convenience stores, coffee kiosks, food courts, malls, the Wal-Mart.

"Life in Malaysia must be so different from life here," I remarked.

"Malaysia does have franchises and big corporations, but it has maintained its culture," he said and leaned toward me. "Maybe one day I can take you there."

I remembered Psycho Nico's prediction.

"New Orleans is the only place I have been in my entire life," I said. "Besides Saint Louis."

"Really?"

"I lived a very sheltered life." I shrugged my shoulders. "It felt safe."

"Do you miss Saint Louis?"

I thought about it, and the truth was that I felt more myself here.

"No," I said optimistically. "Do you miss Malaysia?"

"I miss my mom and dad," he admitted. "And the food: spicy noodle soups; tropical fruit; street food." He patted his stomach. "It makes me hungry just thinking about it."

"Can you find the right ingredients here?"

"Most of them. There is a very good Asian grocery store that my friends and I go to."

"Are you planning to go back to Malaysia?"

"No." His face fell. "That is something that really disappoints my father, but I want to make my own way and my mother understands that I have better opportunities in America."

"She must miss you," I said, a tinge of longing for my own mother pulling at my heart strings. Even though she wasn't perfect, she was still my mother and, deep down, I wanted to love her.

"She misses us both, me and my brother, Krishna."

"You didn't tell me you had a brother!" I swatted his arm with the back of my hand.

"He lives with me," Taj said. "He's working on his bachelor's at Loyola, so I rarely see him. He spends most of his time on campus—studying, working—but he also has a busy social life. That's why he loves living in the French Quarter with me."

"So you all split the rent?" I asked.

"No, he also likes that I pay the rent," Taj said, smiling.

I smiled, too. "Nice."

There was a long pause in our conversation. I looked up from my conjure making and saw Taj on his feet next to me.

"What?" I finally asked with an awkward smile.

"What are you afraid of, Sophie?"

"What kind of question is that?" I thought he was teasing.

"An essential question," he said.

We'd had our share of serious conversations, but this one suddenly felt more intimate. And scary.

Finally, I decided to put it out there. "The dark."

He considered my answer.

"Ridiculous, huh?" I said, glossing over my admission.

Taj shook his head. "It tells me that you, too, believe in the unexplainable. Even if your reasoning mind refuses such ideas."

Bam! He hit the nail on the head. I said nothing more, clamming up like I always did. He was breaking down my barriers and I was patching up those walls.

Eventually, Taj emptied his box of inventory, broke the box down, and threw it in the dumpster in the alley. When he came back in, I tried to get the conversation going again.

"What's your favorite American food?" I asked.

"Hot wings. I love watching baseball and eating hot wings."

"That is about as American as it gets."

"America has so much variety to offer. I have been in thirty-five of the states and every single one is so different."

"Thirty-five?" I asked. "Not even from this country and you've traveled way more than me. I need to get out more."

"I went on two big trips while I was an undergraduate because I thought I may return to Malaysia after graduation. On one trip, I visited the East Coast with a group of friends;

on the other, the West Coast. On our West Coast trip, we drove so much in two weeks that we had to pay extra for the rental car even though it had unlimited miles on the plan. The company said we put too many miles on it."

"Wow."

On his adventures, he'd visited the Statue of Liberty, the Smithsonian, the Capitol, and beaches in Florida and California. He told me about how he had gotten blinded by sparks from a pyrotechnic show in Las Vegas and his friends told him to sleep it off in the minivan, so he didn't get to see anything else in Las Vegas. He had watched the sun rise over the Grand Canyon. He had seen the sun set over the Rocky Mountains. And he had driven the vast landscapes of the southwest and the Great Plains stretching out in all directions.

He made me want to try new things. No one ever made me feel as free as he did.

"What kind of food do you like?" Taj asked.

"Day-old spaghetti and mint chocolate chip ice cream."

He turned his nose up.

"Not together," I gushed. "But sometimes I will eat my spaghetti and then the ice cream for dessert. Wow. After hearing about your adventures and eclectic tastes, I am bor-ing."

"Well, I still like you even if your favorite ice cream is mint chocolate chip." Taj grabbed his cup from the office desk and poured some water from the cooler in the back corner.

"What are you doing, Taj?" I asked, amusement in my voice.

"Getting a drink of water."

I giggled. "That's not drinking water, it's holy water. For our spells."

Taj stood still for a moment, contemplating what to do with his full cup of holy water. Then without warning, he downed the water like a shot.

I stared at him with wide eyes, and we both busted out laughing.

"It's a blessing in my country," he said.

I wasn't sure if he was teasing or if it really was a practice of Hindus to drink holy water, but it got me laughing even harder.

The bell jingled as a customer entered the store.

"I'll get that." Taj set his cup down and hurried to the front.

I watched him walk the customer around the store, picking up a few items, including a love gris-gris like the one I was conjuring. He was so compassionate, listening to her stories about love trouble and when she left the store, he held the door open for her. Guys didn't do that anymore. Older guys, maybe, but not many guys my age. He grabbed a duster from behind the counter and started cleaning the shelves. Attentive, smart, funny . . . and he cleans.

"What was that customer's story?" I asked, wanting to talk more.

"She lost her husband a few years ago and says she is ready to love again."

"She's putting a lot of faith in this." I held up the love gris-gris I was working on.

"Don't you believe in your own magic?"

"Maybe there's some sort of psychological benefit, like a placebo. If they believe in it, it works, or maybe it just gives people the courage to take action."

Taj grinned. "I would like to have that one when you are finished." He pointed to the tiny cloth bag I was working on.

"Absolutely not." I tied the thread around the top of the gris-gris bag, then he grabbed it and stuck it in his pocket. "Hey! Taj!"

"Sorry, boss." He walked toward the front of the shop, and I pursued.

"Voodoo quiz," he said, changing the subject.

"I don't want to play right now," I said. "Give it back." I eyed his pocket, but didn't feel near brave enough to go fishing for the love spell.

"Excuse me, Miss," Taj said, mimicking a tourist's voice. "I need a voodoo doll."

"Seriously. I don't want to play voodoo quiz," I whined and stomped my foot for emphasis.

"The kind with those little pins." Taj wasn't going to give up.

"Ugh, all right." Whipping up my very best authoritative voice, I said, "Actually, the dolls with pins have European roots, but we do sell them in the bins up front." I pointed out and added playfully, "For the tourists."

Taj shook his head. "Consumerism drives the voodoo doll."

"We do have these messenger dolls, though, which are used locally." I grabbed one of the simple cloth dolls from the shelf and tossed it at Taj.

He held it up and waved "hello" with its little hand. Then tossed it back to me.

"What's the difference?" He feigned ignorance.

"No pins, for one. Instead, they have a message attached with string," I said, pulling at the piece of paper tied to the doll. "You leave the doll at a crossroads or at the cemetery and the belief is that the doll will take your message to the Other Side. Basically, the messages ask the loa to intercede in the natural course of events."

"What are the low-ah?"

I couldn't tell if he was still role playing because we may not have covered the loa while studying.

"Are you serious?" I threw the doll back at him and he placed it back on the shelf.

"No." He laughed.

Of course he knew. He had been telling me all about Malaysia and, since his family was Hindu, he compared much of the voodoo elements to his family's Hindu beliefs. Like the many minor gods in Hinduism, the loa were a hierarchy of spirits that had different personalities and powers.

"I'm gonna tell you about them anyway," I sassed, grabbing a duster to tidy the shop while I practiced my spiel. "In voodoo, the loa act as intercessors to God, kind of like saints in Catholicism. And actually, in New Orleans, Catholicism and voodoo work really well together. That's why Marie Laveau was so popular, and so powerful, in both communities."

He smiled at me with his irresistible grin and tilted his head to the side playfully, cleaning but never taking his eyes off of me. My breath caught and I stared back for a bit, before slowly turning away. I didn't want to, but these little flirtations—is that what they were?—were crossing into dangerous territory. Taj was my employee. I was his boss, for God's sake.

"Now it's your turn," I said. "What would a customer ask a loa for help with?"

"The usual things that people want from God: health, wealth . . ." He paused until I looked at him again. "Love."

I blushed and bumped a holy candle with my duster. Luckily it wasn't one in a jar, and the wax just made a dull thud when it hit the floor.

The candle was damaged, so I tossed it in the trash and wrote a note to adjust inventory.

Taj considered something for a moment. "You are different since that first time we met at Night Creatures."

"How do you mean?" I asked.

"You were so . . ." He put his duster in the air, trying to grasp the word. "Resistant, I suppose."

"Resistant?"

He nodded earnestly.

"Resistant to what?" I asked indignantly.

Amusement sparkled in his eyes. "We can talk about something else," he suggested.

"No," I insisted. "Tell me."

He studied me for a moment. "I have a feeling I should change the subject."

I shook my head and grinned. "You can tell me."

"Resistant to . . . trusting others . . . being open to something new . . . to friendship." He stared at the statue he was dusting. If he could clean it by looking at it, it would be the cleanest thing in the store. Not taking his eyes off the statue, he breathed, "To love?"

I just wanted to grab the statue he was cleaning, throw it over my shoulder for dramatic effect, and kiss the hell out of him. My fingers itched to reach for the statue, but as I began moving my arm, Taj stopped dusting. He settled the statue on the shelf, then turned toward me, boring a hole into my soul with those big brown eyes.

Ugh. My heart lurched and I thought I might pass out. I turned to put some candles on the shelf, avoiding the eye contact. Taj knew me. That was the bottom line and it made me feel emotionally naked, so I covered up the confusing feelings, deciding to use humor as a shield.

I pointed the duster at him and joked, "You're fired."

"Either way, I like you," he said with absolute sincerity.

And it absolutely melted my heart. I turned away.

Say something, my inner voice urged. But the front bell rang again, ruining my chance.

I quietly said, "I'll go get that." Stupid me.

"Hey, Sophie," Taj said. "I mean it."

I nodded. *Ugh, why can't I just tell him?*

With my back to him, I mouthed the words, "I like you, too."

Chapter 13
Chrysalis

"If clothes are a representation of your inner self, what are you saying here?" Poppy asked from the doorway of my bedroom.

Glancing down at my shabby pajama pants and T-shirt, then at the clock that read 11:00, I realized I'd spent the whole morning reading about mind changing subjects.

"What? I'm comfortable." I snapped shut *Voodoo Spells for Dummies*.

"Comfortable." Poppy smirked. "Yeah, that's gonna get you a man. Take a look at me." She slowly twirled, hands on hips, sporting a trendy black tank and a flowered silk skirt with black tulle peeking from underneath the hemline. "I call this style Bohemian Eclectic. It says 'I'm fun, I'm free, I enjoy life.' What you're wearing . . ." She waved her finger in my general direction. " . . . says, 'I don't care. Just leave me to tend to my 18 cats.'"

I examined myself in the dresser mirror and saw a young woman who wanted to be invisible, never wearing colorful clothes and hiding behind long, lifeless hair.

Poppy sat on the bed next to me and pulled my hair back at the nape of my neck.

I held my chin up and noticed good bone structure and clear skin.

"When you reinvent the body, you reinvent the mind," she said. "What you need is a makeover, girl."

"You're right," I acknowledged.

"Of course I'm right. I'm always right." She released my hair and stood up abruptly. "Now go get ready."

After a hot shower, I felt so refreshed, but when I wiped the fog off of the bathroom mirror, I saw the same old Sophie. Glasses. No makeup. Comfy, shapeless black slacks. A white oxford shirt that only served to wash me out and hide my curves.

How did I want others to see me? I turned at different angles, checking out my reflection, and considering this question before standing tall. *I am spontaneous*. After all, I'd moved to New Orleans. *I am confident*. I had taken ownership of my family business and had my first mind change under my belt. Pulling my hair up into a loose chignon, I examined my face more closely. I tilted my head to the side and pursed my lips. *I am pretty*. My facial features were symmetrical and my violet eyes were unique. My olive complexion gave me the best of both worlds, because my skin would naturally lighten in the winter but give me a dark tan in the summer sun.

I smiled and flipped off the light, excited to experiment with a new look.

Before leaving the apartment, I grabbed the only interesting article of clothing that I did own, a red trench coat that skimmed my thighs as I walked. Definitely something I could work with.

"Can't I come with?" Poppy peeked over her magazine when I was at the door.

I shook my head. "I need to do this on my own and you will just try to morph me into a miniature version of you. I'm not ready for all that Bohemian Eclectic."

"I'm only letting you leave this apartment if you agree to let me go with you next time."

"Okay, okay. Bye," I sang and quickly shut the door before she could argue her case anymore.

On the way to the mall, I got distracted by a neat little antique shop and picked through their shelves of old books.

As I scanned the classics and pushed aside paperweights like *Moby Dick* and *War and Peace,* I noticed two penetrating eyes peering at me from the opposite side of the shelf.

"Jacques," I said. In a blink, he was on my side of the shelf, standing right next to me.

"Fancy meeting you here, *ma chérie*. What brings you to a dusty little place like this when you could be in your dusty little voodoo shop?"

"None of your business," I stated coldly and searched through the books, avoiding his bizarre eyes.

"I come here to treasure hunt," he said simply.

That piqued my interest because, I felt the same way. Digging through discarded things was interesting, and—if you found something good—it could be exhilarating. I turned to him and tried to read his expression.

He explained, "I buy up what I like and then profit from it or keep it in my apartment rooms for the pleasure that it gives me." He assessed me like I was a quality piece of merchandise; slowly down, then up, and I thought he may grab me by the arm like he had at the shop. To dominate me. Or charm me in some twisted, outdated way. But he didn't.

"I don't really see anything," I said abruptly. "I gotta go." I wanted to get away from him. And I *did* need to find some new clothes or Poppy would never let me hear the end of it. "My business partner needed me to pick up some things."

"Well, *ma chérie*." He held his hand out to me. "What are we buying?"

He intended to go with me? Absolutely not.

"Um—" I couldn't come up with a lie. He raised an eyebrow, still holding his hand out to me. I blushed and admitted, "She thinks I need new clothes." I paused and confirmed, "I *do* need new clothes."

"And we shan't disappoint her."

Shan't? Did people actually still use that word?

He gently took my hand and kissed the knuckles with soft lips, transporting me straight into a Victorian romance novel. Did men really act like this in the modern, real world? I snapped out of fairy-tale land.

"I can shop on my own," I asserted.

"If you indeed could"—he gestured to my appearance—"you would."

"Thanks," I said icily and walked toward the door.

He followed.

"Normally I would not speak so frankly," he said, "but I know that you are a strong woman who can take criticism and apply it precisely. Am I wrong in assuming this about you?"

"I am a woman, Jacques," I pointed out. Pulling on my sassy pants, I added, "So, yes, I can get my feelings hurt."

As I faced him, I noted his perfectly tailored slacks that highlighted a slim waist and a fitted dress shirt that hugged a perfectly built torso. He did have an eye for fashion.

He offered his elbow, and I held up one eyebrow. Really?

When I looked at him, though, an excitement rose inside of me. Jacques was so different than any other man I'd met. I felt transported back to a time when men wanted to make women feel feminine and every bit the damsel-in-distress, even though I considered myself an independent, modern woman. And when he touched me, I felt confused in a delicious sort of way.

I did dust my skin with mind change powder, I assured myself. *And I'd be careful to stay in public.*

I tentatively placed my hand into the crook of his arm and those eyes somehow convinced me it would be okay. We walked a block down and Jacques pointed to the sign hanging above the door that said "Saint Germain Shoes."

"One of my favorites," he said and smiled.

Wow, a smile, I thought.

"A family business?" I asked.

"I handpick all the shoes so that I know they are of the highest quality. This is the only place I buy for myself."

A monarch butterfly floated through the door and landed on my hand as I held a pair of black pumps from the display. I stood completely still, transfixed.

Jacques commented, "If a monarch lands on you it means you descend from royalty. Did you know that the word chrysalis actually means 'gold' in Greek?"

"In English it means 'showy,'" I stated.

"*Touché.*"

The butterfly floated into the air and out the door.

I asked, "Do you speak Greek?"

He nodded. "As a boy, I learned Greek and Hebrew. Then I went to university in Europe and spent much time traveling, so I picked up French, Spanish, Italian— No, no, no."

"What?" I scrutinized the black pump on my foot.

"Not those."

I thought they were a beauty basic, but I took it off and set it back on the display.

"Try these instead." Jacques pulled out a pair of four-inch patent heels that oozed sophistication.

I slipped them on and instantly felt sexier and more confident as they pushed my posture up, up, up. They were incredible shoes, but I would have never chosen them for myself.

"Okay?" I said, meaning for it to come out as an assertion, not a question. But Jacques took it as a confirmation and swiftly signaled the clerk who came over holding three more boxes of shoes in my size: ballet flats, boots, and red, peep-toe heels.

"What do you think, *ma chérie*?"

They all fit perfectly. I posed in the mirror in the red ones.

I asked, "How do they look?"

"Superb, of course."

"Okay," I said, my confidence growing.

He abruptly said, "Put them all on my account, Gilles." The clerk nodded and boxed them up.

"No. Let me—" I started to say, but Gilles completed the transaction and put the receipt in the bag as I fished for my credit card.

"It's already done," Jacques said smoothly. "Your love potion has been doing so well for me, it is the least I can do."

Hopefully, he wasn't testing the love potion out on me. He was beautiful, but definitely not for me. Too overbearing.

"Shall we continue?" Jacques held his arm out to me, grabbed my bags, and nodded to Gilles.

My view of Jacques slowly did a complete one-eighty over the course of the day. We shopped, walked, talked, and I saw a whole new side of him. *Maybe he hadn't meant to scare me at the shop*, I thought. *This was just his way*.

This Jacques—the polite, dashing man I'd first met at Grandma Seraphina's funeral—was a true gentleman. He refused to let my buy anything, and I ended up with an entirely new wardrobe including designer bags, clothes, shoes, and even, lingerie. Shopping for the lingerie definitely made me leery, but he sat patiently in the waiting area while a sales woman fit me with exquisitely made undergarments.

When I was done, I stepped out of the fitting room, wearing one of my new dresses and the red heels. I felt poised and sexy.

"All finished," he claimed satisfactorily. He whipped out his phone and ordered, "I want you to deliver Miss Nouveau's purchases to her apartment." He ended the call and turned his undivided attention back to me—the entire day he'd given me undivided attention. "How do you feel, *ma chérie*?"

"Great, actually." I felt like a million bucks, right down to my high-end skivvies.

After we ate, he fingered a lock of my hair and frowned. "This needs some fixing, I believe." Before I could blink, he whipped out his phone and made a call to his personal stylist.

We walked into the boutique salon and I spun in the beauty chair as the man, in a tight V-neck tee, cut my hair, colored it, and did my makeup to complete my transformation.

"What do you think?" the stylist asked as he spun my chair to face the mirror.

I couldn't believe it was me staring back. The girl from the bathroom mirror this morning was gone and replaced by a chic, put-together woman. My waist-length auburn hair was gone. At my request for "a big change," the stylist had dyed it a deep blackberry color and cut it just above my shoulders. He parted it to the side in a messy bob style.

The stylist measured the ends one more time and said, "I love this color against your gorgeous olive skin."

"You are stunning," Jacques said.

My heart was in a whirlwind. Who was this man and why was he doing this for me?

To finish the day, we had coffee and dessert at a rooftop restaurant overlooking the Mississippi. The sun sank into the river in a blaze of magenta and aubergine.

I remembered Taj, and guilt collected in my gut. Spending the day with Jacques felt like some kind of betrayal. What did Jacques want from me? Some kind of relationship? Friendship? What? I wasn't the kind of girl to have romantic trysts if that's what he had in mind.

"You are so quiet, *ma chérie*," Jacques said as he delivered me to my doorstep. The Jacques I had encountered at the shop had completely vanished into thin air.

"Sorry," I said. "Just thinking." I shook my head and looked him in the eyes. I wasn't so scared of his eyes anymore. "Thank you," I said, pleasantly surprised by how good of a day it had been. Maybe I misread Jacques before.

"There is one more item," he said, revealing a Tiffany box from his jacket pocket. "Something I found while you were getting your hair cut."

I put my hands up to decline. "You've given me too much already."

"Take it," he said softly.

Delicately unraveling the bow, I opened the box where sat a butterfly ring with delicate wings made of sparkling diamonds and threads of inlaid gold.

My breath caught. I held the box, unsure what to say, unsure what to do. He took the box from me and slipped the ring on my finger.

"Chrysalis means gold," he pointed out.

"It also means showy," I said softly, teasing. I fingered the edges of the butterfly's delicate wings, examining its glittering diamonds. *Knowing Jacques, those are real*. And then my guard went up trying to understand this lavish gift. Was it an apology for how he handled me at the shop? If I had, in fact, seen him with the missing blonde, was he trying to buy my silence? Was he straight up trying to buy me? I raised my eyes to his, searching, and that strange, immediate calm settled over me.

No. This was the genteel Jacques. This Jacques wanted a new start. Maybe this whole day, all this extravagant treatment was his way of starting fresh. I could certainly understand the need for a clean slate because that was why I was here in New Orleans.

"You have emerged from your chrysalis," he remarked, slipping the ring on my left middle finger and delicately kissing my hand. "You are a revelation, *ma chérie*." He bowed gracefully, smiled that deliciously mischievous smile, and walked away into the night.

I pulled Jacques' business card from the bottom of the Tiffany box. He had written a note on the back that read:

My Voodoo Butterfly,
May I call on you soon?
—Jacques

I walked slowly up to my apartment trying to process

this completely different side of Jacques. I leaned against the door to close it, still deep in thought.

"Oh. My. God," Poppy said, shock spreading across her face.

"What?!" I fiddled with the ends of my newly shorn hair. "You don't like it." I panicked, pulling at my new dress and rethinking the red peep toes. "It's the shoes, isn't it?" I shook my head. "Red's too much."

"You cut off all of your hair." She pulled the ends of my shaggy bob to check the length. "And it's dark purple," she said incredulously.

The stylist had dyed it the shade of blackberries to match my violet eyes. I really liked it, so my muscles tensed, wondering what Poppy thought.

She shook her head saying, "I absolutely . . ."

"Don't say it! I will get it dyed back tomorrow and it will grow back! I knew it was stupid to even try something new!"

"Sophie, stop! I was going to say I love it. I never would have thought you would go for something like this, but you look amazing. With your stylish shoes and fun accessories." Her bright smile faded a bit and she asked, "Do you feel like this is really you?"

"I had a little help," I admitted.

"What do you mean?"

"I ran into Jacques Saint Germain and he showed me around town. He even brought me to his stylist. I've never met anyone with a personal stylist."

All my bags were scattered around the living room, with the contents laid out on the couch and chairs.

"Looks like you've already seen my new clothes," I said, irked.

"How could you afford all of this?" she asked.

"Actually, Jacques paid for it all." It was really none of her business.

"What do you mean he paid for it?" She put her hands on her hips. "What does he want in return?"

"I guess he wants to take me on a date," I said, pulling his business card out of the Tiffany box so she could read the note, too. "What do you think?"

"I think this is all a little too Cinderella," she said, examining the card more closely.

"Yeah," I confessed. "I'm not so sure it's me either." I shoved the merchandise aside and plopped down on the couch.

Poppy sat next to me.

"Well, you do look gorgeous." She paused. "Give it some time and we can always go shopping for different clothes. Don't forget that you owe me that." She nudged me and I smiled.

She handed the card back to me and I tried to decide about the date. After a few moments of indecision, I tossed it onto the coffee table. I needed to think over everything that had happened in my recent past: new city, new home, new business. A new guy might just push me over the edge.

But what about Taj?

Chapter 14
Failure

All week I avoided Taj at work because, after that note from Jacques, I was straight up confused. I didn't want to lead Taj on and then turn around and date Jacques. Why was I so torn? Taj should be the easy choice, right? Of course, Taj wasn't an official dating choice, because he hadn't even asked me out. *Hmm. Maybe I was working that relationship up in my head.*

One day at work, I hid in the back room while Poppy and Taj worked with customers up front. I was supposed to be checking spell ingredient inventory, but I couldn't stop thinking about this love triangle. Could I even call it that when I wasn't sure if Taj was a part of it? I ripped a piece of paper from my voodoo notebook and drew a line down the middle, labeling one side 'Taj' and the other 'Jacques.' *This is so stupid.* But necessary, I decided.

On Taj's side of the paper, I easily wrote bullet points:
—makes me feel safe
—makes me laugh
—cute
—easy to be with
—compassionate
—can talk about anything, which turns me on
—teaches me new things
—I can be myself
—great smile
—makes me want to be a better person

On Jacques' side, I struggled to make a list:
—exhilarating
—scares me
—sexy
—confusing
—dangerous?
—pushes me
—player?

Obvious choice? Taj. Especially since all of his bullet points were pros, whereas Jacques had almost all cons and question marks.

Friday night, at Seraphina's House of Voodoo, my stomach churned for another reason. I was going out for a "real" mind change. Poppy would go with me, but it would be a much more complex and dangerous target than Christy, my first mind-change target, had been. We'd also go out after midnight, because more crime occurred then.

Poppy drilled into my brain, "Seraphina always said no good can come after midnight."

So we would seek out a more difficult target to up the ante in my training.

Sitting behind the checkout counter, I tried to busy myself with paperwork, but my brain kept envisioning the perfect mind change like a runner visualizing the perfect race.

"Are you wearing contacts?" Taj asked, interrupting my anxiety-ridden thoughts.

I blushed. He'd noticed.

"My first pair," I admitted.

"And you have been wearing makeup. I wasn't sure because I haven't seen much of you this week," he said lightly.

Guilt settled at my core.

"It's new," I said, glancing at my smoky eye shadow and blood red lipstick in the mirror by the Voodoo Jewels. "I'm still not sure if I like it."

"What do you mean?" Taj asked.

I hesitated, guilt settling in the pit of my stomach. Then I realized I hadn't done anything wrong and I didn't want to hide anything from Taj.

"Jacques gave me a makeover," I said.

Taj knew who Jacques was because I'd told him about the strange behavior Jacques exhibited the day he came in for the love spell. Didn't exactly paint the nicest picture of Jacques.

"You seem so . . ." Taj studied my new wardrobe, searching for the right word. "Different."

"You don't like it?" I asked nervously. I pulled at my new cashmere sweater.

"You look really good," he said, the compliment making my heart flutter. "It's just hard to believe that you are underneath this new façade."

"I'm still me," I said. "Just trying something new." I opened a FedEx box and began unpacking the Voodoo Jewels that had come in a shipment, arranging them on the spinning display rack.

He came over to the counter and helped me untangle the jewelry.

"I admire your willingness to change. Try something new," Taj admitted. "My family would never leave Malaysia and they didn't understand why I wanted to come to school in America."

"My move to New Orleans was definitely not as momentous as yours was," I said, shrugging off the compliment.

"You chose to take a risk and run this shop, even though you never met your grandmother," he said. "That shows a real dedication to your family's legacy."

My cheeks flushed underneath my new blush, probably making me turn radioactive pink.

"Oh," I said, busying myself with a stack of earrings. "I'm just doing what anyone else would do."

"Not everyone." He shook his head. "You could have sold out so easily. You own a building in the French Quarter. Prime real estate."

That thought had never crossed my mind.

"This is the only connection I have to my family," I explained. All of my family members had passed, but I felt a piece of them every time I stepped into the shop. Regret at not knowing my family while they were alive settled over me. I glanced the Voodoo Jewels and then scanned the shop, realizing much of the inventory that my grandmother had touched had been sold by now. I took a deep breath and the incense scent, which always hung in the air, calmed me. This is where I belonged.

"You okay?" Taj asked.

I nodded, swallowing down my emotions.

"You sure?" he pushed.

"Yep," I whispered and focused on my work. "Could you break down that box?" I pointed to the empty box on the counter.

"Sure," he said, walking it to the back office. When he returned he told me, "I see how hard you work. You are determined to succeed with your business. You are smart, you learn fast." Taj made his way around the store, straightening merchandise in the bins and on the shelves. "When's the last time Waldo ate?" he asked, pointing to the boa constrictor by the front door.

"I gave her a mouse yesterday, so she's good."

He wanted to tell me something. I could feel it.

He finally said, "I guess it's just, well, it's really none of my business."

"What?" I asked, completely oblivious.

"I do not trust Jacques. I don't trust him," Taj said with a measure of ferocity I'd never heard from him before.

That's so unlike Taj. And completely hot.

"And him taking you on that shopping spree?" He let out a disgusted sigh. "Helping you to be . . ." Taj waved his hands indicating my new outfit. " . . . like this . . . like some dress-up doll. I thought you were your own person, Sophie."

I shot him the stink eye. *Watch it, buddy*. But, he was right, and I liked that he was being so straightforward. A lot. I'd never seen him like this—all passionate—and it made my heart do somersaults. I stopped fiddling with merchandise and looked directly at him. If this were a romance novel, instead of my real life, he would stride over to the counter, take me in his arms, and kiss me with wild abandon.

Instead, he stood across the shop looking at me and began again, this time with his typically soothing voice.

"Can't you see that he's changing you?"

A shot to the heart. I knew Taj was right, but if he wanted me, why didn't he try to pursue me the way Jacques had? I turned back to my work, stocking the Voodoo Jewels, and putting my emotional armor back in place.

Though I couldn't make eye contact with him, I did ask quietly, "Are you jealous?"

"Yes."

I froze.

He walked over to me and took my hands and I absolutely melted. Where was my armor? Speechless, I could only search his lovely eyes. Unlike Jacques' eyes, which almost took away a part of me, Taj's eyes drew me into a place that felt like home. I wanted him to keep his eyes on mine and I liked the feel of my hands in his.

But then the shop door jingled open, bringing in a customer, and I reluctantly withdrew my hands from his, and even as I helped the customer, my hands still tingled from Taj's touch.

Nothing more happened, but I ran the incident through my head after Taj left for the evening.

As Poppy printed out the day's sales figures, she interrupted my thoughts with a question.

"You know what Taj told me?" Poppy said, that mischievous grin plastered across her face. She was definitely Team Taj.

"I'm sure you're going to tell me," I said, sweeping up the floor.

"He watched you with a customer the other day. It was a woman who was having back problems and you spent, like, an hour with her."

"We decided on Seven Herb Bath," I said. I remembered the woman very clearly. "She was hunched over in pain, poor thing."

"That's exactly it, Sophie," Poppy told me in her "duh" tone. "Taj notices how good you are with the customers. He said he loves how much you really care about the people who come in here."

A Mona Lisa smile crossed my lips but, not one who takes compliments easily, I concentrated on my sweeping.

"You do," Poppy said. "You really listen to people. That's something that can't be taught, it just is who you are."

"Thanks," I said, concentrating on the floor. My heart was ready to burst from my chest with excitement. *He noticed.*

"That's why you'll make an excellent Mind Changer," she insisted.

Poppy stapled a stack of papers and filed them away. "Hey, you still having those nightmares?" she asked.

I nodded.

Poppy remarked, "I wish we could figure those out."

"Me, too."

"Let's close up."

I'd gotten used to the routine: say our protection prayers aloud, shut down the computers, check the doors and windows, turn out the lights. We had gotten so good at working together, but every time we prepared to walk out the front door, I remembered that death threat. *My* death threat that would forever be seared into my brain:

Death is coming for you.
You are helpless to resist.

A chill ran down my spine.

"Ready?" Poppy placed her hand on my shoulder and I jumped about a mile. She dangled the key chain in her raised hand.

I ran some prayers through my mind, because tonight the dark terrified me even more. Would the prayers and spells protect me during the mind change? Poppy nudged the stuck door and the hinges creaked just like in a horror flick. The dark, silent street awaited us.

I wiggled my arms and legs, the runner in me shaking out pre-race jitters. All of my senses stood at attention because of this stupid mind change attempt. *Maybe I should just forget it. Try again some other night.*

"Are you coming?" Poppy waited for me to come outside.

I scanned the periphery for shadows, like some kind of action-movie hero, as Poppy locked the door. The darkness made the hair on the back of my neck prickle. I swung my head around, thinking I spotted something creeping around the corner, only to see a normal shadow retreat into normalcy. Was the dark playing tricks on me? Would it send out claw-like, gripping hands when I turned my back on it?

Poppy strode away and I jogged to catch up with her. We skirted the building, taking care to stay within the protective circle of the sidewalk. I wanted to hug the wall, literally put my hands around the building, knowing that I had a bubble of voodoo protection from whatever was out there.

I thought again of the death threat, my hands balling into fists, my heart pumping with adrenaline, readying myself for attack. Time stretched into slow motion and when we finally reached the back door, I scanned the surroundings for danger as Poppy unlocked the apartment door.

So far, so good.

Footsteps echoed in the alley and I jerked my head toward the intruder. A neighbor waved and dropped some trash in the bin. I sighed and raised my hand in response.

"Hi there," Poppy said cheerfully, not even noticing my frazzled state.

I thought about how tonight's mind change would be different. Unlike the trial run at Café Du Monde, we'd be doing this at night with no one else around. Poppy said it was best to work one-on-one with the target to avoid too much attention from bystanders. Christy's mind change had been subtle, but at night, violent offenders would gather too much public attention. The thought of being alone, in the dark, with aggressive attackers made me sick to my stomach, but Poppy assured me that she would train with me until I felt comfortable enough to go out on my own. When would that be? *Never*, was my gut response.

Upstairs in our apartment, Poppy dusted my skin with powder and ran through the plan for the umpteenth time. She would be the bait while I hid in the shadows behind her, ready with a fistful of mind-changing powder. I could either a) throw the powder at the assailant, or b) touch the person with my powdered skin.

"What if this doesn't work instantly? Christy's response was so delayed," I said, picking my fingernails.

"That was because you doubted," Poppy reminded me.

How could I be sure that I'd have enough faith in my supernatural power, this time, for it to take effect at all?

"I'm taking this just in case," I said, holding up my pepper spray key chain.

"That's ridiculous. The powder is much more powerful," Poppy said matter-of-factly.

"I'm taking it."

"Whatever."

I refused to put one hundred percent of my faith in voodoo, which made me wonder why my Grandma had so much faith in the delicate powder.

"Do I need to say the words from the spell?" I asked.

"No, the words are already imprinted on the powder when we make it in the shop."

Over the past weeks, I had memorized the incantation, which I'd jotted down in my voodoo notebook.

Butterfly wings mixed with bone dust
Take these innocent lives we must.
The sacrifice is great to evade harm's way.
God change your mind from night to day.

"Ready?" Poppy asked.

"Ready as I'll ever be," I said, lacing up my running shoes. If I needed to run, I wanted to have good shoes on my side. And my pepper spray.

When we walked into the alley, the flickering gas streetlamp weakly illuminated our path. Poppy had decided the location of this first official mind change attempt weeks ago, but would not name the place for fear that I would research everything about the spot and scare myself silly. She was right.

"The house carries a heavy darkness about it," Poppy said. "So we cannot let that affect us. Hold on to the light inside of you, okay? Almost there."

I followed closely, glancing over my shoulders at intervals to be sure no one—or no thing—was following us. The shadows on the sidewalks and buildings stretched like phantom hands trying, I was convinced, to grab at our heels or pull at our clothes.

"I hate the dark," I said, "Why did I even think that I could do this?"

"No negativity, Sophie. I am right here with you." She stopped and looked across the street, "That's it."

A mansion with prison-gray plaster walls rose three stories above the street, its second level roped in by an exquisite, black iron rail. Tar-black shutters outlined the second floor windows.

"Of course it would be dark and ominous." I said.

"Shh," Poppy hushed.

The top floor windows were barred with white window grills, but peculiarly, one of the windows was completely bricked in.

"Why would someone block out that window instead of just replacing it?" I asked as we crossed the street to stand underneath the black balcony above.

"Never mind about that," Poppy said. "Oh! Did I tell you what Father Malachi said about Christy?"

I lifted my eyebrow. She wanted to talk about this right now?

"She got promoted to manager at Café Du Monde," she said enthusiastically. "Isn't that great news?"

"Really?" I asked softly, wondering if I possessed the power to change Christy's life, could I change the world for the better.

"Yes, really," Poppy said. She nodded at me and gave me a quick, tight hug. "We can do this. You can do this."

The tidal wave of emotion in me surged in a powerful and affirming way. Yes, I could do this.

Poppy flipped through a book. *Holy Bible*, the spine read.

A gust of air screamed through the street, then fog spilled like waterfalls from the rooftops of the row houses surrounding us.

We had positioned ourselves at the corner of the mansion, so I could hide around the side of the building. The cold, dampness of the masonry seeped through my jacket and chilled my back.

The gaslights lining the sidewalk winked out. Poppy pulled out a key chain light to help her read.

"You who dwell in the shelter of the Most High, who abide in the shadow of the Almighty, say to the Lord, 'My refuge and fortress, my God in whom I trust.' God will rescue you from the fowler's snare . . ." Poppy shouted out into the street like some kind of soap box crazy.

Immediately a set of footsteps echoed against the tall row houses. We were covered in absolute darkness, except for a blood red moon high in the sky. The footsteps, along with an intermittent tapping sound, came closer. *Tap. Tap. Tap.* The footfalls didn't faze Poppy one bit.

" . . . You shall not fear the terror of the night nor the arrow that flies by day, nor the pestilence that roams in darkness . . ."

The streetlamps flared brightly and a shadow stretched in the wake of the flames.

I peeked around Poppy and saw that a man holding a cane loomed twenty feet from us. I couldn't see his face because the strange fog encircled him. The preternatural mist filled the street, slinked toward us, and wrapped itself around our ankles. It felt bitterly cold.

Poppy looked up at the shadow man but did not stop speaking the words. He did not move. He was toying with her, but I could not tell if the man had seen me crouched in my hiding spot.

"No evil shall befall you, no affliction come near your tent . . ."

The shadow man stepped toward us, flanked by the fog, and, as he approached, I could see that he wore a bull mask, obscuring his identity.

Poppy handed a bottle of holy water back to me. I considered reaching for my pepper spray, weighing my options for about two seconds: pepper spray, holy water . . . holy water, pepper spray. *Forget the pepper spray.* The holy water vial shook in my hands as I fumbled to open the cap and anoint myself with a quick sign of the cross.

" . . . For God commands the angels to guard you in all your ways . . ." Poppy's voice rose and dozens of pigeons shot into the air from their perch underneath the balcony and I stood up before it was time. With a loud burst, their wings banged against my head and shoulders as their gray feathers rained down on me.

"Get the powder!" Poppy whispered sharply back at me and quickly turned her eyes back to the figure.

I dipped my hand into a pouch and pulled out a handful of mind-changing powder, readying myself to jump from my position.

" . . . Whoever clings to me I will deliver; whoever knows my name I will set on high. All who call upon me I will answer; I will be with them in distress; I will deliver them and give them honor. With length of days I will satisfy them and show them my saving power."

Poppy slammed the book shut.

The figure swung his cane, hitting Poppy below the knees, knocking her feet out from underneath her. She hit the ground with a sickening thud.

"Poppy!" I screamed, running at the man full speed. I clipped him with my shoulder, dropping my handful of mind-changing powder, and skidded to the ground myself.

The fog swooped in, so I lost sight of Poppy, even though she was within arm's reach.

"Sophie," she strained to say my name because the wind was still knocked out of her.

I searched for her with my fingers, but couldn't find her so I grabbed another handful of mind-changing powder.

Our attacker grunted, like he'd been punched in the gut. The cane skittered across the pavement.

"Poppy!" I whispered loudly, fear choking me. "Where is he?"

And then the next attack.

Something strong—really strong—knocked me to the ground. My gut seized as I had the wind knocked out of me and I struggled for air. In a blur, I was up against the building with my face held to the cold, damp wall. I tasted gritty mortar at the corner of my mouth. The smell of centuries of decay filled my nostrils and I couldn't breathe. Gasping, I gripped the powder in my hand as tightly as I could, knowing it was the only thing that might save me. Out of the corner of my eye I could see the dropped vial of holy water lying on the pavement just out of reach. Twisting, squirming, fighting hard to break free from the powerful being, I could not get away.

It leaned in, hot breath at my ear. "There are creatures out here, *ma chérie*, that will kill you so fast." Whispers from human lips, not demon lips. "You would not even know what hit you."

The man let go and I simultaneously spun, hurling the powder with all my might. But he vanished. The footsteps retreated and the fog slipped away.

My peripheral vision detected a dark shape fly over the ridge of a row house across the street. My body shook violently with anger, fear, and adrenaline.

"You okay?" Poppy gasped, struggling to her feet. Her knees and palms were all skinned up.

"Oh my God, you're hurt!" I screamed. It wasn't enough that he'd tried to harm me, but he injured Poppy in the process.

"Why didn't the powder work?" I demanded. My knees buckled and I sat on the ground, staring. "I can't do this . . . I just . . ." I said, my voice cracking. I wanted to run away, leave New Orleans forever, and then I immediately gritted my teeth, hating myself for even thinking it. But this was way too hard. The danger, too real.

"I'm too weak," I said, tears streaming down my flushed face. My heart still raced from the attack.

"Sophie," Poppy said emphatically. "You are not weak." She sat down next to me and said softly, "Mind changing is dangerous work. You face the things of peoples' nightmares."

This wasn't really making me feel any better. I stood up abruptly, feeling the flutter of panic in my chest. *We have to get out of here. It's not safe.*

Poppy jumped up to keep pace with my quick steps. I didn't know where I was going. *Away.*

"It's scary," she said. "You are not weak. Don't ever think that about yourself."

Dizzy and hyperventilating, I stopped and bent over, trying to catch my breath. Finally, I managed to say, "I am so not ready for this."

"Girl, you better get ready," Poppy said with so much resolve there was no way I could question it.

I stood up and glared at her.

"How can you be so nonchalant?" I snapped. "We could have been killed!" I pointed back to that terrible dark building. *This was just supposed to be a trial run. Just practice.*

"Your purpose will protect you," she said simply and with conviction. She held up her battered hands to show me her battle wounds. "I gotta go get these cleaned up. We can talk more at home." She turned on her heel, stepping through the wisp of fog that remained at our feet.

"So not ready," I repeated, staring in shock at my own still-trembling fingers.

Chapter 15
Thanksgiving

Once we got back to the safety of the apartment, my emotional dam burst. "Why didn't all your protection hocus-pocus work?" The skeptic in my head, showing up after weeks of silence, shouted, *See! I told you this was a bad idea!* "And what about the Mind Changer powder?" I wiped away some tears, but refused to completely break down.

"What if they did work and they prevented things from being much worse?" Poppy stayed calm, standing behind her beliefs.

"You're being way too blasé about all this. We could have been killed!" I stomped off to the bathroom and shouted over my shoulder, "I'll be right back. We need to get you cleaned up."

I returned with a handful of first-aid supplies: a wet wash cloth, a bottle of peroxide, bandages, antibiotic ointment, ice packs.

"Maybe the spells couldn't work because we are dealing with something that is not human," Poppy suggested.

"What does that even mean?" I cleaned dirt and blood from her right hand.

Poppy stared into blank space, working through something in her mind.

"When I get to the shop tomorrow, I'll look in my reference books," she said.

"And what am I supposed to do about this?" I nodded to a familiar ivory envelope on the coffee table with its blood-red wax seal still intact. It had been taped to the apartment door when we returned from the mind change attempt. My name was scrawled across the front of the envelope in precise calligraphy, but I didn't need to open it to know what it said.

"I'm not opening it," I said, putting peroxide on a fresh cotton ball and dabbing at Poppy's wounds. Where had I seen that calligraphy before? It seemed like I'd seen it somewhere else besides the death threats. "Are you sure you couldn't see his face, Poppy?" I asked softly.

She shook her head. "I'm sorry, Sophie. That bull mask never came off."

"What did I ever do to this guy? And if he wants to kill me, why didn't he just do it tonight when he had the chance?"

"Let me see the note," Poppy said. She broke the seal, and I clicked my tongue in annoyance. She flipped the piece of paper over, examining it like a scientist inspecting a piece of forensic evidence.

Applying ointment to the scrapes on Poppy's knees, I ran the events of the night through my head and one thing didn't make sense to me.

"Did you say that he held you down?" I asked to clarify.

Poppy nodded.

"How could he hold both of us at the same time?" She'd been on the ground and I was up against the building. I shook my head, the incongruous information making me even more confused.

"It happened so fast," Poppy reasoned.

"Maybe he was working with someone," I suggested. But I hadn't heard or seen anyone else.

"He had his foot on my back, so maybe he could have held you, too, with his upper body."

"Maybe . . ." I placed a large bandage over each of her knees. She sucked in her breath through her teeth. "Sorry," I said.

"It's okay."

"Did you hit him?" I asked, remembering the loud grunt after Poppy had gone down.

"Nope," she replied. "After he knocked my legs out from underneath me, I was down for the count."

"Didn't he drop his cane though?"

Poppy held a hand to her head, racking her brain, and sighed. "I'm sorry, Sophie. I just can't remember all the details because I was in a lot of pain."

"I know." Guilt twisted knots in my stomach as I assessed Poppy's injuries, her body bruised and bandaged. I had to figure out what happened and who this monster was.

I wondered about the shadow I had seen flying over the rooftops. No person could get to the third floor that fast, even if you could find a way to scale the building.

"I feel like my mind is playing tricks on me now," I said. "Like it was just a bad dream."

You'd think that all the adrenaline would have imprinted the attack in my mind in precise detail. But my memory of the event was fading fast.

"I don't know exactly what happened either, but it is strange that the powder wouldn't work," Poppy said, scrutinizing the writing on the card even further, trying to find out some kind of clue.

"I guess none of it got on his skin," I reasoned, not wanting Poppy to know how skeptical I felt about the spell now.

"We do have one clue. We know what his voice sounds like," Poppy said.

"I kind of feel like that's fading, too." I remembered abruptly what the attacker had called me: ma chérie. I sat straight up. *Only one person calls me that. Jacques.*

"What?" Poppy asked, setting an ice pack on her knee.

I pushed down the intuitive jump. I reminded myself that I never got a look at the attacker's face and I was under incredible stress all night.

"Nothing," I said softly.

"We know that he has nice stationery." Poppy held the card up and then tossed it on the coffee table. "We need some chamomile tea."

She stood up slowly.

"No, no," I said. "Let me get it."

"I'm okay," she said and hobbled to the kitchen. She'd taken the brunt of the attack, and my heart welled with guilt again. *It should've been me that got hurt.*

"Aren't you scared?" I asked.

"I know we're safe in here. Grandma Seraphina was never attacked at home."

The fear in my heart didn't trust that I was safe. Anywhere.

"I just don't know," I mumbled.

"What don't you know?" Poppy asked, filling the kettle with water.

"At first I thought I could just be happy running the shop. But now . . ." My voice trailed off. *Should I give up?* I finally plucked up the courage to at least pick up the note.

"What are you saying, Sophie?"

"I'm not built for adrenaline and danger." *I'm a survivor, not a thrill-seeker.* I inspected the letter with its deliberate calligraphy on its deceptively beautiful ivory paper. The wax seal, like a drop of coagulated blood, embossed the image of an hour glass running out of time. I opened the message and read the words:

On Death's list, you stay.

The next few days passed as a blur. I kept to myself, letting Poppy or Taj help customers while I mixed potions in the back and sent out online orders. It felt like the times growing up when I laid low until my mom was done with a drinking binge.

I was scared. I wanted to survive. The whole time, a poisonous idea had taken root in my mind: *I need to run.*

"I'm moving back to Saint Louis," I finally confessed to Taj and Poppy before I left the shop for the day.

"What? Why?" Taj sputtered. Shock and confusion settled across his face.

I turned to Poppy because Taj didn't know about the supernatural side of my job description. Shop owner by day, voodoo priestess superwoman by night. He could never know about my secret life, or about my secret feelings for him.

"Sophie," Poppy said sharply. "You need to give it time at . . . the shop." Poppy's voice went up indicating that, "the shop" was code for mind changing. "The shop,"—the inflection again—"is stressful for someone who is not as familiar with this kind of work. You came from a very different upbringing, but it is in your blood to . . ." She paused. " . . . be responsible for 'the shop.'"

"I may have been born into this . . . line of work . . . but it's too much . . . responsibility," I explained, choosing my words carefully. My shoulders slumped in defeat. I hated giving up. Seraphina's House of Voodoo and mind changing had been a part of my family's heritage for generations and I was just walking away.

"Maybe it's a good sign that you're scared because it shows that you are willing to take some risk and, God forbid"—she threw up her hands—"have some excitement in your rigid, scheduled life."

"Did you ever think that maybe I like rigid and scheduled even if it means that it's—"

"Boring!" Poppy accused.

"Safe," I hissed and made a slashing motion with my hand across my throat because I wanted to end the conversation.

Taj's confusion changed to suspicion, so I told him, "You know, the store could get robbed and crime has gotten really bad down here." I turned on Poppy again, "I watch the news. I know."

"I wish you would have told me that this is why you've been so quiet the past few days," Poppy said.

"Well, it was my decision to make." I crossed my arms over my chest and Poppy did the same. Stalemate.

Taj intervened, "Obviously there is something going on between you two. But, Sophie, you and Poppy can work this out." Taj's composure calmed the storm within me and I just wanted to change the subject.

"What are you doing for Thanksgiving?" I asked him.

Poppy grabbed the broom from the back room.

"I'm gonna go sweep the front and back doorways," she huffed. As she walked away, she muttered, "Mama Marie and Papa Legba, help me."

Taj watched Poppy sweep furiously and then turned slowly to me with wide eyes. When I refused to acknowledge Poppy's tantrum, he relented.

"Sophie," he said.

I knew he'd try to talk me out of leaving.

"Do you celebrate Thanksgiving?" I pressed.

"Normally my brother and I have turkey curry with friends."

"Do you two get home for the holidays?" I asked, clicking print on the computer to get the day's sales figures.

"Don't do this," he said, trying to talk me down.

I raised an eyebrow and waited for his answer. I was changing the subject and that was that.

"Actually, we have not been home in three years," Taj said.

A heaviness settled over the conversation and I wondered if he was homesick or if he was mad at me, too, for leaving.

He turned to put some candles on the shelf. "Sophie, don't go."

The look he gave me melted my heart.

I stood up and began arranging things to avoid eye contact. I really, really liked Taj, and Poppy, and I didn't want to hurt them, but I knew my leaving was going to impact them just like it was me.

"I'd like to hear more about your family," I said softly, trying to distance myself from my strong feelings for him and disconnect from this new life that was trying to hold me to New Orleans and the life of a Mind Changer.

Taj cocked his head to the side and waited for me to tell him what was going on with me. I wouldn't do it. I'd already put Poppy at risk and I couldn't endanger Taj, too. He went back to busying himself with the candles.

He finally relented, saying, "We would fly home more often if plane tickets were not so expensive, but I try to call Amah about once a week. Krishna talks to her less often, but my mom and I are very close and we will stay on the phone for hours. I miss her, especially her cooking." His voice like a sad song, he continued. "When I go home, she makes my favorite dish, rasam, which is a spicy and sour broth garnished with tomatoes. You pour it over rice and serve it with a meat curry. So good."

I kept my fingers busy with work, but eyed him to make sure he was okay.

He pinched the bridge of his nose and then let his arm fall to his side. He was upset with me.

"My mother and I weren't close," I admitted. I'd always wanted to escape my mother, but she was too sick and I didn't want to turn my back on her. Then I realized that I had my mind set to turn my back on Poppy and Taj. "Is that natural?"

"Is what natural?" He placed a vial of snake oil on a high shelf.

"You're so connected to your family," I commented. "Or are you just saying that to impress me?" Then my lips twisted into a smile so I could lighten the mood.

He didn't see me smile. He focused on his work, I think, to avoid looking at me.

"My family's my world," he said simply.

The phone rang, interrupting what had become an intimate moment and I did not want to walk away, but we were at work. I reached for the phone. "Seraphina's House of Voodoo, how can I help you?"

The customer wanted a love potion, so I gave her my suggestions and she said she'd be in tomorrow morning. I hung the phone up.

"Sorry," I said to Taj, trying to regain my train of thought.

"I think you were about to take pity on me and invite me to Thanksgiving dinner." Taj brightened a little, trying to put on a happy face.

"It will just be me, Poppy, and Father Malachi. Do you want to invite Krishna and your friends, too?"

He smiled his beautiful, from-the-inside-out, smile. "Let them eat turkey curry."

Poppy stirred the turnip greens in a saucepan on the stove. She was in charge of the Thanksgiving feast's vegetarian elements and I offered to roast the turkey. She about broke her jaw on the floor when she found out I could cook.

Turning her attention to another saucepan, she tossed in some butter along with the Holy Trinity of Cajun cooking: diced celery, onion, and green pepper.

"What are you making now?" I wondered what she would try to whip up last minute.

"Red beans and rice. It's tradition." She stirred the pot and poured in the beans. "Sophie, you have to stay. You're power's just blocked. Temporarily. All you have to do is believe in yourself and I know the spell will work."

I rolled my eyes. I wished she would stop it already. I was leaving and that was that.

"Easy for you to say," I retorted. "You're not the one getting death threats."

"Are you serious?" She raised her eyebrows. "Because as I recall, I was attacked out there, too, when I was trying to help you. And I face the same danger that every other human faces on a daily basis. No one knows when their time is up on this planet. If you don't believe you can do this work, you can't. If you don't believe in yourself, you can never be and do and have all the things you desire. Believe in yourself and you will become the Mind Changer."

Believe, believe, believe. She sounded like a freaking broken record. I thought I *was* believing, enough anyways.

"I guess I just don't get this—this—magic," I stuttered, frustrated by the fight that was brewing. "Or religion, whatever voodoo actually is," I said sharply.

"Well there you are. Doubt." She pointed at me with a wooden spoon. "Until you can acknowledge that humans don't have all the answers and that there is a divine energy at work, then you won't be able to draw on that God energy. And your magic will not work." Poppy turned back to the stove, checking on her vegetarian red beans and rice.

A thought occurred to me; I knew it wasn't right but I voiced it anyway.

"Are you jealous?" I asked.

She flipped back around, her eyebrows up to her hairline.

Oh boy, I just unleashed the dragon. But I pushed the point anyway, because I was pissed that she kept trying to force me to do something I didn't even necessarily want to do.

"This is stupid," she said, more than annoyed. "You're being stupid."

"Do you want to be the next Mind Changer? Because if you do, take it. I officially bequeath the position to you."

"How. Dare. You." Poppy pointed an accusatory finger at me. "I have helped you in every way that I know how, because you're Seraphina's granddaughter."

"It just feels like you're constantly breathing down my neck. 'Be the Mind Changer, be the Mind Changer, be the Mind Changer.' I never wanted any of this, but you seem to think that just because I am a Papillon woman, I have no say about my own fate." I pointed a finger at my chest. "I make my own destiny!" Then I turned the accusatory finger in her direction. "Not you."

"No!" Poppy barked at me.

"'No' what? I don't get to decide what I do with my life?"

"No, I am not jealous of you," Poppy said, frowning. She came over to me and put a hand on my shoulder. "You are like a sister to me."

I chewed my lip.

"I know," I said.

The doorbell rang.

"That's Father Malachi," she said. "Can you buzz him in?" She retreated to the stove.

"Yep," I said, walking into the entryway. I pressed the button and said as pleasantly as I could, "Hello?"

"Malachi here," was the reply. I buzzed him in.

"You know I can't do it anyway," Poppy said, frustration still lacing her voice.

I nodded. "Only the Papillon women can," I said, pulling the door open.

"So it's a moot point," she shouted over her shoulder as Father Malachi reached the landing in front of me.

"Welcome," I told him.

"Thank you, Sophia," he said, handing me a tray of sweet potato casserole. "Be careful, my dear, it's hot."

Father placed his hat on the hall tree while I brought his side dish into the kitchen.

Poppy shuffled to the side so I could put it in the oven. I checked on the turkey which had browned to perfection, the smell of sage and onion wafting up. She clinked the spoon on the side of the pot loudly and I rolled my eyes at her.

"Father Malachi, we're so glad you could join us," Poppy said, giving Father a big hug when he entered the kitchen.

"It was so nice of you all to invite me. Normally, Seraphina would have me over—of course you know that, Poppy—and this first Thanksgiving without her is—." He didn't finish, but his shoulders drooped and he sighed. "May I use the restroom?" he asked, his voice strained.

"Sure," I said and pointed toward the hall.

Poppy wiped her eyelashes then brushed her fingertips on her apron. We didn't talk for several minutes until Father came back and sat at the kitchen table. I busied myself with setting the dining room table.

I heard Poppy say, "Did Sophie tell you that she's leaving us on Monday?"

As I arranged the place settings, Father stood in the doorway, waiting for me to respond.

In my defense, I said, "I really am the worst person to be a Mind Changer. It's like I have to be Wonder Woman, which—clearly—I am not. In fact, I am probably the anti-superhero."

"Aren't they all?" Father asked, smiling at me.

"What do you mean?"

"Even Superman struggles with Kryptonite. Think about the positive changes that your special powers can bring into the world, before you turn your back on your destiny."

I never wanted to be Wonder Woman, but then again, I never thought superheroes could actually exist in the real world. Mind changing and voodoo, whether it really worked or not, was upending my perception of what could exist in the world. Did I want to be responsible for the power I could hold over voodoo believers? Not really. Did I want to drop the ball on generations of family heritage? No. Did I want to leave Father Malachi, Poppy, and Taj? Absolutely not.

Just then, the door bell rang again.

"That must be Taj," I said, running over to answer the intercom, glad that I didn't have to be grilled by Poppy or Father Malachi while Taj was here.

But for the rest of the afternoon, my mind kept coming back to what Father Malachi had said about superheroes. If being the Mind Changer meant that I could still be human, then maybe I could free myself of the pressure of being perfect and then I could access the power that Poppy kept telling me about. I *could* do a lot of good in the world if I would listen to these intuitive nudges and connect to such a purpose-filled life.

Taj had brought two bottles of wine and, as we drank and ate, I relaxed into the day. No one tried to convince me to stay. I think everyone must have wanted to enjoy the day as much as we could and really revel in the moment. As Poppy and Father Malachi talked about Seraphina, and Taj shared stories of faraway Malaysia, I felt like I had a family for the first time in my life. Could I really turn my back on that? After a dessert of tofu pumpkin pie and organic vanilla ice cream, we packed up leftovers for Taj and Father Malachi to take home.

"This was the best holiday I have ever had," I admitted, hugging Father Malachi, as he stood to leave.

"It was a splendid feast. If you do decide to go, Sophia, I hope that you will come see me one last time."

"I would never leave without saying goodbye to you. You have helped me so much, Father."

Poppy walked Father Malachi to the door and Taj watched me intently from across the dining room table.

"What?" I asked playfully. The free flow of wine all afternoon had me pretty buzzed.

"So you really want to leave New Orleans?"

Definite buzz kill. I frowned.

"I don't want to leave, but I don't belong here." I sat

quietly for a moment, a deep, inner voice telling me to stay. Of course I ignored it.

"So you will leave all of us?" He held out his hand to me across the table.

Cautiously, I placed my hand in his and warmth immediately filled my arm and spread through my body. He put out his other hand and I took that one, too, feeling the same tingling sensation course through my veins. He intertwined his fingers with mine. Holding his hands felt wonderful. Natural.

"Thanks for coming," I said, genuinely thankful that we could spend such a perfect day together.

"Let me do one thing before you go," he said softly, tilting his head to the side and looking into my eyes.

"What?" I asked softly.

He squeezed my hands. "Convince you to stay."

Chapter 16
My Bright Light

Taj picked me up at my place for a night on the town.

"Just to keep things straight, this is not a date," I emphasized. "I'm your boss, you're my employee, and you are merely helping me complete my New Orleans to-do list before I move back to Saint Louis."

"But since you are leaving New Orleans, my job is not in jeopardy, really."

Good point, Taj. My heart didn't want to leave this new existence that held so much untapped potential for me, but my head reasoned that I needed to go back to where I came from. The bottom line: I was walking away from this life. Away from Seraphina's House of Voodoo and the responsibilities of a Mind Changer. Away from my new friends and away from the possibility of romance. *It's simpler this way. And safer for my friends*, I convinced myself.

Taj brushed a piece of my hair back from my face and said, "I like this color better."

Pulling away from him, I fingered the ends of my hair which were dyed back to my original brunette shade. Taj's touch flooded my heart with regret. How could I leave him? Not only had he become my friend, but I felt such a strong magnetism toward him. He was easy to be with. Not to mention, easy on the eyes.

"I decided to grow it out again, too," I said.

"You don't like it short?"

"I'm glad I tried it, just not sure it was me."

We came around the corner and crossed Chartres Street. I didn't want to overstep my bounds, only to hurt Taj when I left in a couple of days, but he'd been insistent that he show me the New Orleans I'd be missing if I left. I couldn't tell him that the biggest thing I'd be missing was him.

Banter about work turned into long periods of silence and I nervously bit my lip, sneaking peeks at Taj out of the corner of my eye. Even in the silence, he walked confidently, his posture upright and his shoulders at ease. His easy disposition made me love being around him. I inched closer longing for the courage to slip my hand into his, but I just couldn't. *You have to leave*, my subconscious reminded me. Still, I was allowed to enjoy myself a little.

"I'm thinking about getting a tattoo," I confided.

"Really. What of?"

"A butterfly."

"Why a butterfly?"

"I don't know." I deflected because if I told him about Jacques calling me his voodoo butterfly, then I'd definitely ruin the night. "I feel like I've really undergone a transformation since coming here."

"It's good to be spontaneous," Taj said.

"That's what Poppy told me," I replied.

"Does she have a tattoo?" he asked.

"She has a needle phobia, so no piercings or tattoos for her."

Taj smiled and raised his sleeve revealing a tribal band. *Nice bicep*, I thought, my core filling with desire.

"I wouldn't have pictured you with a tattoo," I said.

He rolled his sleeve back down. "I got it during my undergraduate years."

"Maybe you can come with me to get mine," I said, looking up at him through my eyelashes.

"It's a date," he said brightly.

Our eyes locked for a moment and then I broke the eye contact because it was too intense for me. A row house ahead of us flipped on their Christmas decorations and I caught my breath, awestruck at the beautiful over-the-top display.

"Wow," I said in spite of myself.

The third floor blazed with white twinkle lights, spelling *Peace Y'all* surrounded by animatronic doves taking flight. I thought of the two turtle dove feathers—representative of a strong, lifelong bond—wrapped up in the love spell gris-gris. The second floor showcased two trumpeting angels in the same dazzling white lights. And icicle lights hung below the balcony at street level.

Magically, as if on cue, other light displays sprung to life. The gas streetlamps shone proudly with red velvet bows tied under their chins. Darkness descended on the city, but the tiny sparkling lights made the streets glow with Christmas cheer.

Taj wrapped his hand in mine.

My face instantly heated, but I didn't want to pull my hand away.

I shouldn't, I thought, but his touch felt so sweet. So secure. *Maybe this could work? Maybe if I just gave up mind changing, the death threats would stop.* I was so upended. I wanted to stay, but how could it work?

"Do you like Cajun food?" Taj asked as we rounded the corner of Royal and Saint Peter Streets.

I pointed to my mouth. "I make it a rule not to inflict pain on myself."

"Can't agree." He shook his head. "The hotter the better."

The way the words rolled off his tongue, made my temperature rise.

"But I'll try anything once," I said, raising my eyebrows.

"You are so open-minded. Not everyone will try new things," he said. "I love that about you," he said without skipping a beat.

The "L" word! I know he didn't say, "I love you" specifically to me, but still. My palms got clammy and I hoped he couldn't tell since we were still holding hands.

"Not all Cajun food is spicy hot," he said, "even though it is full of spice."

He didn't skip a beat and continued on as though he never said the word "love." And *I* loved *that*. No games. No stress over what you can and can't say in a relationship.

"I am excited to see what you think. It's this place right up here." He pointed to a café with floor-to-ceiling windows lining the sidewalk. Above the door a sign read, *Eat Y'all: A Cajun Kitchen*.

The hostess sat us by the window. Light from a single white votive, set in the middle of the table, danced around our table, reminding me of the votive I'd lit at the cathedral during Grandma Seraphina's funeral Mass.

As Taj helped me out of my coat, he mentioned, "When the weather is warmer, they open the windows so you can people watch."

"It's perfect." I sat and smiled up at him as he pushed my chair in for me. The gesture made me feel like a real lady. "Even though I've never traveled," I admitted, "when I walk through the streets here, I feel like I'm in Europe."

"Does it make you want to travel more?" He asked.

"I like the idea of seeing the world, but I don't think I'm adaptable enough." *That's why I have to leave*, my subconscious prodded. *I'm no good at change*.

"I have to disagree," Taj said. "You have adapted to life here very well."

Maybe Taj was right. Maybe I wasn't giving myself enough credit for the new life I'd undertaken here.

The waitress came over and Taj asked me, "May I order?"

"Sure. But nothing too hot."

As Taj ordered, I pictured him kissing me, taking me into his arms and boldly pressing his lips to mine. I crossed my legs and leaned toward him, imagining what it would be like to be his girlfriend. I loved how he was taking charge on this date. Taking care of me.

"I heard you order gumbo. Isn't that spicy?" I teased, but really, it was my Type-A self trying to take control of the situation and I refused to let Type-A Sophie ruin this night for me.

"Don't you trust me?" he teased.

I do, I thought automatically. And that was the truth.

"The spicy gumbo is for me and the etoufée is for you."

The waitress placed two dark beers at our table. "Two NOLA brews."

Taj indicated for me to choose a glass. "Ladies first."

Grabbing the ice-cold pint glass, I sipped the smooth ale, letting it swirl around my tongue and noticed a subtle nuttiness to the flavor. I wasn't a beer connoisseur by any means, but I could appreciate that it wasn't bitter or dry. I nodded my approval and relaxed back into my seat and let the mellow effects of the beer sink in.

"Do you know what's in etoufée?" Taj asked, taking a sip of his beer.

I shook my head and smiled shyly. My prior insistence that this was *not* a date was slipping away and I began to imagine myself as Taj's girlfriend.

"It's a bed of rice smothered in a shrimp gravy." He used his hands to explain—I loved that. Taj pointed to the next table's order as the waitress served them. "There's some."

A rich tomato-colored gravy with huge, sumptuous shrimp sat atop a mound of white rice. The aroma of the Cajun trinity filled the air and I closed my eyes to savor the smell. Maybe it was the beer making me feel heady, but my senses sprang alive.

"It's a good thing I brought you out so that I could educate you about where you came from," Taj ribbed me.

"*Touché*." He was right. I didn't know much about my roots and now I was walking away from my family's hometown. I stared at my hands in my lap.

"What are you thinking?"

That I don't want this night to end. I didn't answer.

After a moment, he said, "We always talk about me and my family, so tonight let's talk about you." Straightforward as always, Taj had stripped me down to the core.

"Because I'm such an amazing topic of conversation," I deflected.

"To me you are."

My stomach tightened.

He continued. "I want to know more about you. Like for instance, why this physical transformation?" He indicated my hair and makeup.

Tensing slightly, because I normally kept conversation light at work, a voice inside of me softly plied, *Taj is safe. Open up to him.* My shoulders relaxed away from my earlobes.

"Can we get another one of these?" I asked him, tapping my almost-empty pint glass.

He raised his hand and the waitress hurried to our table.

"Two more NOLAs, please. Thank you."

Here's to bearing my soul. I swallowed the remainder of my beer and said, "The transformation . . . it goes back to something in my past."

"Okay," he said.

I searched his dark brown eyes. *Just jump. You can trust him.* The overall din of the restaurant retreated to the background and it became just me and Taj in the world at this moment.

The little Sophie inside of me emerged, speaking quietly. "My mom drank too much. She couldn't hold down a job and we never had much money."

He leaned forward, nodding, encouraging me to say more.

"When I needed new clothes, we'd shop at thrift stores. In middle and high school, kids can be pretty judgmental about the clothes you wear," I said. "Especially girls."

"I'm not sure I understand," he said. "In Malaysia we wear uniforms."

The waitress brought us two fresh ales and Taj nodded thank you.

"Well," I said, not really wanting to launch into a full conversation about women and body image in America. "Let's just say that I haven't cared about 'my look,'"—I did air quotes—"since I was probably twelve."

"It must be hard to grow up in a culture where so much is placed on your appearance and not your character."

Even though he hadn't grown up here, he understood completely. My jaw nearly hit the floor.

"Was it hard to make such a big change then?"

"When he cut my hair, I had to close my eyes," I admitted. "I miss my long hair."

"I like you either way." Taj's eyes locked with mine and he clenched his jaw slightly.

He sees me, I thought. *The* real *me*.

The waitress dropped off our food, but her being there barely registered on our radar, because our conversation had brought us to a whole new place. I trusted Taj.

"What do you think of the etoufée?" he asked after I'd savored the first bite, the aroma of celery and onion filling my palate.

"The etoufée," I emphasized my new vocabulary word with a raised eyebrow, "is wonderful. Thank you."

"Want to try some spice?"

"I don't think I can handle that," I said, pointing at his gumbo with my fork.

He held out a heaping spoon of andouille sausage, chicken, and okra and waited for me to take it.

Just go for it, I thought and I accepted the spoon from him, sniffing the concoction first. The deep brown roux smelled savory and spicy. I put the bite in my mouth and closed my eyes, preparing for my taste buds to catch fire. The hot pepper seeped into my nostrils and tingled my throat, but the flavors of the vegetables, meats, and other spices, balanced out the heat.

"That is really good," I said, pleasantly surprised. Even though it was hot, the zing excited my senses.

Red pepper will keep the love life spicy, Poppy had said when she added it to the love potion.

I pinched my eyes closed, trying to ignore any ideas about love.

"I love okra. My mom uses it in her soups and curries," Taj said. "You sure it is not too hot?"

"It's not so bad," I admitted.

"Another taste then?" He scooped up some more gumbo and held the spoon near my lips. The seduction of offering to feed me himself made my stomach muscles clench with anticipation. A heat charged through my entire body. I opened my mouth to take the bite, feeling ridiculous at first—like I was in some romantic comedy—but then something romantic, sensuous even, filled me the moment Taj placed the bite into my mouth. The spice in the gumbo made my lips tingle, and a buzz of senses filled me from head to toe. I closed my eyes and savored the feeling. I imagined the pinch of red pepper on top of the other ingredients in the gris-gris bag.

Enough denial, I told myself and then opened my eyes to drink Taj in. I wanted him. I had wanted him for a long time. An urge bubbled up inside of me and I wanted to do something that I would never normally do. I placed my hand on the table with the palm up, in the space in between us, asking him, without words, to put his hand in mine. *This is worth it. I have to stay.*

"Can I have more?" I asked.

He looked down at my hand and then at the empty gumbo bowl, realizing I meant that I wanted more in a relationship from him. Taj placed his brown hand in mine and our fingers naturally and beautifully intertwined. Then I felt my body lean forward, almost automatically, and I did another thing that I would never do. I lightly tugged his hands toward me to let him know he should lean forward, too.

And then I kissed him. It was a sweet and soft first kiss that made me feel at home and I closed my eyes for the few moments that it lasted. When we pulled away and I opened my eyes, his eyes found mine.

"You're different. There's something I see in you..." he struggled to find the right words. "I can't explain it."

We were still holding hands, so I squeezed his hand with mine, willing him to guess my secret identity all on his own. Then I couldn't be blamed for giving up myself as the Mind Changer.

He released my hand and rubbed his thighs with his palms, something making him nervous. He averted his eyes.

"I don't know," he said. "Maybe there is something of myself that I am seeing in you too." *What did that mean?*

His eyes met mine again and I wished with every particle of my being that I could, at that very moment, read his mind. Unfortunately, I was a Mind Changer, not a mind reader, and I couldn't risk showing him my whole self including my paranormal side. Not yet at least.

The waitress came to clear our dishes, "Can I get you anything else, babies?"

"Two more beers, please," Taj said, never taking his eyes off mine.

Life carried on around us: other diners ate and talked, pedestrians passed by the window, but we were in our own world. Just me and my Taj.

He had done it, done what he'd said he'd do: convinced me to stay. But more than that, during our time working together, he'd worked a miracle. He'd gotten to know the real me. The me that I had kept hidden for so long, so that I didn't have to risk being in relationship with people. The strain of my relationship with my mother had caused me, at a young age, to clam up and not let people in. I thought the inner me was a haunted place where no one would go, but Taj had fearlessly opened the door and begun to explore the hidden desires and fears housed there, chasing away the dark with his bright light.

Chapter 17
Haunted

Taj was cooking Malaysian food for me at his apartment. It was the first time I'd gotten to see his place and I was pleasantly surprised that it wasn't the typical bachelor pad. Taj kept the place tidy and the decor felt homey, yet exotic. The hibiscus in the corner of the living room caught my attention and I walked over to it, cupping one of the blossoms in my palm.

"Hibiscus is the national flower of Malaysia," Taj said. He was standing in the kitchen, but could see me with the open floor plan.

"Really," I said, considering Nico's outlandish prophecy. *You were from Malaysia in a past life and you will be returning there in this lifetime.* "Hmm. Malaysia." I sauntered over to the stove and peeked into the pot that Taj was stirring. "More spice?"

"Curry Mee. And, yes, it is spicy," he said.

I eyed him suspiciously. "You know how I feel about abusing my taste buds."

He protested, "Check out this broth. Smell it and tell me you can say no to that."

Leaning over the pot, I inhaled the bubbling pot of mysterious pumpkin-colored broth. "Is that red chili?"

"Yes." The bright red oil beaded into tiny delectable bubbles which swirled around yellow spaghetti-like noodles. "Would you mind chopping these?" He pulled a handful of fresh green beans from a strainer in the sink and set them on a bamboo cutting board.

"Sure," I said, reaching for a knife from the block. "How long should I cut them?"

"About an inch."

"So where's Krishna?" I asked. "Your mysterious brother that I have yet to meet."

He sighed and dramatically dropped his head back.

"I know," he said. "That boy is always out doing something. Tonight is the French Quarter pub crawl, I think." He concentrated on his Malaysian concoction again.

"What kind of noodles are those?" I tasted a bit of green bean, the fresh flavor awakening my salivary glands.

"Egg noodles. The broth is chicken stock, coconut milk, curry paste. Go ahead and toss the beans in."

Using the knife, I scraped the pile of fresh beans into the bubbling broth.

"And cut these into quarters." He handed me two shelled hard-boiled eggs. "There's also lemongrass . . ."

What a weird combination of ingredients.

". . . chicken pieces. And fish balls."

"Excuse me?" I almost cut my finger with the knife. "Fish whats?"

"Try one." Taj fished a fish ball out of the bubbling opaque orange broth. It looked like a tofu-colored ping-pong ball. He offered it to me.

I turned up my nose. "What are they?"

"It is basically a processed food made from fish. Here, taste one." He blew on the fish ball until it was cool and took a bite himself as proof that it was edible.

My head said, *Don't eat that! It is unrecognizable as food*. But the braver inner Sophie, the Sophie who'd learned to trust her hot new boyfriend and enjoyed trying new foods—new everythings with him—said, *Why not?*

I allowed him to spoon it into my mouth and thought about the taste. "Definitely fishy but not overpowering. Kind of the texture of an omelet."

"A bit firmer than squid, though not as chewy."

"It's not bad," I admitted. "Terrible name, though, fish balls." I scrunched up my nose.

Taj placed some noodles in the bottom of an empty bowl, followed by a couple of chicken pieces and a few fish balls. He ladled some broth over everything and garnished it with fried onions, an egg quarter, and a few green leaves. "Cilantro. We call it coriander in Malaysia. Lime juice?"

"You're the chef," I said.

He finished it off by squeezing a wedge of lime on top. Not my idea of the perfect mixture of food items, but Taj hadn't steered me wrong so far.

"Thank you," I said, setting my bowl and wine glass at the table. "You know"—I avoided his eyes, so I could garner the courage to say—"I really like this."

He sat down at the chair opposite me. "Like what?"

"I like trying new things with you." I twirled some noodles between a fork and spoon, and tasted the delicious flavor explosion. "I like . . . being with you." *There. It's out there. I said it.* Since I'd said it, I could finally look at his face to gauge his reaction.

He had an enormous smile plastered across his face and I loved it.

"Same," he said.

My heart melted to my toes and the same goofy smile spread across my face.

As we sipped wine, spooned broth, and slurped noodles, Taj told me about the rubber and oil palm plantation he grew up on and how, at age eight, he single-handedly killed a king cobra that had slithered into their bathroom.

"What?" I choked on my soup.

"I was more scared of my mom," he said, giggling.

His infectious laugh got me giggling too. He told me about his two brothers and all the trouble they'd put his mother through. His subtle accent floated in the air, settling into my chest. The beautiful words rolled off his tongue and made my heart go pitter patter.

"So what do the people there believe in?" I asked.

He smiled a half smile at me.

"What?" I asked.

"It's strange that you doubt God, but are so interested in religion."

"We can talk about something else," I said, swatting away his true statement because I didn't want to deal with it. The idea that other people had faith was so fascinating to me. It didn't matter which religion, it was just that I wanted to understand how people got connected to God.

"It is fine," Taj reassured me.

"I just feel like I can talk to you about anything." I shrugged and ate the last fish ball in my bowl.

The truth was that I felt at home around Taj. Whenever he looked at me with his soft, reassuring eyes, peace ran through me. And even more than that, he was opening my eyes to so many new ideas because his worldview was so foreign. Strange that I could feel a world away and at home in the same instant.

He took my hands in his, intertwining our fingers. My hands warmed in his and the affection he showed me completely unraveled me, but I tried to not show it.

"Hinduism's gods serve humanity in a variety of ways."

"Like voodoo's loa?"

He nodded.

Damn! How did he always remain so composed? Meanwhile, he had the power to set my body on fire.

Taj kept the conversation on track, while I simmered. "And images of Hindu gods are placed in every Hindu's home. Like the framed picture of Marie Laveau in the shop."

I remembered that Mom always kept a picture of "The Last Supper" in our dining room. No matter where we lived, that picture stayed with us. *A good memory of Mom*, I thought momentarily. Maybe being around Taj was softening my heart toward my mother.

"Hindus overdo it, though. They cover absolutely every wall with the pictures," he said, sweeping his arms in a wide arc. "And I do mean *every* wall."

I started giggling, the wine's buzz filling my body from head to toe. He topped off my glass.

"Thank you," I said. "So is Hinduism a male-centered religion?" I asked, my inner feminist hoping for more balance than we have in western religion. That was probably one of the reasons I'd rejected faith for so long. Now I was paying for it since I needed faith as a Mind Changer.

"There is an Indian saying, 'God could not be everywhere, so he gave each family a mother.' My mother is certainly the spiritual center of our family and women can even lead spiritual rites like marriage."

"Poppy says voodoo gives a lot of power to women, too. I like that," I said, a conspiratorial smile sweeping across my face. "Girl power!" I raised my fist.

Taj laughed. Then he took a sip of his wine, studying me over his glass, not breaking eye contact.

"What?" I asked.

"You always ask about my family, but you're never forthcoming about your own." He wasn't accusing, just commenting, but he struck a nerve.

"I just don't have much to say about my past." Feeling a little sulky, I rose to clear the table. But he did have a point. *Don't be like that, Sophie*, I told myself firmly. "I don't mean to keep you in the dark, Taj," I said quietly and filled the sink with hot, soapy water. But that was exactly what I'd been doing; shrouding my past in darkness. How could I ever really open myself to someone else unless I had the courage to shine a light on my own shadows?

"I want this to work," I admitted quietly. "So I'll try to share more. But my relationship with my mom isn't something I really like to think about, or talk about." I shrugged. "It's just so . . . It still hurts."

Taj appeared behind me, wrapping his warm arms around my waist and leaning his head on my shoulder. He gently kissed the nape of my neck. I shut off the hot water and turned to him. He pulled me tightly into his arms and pressed his lips to mine, kissing me deeply, reassuringly. I felt safe and warm in his arms. And when the sweet, hot kiss stopped, I leaned against his shoulder, knowing I had made the right decision to stay in New Orleans. Even if I was scared. Even if my life was in danger, I couldn't imagine a life without my Taj. How had I fallen so hard so fast?

"My family likes going to a local Buddhist temple that was built inside of a mountain," he said, giving me the emotional space I needed. In that moment, the power of his love swept over me: sensitive, strong, compassionate, and sexy, to boot. *How'd I get so lucky? Maybe I don't deserve him.*

I pushed down the idea, refusing to let it ruin the moment.

Taj picked up a dishtowel. I washed and he dried.

He spoke more about the temple. "You follow a passage through the mountain and when you are inside, you can look up to see the sky through the mountain's center."

"Sounds like something from a storybook," I said softly. "And your family prays to Buddha when they visit there?" Since his family was Hindu, it confused me that they visited a Buddhist shrine. But maybe it shouldn't surprise me that multiple religions can coexist, since voodoo and Catholicism mixed so well in New Orleans.

"We enjoy the peace and beauty of the place. It also has beautiful gardens, koi ponds, meditation paths." He stacked the dishes neatly in a cabinet.

"So do you attend Hindu temple here?" I asked.

"Actually, Hinduism is too superstitious for me," he admitted.

"How so?" I asked, my curiosity piqued.

"My mom, for instance, goes to a fortune-teller when she needs to make important life decisions."

I immediately thought of Nico, the con artist in Jackson Square, and Gabriel, the harmonica player. Those two showed me that some people did seem to have a genuine psychic ability.

Taj continued. "When I decided to get my education in America, my mom would only allow it once she spoke with her fortune-teller."

I considered his mom's strong faith in reading the stars. What would that be like to completely surrender your life to a force outside of yourself?

"What do you believe?" I asked.

"I believe a person makes their own destiny," he said with conviction.

"Does your mom know that?" I asked.

"She is aware of my skeptical nature, but knows I believe in something greater than myself." He reached around my hips to put the silverware in a drawer next to me. "Excuse me," he whispered into my hair. Then his hands lingered on my hips and he stepped behind me, wrapping his arms around my waist.

My body sighed with delight. With record speed, I rinsed and dried my hands and spun toward him, wanting his lips on mine. Our mouths locked and heat rose to my face. Putting one hand in his hair and the other along his jaw line, our kiss quickly increased from sweet to hot.

Taj swept me up in his arms and walked the few steps into the adjoining living room, setting me tenderly on his futon. He hovered above me, not crushing me. Not overwhelming me. Perfect. He communicated his feelings through his exploring kiss, his electrifying touch. Our bodies entangled. Needing each other. Wanting each other. Our passion stretched out into eternity.

I woke to a pain in my hip and realized it was the bars of Taj's futon digging into my side. Taj, holding me in his arms still, slept peacefully. I watched him for a few moments, drinking him in, before groggily glancing at the clock. 2:50.

"Oh my God!" I scrambled to my feet and grabbed my shoes.

Taj jumped up, too, rubbing the sleep from his eyes.

"It's past midnight! I have to open the shop tomorrow!" I hopped around, trying to put on my shoes, then decided sitting on the futon would be an easier way to get them on. "Shit!"

Taj rubbed my back, making the surge of anxiety within me back down. "Let me take you home," he said softly.

Oh, thank God. After the mind change attempt, I hated walking alone at night.

The night air was thick. A fog settled in the streets, and Taj navigated through the flickering, eerie orbs of light from the streetlights. He put his arm around me, and I snuggled into his side.

"So how many men have you dated?" Taj said, lightening the mood. He always seemed to know when I was anxious and always knew just what to say to put my mind at ease.

"We're gonna play this game, huh?" Smiling up at him, I remained mysterious and vague.

"Not many then?" He jabbed.

"Thanks." I tickled him, and he was powerless against my tiny fingers.

"All right, all right." He raised his hands in defeat.

"For your information," I said, "I went out with a few guys in high school and college. It's just that no one, you know, wanted a second date."

"That's . . . pretty bad."

"Hey! You're bringing my self-esteem down about seventy notches. You know that, right?"

"I'm the lucky one," he said.

I smiled, nuzzling into him.

"It definitely didn't feel good to be . . ." My voice trailed away. I didn't know what word to put in there.

"What? You can tell me." Taj squeezed my hand.

"Unwanted. Undesirable, I guess. I missed out on a lot of normal, teen activities—like binge drinking and dating—because I was taking care of Mom."

He hugged me and whispered into my hair. "You're desirable to me."

I squeezed him back and confessed, "Most of the time I was more interested in reading than in making friends anyway. It worked out."

I glanced across the street and stopped dead in my tracks. There it stood. The corpse-gray plaster and tar black shutters on the dreaded mansion transported me to the night of my failed mind change. My heart pounded in my ears and I felt myself reflexively moving closer into Taj's body, wanting to be safe.

"What is that place?" I spoke of it as if it were a thing or a monster, not a building. The hair on the back of my neck rose and Taj could see that I was getting more and more fearful. He wrapped his arms around me.

"Don't you know?" His question made me realize that "everyone" knew. And his tone implied that the building was not just famous, but infamous.

"We should just get out of—" I started to say. Then I noticed footsteps walking toward us. The fog obscured the walker. My mind raced back to my crazy night at the cemetery. Then the night of the failed mind change. Were these the footfalls of the same person who kept coming after me? The shoes clicked on the cobblestones and echoed off of the tall buildings, their speed and closeness increasing. My heart rate increased, too.

"Let's get you home, woman," Taj whispered teasingly in my ear, completely unaffected by the footfalls. Was it because he was always calm? Or was I just hearing things?

We're only another block from home, I silently tried to calm myself. Taj's hand in mine helped, but my palm grew clammy. *Half a block more.* My throat tightened and I knew that I could still hear footsteps.

"Do you hear that?" My voice came out tiny, choked with fear.

"Hear what?" Taj stopped and turned his head in different directions. Listening.

"Nothing." I tugged on his hand. "I thought I heard something."

As we rounded the corner to my door, we nearly collided with a familiar dark figure.

"Jacques?" I asked, catching my breath. "What are you doing here?"

Taj pulled me close.

"Good evening, *ma chérie*." Jacques removed his old-fashioned brimmed hat and bowed curtly.

The fog swirled around the three of us. I wanted to run to the safety of my apartment, but Jacques continued. "Sometimes I cannot sleep, so I like to roam the streets at night."

"I mean, what are you doing by my house?" I hissed.

Jacques tilted his head and studied me, and then Taj, before answering. "Sometimes I find myself wandering by your little shop, *ma chérie*. You know that the love potion you sold me is working splendidly. Of course, I wish it would work . . ." He looked hungrily at me. ". . . with someone else."

Taj grabbed my hand and stepped in front of me. "Let's go inside, Sophie."

Jacques clicked his tongue, amusement lighting up his face. He ignored Taj and spoke directly to me. "Sophia . . ." His voice the purr of a tiger. "Have you given any more thought to my invitation?"

I remembered the card he had given me at the end of my makeover day. I had stuck it in my wallet weeks ago and forgotten about it with the flurry of confusion: about staying in New Orleans, about pursuing mind changing, about being with Taj.

Peeking from behind Taj's shoulder, I shook my head. When I realized Taj was having to protect me, something just didn't sit right with me. Up until this point, I'd been pretty good at taking care of myself.

Nudging Taj to the side, I stepped forward and confronted Jacques.

"I've had enough of these haphazard meetings, Jacques."

"Haphazard?" he asked, raising his eyebrows innocently.

"You know exactly what I'm talking about. It's starting to feel pretty stalker-ish and I'm not putting up with it anymore. If you want to see me, do it in the light of day and don't scare the bejeezus out of me." I shoved my thumb out towards Taj. "Or my friends."

Taj interjected, "I think you should leave."

His voice was so forceful, so stand-up-for-your-woman. But I was a big girl and could fight my own battles, thank you very much. I dared Jacques straight in his cold-as-steel eyes.

"This is my boyfriend, Taj," I said boldly.

Jacques grabbed the fingertips of my left hand in an unbelievably quick movement.

Taj stepped forward, eyeing Jacques, and clasped his fingers around my other hand. Like some woman in the Victorian era, I had two suitors vying for my attention. My amazing boyfriend, my bright, shining light, captured me mind, body, and soul. But some mysterious force compelled me to keep my fingers in Jacques's hold.

"The offer remains open, *ma chérie*." He addressed me, but his eyes never left Taj's. Jacques kissed my hand and let it drop, before bowing curtly once more and walking into the fog. The sound of his dress shoes faded into the night. Not realizing I'd been holding my breath, I took a long inhale and then breathed out, trying to empty my body of some of the tension from this crazy walk home.

"We should go upstairs," Taj said, surveying the street. He held my hand a little too tightly and I had to wriggle loose from his grasp so I could fish out my keys and unlock the door.

When we were safe inside, I hurriedly locked the dead bolt behind us. Our meeting with Jacques had completely unnerved me, so I flipped on all the lights in the main living areas.

"Please stay with me," I pleaded, realizing Poppy was out.

Taj nodded, his mouth set and his jaw clenched.

"I'm going to check the other rooms," he said firmly. He strode down the hallway and flipped on the bathroom light. *Swish*. He pulled the shower curtain back. *Click, click*. He checked the window locks.

Anger rose in my throat and I headed down the hallway to help him check the bedrooms. *This is my home. I shouldn't be afraid here*. He checked my room and I flipped the light in Poppy's room, threw open Poppy's closet and, hurriedly, knelt to inspect under the bed. All clear.

The adrenaline and fear coursing through my body had me puffed up. I shouted at Taj in the other room, "You know I can take care of myself right?"

No response.

"I can fight my own battles. You can't just step in front of me and be my knight in shining armor or bodyguard or whatever." Exasperated with the whole confrontation with Jacques, I huffed aloud.

"I know you can," Taj said, standing at the doorway.

He pointed under the bed where I was crouched. "No monsters under there?"

I smiled, relieved, and stood up, walking over to him.

"I can protect myself," I insisted, landing a playful slap on his cheek.

"Ouch!" He rubbed his jaw. "That hurt."

"Sorry," I squealed, not knowing my own strength. I added, "But you better watch out because it's hard to put the whoop ass back in the can. That's all I'm gonna say."

I let my head drop back and sighed, rubbing the tension in one shoulder.

"What a night," I said.

We walked down the hallway and he placed his hands on my shoulders, filling me with a new kind of tension. His touch was electric. He sat down on the couch and pulled me into his lap, not saying anything, but I could tell he was furious.

"He's like the Jacques from the story," he said abruptly.

"Story?"

"Remember, at Night Creatures? That first night I met you."

"You got a light for Jacques?" I said, rubbing at the goose bumps forming on my arms. "You don't really believe that do you?"

"There's something not right with him," Taj said.

He pulled me closer and kissed my hair. We sat in silence for a while and then he lifted my chin so I could see his eyes. They sparkled with the beginning of a smile. "Speaking of urban legends, you do know that the house you pointed out is known to us locals as 'The Haunted House,' right?" My body tensed so he rubbed my back. Laughing a little, he said, "It's okay. They're just stories. But the LaLaurie Mansion *is* a huge tourist draw."

Why was Poppy always forcing the paranormal down my throat? I ranted on the inside, thinking of our brush with death the night of my failed mind change. *Did she want to push me over the edge? Was she trying to give me a heart attack?*

"You honestly haven't heard of it?" Taj repeated. His mood had improved, since his big showdown with Jacques, but I still hadn't gotten over the frightening walk home.

I shook my head, staring out the windows of the French doors. I thought I saw a dark shape move across the balcony. I squinted my eyes, but there was no way I was getting any closer to the window to investigate.

"Tell me about it," I whispered, my eyes trying to register the shape in the dark.

"The LaLauries lived there in the 1800s and Madame LaLaurie was known to be cruel to servants. Many would go missing and never be heard from again and it is said that she even pushed a servant girl over a balcony, killing her. Supposedly, she did it because the girl pulled Madame LaLaurie's hair while brushing it."

The story piqued my interest and I stopped searching for the dark figure outside. My eyes were probably tricking me anyway.

Taj continued. "But the house is most famous for the reason why the LaLauries were forced to leave New Orleans." I settled into the couch, feeling safer that Grandma Seraphina had always been protected in this apartment. That and the fact that Taj was here with me, put my mind at ease. "One night, they hosted a party and a fire started. When the firemen came, they searched the third floor, one where no one had ever ventured. And what they found came straight from a horror film."

I leaned forward, settling my chin in my palm.

"Over the years, all the servants who had gone missing in the LaLaurie household, had been enslaved on the third floor. Madame LaLaurie had performed terrible experiments on them there."

I remembered the bricked in window on the third floor.

"They found a female servant carved into the shape of a human caterpillar, her arms and legs amputated and her skin peeled off in strips to give her a segmented body. One man had undergone a crude sex change operation. Another woman had been locked in a tiny cage, and when they opened it, they realized that her arms and legs had been broken and reset at strange angles so she resembled a crab."

I shook my head. "That's crazy."

"At night, people can still hear screams from the building."

A chill ran down my spine.

"And those who have tried to live there, or start a business, never stay. It is too haunted. Most locals will not even use the sidewalk in front of the mansion. They cross to the other side of the street, because, supposedly, the evil of the place attaches itself to anyone who touches it."

I'd felt it's sinister energy when my face was forced up against the building. The wicked taste of mortar in my mouth. The stink of decay filling my nostrils.

Taj rubbed my back and assured me, "It's only a story."

He was right. A building couldn't be evil or good, could it? There was no way it could somehow infect me. I wondered if the mind-changing powder had protected me as it had protected Grandma Seraphina for all those years. A chill ran down my spine.

"Hey," Taj said softly, squeezing me and rubbing my arms as he held me. "You okay?" He kissed the top of my head.

"Can you stay with me tonight?" I asked. "Just to sleep," I said, firmly establishing my boundaries. I didn't want things to move too fast; I just wanted to feel safe in my bed. The nightmares were making it more difficult to sleep, even with my night-light on and my rosary tucked under my pillow, and I just knew, deep down in my heart, that Taj could keep the ghosts at bay.

"Of course," he said.

I leaned forward, and he embraced me in his safe arms when Poppy slammed the door, making Taj and I jump, the ghost story obviously still keeping us on edge.

"So, Poppy," I said, staring her down from across the room, "Taj has been telling me about the LaLaurie Mansion. Ring a bell?"

Chapter 18
Come On, Baby, Light My Fire

Christmastime, or Papa Noel season as it's called in New Orleans, drew lots of tourists and our little shop buzzed with a steady stream of customers. I liked to think Grandma Seraphina would be proud that business was booming and we were carrying the torch for her, especially since she loved the holidays so much. The hard work wore on me, though, and the death threats ran through my head on a never-ending loop, dulling my nerves.

"I need three love potions and nine lucky candles." A woman rattled off a shopping list and then returned to the conversation on her cell.

"No, no, no," she said as I reached for the candles.

"But these are—"

She swatted my explanation away and pointed to her phone. Even though she smiled, I wasn't amused. *Turn it off for two seconds, lady.*

"Help me, help you," I said under my breath. After gathering her order, I led her to the checkout counter, and rang up her items.

"Thanks," she mouthed, still listening to the person on the phone.

I smiled, waved, and hissed in Taj's ear, "I should've thrown in a jinx spell."

A man approached us wearing Christmas tree sunglasses and a boa of gold garland around his neck.

"Do you have any stocking stuffers?" he asked cheerfully.

I laughed a little. "Nice outfit."

He lifted his glasses and winked. "Why, thank you, sweetie."

"We have voodoo dolls, New Orleans gear, and our most popular gris-gris bags in those bins up front."

"What's a gris-gris?" the customer asked, putting his hands on his hips and cocking his head to the side.

His exaggerated body language made me laugh again.

"How can I help?" Poppy asked, swooping in and taking the customer by the arm and leading him toward the stocking stuffers.

Taj nodded toward the glittery garland man. "Festive."

"Definitely cheered me up," I agreed.

"Can you handle the register for a moment?" Taj asked. "I need to get some more candles and incense from the back. They're getting pretty thin."

"Yep." I swatted his butt as he walked away.

"You better watch it, woman," he said, hoisting an empty box above the crowd of customers.

"Sophie?" Poppy yelled to me from the front. "These two need to see the Voodoo Jewels . . . Papa Legba and Erzulie." She pointed the customers back to me.

I raised my hand so they could see me through the crowd in the store.

Just then, Taj came back with a box in his arms.

"I have to help these ladies," I told Taj, nodding to the customers coming my way.

He set the box on the counter behind us and manned the register.

"What does Legba and Erzulie do?" one of the customers asked me as I sifted through the Voodoo Jewels.

"Erzulie helps you in the love department and, let me see . . ." I read the tag on the black and red Legba beads. "Clears obstacles from your life and helps open doors."

They nodded and bought one of each. I rang them up really quickly and whispered to Taj, "Nothing says, 'Merry Christmas,' like the cha-ching of a cash register."

"Does that mean Christmas bonus?" he teased, and put his arm around my waist.

I leaned against him and bumped his hip with mine. I loved working with my Taj.

Poppy grabbed her drink from behind the counter. She said it was water, but I doubted it.

"All I can say is thank God it's Friday," she said. Then she turned to yell out to the customers on the floor, "Fifteen minutes until closing time, y'all. If you need help, this is your last chance until tomorrow." She gave us an exhausted shake of her head and flew around the store to help the remaining customers.

I took a sip of Poppy's water. It stung going down.

"That's not water," I said.

Taj and I exchanged goofy puppy-love smiles. It was kind of gross.

"No," Poppy told a customer emphatically. "You do not ingest these oils and potions." She ticked off the three ways to use them on her fingers. "You carry, bury, or wear them. Do not eat them. Ever. Because some of them contain poisonous ingredients and we cannot be held liable for misuse of the conjures."

"She has said that at least a hundred times today," I told Taj.

"I can't blame her. If someone were to get sick, it could destroy Seraphina's House of Voodoo."

Poppy continued to instruct the customer on the item's use. "You can bury it at your home or near the headstone of a family member. Exactly. That is just what you need right there. You just check out back at the counter." Poppy pointed a customer back to us and the customer promptly knocked over a spinning rack of Mardi Gras beads.

"I got that," I told Taj, squeezing behind him while he ran the register.

The lady told me, "I'm so sorry. Let me set this all down and I can help you."

"It's no problem, really," I said with a smile. "I got it." I righted the rack and then bent down, looping the strands of beads on my arm.

"How do we know Seraphina's heir has any power at all," a woman behind me said. I didn't want to attract attention to myself, so I slowly picked up the beads and eavesdropped.

"She's never been trained," a man replied. "Because Marie sure as hell didn't train her. Marie ran away from the socyete."

"Well I can tell you one thing," the woman said. "I will not accept her as the rightful heir until she proves herself."

"Maybe it's time for power to change hands," the man suggested. "A new family to run New Orleans."

"You know," the woman lowered her voice to a whisper and I strained to hear. "They say Dr. Bones has been working black magic. Allegedly, he's in cahoots with the LaLauries."

I'd picked up all the beads, so I couldn't just stay on the floor. As nonchalantly as I could, I stood and arranged the beads on the jewelry rack.

It didn't work.

The woman noticed me listening in on their conversation and looked down her nose at me.

"Got what I need," she told her companion. Regardless of her icy stare, she didn't seem to know who I was, so I counted my blessings.

"We gonna go get something to eat?" the man asked and they slipped past me on the way to check out. Until they left the store, I busied myself with helping customers, straightening merchandise, and chewing on their conversation.

I wondered who they were and why they didn't want to accept me even though they'd never met me. And who was this Dr. Bones and how was the LaLaurie family involved with him? I didn't even realize any LaLaurie family members still lived in New Orleans.

After the man and woman left, I returned to the counter to help Taj. The bottom line was that I couldn't please everyone all of the time and Poppy had already emphasized the important leadership role I'd automatically take on by being the next Mind Changer. Being a leader would require me to ruffle some feathers, so I'd have to get over it.

"What do you say we get something to eat after work?" Taj suggested, helping me put my anxiety on the back burner.

"Sounds good," I said.

Poppy came back to the counter, so I invited her, too. "Want to go out for some food after this?"

"I have a ton of online orders to work on tonight," she replied.

"I can help," I said and then finished ringing up a customer. "Thank you, ma'am. Any questions, just call the number on the bag."

The woman nodded to me, and I helped the next person in line.

"That's okay," Poppy told me. "I can handle it. You two go and have a good time." She gave me a weird smile and then fluttered off to help more customers. Poppy had been very encouraging of my relationship with Taj because she knew how difficult it was for me to date. She had been nudging me along with over-enthusiasm, I think, so that I wouldn't ruin it.

"Eat Y'all?" I asked Taj and he nodded his approval of my restaurant choice.

We continued checking out the day's incessant line of customers, the register cha-chinging as each person got their Christmas wish.

After our meal at Eat Y'all, Taj and I stood outside the restaurant, trying to decide whether to go home or not. Neither of us felt tired. In fact, we always felt invigorated by each others' presence. Ready for more adventure. Taj wrapped my scarf snuggly around my neck and I leaned into him. He kissed the tip of my nose.

The hair on the back of my neck suddenly stood on end. And it wasn't the chill of the night air. Something felt wrong. I glanced around my shoulder, but there were only a few tourists lined up for the next haunted French Quarter tour.

"Let's go through the square," I told Taj, grabbing the crook of his arm. I didn't want to walk through dark, deserted streets and put us in harm's way.

"But it's quicker this way."

"I hear caroling in the square. Let's go see." The truth was that I knew—with absolute certainty—that I could hear those diabolical footsteps behind me. Again. It seems like they were always with me, but especially at night. *Click. Clack. Click. Clack*. Sharp and unrelenting like the ticking of a clock. We continued in silence for a while, my stomach tense and my breathing shallow. Taj must've known I was feeling too tense because he wrapped his arm tight around my shoulders.

"Woman! Why are you rushing?" he asked with laughter in his voice.

"We need to get near people," I told Taj. *Lots of people.*

"Oh-kay."

The giant Jesus statue rose up behind Saint Louis Cathedral, but the size of this imposing statue with its arms spread wide in blessing was not what caught my attention. Instead, I noticed the even larger presence of its shadow spreading across the back of the cathedral. The ominous, lurking shadow hovered behind Jesus' shoulders making the actual statue of Christ insignificant by comparison.

Another shadow was lurking behind us, too. Something dark and large and powerful. I remembered the force that had slammed me up against the LaLaurie mansion. I was almost running, dragging Taj around by his hand. Then we broke into the crowd that was jammed into the gated courtyard and spilling out into Jackson Square.

"So I was thinking about your fear of the dark," he said.

"It's stupid, I know."

The crowd thickened.

Safety in numbers. I breathed a sigh of relief.

"What I was going to say is that it is human." He stopped and took my face gently in both his hands. Then kissed me sweetly, before taking my hand again.

A few women nearby said, "Aww."

"She is amazing," Taj told the ladies.

I rolled my eyes, smiling, and Taj led me toward the center of the crowd.

"Anyway," Taj said, "fears can be exhilarating, too."

"What do you mean?" I wrinkled my brow. "Like adrenaline junkies?"

"Take the millions of people who go to scary movies, for example. They do not have to go. They choose to go because it is fun for them."

"Adrenaline junkies," I confirmed, casting a glance behind me. No one was following us.

"At least they are willing to face their fears," he said. "Even if they are scared."

But those people don't have death threats hanging over their heads. I wished I could tell Taj right then. Tell him everything. Have him hold me close and say that everything would be all right.

We finally made it into the garden within Jackson Square as "O Holy Night" began. The beautiful music reverberated off of the buildings surrounding us. Thousands of carolers raised their voices in unison and a thick blanket of comfort settled over me. I couldn't hear the footsteps anymore. Maybe it was just my overactive imagination. Maybe. We stopped next to an older couple, who looked to be in their fifties.

"We have rum," the man said, offering us a flask.

I glanced around and noticed everyone holding cups of liquid holiday cheer.

"And we have Coke." The woman picked up a two-liter bottle from under a nearby bench.

"No, thanks," I said, smiling. Their merry attitude was from too many drinks, I knew, but they were clearly having a ton of fun.

They handed us their extra candle and song sheet and, just like that, we became Christmas carolers.

"I have never done this before," Taj said excitedly.

"Me neither," I replied, smiling.

For the remaining few songs, the couple next to us belted out each tune with their etched glass whiskey tumblers in one hand and a lit candle and song sheet in the other hand. In the course of three songs, the two lovebirds: spilled liquor on themselves, nearly dumped their entire bottle of Coke, and caught their song sheet on fire. The man, while trying to put the fire out, accidentally bumped his wife's arm and she spilled holiday cheer all over herself.

She snorted and held her tumbler high. "Song sheets, booze, and open flames. Probably not the best combination."

Mom had never been a happy drunk. *Maybe that would have helped,* I thought. Instead, she'd always turned mean—scary, even—when she drank. I balanced my candle in one hand, warming the other hand with the small flame. Its brightness spellbound me and in spite of the momentary reminder of Mom's nasty addiction, the cheery atmosphere won out, warming my heart. Taj stood behind me, wrapping me in his arms and we swayed with the music. Mom's memory softened in my head. My heart beat strongly in my chest. All the songsters lifted their lights and voices in unison. Joy welled up inside of me as my voice joined with theirs, my spirit connecting to the whole. The security of Taj's arms made my eyes brim with tears.

So this is happiness, I marveled, basking in the warmth of the emotion.

My fear of the dark dimmed and, for that moment, I forgot about death threats. I forgot about looking over my shoulder. With all of the carolers gathered here, I could see Jackson Square for what it was: the beating heart of this mystifying city.

My home, I thought. New Orleans was my home.

Chapter 19
The Dark Side of NOLA

Seraphina's House of Voodoo hummed with holiday cheer and the cha-ching of good business, but with Christmas upon us, I'd been thinking a lot about my mom. One particular childhood memory about a Christmas long ago continued to haunt me.

Clad in my bright red-footed pajamas, the six-year-old me enthusiastically held up a plate loaded with generic brand Oreos, the only kind we could afford, and a glass filled to the brim with milk.

"Mommy, look! I got this for Santa!"

Mommy growled like a bear in her bed. The big, black curtains made her bedroom so dark it scared me. The room smelled yucky, like smoke mixed with her spicy drink. She finally sat up and grabbed her box of "cancer sticks." She flicked the lighter and her face became a Halloween mask. It was Christmas Eve. Mommy got crabby at Christmastime.

"See, Mommy." I set the cookies and milk on her nightstand and flipped on the little lamp. "We can set these out so that Santa will make it here this year. I think he didn't come last year because we didn't put any cookies out. It's not 'cause I was bad. But we have cookies this year. So he should come! Right, Mommy?"

The cancer stick dangled from her fingertips. She leaned over and balanced her elbows on her knees, her head in her hands. After a few moments, she took a long smoke and blew it in my face, making me cough.

"It's all bullshit, Sophia." She hiccupped and giggled, her breath stinky, her voice sloppy. "Christmas is nothing but a bunch of bullshit."

I backed up, my knees shaking, because I knew this was Angry Mommy.

"How old are you anyway, little girl?"

"Six and a half," I whispered, tears making it hard to see. *Don't cry. Crying makes Mommy angry.*

"Well you need to know the truth, Sophia." She pointed the bright red end of the cancer stick near my nose, pointing out every word. "There. Ain't. No. Santa."

She puffed more smoke in my face.

"There ain't no magic. And there ain't gonna be no toys neither. You wanna know why?"

My throat choked. *Don't cry! Mommy doesn't like it when I cry.*

"I'll tell you why! It's because I'm a failure! I am a failure of a mother and I ain't got no purpose in this world." She started to cry.

Angry Mommy became Sad Mommy really fast. Sometimes she did that. She cried really hard and it made me really sad, too.

"Don't cry, Mama." I placed my little hand on her sad shoulder. "Please, Mama. I'm sorry."

"I could've changed people . . ." She put her head in her hands, again, and I worried she'd burn herself with the cancer stick. "Made the world a better place. Not such a shit hole," she said.

Please stop crying, Mommy. My heart hurt when she was like this.

"But I ran away," she said, banging the fire end of her cancer stick into Santa's cookies. "It's too late. Too, too late." She laid down and hid under her covers. She just kept saying, "Too late. Too late. Too, too late . . ."

I didn't say no more about Santa. I crawled next to Mommy until she went to sleep. Then I got up, turned off the lamp, and left my mother in her scary, dark place. And Santa didn't come. Like Mama said.

Now my grown-up heart ached for my mother. Finally I understood her words. *I could've changed people . . . made the world a better place*. Mom had turned her back on New Orleans, on her responsibilities as a Mind Changer, and she'd paid the price for it. If I didn't try to fulfill my purpose, I'd end up in her shoes. I refused to fail. I refused to be nothing. Father Malachi and I had talked about this memory during one of our sessions.

At that time, he wanted me to meet him at the cathedral so he could show me the different people I'd be helping as a Mind Changer.

He held an arm out over the entirety of the space. "*See* them, Sophia. Really see them."

I'd glanced around the church, up and down the main and side aisles.

"On the surface, things are fine, right?" he had asked, giving me some time to consider the rhetorical question. "You see that woman over there? She's got bags under her eyes and a slump in her shoulders. The world has beaten her down. She needs peace. See people, really see them, and you will recognize doubt and fear and hope residing underneath their masks. Sure, Poppy will teach you all of the voodoo tricks to do your job well, but the real trick is to read people. Really see them and you will find what you need to know."

I remembered my mother's haunted eyes. Understood them, even as a small child. All that pain. All that anger simmering beneath the surface. If I only could have helped her out of the darkness, then maybe I wouldn't be so scared of it, too.

"I don't know," I said, full of doubt. Sitting there, in the church, I felt absolutely terrified of even *thinking* I could become a Mind Changer.

"Hope exists, Sophia," Father had assured me.

The beginnings of hope stirred in my heart and I knew that I wanted to believe that. I shoved my hair behind my ears, uneasy by my shifting perspective. The world as I knew it was a sand dune, shifting under my feet with the winds of change.

"God exists," he said emphatically. "You will help people to see the good that is God."

"I don't know how to, Father."

"Start by believing that it's possible."

I felt a twinge of optimism pull at my heart, but it quickly turned to anger. I wanted to retrieve the faith that I had felt when I was little and blindly believed that Santa existed. But blind faith seemed like such a stupid illusion. A belief in Santa or any other mythical creature couldn't help me.

"What am I supposed to believe in Father?"

"In yourself. In your purpose. In God. Faith is a strong force; it breathes miracles into being. Contemplate that and it can be so." He put his hand on my shoulder and got up and walked to a front pew, moving among the other wandering souls. I studied my hands, trying to decide what to do. I knew I had to, at the very least, let go of the anger I had toward my mother. I had to forgive so that I could move on with my life.

"Sophie? Sophie!" Poppy shoved a shoebox in front of my face. "Girl, it's a good thing tomorrow's Christmas and the shop's closed because you need a break."

"Sorry." I shook my head. "I was just thinking."

"Anyway," Poppy said, out of breath. The holiday rush had taken its toll on her, too, and I could see it in her tired eyes. "I need you to deliver this package to Margaret the White Witch."

She took my place behind the shop's register.

"She's already paid for it," Poppy said.

"Got it."

"Hey, Sophie," she said.

"Yeah?"

"Be careful. It'll be dark in an hour." She tapped her finger on her lips. "On second thought, maybe Taj should go with you. Taj!" she yelled through the crowded shop, waving her hand to get his attention.

Everyone looked at us and I pulled Poppy's elbow down abruptly. "I'll be fine. Who is this Margaret the White Witch, anyway? Sounds like we're in Oz or something."

"She is a powerful mambo and was one of Seraphina's closest friends, very respected in our voodoo socyete."

I grabbed the box off of the counter.

"Careful. It's fragile," Poppy said, and then she yelled after me through the store, "Thanks Sophie!"

"No problem," I said and hurried outside, crossing the busy street. Even though dusk approached, the city crawled with activity: street performers peppered every alley and square; fortune-tellers and tea leaf readers hawked their psychic wares in Jackson Square; busty waitresses stood at the doors of restaurants and bars, shouting to potential customers as they passed, "Shots! Shots!" They held up vials of neon-colored liquids. Street sweeping machines ground against the grimy cobblestones after last night's binge. I hopped over a puddle of putrid, foamy water, not even wanting to guess what sorts of bodily fluids were in there, mixed with the cleaning solution that got sprayed on the sidewalks and streets every morning.

Lost cause, I thought. *But I guess they have to maintain.* Momentarily I remembered cleaning up after one of Mom's binges with her fling of the week. I shook my head. *Don't go there, Soph.*

Heading toward the river, a maroon streetcar rushed past my line of sight, sweeping me into another era, kicking up memories of the past in its wake. I watched the streetcar recede into the distance, then I crossed the tracks, heading to the top of the levee.

A park snaked along the levee and I walked along the riverfront for a while. At one point, I noticed that a blue haze had settled over the surface of the water, snaking its way across the river like a sentient being. I shuddered, remembering the strange fog that pursued me my first night in New Orleans. A silent sailboat cut through the mist.

Beyond the fog, maybe a mile or so away, a bonfire burned on the opposite shore. It must've been enormous, though, because I could see it swirling wildly. The flames would grow into a monstrous form and then recede, changing color from pink to blue to white to yellow. Some pedestrians glanced at the fire and continued on their way. Others would stop, but I was spellbound.

A man cleared his throat beside me, appearing from nowhere and nearly giving me a heart attack. I turned to him and noticed his eye patch before politely smiling to acknowledge his presence. He looked straight through me, like I didn't exist, and a boulder of negativity settled in the pit of my stomach.

"That's Coffin Point," he said, pointing with his stubby cigarette. Middle age settled itself across the man's tan skin, lining his face. His coloring suggested too many hours in the sun mixed with some Spanish or Native American lineage. Despite his messy salt and pepper hair and a grizzled five-o'clock shadow, he had the features of someone who had been handsome. Once.

He flung the smoking cigarette butt to the ground and shuffled it out with his alligator hide boots. Shading his one good eye with his hand, he nodded to the strange bonfire on the opposite shore and leaned into the silver-tipped cane that supported his weight.

"That's Madame Delphine's fire," he said.

Not a smiler, but I guess he wants to talk.

"Delphine?" I asked, setting the box down between my feet because it was getting heavy. He glanced down at it.

"Delphine LaLaurie," he clarified.

My blood ran cold at the mention of the wicked woman's name. Momentarily, visions of the poor tortured souls trapped in "The Haunted House" flashed into my mind. The human caterpillar. The human crab. The image of the cold, gray mansion with its iron bars and its black shutters seeped into my brain. And so did the memory of those horrifying footsteps.

Since the man had appeared next to me, an unexpected nausea had began to build in my core. Bile burned my throat. I wrapped my jacket around me tighter and looked over my shoulder just to make sure no one else would sneak up on me. I thought about leaving, but wanted to know more about the mysterious fire.

"Is Delphine a distant relative of the family who built the LaLaurie mansion?" I asked, picking at my nails.

"No, it's her," he said nonchalantly. "*The* Delphine." He pulled a fresh pack of cigarettes from his pocket, resting the cane on his hip, then smacked the top of the pack against the palm of his hand. "The same Delphine who murdered and tortured all of those people." A sinister smile spread across his face.

Is he toying with me? I stared at him, not wanting to back down. He never broke eye contact as he lit a cigarette, sliding the pack in his back pocket.

He continued. "She likes to make her presence known now and again. Most people ignore her fire this time of year, because they think it has something to do with the Papa Noel fires. But, it's her." Adjusting his eye patch, he gave me that unnerving sneer again.

My stomach lurched and I swallowed hard.

"She used to own this town," he said, his tone strangely insistent and proud at the same time. "It's a damn shame what happened to the LaLauries."

Were we talking about the same woman? From what I'd read online, and I'd done some serious research after Taj told me about Madame LaLaurie, her and her husband were sadistic psychopaths.

"The LaLauries will always have their legacy, and I, for one, would like to be a part of it. She'll come back," he said cryptically.

What does that even mean? Then a crazy thought struck me. *Were there others who wanted to resurrect this so-called 'legacy'?* It sounded like he wanted Madame LaLaurie to raise from the dead like some zombie. It was absurd and unnatural. Anyone who would be onboard with that...I had to tell Poppy. Those kind of people would have to be stopped.

"I have a ferry to catch," he grumbled. Taking a long drag on his cigarette, he slowly blew smoke into my face, like Mom had done to me on that Christmas Eve when I was six.

I coughed and bent over, clutching my knees, to keep from retching in public. I waved his smoke away, heard the tap-tap-tap of his cane on the sidewalk, and noticed his gator boots saunter away. The fog of nausea immediately lifted and I stood up slowly, my equilibrium returning, but the fire and the man in the alligator boots had undone me.

The tap-tap-tap of his cane receded, the harsh sound bringing a memory to the surface. The person wearing the bull mask, on the night of the failed mind change at the LaLaurie Mansion, had carried a cane. I'd assumed Jacques was our only attacker, but maybe he hadn't acted alone. I twirled around and hurried away from the one-eyed man as quickly as my feet could carry me.

My fear of the dark settled into my bones as I looked at the sunset sky. Through a layer of gathering clouds, I could just make out the outline of the waxing gibbous moon.

Not much time. If I wanted to get home by nightfall, I'd need to book it. Quickening my pace, I remembered something Poppy had told me in a late night conversation on our balcony. *New Orleans, she never sleeps . . . and never forgets,"* she'd warned me. *Do not get on her dark side.*

I didn't understand this place sometimes. Perhaps I never would. Maybe it was because I hadn't grown up here. But what should that matter? Technically, I was a native due to the fact my family line sprawled back for generations. If blood and history didn't connect me to this city, I didn't know what else would. The final words of Poppy's warning rang in my ears, *Do not get on her dark side,* as I walked, watching Delphine's fire burn on Coffin Point.

Finally, I made it to Margaret's house based on the address printed on the shoebox. This tiny package meant so much to her, a believer in magic. I was understanding more about that kind of power, but the weight of the box felt deceptively insignificant in my hands. I pushed the intercom button at Margaret's courtyard entrance. Peeking through the iron gates, I could see the front of the house covered in aged white plaster. Green vines surrounded the solid wood front door. A peacock-colored decorative wooden balcony swept across the entire second floor.

"Hello?" A pleasant voice crackled through the intercom.

"I have a package for Margaret. From Seraphina's House of Voodoo."

The huge gates clicked open and I pushed through, entering a courtyard with dozens of angel statues placed along rambling walkways. Under the romantic brick archway, concrete planters overflowed with evergreen bushes surrounded by newly planted poinsettias for the holiday season. The fading sunlight cast a shadow of the gas lamp at the archway's peak. The features of this city could change so fast. One little nuance in the lighting, one change in the wind, and the familiar suddenly became terrifying. Bipolar.

Like crazy Madame LaLaurie. The public Delphine, a renowned citizen, who threw extravagant parties for the city's elite. The hidden Delphine: torturer, murderer, monster.

I was glad I was in the safety of this lovely courtyard that overflowed with beautiful plants. Even though it was winter, lovely white flowering bushes filled the air with a heavenly scent. From the courtyard's center came the soft bubbling of a fountain; the space protected from the outside noise and exhaust fumes of heavy traffic. A hush of wind blew through the trees. The golden light of sunset bounced off the brick walls making the air feel warm and cozy. I picked a white flower and held it under my nose.

"Gardenias," a voice said.

I jumped, dropping the flower. Caught in the act of stealing a blossom, I felt incredibly rude. I turned to see an old woman with a heart-shaped face standing in the open front door.

"I'm Margaret," she said.

Suddenly, I remembered her from the funeral second line, but at that time she'd been wearing a huge royal blue hat and walked alongside her friend—*Yolanda*, I recalled.

Margaret's white hair formed a halo around her brown skin. I blushed, trying to stammer out an excuse for picking a flower, but she didn't seem offended. She broke into an easy smile.

"Come in. Come in, my dear," she said and, somehow, I loved her immediately.

"Your order." I held the package out to her.

"Yes, yes. I've been expecting you," she said, her voice like the coo of a dove.

"Margaret!" a woman barked from inside the house. "Who that?"

"It's our delivery from Seraphina's House of Voodoo, Yolanda," Margaret called back calmly. She turned to me and said, "I have tea on the stove. C'mon in."

"Oh, no thanks. It's getting dark and I need to get back." I pointed my thumb over my shoulder.

"Home to your husband," she said certainly.

I laughed, embarrassed. "No husband."

"Someone that you love, then."

"Back to work," I explained.

"Child, you have someone that loves you at home," she said with a sweet-as-pie smile. "And he's meant to be your husband if you would just see that." She laughed and shook her head.

The mystery woman poked her head out and said impatiently, "This juju ain't gonna hold up much longer. I need your help."

Margaret rolled her eyes.

"Yolanda, don't be rude. Say hello to our guest."

With hands on her hips, Yolanda grunted a hello and turned right back inside, slamming the screen door as she went.

"I apologize for my friend," Margaret said. "You can't teach an old mambo new tricks."

"It's fine," I said, waving off the rude behavior. "Well, just let us know if you need anything else."

"Wait." She put her finger in the air. Grabbing some kitchen shears from her apron, she reached up and snipped off a pristine gardenia blossom from a nearby bush. She tenderly tucked the gardenia into my ponytail, the sweet scent clinging to my hair.

"Thank you," I said, gently feeling the bloom at the nape of my neck.

She folded her hands around her middle. "You look like her, you know."

I raised an eyebrow.

"Your grandmother." She patted my shoulder. "We all loved Seraphina. She was so gifted in her special . . ." She winked at me. ". . . work."

My breath caught. *She knows about mind changing.*

"Um." I held my thumb over my shoulder again. "I need to get back. The shop's been really busy."

She nodded and then walked back into the house.

I stood at the porch for a moment, letting the reality sink in. *She knew.*

"Yeah, she's Seraphina's granddaughter," Yolanda's rough-around-the-edges voice drifted through the screen door. "But can she do the magic? That's what I want to know."

Margaret's softer voice was harder to make out, but I think she said something about supporting the "reigning family" and "power" and "tradition."

"We need the Mind Changer," Yolanda said. "That girl looked like, well, like a little girl. You gonna tell me she has enough power to lead us?"

Margaret appeared at the screen door and addressed me calmly and kindly. "Let me know how we can help you, Sophia."

"Okay. Thanks." I swallowed hard and did a one-eighty. *Totally busted for eavesdropping.* Under my breath I muttered, "Of course she knows my name, too." I pushed the iron gate open with a rusty creak. *Who else did you send the dream memo to, Grandma Seraphina?*

Back on the street, the sense of beauty and tranquility of Margaret's place evaporated. As dusk settled, an edgy energy thrummed beneath the surface of the pavement. I walked past other cobblestone courtyards, noticing their shadowy foliage bathed in twilight, and my heart beat faster. So pretty during the day, these places became ominous at night, housing centuries of terrible secrets, just like the LaLauries tried to hide their atrocities. I imagined the firefighters' faces twisting into disgust as they entered the chamber of horrors on the third floor of the LaLaurie mansion. Eventually, every dark secret will come into the light. The truth will be known.

But sometimes the guilty get away, I thought. As was the case of the LaLauries who escaped into the night. *And the victims would never be completely free.*

New Orleans scared me at times, but I was a grown woman. This was my home now and I would face my fears and walk, despite the growing darkness. *I will not run. I will not run.*

"Positive thoughts," I whispered to myself.

I remembered the fun I had with Taj while caroling in Jackson Square. I envisioned the older couple—song sheet alight and covered in booze—and giggled to myself. The familiar, relaxing effect that Taj brought out in me settled around my shoulders.

I love him. The thought stopped me in my tracks. After considering the automatic response to thinking about him, I knew it to be true. In the last month, Taj had changed me. I was the happiest I'd been in my life. He took me on a horse-drawn carriage ride around the French Quarter. We did a haunted New Orleans tour. When the tour paused at the LaLaurie Mansion, my heart pounded and I felt like I could die of a panic attack, but Taj had wrapped his arms around me and kept telling me that it was just a building and we were safe on the opposite side of the street in our big group of tourists. I found myself looking for new experiences and places to add to my New Orleans to-do list so I could keep going on adventures with Taj.

I love kissing him. He never pressured me for more and I felt completely in charge of my body and of my own decisions. Now *that* felt sexy. To have him to cuddle up against and never worry that he would take advantage of me, force me to do something I really wasn't ready for, or threaten to find another woman because I wouldn't put out fast enough. Maybe because he was foreign, there were no head games.

Taj brought me peace, but my mind would occasionally creep back to a deep, dark fascination with Jacques. The sexual chemistry buzzed around me like a fat fly. No matter what I did, I couldn't get Jacques completely out of my head.

Coming back to the present, I nearly stepped on a teenage girl with a fringe of ginger hair. She sat amidst a nest of carefully displayed artwork. I wondered when she'd eaten last. Her lumpy cardigan hung from her bird-like frame. Looking into her face, I recognized the hardness that I knew all too well. *Survivor*, the set of her jaw said. *Like me*.

I wanted to help her, and I briefly considered trying a mind change. But I hadn't reapplied the powder since the morning and I doubted it would still work. Leaning closer to examine her art work, I noticed the mixed media collages were made with different types of papers, inks, and paint.

"You made all these?" I asked, and her freckled face brightened. She held one out to me.

"They're found art," she said meekly.

I once was lost, but now am found.

"They're beautiful." I handed the one she gave me back to her. "How much?"

She summed me up and then named her price, "Thirty dollars."

My eyes floated over the dozen or so paintings and one kept catching my eye. It was made from a brown paper bag and when I flipped it over, the back said, HOLD BOTH HANDLES.

My mind slipped to the memory of my mother not accepting who she was, not having a handle on her life.

I have to get a handle on mine.

Pasted in the upper right corner was a picture of a partridge, torn from a yellowed encyclopedia page.

Mom tried to fly away, but I'm staying. My heart swelled with pride that I'd had the courage to do what my mom could not: face my destiny.

I scanned the swirling penmanship across the bottom of the page: *Partridge and Tangerine, Sierra Hart.*

"A partridge in a tangerine tree," I remarked. The picture was sweet.

Like my Taj. At the mere thought of him, my heart fluttered and I happily fished two twenties from my purse.

"Keep the change," I said.

As soon as the girl's hand touched mine, a charge leapt from my fingers to hers. A beam of pure white light, only visible for the snap of a second, bridged between us.

"Sorry," I said and checked my hand. "Static, I guess."

The girl looked at me with the eyes of a child; she recognized something inside of me.

"It's not static," she said firmly, her lips pressed into a thin line. "I have to go home."

I tilted my head, trying to understand. The whole interaction was becoming weird. I rubbed my hand on my pants, because it felt like it was crawling with thousands of tiny ants.

"With my parents," she added resolutely. She shuffled all her artwork into a pile and shoved it under her arm. "I can't stay out here anymore. I want to go home."

"O-Okay," I stuttered.

"Thank you." She hugged me, turned, and walked quickly away. Every now and then she'd turn back and find me. And then she disappeared into the distance.

What the . . . ? I studied my hand. Nothing visibly different, but it thrummed with a new—I don't know—energy. Each time my heart beat, I could still feel power pulsing through my veins. I glanced over my left shoulder and towering across the street was the statue of Joan of Arc, illuminated by flood lights.

Love! A sharp whisper intruded into my ear canal, my earlobe tingling.

I whipped my head around, looking over each shoulder, but no one was there.

Power!

The voice again. My eyes searched the Saint Joan of Arc statue. She stood sentinel, unmoving and committed.

Love . . . power, the voice urged with a softer intonation. I closed my eyes and tried to connect the words. Suddenly, it hit me. Right before I bought the painting, I'd been thinking of Taj, feeling his love. And when I touched Sierra, all that love surged inside of me.

"No way," I whispered, holding my hand in front of me, turning it from front to back. *But the powder. . .* I examined my hand once more. *It should have rubbed off by now. It . . .*

I took off running toward Seraphina's House of Voodoo to tell Poppy. A smile spread across my face. And I felt like that six-year-old, Santa-believing kid again. The one who knew with certainty that magic can be real.

Chapter 20
A Second Strike

After my unexpected mind change with Sierra, the street artist, I felt invigorated with a new energy. *I can do this. I can become the next Mind Changer.* A huge smile spread across my face as I hurried toward the apartment and, as I approached the alley, I fished my keys from my purse. Unexpectedly, the aroma of pipe tobacco filled the air around me, and I knew Grandma Seraphina was near. I closed my eyes, taking a deep whiff of the sweet smoke, and pretended Grandma's arms were wrapped around me.

Suddenly, strong hands pushed me from behind. I skidded to the ground, dropping my keys. Out of the corner of my eye, Taj's picture fluttered to the cobblestones.

The death threats.

Fear choked me. My hands and knees throbbed.

The night at the LaLaurie Mansion. Jacques.

I clenched my teeth and faced him. But it wasn't Jacques. Instead, a white guy with a grizzled beard hovered over me. My mind reeled trying to understand who this man was and why he was the one threatening me. I prepared myself for another blow.

"Well, well," the man slurred.

Fear held me captive. My mind fumbled to make a plan, but nothing made sense. No way to escape.

"What do we have here?" The man spit on the ground next to my head.

"What do you want?" I said.

He knelt down next to me. Grabbed my hair. Yanked back.
"Ow!" I screamed. "Help!"
He pulled me to standing. Shoved me back against the brick wall.

My breath, short and desperate, I screamed again. "Help me! Somebody please!"

Backhand.

"Quiet!" he said, wrapping his fingers around my throat. "You're gonna die." He cracked the back of my skull against the masonry wall.

Dazed, I remembered the night of the failed mind change. This man who wanted me dead had shoved me against the cold, gritty mortar at the LaLaurie Mansion. A moment of lucidity. *Now he's going to kill me.*

He plastered his body against mine. Looked at me with dark eyes. Imposing brow. Forced his scruffy face against my neck. Breath drenched in bourbon.

I turned my face, gagging.

"How about a little kiss?" He yanked my hair back, grabbing me at the nape of the neck.

Survive! Gritting my teeth, I fought back. Kicked. Screamed. Scratched.

Too big. He's too—

He tore open my shirt.

The mind-changing powder, I thought desperately. *Should've reapplied.*

Heavy breathing. Disgusting kisses . . . on my neck . . . face . . . breasts.

My mind left. Escaped.

He licked my cheek.

Bile filled my mouth. *I don't want to die like this.*

"Mmmm, you taste—"

I vomited.

He released me, just for a second, and stared at his shirt.

Run! my adrenaline told my muscles. I surged forward.

"You bitch!"

Too late.

Another backhand. My face throbbed.

He pinned me to the wall again.

I jutted my chin out, refusing to cower. Blood slid down my nostril.

"You puked on my new shirt!"

My body strained against his hold. He looked down at his waistline. "I'll teach you a lesson."

He fumbled with his belt buckle.

Now!

Summoning every ounce of energy I had left, I swung and hit his jaw. Hard. A shimmery dust exploded around my hand. Upon impact, a few sparks rained down. They hit his skin and then smoldered.

Belt and zipper wide open, the man stumbled back. He shook his head, was about to go down.

My hands, balled in fists, shook.

"She's mine!" A shadowed man swooped in between me and my assailant, delivering a knockout blow. The thug staggered. Dropped to his knees. Then fell face first on the concrete.

Blackness edged in around my eyes. Lightheadedness. My knees wobbled. But before I fell, my rescuer wrapped his arms around me. Slowly, my eyes adjusted and I was looking into those terrible, enchanting eyes.

"Jacques," I murmured.

"Are you okay?" Jacques asked with a quiet tenderness that I'd never heard from him before.

I wanted to melt into his arms. Stay there forever.

I nodded.

"Ow." I put my hand to my aching head.

Jacques delicately sat me on the ground near my door.

"Sophia, I am right here," he reassured me, holding his hand to my cheek.

I blinked in response.

Jacques turned on my attacker, who was now moaning on the ground.

The survivor in me wanted to escape. Crawl into my apartment. Be safe. But my body just couldn't.

Instead, I watched Jacques circle around the man like a bird of prey. I knew he would kill him.

Swiftly, Jacques pressed his face within inches of the man's face.

I watched. Captivated.

Jacques stood, towering over his quarry and then, surprisingly, he backed away.

"It's not your time, or I would finish you myself," Jacques said through gritted teeth. He took a deep breath, smoothed back his ever-impeccable hair, and straightened his jacket.

He ordered sharply, "You will turn yourself into the police."

"I will turn myself in," the man repeated, entranced.

"You will confess to all the rapes and murders for which you are guilty." Absolute ice hung in Jacques' words.

"Confess everything," the man said, his voice monotone.

Jacques pointed. "Now go."

The man stood, gazed at Jacques, and then stumbled away, in the direction of the police station, I guessed.

Jacques walked toward me, stooped to retrieve Taj's present, and handed the picture to me.

"How? What?" I bumbled.

"Never mind, *ma chérie*. Let us get you inside."

With that, he lifted me into his arms as if I weighed nothing. He kicked my keys off the ground and into his hand, unlocked the door, and carried me upstairs. When we were in the safety of my apartment, he deposited me on the sofa.

"Ice," he said.

I blinked, and he had magically created bags of frozen veggies. I propped myself up on the couch, completely confused. They were from my freezer, of that I was sure, but I couldn't understand how he'd moved so fast.

I must have hit my head harder than I realized. I placed the bag of peas across my knees and held the icy bag of corn to my face.

"Thanks," I said.

He nodded and left the living room again. In a blink, he was kneeling beside me with a cotton square covered in peroxide pressed to my elbow.

"Where'd you get that?" I asked.

"Your bathroom, of course."

"That was fast," I whispered.

"You are injured. Should I not be quick on my feet?"

A concussion. That explains his speed. I'm not thinking straight.

The corner of Jacques' lip curled in amusement.

I blurted out, "How do you know your way around my house?"

"Do you really believe that I am not smart enough to guess that first-aid supplies would be in your bathroom medicine cabinet?"

I smiled and gave up trying to explain Jacques' superhuman speed and intuitive faculties. Obviously, I was still out of sorts from being knocked around.

The door buzzed, and I yelped, my heart hammering in my chest. He looked into my eyes, and I immediately felt calmer. *Why does he have this effect on me?*

He stood, walked to the apartment door behind the couch, and pushed the intercom button.

"Yes?" he said, his usual smooth voice. Unruffled, even after facing a thug.

"Is Sophie there?" Taj's voice rang through the intercom.

"Yeeeees," Jacques purred.

"Can I talk to her?" Taj said, an edge in his voice.

Jacques turned to me for an answer. I nodded. Jacques pushed the button to unlock the door. Footsteps blasted up the stairs.

Great. I knew Taj would be *so* happy to see Jacques, especially alone with me in my apartment.

Again, magically appearing by my side, Jacques placed his hand on mine. Peace instantaneously filled my arm and coursed through my entire body like a deep, still river. The door flew open, rattling on its hinges. I wrenched my fist away from Jacques.

"Sophie!" Taj shouted and looked wildly from me to Jacques to the ice packs and bandages.

He turned on Jacques. "What the hell happened?"

Then Taj knelt by my side and took my hand. "Are you okay?"

Guilt rose in my chest about allowing Jacques to hold my hand, allowing Jacques to have such a hold over me at all, that I barely nodded. Taj delicately took my chin in his hands and put his lips to mine. After a soft kiss, he breathed a sigh of relief.

Taj turned to Jacques, who sat at my other side. "What the hell happened?"

I finally found my voice. "Someone attacked me in the alley. Jacques saved me."

Taj lifted the frozen veggies to inspect the damage. "We should get you to the ER."

"No, no. I'm fine," I said.

Taj wrinkled his brow.

"Really." I tried to sound convincing. "It's just some bumps and bruises. Nothing broken."

"Sophie," Taj said firmly, "you could have a concussion."

"She hit her head pretty hard," Jacques agreed.

Each man knelt at my feet and I turned from one to the other. *Really? Now you're gonna team up?*

Clenching my eyes, my head a wreck, I pleaded, "I just want to get cleaned up and go to bed."

Taj pressed his lips into a thin line. Not happy.

"Are you sure?" he asked.

I nodded and after a nice, long awkward silence, Jacques rose to his feet.

"It appears as though you are in good hands, *ma chérie*. So with that, I will take my leave." Jacques bowed curtly and turned to go.

"Wait." I touched his hand and that captivating tranquility swept through me once more. "How were you there at just the right moment?"

"Out for a stroll. Fortunate that I would be at your door."

"And I couldn't sleep, either," Taj said. "Something made me feel like I needed to come over here and see you."

"Look at that, *ma chérie*. Two guardian angels to watch over you."

I smiled slightly, knowing he was right. There was no way I could have fended that guy off. I didn't even want to think about what could've happened.

"Thank you, Jacques. So much," I said.

"My pleasure," he replied, grabbing his hat before he let himself out.

"I still do not trust that guy," Taj said as soon as the outside door clicked shut. He muttered something in a foreign language and held a cool cloth to my forehead. "Hold this."

I did. And he proceeded to clean the cuts on my hands, before gently placing bandages on the wounds. He put the frozen veggies on top of the bandages to help the swelling.

"Could you get me some aspirin?" I asked. Even though I tried to put on my brave face, everything was throbbing at this point, and I just wanted to cry.

"Sure. Where is it?"

I pointed toward the hallway. "Bathroom cabinet."

Poppy walked through the door and the first words out of her mouth were the same as Taj's. "What the hell happened?"

"I must have that effect on people." I laughed a little and pain stabbed me everywhere. "Ow."

Taj came back with the aspirin and nodded his acknowledgement to Poppy.

"Tell me everything," he said firmly. "Every detail."

Poppy sat down in the wingback chair, her eyebrows upturned with concern. Taj sat next to me and took my hand in his.

"There really isn't a lot to share. I wasn't being alert. Stupid, really."

Taj squeezed my hand. "You're not stupid, Sophie."

Poppy shook her head, still disbelieving the state I was in.

I continued. "A big guy—he was drunk—he knocked me down."

"The same guy?" Poppy asked, and I knew she was talking about the night at the LaLaurie Mansion.

She covered her mouth, immediately knowing she shouldn't have let that slip in front of Taj.

Whoops.

I didn't want Taj to worry, so I'd never told him about that night. And now he'd know I was hiding things from him. And, the fact was, I *was* hiding things from him. Much bigger secrets. Everything about my double life as a Mind Changer would forever be an inevitable shadow in our relationship.

I said quietly, "I don't know if it was him."

"Wait a minute," Taj broke in. "This happened before?" Taj was more puffed up than I had ever seen him. He always stayed calm and serene, so seeing the display of testosterone would have been a turn-on if my whole body didn't hurt.

I decided to tell him the truth. At least as much as I could.

"I think it was the same guy," I said softly. "But I can't be sure. His voice sounded, I don't know, different." I doubted a lot. I doubted that the grungy man reeking of alcohol could be the one who wrote those eloquent death threats.

He was right outside my house, I thought, fear choking me. My head was swimming with pain. *Maybe I do have a concussion.*

"I want to know about before," Taj insisted.

I sighed. "One night, Poppy and I were out walking..." Taj's eyes bored into me, so I looked down at my lap, busying myself with the ice packs. "And we were... confronted. Near the LaLaurie Mansion."

I could never tell him the real reason why we were there. How would a conversation like that go anyway? *By the way, Taj, I'm a supernatural superhero. You know those powders and spells that we sell down at the shop? Well, they're not really just for tourists. They actually work. And I have the power to make them work. And more than that, I'm a powerful voodoo priestess who knows how to exorcise peoples' demons.*

Yeah, that wouldn't be a total turn-off or anything.

Instead, I finished with, "That's why that place scares me." I raised my eyes. Betrayal settled across his face. He'd always been so open and honest with me and I'd kept such a big secret. So many secrets.

"What about this guy?" Poppy interjected, steering me back toward the crisis at hand.

I recounted, in as much detail as my dizzy head could remember, the horrible episode and Jacques' last-minute intercession.

"Sophie, we have to call the police," Poppy said unequivocally. "You have to catch this guy or he may come back."

"He won't come back." I remembered the bizarre exchange between Jacques and the attacker. He would turn himself in, I knew that with one hundred percent certainty.

"What do you mean he won't come back?" Taj asked,

his voice rising. "He'll do it again. If not to you, then to some other woman."

"He won't."

"Talk some sense into her," Taj pleaded with Poppy.

Poppy didn't say anything. She stared at me long and hard and I knew she wanted to talk about this without Taj in the room. I sighed, knowing what I had to do, and took the ice pack off my head.

"Taj," I said. Those brown eyes stared into me, and I swallowed hard. "I've been through a lot tonight. And to tell you the truth . . ." The pain of telling yet another lie stabbed my chest. ". . . I just want to get cleaned up and go to bed."

"Are you sure you do not want me to stay?" He took my hands in his. Those sad, adorable brown eyes wrenched my heart.

Poppy deliberately extracted another ivory envelope from her purse and held it up so that I could see it, but Taj couldn't.

Crap. She slipped the note back in her purse.

Taj definitely had to go, even though I really wanted him to stay, wanted to fall asleep in his safe arms. *Another night sleeping with the lights on,* I guessed, all the terrifying elements of my life piling on top of one another: my nightmares, the attack, and, now, another death threat. I wanted to cry—a full on cry complete with shoulders slumped, head in hands, nose running, just to let it all out—but I had to convince Taj that I was okay and that he could leave me.

"Poppy's here. I'll be fine," I said through the lump in my throat.

He tenderly held his hand up to my face, looping his thumb behind my ear, and gave me a long kiss. When he pulled away, I gave him the biggest brave-girl grin I could muster.

"Thanks for being my knight in shining armor," I said.

Poppy waited until he descended the stairs and closed the door at the street. She pushed the curtains aside to watch him go and then pulled the envelope from her purse.

My heart plummeted. "Where did you find that one?"

"In the mailbox." She turned it around in her hands, before reluctantly giving it to me.

"When did you check the mail?"

"Right before I came in."

"Have you opened it?" I asked.

She shook her head. "I didn't think I should."

I slid my finger underneath the seal, as tears collected. This was all too much. This whole night. Just too much. I gritted my teeth, trying to hold back the tears, but a few splashed on the calligraphy, smudging the writing. The message read:

Mortality: the only certainty.
Your time is nigh.

Below that was an additional message, an afterthought on the part of the writer.

This need not involve those you love.

I crumpled the paper into a ball and threw it across the room. Furious tears streamed down my face and Poppy snuggled next to me on the couch, putting her chin on my shoulder.

"My protection spells aren't working," she said. "And neither is the mind-changing powder."

The powder. I'd almost forgotten about Sierra's mind change.

"But the powder did work." I shifted to face her, wiping the tears off with my sleeve. "Before it didn't, it did."

Poppy pulled open one of my eyelids and looked at my pupil. "Sophie, are you sure you don't want to go the hospital?"

I ignored her and pointed to my mom's cigar box of goodies on the book shelf.

"Can you give me that," I said.

Poppy handed it to me.

"This strange man was talking to me about Delphine's fire," I said vaguely. I remembered his eye patch, the black cord slightly digging into his tan skin. Pulling the object I wanted from my mom's box, I slowly unwrapped the black fabric from around the glass eye. Looking into its pupil, my mind saw the blackest darkness I'd ever seen and heard a shrill scream from some female thing that couldn't be human.

"What's that?" Poppy asked, interrupting the weird vision.

"Nothing." I hastily wrapped the eye back up, because it was giving me the creeps. I didn't know if I would ever understand that strange object's part in the puzzle that was my mother's past. I told Poppy about Margaret the White Witch knowing my name and implying she knew about mind changing.

"Of course Margaret knows," Poppy said. "She was one of Seraphina's closest friends."

"So do a lot of people know?"

"Just me, Father Malachi, Margaret and Yolanda." She ticked the names on her fingertips. "We were all Seraphina's allies. And now we're yours."

When I explained my encounter with Sierra Hart, the teen artist that I bought the painting from, Poppy perked right up.

"That's more like it." Her voice went up an octave.

"I thought for sure that the powder would've rubbed off during the day," I said skeptically.

"No. There's no need to reapply it throughout the day." She sat straight up and lightly clapped her hands quickly. "You did it, Sophie! All by yourself!"

I smiled and rolled my eyes. But the pride I'd felt as I ran home with Taj's picture returned to me momentarily.

Then the dark cloud of the man pushing me to the ground zapped my brief feeling of triumph.

"So why didn't it work when that guy attacked me?" I asked.

Poppy fell back against the couch, puzzled. I couldn't think of any reason for why the spell would work for one person and, then, moments later fail me. Suddenly, Poppy sat straight up and pointed a finger at me.

"Do you love him?"

"Wha—? No! He was so repulsive that I threw up on him," I said.

"No, no, no." She waved my line of thinking away. "Taj. Do you love Taj?"

Silence.

A smile tickled my lips and I held my fingers to my mouth.

"You do." She raised her eyebrow. "Well that changes everything."

"What does Taj have to do with my work as a Mind Changer?"

"Love is the key."

I shook my head, waiting for the explanation.

"You finally know how to unlock your power," Poppy explained. "Your love for Taj. Maybe if we use that love to your advantage, you could be . . . unstoppable."

I remembered the full and wonderful feeling of love that I'd felt when I'd been with Sierra, thinking of Taj. And then love's exact opposite: overwhelming oppression of fear, when I was victimized.

"I think you need to go get some rest." She helped me to my feet, checking the lock on the door as I hobbled toward the hall. She deposited me in the bathroom, taking my ice packs, and handing me a clean towel. "I'll put some fresh ice packs in your bedroom, sister," she said, the word "sister" making me feel all warm and fuzzy.

Then I faced myself in the mirror. I looked like shit. My jaw was red and swollen. Dried blood caked around my nostrils. I examined my knees, which were tinged violet around the bandages. I considered just giving myself a sponge bath, so I didn't have to reapply my bandages, but I needed a shower. Needed to wash away the dirtiness of my attack: the blood and tears and terror of it.

As I stood under the healing water, Poppy's word "sister" rang in my ears and made me smile, the mere word filling me with warmth and making me feel whole. Then I thought about Taj. *I love him.* That made me beam and I reached my hands to my cheeks, feeling the happiness on my face. But grim darkness fell on my heart and my smile vanished when I thought of that malevolent piece of paper crumpled on the living room floor and those hateful words: *This need not involve those you love.*

I shut off the water, wrapped myself in a towel, opened the bathroom door, and nearly crashed into a dark figure in the hallway. My adrenaline surged and I pushed the figure with all of my might.

"Sophie," he said as I turned to run.

"Taj?" I recognized his voice as he wrapped me in his arms.

"You need me," he said. "I will sleep on the couch if you want."

I eased into him and tears began flowing down my cheeks from sheer happiness and relief that I didn't have to be by myself to face the dark.

"You can sleep in my room," I said, wrapping my arms around his neck.

I love him so much.

I curled my fingers around his and led him to the bedroom, turning off the lights because I wasn't afraid of the dark. My love was with me. I settled into the arms of my Taj. His peaceful presence eased my mind, except my busy brain tried to connect the dots between the attack tonight and the one at the LaLaurie Mansion. I thought, for sure, Poppy and I had been attacked by Jacques that night. *But why would he save me tonight? Were the two attacks even connected?*

The guy tonight seemed way too drunk and sloppy compared to the man in the bull mask on the night of the failed mind change.

That night the supernatural fog had shown up, too. Tonight, no fog. *And what about the one-eyed man?*

"You okay?" Taj whispered in my ear, noticing I hadn't fallen asleep.

"Yeah," I said, snuggling into him.

Something more than the attacks made me anxious.

My mind itched with the information that the man in the alligator shoes had put in my head. It had sounded like he wanted Madame LaLaurie to be resurrected. From what I'd read, *zombis* were a part of Haitian voodoo lore, not New Orleans voodoo. Was it truly possible to reanimate the dead?

Chapter 21
Sympathy for the Devil

Throughout the night, I tossed and turned, my body aching from the assault, my mind spinning from the most recent death threat. Had the man in the alley been the one to send the note? Deep down, I knew the answer. *No.*

The letters had all been too eloquent, the stationery too elegant. The brute last night wouldn't have bothered with fancy notes. Every time I awoke, I would look over at Taj in my bed and I would feel safe, but I knew that Taj wasn't safe being around me anymore.

This need not involve those you love. The note's final words repeated on a constant loop in my head. The stakes had been raised. Now, by staying in New Orleans, I was not only putting myself at danger, but was risking the lives of those that I had grown to love: Taj, Poppy, Father Malachi.

Living the life of the Mind Changer was now a selfish dream, harmful as much as helpful. And with this new thought infecting my brain, I also had to consider what being a Mind Changer really meant for my targets, too.

"Is it right that I am taking the free will of people?" I asked Father Malachi and Poppy.

It was Christmas Day, and Taj would be here any minute. Since he'd stayed overnight, he needed to go home and change, so he'd left earlier. Meanwhile Poppy bustled around the kitchen as Father Malachi sat, sipping a cup of coffee at the kitchen table. We'd asked him to come over a little early to talk about the previous night's attack. Without Taj there, we wouldn't have to tiptoe around mind-changing topics.

"Even if they are like the guy last night"—I fumbled for the right words—"Maybe . . ."

"You mean your would-be rapist?" Poppy interjected.

"I'm not God. I can't chart the course of someone's life," I said sharply and then turned to Father Malachi. "Is it right to take away someone's free will, even if they mean to do harm?"

Father opened his mouth to speak, but Poppy jumped back in before he could say something.

"Damn right it's right! Last night is a perfect example."

I had never seen Earth Mama Poppy so upset. She frowned as she stirred some black-eyed peas on the stove.

"Such a shame that you would have to undergo such a horrific experience," Father Malachi spoke thoughtfully. "Still, free will is a God-given right."

Poppy flipped down the oven door with an overzealous thud to check the Christmas ham.

"I know there are bad guys," I told her. "I know people do evil things, but people should have the freedom to choose their actions. Right?"

"Stop it! Stop right there!" Poppy pointed a spoon at me, "You were assaulted. Remember that! You were defending yourself."

"I am *trying* to understand the bigger picture here. Would you just, for one second, let me talk this out?"

Poppy rolled her eyes and turned back to the side dishes that were bubbling on the stove.

I continued. "And now with this new death threat." I smoothed out the wrinkly note on the table. "It's one thing for me to take *my* life in my own hands, but I cannot just ignore the fact that this person could hurt either of you to get to me."

"I'm not scared," Poppy said defiantly.

I looked at Father Malachi who was listening, but not contributing much to the conversation. I paused, trying to read his face, wanting to know his perspective, but I just couldn't tell what he was thinking.

Eventually, I said to Poppy, "I'm struggling with what to do."

"Think about all the rape victims who won't have to live with their personal demons," she argued. "They would never have to question what they did wrong. Families of would-be murder victims would sleep peacefully knowing everything is safe in their world. You would know that you changed the murderer before he could commit the crime. Our world could be happier."

"You said yourself that voodoo maintains a belief in the balance of positive and negative energies at work in the world," I said. "What if even more evil is perpetuated in order to compensate for the evil that I transformed into good?" I imagined the toys that hold two different-colored liquids and when you turn them top over bottom, the two liquids mix and swirl trying to reach equilibrium. This whole mind changing business was becoming complicated and muddied.

"The good stays good," she answered, shaking her head with certainty. "You just don't get it do you, Soph?"

"You're right. I don't." The next part I knew would sting, "Sometimes I wonder why I ever left Missouri."

Poppy slammed a lid on a pot and took a deep breath.

"Because your life there was mean-ing-less." She enunciated each syllable.

"At least things were consistent."

"Yeah. Consistently boring. You had no life back there." She pointed with a spatula. "And now you have a purpose and people who love you."

"And that won't matter if my work makes you all targets to a madman."

She let the hand with the spatula drop to her side.

"And how do you know my life before was meaningless?" I asked angrily. To me, as the child of an alcoholic, consistency provided safety, and trying all these new things in New Orleans was overloading me. In a way, Poppy was right. I wanted to succeed as a Mind Changer to avoid my mother's fate, but there was no way in hell I'd endanger the people I loved.

"Forgive me for interrupting, my dear, but may I say something?" Father Malachi finally cut in and I was happy to hear his input. "Seraphina once told me that the mind-changing spell frees people from trapped emotion. We bottle our deepest feelings and don't deal with them for years and we expect for all of that power to dissipate? No, no. Mind changing helps people free their minds of repressed emotion. Instantaneously, they can see a better answer because they are not blocked by their negativity. So maybe you need not think of it as taking a person's free will. Instead, you are freeing the person. Think about all the eulogies at Seraphina's funeral. Those people became her children in a way because she helped them into the light."

Supporting free will. I'd never thought about it that way.

"But what about *your* safety, Father?" I asked.

"I am an old man. I've lived a good life. I have to believe that God's will be done and I believe your work is God's will."

"What about Taj?" I asked.

Father made a steeple with his fingertips, and I could tell he was mulling it over.

Poppy said, "For the record, I still think the universe is better without the pieces of shit like that guy last night. And," she repeated, "I'm still not scared."

"I can't stop thinking about the attack at the LaLaurie Mansion, either," I switched gears in the conversation a bit. "And yesterday I ran into someone who said something about the LaLauries coming back into power. Are there other families vying for power now that Grandma is passed?"

"Who said that?" Poppy asked sharply.

"Some guy with an eye patch and alligator boots. Don't know who he was, but I felt really sick when he was talking to me. What's up with that?"

Father Malachi and Poppy gave each other sideway glances.

"What?" I asked. "I feel out of the loop here. Again."

"Seraphina worried that a rival family would take over when she was gone," Father Malachi said. "She had all but given up on your mother, Sophia. And how was she to know that you would show up to take her place? She believed this could be the end of the Papillon reign."

"That guy with the eye patch was determined that Madame LaLaurie herself would come back. Poppy," I addressed her directly because she'd become so quiet all of a sudden and Poppy never held back saying what was on her mind. "Is that possible?"

"No way," she said firmly, then backpedaled. "Well, there is an urban legend about Madame LaLaurie." She paused.

"And," I prompted her, waving my hands in the air.

"The story says that when she ran away from New Orleans with her husband, they went into the swamps," Poppy said. "Supposedly, while they lived there, they met a hoodoo doctor who helped them learn black magic. According to the story, Madame LaLaurie learned how to preserve her soul outside of her body; her hope was that she could be resurrected and take over New Orleans."

"Well, hell," I said, then clamped my hand over my mouth. "Sorry Father."

Father brushed away my apology, saying, "That *does* sound bad."

"But it's just an urban legend," Poppy asserted. "No one has the power to raise the dead. There are rules in nature that have to be observed."

"What about *zombis* in Haiti?" I asked, knowing what I'd read, but wanting her experienced voodoo opinion.

She laughed. "That's absurd. They've all but discounted the stories through scientific evidence."

"Oh, now you're gonna get all scientific?" I countered.

"It's just not possible," she said firmly. The doorbell rang.

"That's Taj," I said.

I walked toward the door, the one-eyed man's words echoing in my mind, *She'll come back*. He had said it with one hundred percent certainty.

"Hello?" I asked through the intercom.

"Woman, it's me," Taj's bright voice replied.

I buzzed him in, and as I opened the interior door to let him in, Taj produced a bright bouquet of flowers from behind his back.

"Thought I would contribute to the meal." He held up a bottle of red wine with his other hand.

"Hi." I sighed, giving him a hug, inexplicably happy that we'd be spending the holidays together.

"How are you feeling?" he asked, inspecting the bruise on my cheek.

"I'm okay." I choked back some tears and then reached for the wine bottle. "We need to open this up." I didn't want to rehash the attack for the umpteenth time. I wanted to enjoy myself.

Poppy handed me the corkscrew and Taj gingerly took the bottle and opener from my hands, offering to help. I wiped some tears out of the corners of my eyes and Taj kissed my forehead.

I thought about my mother and realized I could end up like her if I left. Maybe she ran away because she was scared of her responsibilities as the Mind Changer. But perhaps she had actually faced the same dilemma I now faced: become the next Mind Changer and put those you love in danger or choose to run away instead. At that point, she would've been pregnant with me, wanting to protect me.

Taj held out a glass of wine to me and noticed the

bruises on my hands. Anguish crossed his face. "Are you sure you are okay?"

I nodded, and gratefully took the ruby elixir.

With the dinner spread on the festive table and wine pouring freely, the conversation lightened. Like at Thanksgiving, I basked in the warmth of my new "family," but I had a sharp awareness that next year I could be alone. *If I do the right thing and protect these people that I love so much.*

"Is that snow?" Poppy asked with surprise, interrupting my nagging thoughts.

Everyone rose and peeked out the windows.

"Do you all get snow here?" I asked.

"This is the first time I have seen snow since I became pastor at Saint Louis Cathedral," Father Malachi said. "That was over ten years ago."

"It's rare. Never accumulates," Poppy said, gawking out the window with the wonder of a child.

"Let's go out on the balcony," I said excitedly.

We filed outside and held our hands out, faces to the sky, feeling the snowflakes touch our warm skin before fading like a quiet memory. The flakes gathered in our hair and on our eyelashes. Looking up into the sky, I opened my mouth to taste the cold tickle of snow on my tongue.

The snow continued, off and on, for a couple of hours and by the time it was coming to an end, Father Malachi had left and Poppy had gone back to her bedroom to read. Taj and I sat on the couch. I leaned against him, holding a pillow to my chest and folding my feet on the couch beside me. We sipped wine and watched the gentle flakes fall.

"I almost forgot," I said, setting my goblet on the coffee table. "Your present." I excitedly hobbled back to my room to get the "Partridge and Tangerine" picture, which had also suffered an injury, a tear to its corner. That morning I'd carefully taped the back of the piece of art, hoping to conceal what had happened.

"I got this for you," I said, searching his face for a reaction.

He held the paper quietly, lightly fingering its torn edge. He swallowed and turned to me.

"I love it," he said.

Taj set it down on the table and cupped my face with one hand. I leaned in for a kiss and that all-too-familiar voice buzzed in my ear: *stay, stay, stay*. I never wanted this moment to end. He eased back on the couch and pulled me onto his chest. I snuggled into him, trailing kisses up his neck, along his jaw. I wanted this to be my life. All of it: mind changing, family . . . love.

My mouth found his again and heat coursed through me. I clutched his hands and I could feel our hearts pounding in unison, professing with each beat, *I love you, I love you, I love you*. I had never known love could be like this. I wanted it. I wanted Taj. Forever.

Chapter 22
Those Three Magic Words

Taj opened the door to his apartment and the spicy deliciousness of Indian food welcomed me.

"This is going to be the best turkey curry you have ever tasted," he said.

"And the first," I replied, stepping through the door and wrapping my arms around him.

"Welcome, Sophie," an Indian woman, about my age, walked toward me with open arms.

I gave Taj a sideways glance.

"This isn't Krishna," I said, my mind whirling to make sense of this gorgeous twenty-something woman in his apartment.

He smiled and shrugged. "Surprise?"

The woman embraced me and said, "I have heard so much about you and now we finally meet."

"Sophie, this is my friend, Avinash," Taj introduced us. "Avinash, Sophie."

"Please, call me Avi," she said, holding her hands together in prayer position and bobbing her head side-to-side.

"Avi owns this whole building, including the souvenir shop downstairs," Taj said.

"Ohhhh," I said. *She better not be trying to move in on my man. Now that I actually have one.*

Two guys came walking out of the kitchen and into the living room where we were standing.

I recognized them as the friends in Night Creatures on that first night that I met Taj.

"You weren't kidding, bro!" The guy with wild, curly hair gave Taj a low five. "She is pretty."

The other guy, pushing the tortoise-rimmed glasses up on his nose, gave me a half-smile.

"Sophie, this is my brother, Krishna." Taj pointed to the first guy. "And this is Avi's brother, Deepak."

"Deepak's like an honorary Jahan brother, though," Krishna said, wrapping his arm around Deepak's shoulders and tousling his hair. After the introductions, Deepak and Krishna resumed the video game they had been playing and I followed Taj and Avi into the kitchen. The realization hit me. Taj was introducing me to the important people in his life, which was a big step in our relationship.

"Please, Sophie." Avi indicated a chair in the kitchen. "Make yourself comfortable."

"Can I help with something?" I offered.

"We're fine," she said. "Just sit and relax."

Taj poured some white wine into a pint glass.

"Nice stemware," I said.

"Only the best," he replied.

He and Avi worked effortlessly on the meal, handing each other vegetables and cooking utensils, while carrying on an incessant conversation in their language. I watched how close they stood to each other and how familiar they were as they laughed at intervals, and it made me wonder if Avi had ever had romantic feelings for Taj. Or vice versa. A twinge of jealousy rose up in my throat. Avi turned to the stovetop to stir the curry and Taj came over to give me a kiss. I held him there as long as I could.

"That was nice," he remarked with fire in his eyes. When he turned to grab some ingredients from the fridge, I swatted his butt.

"So how did you decide to start a souvenir shop in New Orleans, Avi?" I asked, wanting to know more about Avi and actually be a part of the conversation. Not to mention, I could get a better grasp of where she and Taj stood on the friends/more-than-friends spectrum.

"Taj and I both went to school in New Orleans and I just fell in love with the culture here. I think we both did." She smiled at Taj, and he nodded. "After I finished my bachelor's I wanted to start a business, invest in commercial real estate, and decided that a souvenir shop would be a good moneymaker. There are four apartments in this building, too. Taj and Krishna live in this one, my brother and I live in another one, and I have two other tenants."

"I just inherited a family business of my own," I said. "Maybe you could give me some pointers."

"Sure. We should do coffee sometime."

"That would be wonderful," I said, wrapping my fingers around the pint glass. "Are you from India, Avinash?"

"Actually, I am from Malaysia. Taj and I grew up together on the rubber plantation where our families worked."

Another twinge of jealousy at the fact that they'd known each other their whole lives.

"My family is not happy that I decided to stay in America," she continued.

Deepak and Krishna shouted at the TV, upset by some turn of events on their game. Taj went to investigate what had happened.

"Boys and their games," she said and rolled her eyes.

I smiled and took a sip of my wine, then asked, "So are there hurt feelings since your family wants you to go back to Malaysia?"

"They respect that I am an independent person. So they know they have to let me go." Avi shrugged matter-of-factly. She knew what she wanted and went after it. Her drive made me think about my own ambition to be a successful businesswoman and conjurer and I admired her for that. The corners of my mouth turned down as I reminded myself that I needed to walk away. The life of a Mind Changer, even if best for me, was too dangerous for Taj.

"Boys!" Avi sounded like a mother calling to her sons. "Food's ready." She washed her hands in the kitchen sink, grabbed a towel, and then tossed it on the counter.

"Ready?" she asked, smiling infectiously.

Over the course of the evening, I fell in love with Avi myself. She felt like the older sister I never had and I could see why Taj would feel the same way.

The turkey curry was delicious and I sopped up every last bit of it with my naan bread. The Indian flat bread's soft and bubbled surface formed pockets that perfectly soaked up sauces, plus you could use it as a utensil to pick up pieces of meat and vegetables.

"That was incredible," I said, barely able to breathe because I was so full.

"I'm glad you liked it. It is an improvisation of my mother's chicken curry," Avi said.

"A mixture of your mother's and *my* mother's recipes is what you mean to say," Taj interjected.

"You will get better at eating." Krishna teased me for my inept ability to eat with my hands. Taj and his friends had all eaten with their hands and I had decided to do the same to get the full cultural experience.

"The trick is to make a scoop with your fingers and then push the food into your mouth with your thumb. Like this," Taj demonstrated skillfully.

My initial bite, on the other hand, had me shoving my entire hand into my mouth, throwing my head back, and ending up with curry dripping down my chin and wrists. Deepak laughed quietly at my efforts but looked pleased. After the meal, all the boys cleaned the dishes while Avi and I talked.

"We're planning on going to Night Creatures after this. You want to go?" she asked me.

"Actually," Taj interjected, "I was hoping we could have some alone time."

"Ah," Avi said.

"We can take a hint, bro," Krishna said, throwing the dishtowel at Taj. "All finished here anyway."

Deepak meekly waved, Krishna gave me a huge bear hug, and Avi gave me one more hug before they all walked out the door.

"I forgot to bring this over yesterday." Taj handed me a box with red and green wrapping paper sticking out at odd angles.

I giggled, shaking the box slightly by my ear.

"Nice wrapping job," I teased.

"Not the prettiest," he admitted. "It is my first try."

I pulled at the seam to tear the tape loose to unveil an iPod box. My mouth dropped open.

"Taj," I said, "it's too much."

"I wanted to. Anyway"—he turned on the device and scrolled through the music files—"Poppy helped me put all of your music on here."

He pointed out my AC/DC and Led Zeppelin albums.

"You did that behind my back? How sweet," I said, excitedly scrolling through the music files. "This will be great when I go running." I shot him my best sultry impersonation and tantalized him with a kiss. We were so crazy in love, and I wondered if I was even doing these new facial expressions, like sultry, and new gestures, like tantalizing kisses, justice. Maybe I came off as a complete goof, but I was Taj's goof. And he didn't seem to mind.

"Thank you," I said, our lips nearly touching still.

"It was nothing." He looked at my lips with hungry eyes and shook his head.

Naughty or nice thoughts? I wondered.

He grabbed the iPod again and showed me the screen.

"I added some of my own music, too. Michael Jackson, The Beatles, and other classics you neglected to include in your music library."

Taj had good taste in music. Different than mine but good.

"Thank you."

"How are we doing on the New Orleans' list?" Taj asked, relaxing into the futon, setting his arm around my shoulders.

"Everything's been checked off for a while. But you, ahem, *we* . . ." I leaned in and kissed him playfully. " . . . Keep adding things. I wonder why."

"No idea." Taj lifted his eyes to the ceiling, the picture of innocence.

"Hmm," I said. I knew full well that he was trying to come up with more reasons to convince me to stay. Maybe deep down he knew that something was wrong. And something was wrong, I reminded myself. I stared down at the iPod and got serious, thinking about the danger that my staying in New Orleans was posing for Taj. Without him even knowing it.

Taj took the iPod out of my hands and set it on the table. He pulled me toward him and I laid my head on his chest. We lay there for a moment and I breathed in the exotic smell of him. Like peace-inducing incense, it focused me in the present moment. I snuggled into his soft T-shirt.

"How did your to-do list start?" he asked.

"In high school," I said. "I fantasized about running away to see the world. I still have that list. Somewhere."

"What's on it?" Taj pulled me onto his lap and intertwined the fingers of his hand with mine.

"Pick a tulip in Holland, climb the stairs of the Colosseum, sip café au lait in Paris. I actually believed I could do those things. Naïve, huh?"

"No." Taj slipped his fingers through my hair and then drew me forward so my lips met his. "Everyone must dream."

He kissed me again, softly. "And it can be good for a person to run away from home." He smiled. "Look at the good it has done for me." Another light kiss.

"Yeah, you're working at a voodoo shop . . ." This time I leaned in and pressed my lips to his. " . . . learning no valuable skills." I teased his lips with mine.

"I found you. That's all that matters to me." He hugged me close to snuggle into my neck and breathed deeply. We sat like that for a moment. Completely content.

Then he tilted my chin up and searched my eyes. "I need to tell you something."

I nodded and settled on his lap, facing him. His uncertain hopefulness charged the air and made my stomach drop. *Oh no.* I knew where he was headed. *Too soon.* It had only been a few weeks since we started dating. I wanted to raise a warning flag. Wave a stop sign in front of him.

He tried again. "I think . . ."

I cringed on the inside, but held his gaze. Deep down, I wanted him to say it, too, but I didn't know how to deal with it. *It's too soon.*

"I love you."

There. He'd said it. And I couldn't say it back. The silence stretched out between us. A chasm of unfulfilled contact.

"What are you thinking?" He pushed my bangs back to the side with one hand and then the other hand came up to hold the side of my face.

I leaned into the hand for support. "You don't want to be with me," I said with downcast eyes.

No one wants me.

"What are you talking about? Of course I do."

I nodded and then wiped the tears from my eyes, a smile of pure joy crossing my lips, filling my heart. Taj had completely disarmed me and I no longer wanted to put on my emotional armor. I cared for him. Of that much I was sure, but I just couldn't go there yet. I couldn't say those three magic words.

"Taj . . ." I struggled to find the right thing to say. "I'm just . . . I'm just not ready . . . to say *that* yet."

His smile faded and he searched my eyes.

Placing a hand on either side of his face, I confessed, "But I want to someday. When I feel it's the right time for me."

Why couldn't I just be brave? At a time in my life when I was immersed in darkness, Taj pulled me into the light. He wrapped me in his love and I felt whole. But love would not have me and I didn't know how to have it. I closed my eyes and curled into his lap so he could hold me for a little while longer. I was so scared that I would lose him and I wrapped myself around him, holding on tight.

"I can wait," he said. He kissed the top of my head and held me with strong arms. "I can wait."

Chapter 23
New Year's Eve

The next morning I had to clear my head, so I decided to go for a run. I loved Taj and he loved me. I knew that. But I couldn't protect him from whoever was writing the death threats. Deep down, I knew what I needed to do. Leave town in order to protect him. Not bothering to tell Poppy where I was going, I bounded down the apartment stairs, hit play on my new iPod, and took off at a sprint. Before I had even gotten a block, the familiar whispers started in.

True love, they murmured. *Power*, they insisted. Blood rushed to my cheeks and my heart rate quickened as I increased my speed, but even running did not help me outrun the truth of the words. The whispers spoke clearer, louder, and in time with my stride, *True-love. Pow-er. Stay-here. Stay-here. True-love. Pow-er. Stay-here. Stay-here.*

One mile. I stopped to catch my breath and the thoughts took over. *It will be my fault if something happens to him. I just need to get away from New Orleans before anyone else gets hurt.* I started running again.

True love. Power, the inner voice insisted.

I wanted to scream, "I know!" I'd heard the same message again and again since Poppy and I'd uncovered the source of my strength as a voodoo priestess. Love would be my sword and shield. Love would power the mind-changing spell.

True love. Power, the voice repeated.

"Ugh!" I said and pushed my feet harder against the cobblestones. *I refuse to listen to imaginary voices.* More than that, I refused to put Taj's life in danger. I ran through the necessary steps in my head of how to ensure his safety. First, break up with him. I sighed, wanting to cry, at the mere thought of hurting him. Second, in the short term, I needed to avoid him at work. Until I figured out a way to get my life back on track in Saint Louis. It would take at least a few weeks to get an apartment lined up.

Poppy will never let you go either. She was too insistent that I take over as the next Mind Changer. Plus we'd grown so close over the past couple of months. Despite holding back my stinging tears, my nose began to run. I focused on how I would avoid Taj at work. I'd just tell Poppy that Taj had told me he loved me and I needed space. She wouldn't like that either, but as my friend, she would have to understand that I was freaking out about his profession of love. Even though my head tried to say it was too soon for such an admission, my heart warmed and beat faster. No, it wasn't too soon. Not at all.

A deep loss settled in my gut. Already, I was disentangling myself, mentally, from this wonderful life that I'd found here. But it had to be done. There was no other way to save the people I loved.

The Beatles' hit "Let It Be" blared in my headphones, talking about "words of wisdom" and encouraging that there would be an answer. For me there would be no easy answer.

Third, I realized, *I have to hurt him. That's the only way he'll stay away.* I thought of Poppy and Father Malachi. *I have to hurt everyone that I love.* Stopping abruptly, I leaned onto my knees for support. I gasped for air. My heart ached and I couldn't make it stop. A solitary tear seeped down my cheek and I rubbed it out. *Don't cry*, I steeled myself. *Or you'll never get through this*. I gritted my teeth and drove myself forward again.

The inner voice droned on. *True love. Pow-er. Stay here. Stay here.*

With determination, I sprinted back to the apartment. I knew what I needed to do. I clicked off the music and ran up the stairs, bursting through the door and grabbing my purse. Ignoring the mantra in my head, I pulled out my wallet and searched for the card. It was the only way.

I have to save Taj, I thought desperately, dialing the phone quickly, so I wouldn't change my mind.

"Hello?" The man on the other line picked up after just one ring.

"Jacques? It's Sophie. I'd like to take you up on your offer."

New Year's Eve was my big date with Jacques. Leaning into my bedroom mirror, I dabbed blush on the apples of my cheeks and thought about the previous few days since I'd set up this date, which consisted of me avoiding Taj at all costs. I had let all his calls go to voicemail and had rearranged my schedule so he worked with Poppy instead of me.

Coward. That was what I saw in the mirror. My stomach churned thinking of how my date with Jacques would absolutely break Taj's heart. *Taj*, I thought longingly and searched my eyes for some way to get around doing this. Finding no other answer, I turned away from the mirror and dropped my makeup on the dresser. I didn't know how I would make it through this night, but I had to be a convincing date. I sighed, scanning the designer clothing packages on my bed.

"Where to start?" I asked myself.

Jacques had flown in an outfit from New York. His messenger delivered everything to the store yesterday, assuring me that, "Monsieur hand-selected each piece himself to fit perfectly."

It would have seemed strange—scary, even—that Jacques knew the size of my body so well, but since he had taken me shopping for a new wardrobe, of course he knew all of my sizes. The biggest white box was tied with a black silk ribbon. Untying the bow, I carefully opened the white tissue paper to unveil a strapless black dress. Stepping into it and fitting it up and over my body's curves, the soft fabric kissed my bare skin. I zipped it up over my black strapless bra and matching underwear. The lingerie was mine. If Jacques had included lingerie I would have canceled the date and come up with a new plan.

"This has to work," I reminded myself, focusing on the task at hand. I searched my face in the mirror again. Breaking Taj's heart made me feel like a monster. I turned away, busying myself with the next package on my bed, trying to ignore all the feelings tearing me up on the inside. A bright blue Tiffany's box contained chandelier earrings which dripped diamonds down my neck. Dressing so extravagantly would have been fun if it wasn't coming at such a high cost. I was breaking the heart of the man that I truly loved.

With the enthusiasm of a robot, I pulled the last box off the bed. Prada shoes. Steadying myself on the headboard of my bed, I wriggled my toes into the strappy black sandals. The sexy footwear lifted my insteps which flexed my calves, lengthened my legs, pushed up my bottom and thrust my chest forward.

"That should do it," I said to my reflection. Jacques had successfully transformed me into his little dress-up doll. Again. Taj had been right. This so wasn't me. But it would satisfy Jacques and that's what I needed in order for my plan to work. Dabbing on some rich red lipstick, I reassured myself that, like chain mail, this façade would protect my vulnerable heart from turning back. I knew what I had to do.

Poppy walked in as I was applying mascara to my false eyelashes.

"Hey, sexy mama, going on a date with Taj?"

"Actually . . ." I jutted out my chin and hardened myself against her response. "I'm going out with Jacques."

Poppy's smile flipped upside down and her voice deadened. "What?"

"Jacques saved my life and I wanted to at least have dinner with him to show my appreciation."

"You better cancel," she said matter-of-factly and sat on my bed. "Sophie, you're gonna screw up everything with Taj."

"I need a break from Taj," I said.

Her cheeks flushed beet red, and luckily I had prepared my preemptive strike. Holding my hands up to defend against her verbal blows, I reasoned, "Everything's moving way too fast with Taj. He told me he loved me."

"So that's why you're avoiding him at the shop. Look, Sophie, Taj is a really great guy and he loves you. So what if it seems too soon. At least he is brave enough to say it."

"I'm not ready to get serious with Taj," I said flippantly, amping up my performance.

"Bullshit," Poppy said. The bullet struck my heart. She was absolutely right, this was all bullshit. My lying and her anger made me want to crawl into a hole and die. "You are making a big mistake. I don't know why, but this is all," she waved both hands in the air, "bullshit."

"It's my life," I snapped. "And it's really none of your business, is it?" I did one last makeup check in the mirror to complete the I-don't-care act. I glanced her reflection in the mirror: arms crossed, head cocked to the side. She rolled her eyes.

"Whatever," she said.

The clock chimed seven and, simultaneously, the door buzzed.

"That's Jacques," I said, mentally arming myself against more of Poppy's protests.

"For what it's worth, girl," Poppy said. "And it doesn't seem like my opinion matters much to you anymore. I do *not* trust Jacques. I don't care if he did save your life." She got up, went into her room, and slammed the door.

I breathed a sigh of relief that she'd bought it. Lying hurt my heart, but it had to be done. I straightened, assessed myself one more time in the mirror, and strode out to meet my date.

Jacques did not eat. He merely pushed the food around with a fork and sipped wine continually from his cut crystal chalice. The deep red wine coated the side of the glass every time he took a sip, making me wonder if it was mixed with something.

"Pinot noir," he informed me from the opposite side of the ten-foot long table in his expansive dining room. "From the French meaning 'pine' and 'black.' The grapes grow in clusters shaped like pine cones."

I nodded and smiled, the awkward silence recommencing. The pinot noir tasted dry and bitter to me, so to cleanse my palate I took a forkful of rare steak. Jacques said rare was the only way to enjoy steak. It was cooked nicely, but every time I cut into it, blood would pool on my plate.

Taj and Avi had served a chardonnay on turkey curry night, I remembered. The wine, fresh and light, had perfectly matched the food and the atmosphere of the party.

Pushing my unfinished plate away, I sipped my wine quietly. Immediately, the butler swooped in to clear our dishes. The magnificent grandfather clock in the corner *tick-tick-ticked*, interjecting into the silence.

Jacques swirled a finger around the edge of his chalice. "Another glass, my dear?"

I nodded enthusiastically, wanting to feel a buzz that would at least take the edge off. Since I was by no means a heavy drinker, the second glass would help if I drank it fast enough. The butler abruptly appeared at my elbow to refill my cup, startling me.

"Thank you," I said awkwardly. I wasn't used to having someone serve me on hand and foot. "You have a beautiful place," I nearly had to shout to Jacques, because he was so far away. He nodded, not helping me keep the conversation going.

I scanned the room as I desperately searched for something to talk about. Silk draperies dressed the floor-to-ceiling windows. Rich wood paneling skirted the room. Hungry flames leapt from the carved marble fireplace.

This night's gonna drag on for-e-ver. Momentarily, my mind returned to my list for the perfect man when I was making my first love potion. I'd hoped for a guy who understood me, allowed me to speak my truth, allowed me to be myself. Jacques just wasn't doing it for me.

I sighed and then tried again. "The painting." I pointed to Jacques' portrait above the mantle. "It seems like it's from another time." In the portrait, Jacques was dressed like he should be attending court with King Louis and Marie Antoinette. The candles flickered on the long table, but my observation was met with silence. In the dim lighting it was hard to read Jacques' expression.

He cleared his throat, tossed his linen napkin on the table, and stood.

"Shall we dance?" Jacques' voice echoed in the massive room.

"Dance?" I smiled, not understanding such a strange request. I glanced around the room, noting the hulking furniture.

"Not here, *ma chérie*. I have a ballroom."

"Oh." *Of course you have a ballroom.*

He walked to my end of the table and held his arm out. I took it and rose from my seat. Leading me down a long corridor, he gave me a tour of his grandiose home as we passed each room.

"Drawing room, reception room, library . . . aviary . . . all designed by me, personally," Jacques stated.

Of course you have an aviary. I nodded. It was an impressive home, but it felt so uptight. I was afraid to talk too loudly or, heaven forbid, break something.

My mind wandered back to Taj's cozy kitchen. All five of us huddled around Taj's tiny table with Krishna teasing Deepak for being so quiet and Taj and Avi laughing about their childhood adventures around the plantation. The dishes of curry, naan, korma, and rice circulating along with the lively conversation.

"And finally," Jacques said, after we ascended to the top floor of the mansion, "the ballroom. I like to entertain, so I decided to spend the majority of my renovation budget making this room the *pièce de résistance*. What do you think?"

I stood, speechless, in the room's vastness.

He picked up the slack in the conversation. "The room measures seventy feet by thirty-two feet, so there is plenty of space for people to move around comfortably at my parties." The blue on the walls was the color of the sky on a summer day. I still hadn't said anything, so he cleared his throat and continued. "These murals were painted by an artist friend. They depict pastoral scenes from some of my favorite places in Europe; landscapes of the Irish coast, Provence, Tuscany, the Cotswolds of England, and, last but not least, the Rhine River Valley. My decorating tastes tend toward the European, but I feel most at home in New Orleans. These paintings are just a reminder of the Europe that I once knew." His voice sounded far off and, since Jacques did not look more than forty, I wondered at his nostalgia.

"The chandeliers are gorgeous," I said, finally finding my voice. This room, too, was lit by candles, but the crystals of the chandelier shone like fireworks.

"Swarovski," Jacques voice echoed in the empty luxury of the ballroom. "The fixture handmade to my exact specifications. It really makes the room sparkle and completes the space. Don't you agree?" With his hands clasped behind his back, he waited for me to respond.

I nodded.

"It's so quiet." I rubbed my bare arms, chilled.

"Mmm." He nodded, smiling, as if pleased with my observation.

Again, I found myself comparing Jacques with Taj. The quiet loneliness of this extravagant home didn't hold a candle to Taj's lively party where Avi told me that Taj's parents and her parents had been friends forever. She'd described Taj like a little brother. They'd grown up fighting and playing like real siblings. When Avi's parents wanted her to come to school in America, they convinced Taj to apply, too, so he could watch over her.

Jacques looked at me with curious amusement. "Too much wine or is my company boring you?"

"I'm sorry." I smiled, too, but with embarrassment. "Maybe I did have too much wine." Rubbing my forehead with my fingertips, I wanted to disappear. But I needed to convince Jacques this date was real. That my feelings for him were real enough.

"We could sit down." Jacques motioned to a fainting couch positioned along the wall. The piece of furniture brought to mind images of wallflower debutantes perched on the periphery, hoping to be courted and fill their dance cards.

Play the part, I told myself.

"Maybe a dance would be good," I said, mustering up some courage to be the woman I needed to be. "Get the blood going."

"Excellent," he said, savoring the word. "I know just the song." Jacques went over to a sound system built into the wall. "When I have parties, I always hire local musicians, but this will do for our needs." He turned up the volume, and I heard a low hum before the first notes.

The round, rich tones of Etta James' voice swelled from the speakers.

I smiled and teased, "You like Etta James?"

"This song seems appropriate."

"How so?" I asked, swaying to Etta's "At Last."

"Because you have come to dine with me," he said, "at last."

I blushed at the sweet remark. The truth was that I had blown him off for months, even after he had been so generous, showering me with a lavish new wardrobe. Even after he'd saved my life. The smile left my lips as I realized that I could be hurting Jacques, too. And even though he wasn't as close to me as Taj, he was still human. Right?

He grabbed my right hand in his and, draping my left palm on his shoulder, stepped very close to me. I had decided to wear the butterfly ring, and I peered at it to regain my focus.

"Do you like the music in New Orleans?" I asked, putting my game face on and smiling brightly. Being so close to him made me nervous and I needed to try again to make small talk.

"It is one of the reasons that I fell in love with the city. If you would like, I could bring you to Preservation Hall for a concert. It's a no-frills dive with limited seating and a dim, dingy atmosphere."

"A dim, dingy dive." I nodded. "You really know how to sell the place."

He smiled. "The music is what people go for. It will change your world."

With the final notes of "At Last" fading, Jacques pulled me close, and then dipped me slowly. His strong arms held me and I leaned far back, elongating my neck, feeling exposed, trusting he wouldn't drop me. One last fading memory played in my head from turkey curry night . . .

During dinner, Avi, Taj, and the guys spontaneously jumped up to dance to a favorite Indian song on the radio. They turned up the music in Taj's living room and they did their foreign, energetic dancing like something out of a Bollywood movie. I got up and danced, too, shaking my groove thang and letting loose in a way that I would normally only have done in the privacy of my own bedroom. It was absolute fun and freedom.

My inner voice crept in again. *True love. Power. Stay here. Stay here.* The memory almost made me give up and go running back to Taj. Right that instant. But Jacques yanked me back up into his arms, pulling me tight against his body, and shattered the memory into a thousand pieces. I looked into Jacques' eyes. Those delectably frightening eyes.

I tilted my head to the side.

He bent to my lips.

I closed my eyes.

He kissed me. And it took my breath away.

Chapter 24
Mardi Gras

Darkness. Water. Drowning. The same nightmare, yet somehow different. This time, a storm raged all around me. The air, thick and greenish, weighed heavy on me as I struggled to keep my head above the water. Lightning shimmered. The sky rumbled. The wind whipped the clouds into a rotating mass. A finger-like projection dropped down from the cloud, touched down at the water's surface, and a whirlpool formed.

Barely staying afloat, I kicked away from the widening vortex, desperately grabbing a nearby fallen tree. The whirlpool swallowed everything around it. Greedy. Hungry. My muscles weakened and I couldn't fight the current any longer. The vortex roared, its mouth open wide. Panic filled my heart. I just wanted to give up. Be done with the terrible nightmare once and for all.

And the darkness . . . always the darkness. Death's shadow enveloped me. I searched the bank, hoping someone would save me, but the only thing I could see was the current eroding the dirt from the roots of the tree I clung to. I had no protection against Mother Nature.

A lightning strike momentarily illuminated the horrifying scene. The entire river was full of debris. Everything was being sucked into the vortex, pulled down to the depths.

Another flash of lightning. I swore I saw corpses with stringy hair and empty eye sockets directly below the surface of the water.

Another lightning strike. A huge rectangular box catapulted from the bank and into the river. It floated slowly past me. A coffin. Another popped from the ground with a sucking noise. Then another popping explosion. And another. And another. The coffins should not have been laid here. They burst from the ground like balloons being held under water.

Why would people bury the dead in a place where they could not stay buried?

Finally, lightning struck the bank near the tree that I clung to. The roots exploded. The tree broke free. It floated toward the whirlpool. This was my ferry ride to the underworld.

Where's God? It didn't matter. It was too late. There was nothing I could do but hold on tighter. The tree's top sank into the violently swirling water. And then I was falling, too. Falling, falling. Falling into the darkness.

I awoke, heart slamming against my chest.

Stay! urged the familiar sharp whisper of the voice in my head.

I ignored it. The sweetness of pipe tobacco filled my nostrils, and I waved it away.

"I have had it," I said, throwing my covers off and sitting upright in bed. My eyes slowly adjusted to the dim morning light and I stood up. Today was the day. I couldn't stand this state of limbo. Since making up my mind to move back to Saint Louis for the sake of my friends' safety, I'd signed a lease in my old apartment building and set things in motion for my transition back there. All that I needed to do was tell Poppy, Father Malachi, and Taj. I placed my face in my hands and sat back down on the bed.

"No." I stood up again. "I can do this." I steeled myself. I had to go through with this step. I had to hurt the people that I loved.

Poppy first. I rushed down the hall and into the kitchen where she was making coffee.

"I'm leaving New Orleans," I barked at her.

"Well good morn—" she said, kidding, but I stopped her short.

"Tomorrow," I said firmly.

She stood with her mouth still in mid-sentence. I couldn't let her talk me into giving up my plan.

"I can't stand it here," I said monotonously. *Show no sign of emotion.* "I'll sign my part of the inheritance over to you." I turned away, walked down the hall, and locked the bedroom door behind me.

"Sophie!" Poppy rapped on my door for a good fifteen minutes, repeating my name and phrases like, "Let's talk about this" and "Be reasonable" and "Why are you doing this?"

To drown her out, I put some AC/DC on and turned the volume all the way up. I'd have to open the door eventually, but at least I could avoid her for now.

"It is because I said I love you," Taj said.

Poppy had called him almost before I could get the words, "leaving New Orleans" out of my mouth. And here he was, watching me pack up, doing exactly what I knew he would do. Trying to make me stay. I tossed jeans and tank tops into my open suitcase.

"I told you I love you and it scares you," he pressed.

"And almost being raped and killed couldn't be an obvious reason for why I'm scared," I said with too much bite. It had to be done. I knew Taj would be the hardest. I threw some socks and underwear into the suitcase to fill the space around my clothes.

Poppy piped in from her room across the hall, "But you weren't killed." She showed up at my door and peeked in. "Stay, Sophie. Don't run away from your work here."

Do not make eye contact. Head down and focused, I grabbed Grandma Seraphina's shawl, thought about packing it, but then realized I should cut all ties with my life here. I didn't need to think about my family, because they were all dead. That was depressing. But that was life. And I didn't need to remember New Orleans or the friends I had made here because it would be too painful.

Still holding the shawl, I squinted at Poppy. "Here." I shoved it into the space between us. "Take it."

She shook her head and returned quietly to her room.

I turned my attention back to Taj. "Look. I'm not a businesswoman," I said, surrendering. "I can just move back to Saint Louis and see if I can get my life back on track."

"Why?"

Ignoring his question, I put my knee on my overfilled suitcase to zip it shut. On the inside I was a wreck. My heart cried out for Taj's arms to be around me. I wanted him to kiss me. But I had to keep my armor on. *Do not make eye contact.*

"Sophie, take a chance," he dared me, trying another approach. "Stay. Even if it scares you."

I dropped the suitcase by the door and gave him the dead eyes.

"Be who you were born to be," he said, interlacing his fingers in mine. His hands in mine felt so good.

"Who was I born to be?" I asked breathlessly. He, literally, was taking my breath away with his intensity. Another minute longer and I would give in. *Don't do it*, my subconscious instructed me desperately. *You must leave. To save him. To save all of them.*

Taj moved his face close to mine.

"A smart businesswoman," he whispered through smiling lips. He knew he was breaking me down.

I sighed.

He took a step closer to me and continued. "A smart businesswoman whose specialty is love spells and voodoo dolls."

Do not smile back, Sophie. Dead eyes. Be a cold, hard—

"And—" He stopped. He turned away and I knew, in that second, that I'd done my job well. I made him believe that I didn't love him.

"What?" I demanded. Inside, my heart collapsed. *Say it. Please.*

"Forget it," he said. "I can see you've already changed your mind."

All the air was sucked from my soul, leaving an empty, destructive vortex just like in my nightmare. And then I let him walk out of my door and he quietly let himself out of my life. Forever.

I slammed my bedroom door shut and locked it to keep up the pretense. I didn't need Poppy coming in here. Seeing me fall apart. I laid on my bed, cranked up my music, and cried until I ran out of tears. Until there was nothing left of me but a cold, hard suit of armor.

"To hell with it," I said, shutting my laptop and getting to my feet. It was Mardi Gras and I needed to get out of this pressure cooker of an apartment. *Carpe diem*, I thought bitterly. I'd have one last hurrah and just drink my problems away. *I don't need anybody*, I reminded myself in the mirror. I'd always been on my own before and I survived. Solitude felt familiar. Comfortable.

Jacques had sent an invitation for his Mardi Gras party, but I'd never gotten back to him. I thought I'd be gone by now, but leaving this city had become vastly more difficult than I realized. New Orleans had me in her clutches. Ever since I'd been stuck in this limbo, things had cooled between Jacques and I anyway. Mainly because he had been called away on several business trips since our dinner date at his house. I thought of him sometimes. We did have some kind of connection or chemistry, if I could call it that, but Taj's face was forever in my mind.

Slipping into the Chanel dress from New Year's along with fishnet stockings, wool socks, my boots, and my red trench coat to keep warm, I set out at about noon with my "to hell with it" attitude. I knew underneath my costume-armor, I didn't want to do this. I didn't want to walk away from my new life here. The death threats spun in my head momentarily, but I no longer cared about my own safety.

"Let that bastard kill me," I said under my breath, hurrying down the stairs. When I got in the alleyway, I shouted to the rooftops, "You want me? Come and get me! I'm gonna go get drunk!"

"Sophia!" a voice rang out, startling me into dropping my keys.

"Shit," I said, not expecting an actual response.

Gabriel's smiling face peeked around the corner. "Baby, the mighty hand of God will reach down from the heavens and pluck you from the clutches of Death!"

I focused on locking my door.

"Gabriel, I don't want to hear it." I put a hand up, refusing the message and striding past him.

"Ask for God's help, Sophia!" he shouted after me. The echo of his final words rang in my ears and I turned to get one last look at him. But he was gone.

The Mardi Gras revelers were already out in full force, and I quietly slipped into the crowd. At my first stop, the French Market, I meandered through stall after stall of junk and treasures. Hawkers sold everything from fake designer sunglasses to X-rated shot glasses. I purchased a Mardi Gras mask with emerald feathers. Half-heartedly smiling, I told the vendor as I handed over my money, "This will help me disappear."

More and more partygoers and tourists emptied into the streets from their apartments and hotels. *On to the next item on the list*, I thought, *Pat O'Brien's specialty*.

"I'll take a hurricane," I told the bartender at the to-go window. He handed me the fruity drink garnished with a maraschino cherry and orange slice. The drink tasted of alcohol, more alcohol, a tiny bit of juice, and more alcohol.

"Happy Mardi Gras." A woman in a corset raised her glass to mine.

"This should do the trick," I said, emptying my cup in a single, long draw. She nodded, and I headed down the street, waving goodbye to corset lady. A couple of blocks down I decided to grab a bite at another bar and settled at a table by the window so I could people watch.

The server bussed the dirty glasses from my table. "What'll you have?"

"I'll take a hurricane and a crawfish po' boy. Last chance to get one," I told the server.

"Sure thing." He smiled and took my menu.

The warmth of alcohol flooded my cheeks and I knew the hurricane was working its magic. I looked out the window, a rum haze settling on my brain. Passing by the window were a parade of characters: a transvestite in a tutu and heels; a metallic birdman; skeletons in top hats; harlequins; pirate dames and scallywags; Napoleon and Josephine. Fake boobs; real boobs; wax lips; wigs of every color; bunny tails; kitten ears; superhero masks; tiaras.

After my third hurricane, I wanted to be swept away by the crowd, so I joined the celebrants in the street. We swarmed down Bourbon Street where the crowd thickened into a solid mass of people. Drunken women popped up on shoulders like Jack-in-the-Boxes, peeling their shirts up. Men shouted and dangled beads from the above balconies. Behind my mask I felt like I could do anything. Just not that.

"There's not enough alcohol in the world," I said as another woman flashed her boobs and the crowd screamed. I decided to point myself in the direction of Night Creatures for one last Purple Potion. For old times' sake.

A man in a hat, mask, and cape swung around to face me, brandishing a sword, and my heart skipped.

"Oh shit!" I squeezed my eyes shut. "Just kill me and get it over with!" I screamed, throwing my hands up.

"Say what?" He asked.

I peeled open one eyelid. And then the other.

The man's gold-toothed smile turned upside down. "No!" He realized I held my hands up in surrender. "I'm not gonna hurt you."

"You're not?" I lowered my arms.

"No," he said, extending his hand.

I placed mine in his and he politely kissed my knuckles.

"My lady, I'm the Ghetto Zorro," he said with a flourish of his cape. "Want some beads?"

Not trying to kill me. I bounced back to reality, "Not bad enough to do whatever it is that you want me to do."

"Take it easy now. These are free of charge," he said, draping some yellow, green, and purple beads over my head.

"Oh." I felt my cheeks heat in embarrassment. "Thanks."

He bowed then, with a spin and a dramatic flutter of his cape, he disappeared into the crowd. Shouts from the balcony above got my attention. A blow-up doll came my way, and I hit it with both fists, sending it onto the crowd's fingertips. I giggled and my head spun. The Mardi Gras scene came at me in the flashes of a sensory montage.

Cups raised. Hurricanes and mint juleps sloshed. Gray, mucky water pooled.

Music blared. Couples grinded. Lovers searched, all hands and lips and tongues.

Street performers worked the crowd. I stopped to watch a trio of jazz musicians play saxophone, trombone, and clarinet. Beads on their necks, dress shoes on their feet, sweatshirts to keep warm, and sailor caps for showmanship.

I'm gonna miss this place. Swallowing my sadness, I threw a tip in the open clarinet case at their feet. The men nodded at me and belted out more jazz notes. I turned on my heel to drink one last Purple Potion.

Chapter 25
Murder

Sitting in Night Creatures I watched people in the street, my mind blurring from the Purple Potion I was sipping. I pulled the Mardi Gras mask from my eyes. Today had been a good day and I was anticipating crashing in my bed, until I saw two familiar figures walking toward me.

"Oh boy." I turned my back to them, throwing back the rest of my drink. Moments later Poppy sat in the chair to my right and Taj sat silently at my left.

"We've been searching the whole damn city for you," Poppy snipped at me.

"I wanted to be alone," I snapped back, raising my glass to get the bartender's attention for another drink.

"How many of these have you had, girl?" Concern softened her voice.

"Lost count. Before the purple ones I was having pink ones." I smiled, realizing how light and fun drunk feels. "No wonder my mom drank. She wanted to feel like this all the time."

"Okay, it's time for you to stop." Poppy turned to Taj and said, "She needs water."

"I don't like water. I like fruity, colorful cocktails." I wrapped my lips awkwardly around the straw, poking myself in the gum. "Ow." *Sip, sip, sip.* "Mmmm."

Taj placed the glass of water in front of me and sat quietly by my side again. I glanced out the window, avoiding eye contact with either of them. *You hurt him. You stupid, stupid girl*, my subconscious scolded. Then a familiar figure stepped into the frame of the open window by our table.

"Jacques," I said, my mouth gaping at his drop-dead gorgeousness with his tailored tux, perfectly tousled hair, and flawless skin. He didn't say a word. Just stood there, the crowd breaking around his strong, unmoving presence.

Poppy cleared her throat to regain my attention and Taj grunted his disapproval.

I needed to get rid of them, I thought desperately, *or they'll convince me to stay. And that is just too risky. For all of us.* I swallowed the lump in my throat.

"*Ma chérie*, you never returned my phone calls," Jacques remarked, the ever-present trace of a smirk at the corner of his lips. "And I have heard that tonight is your last night in town."

I squirmed in my seat.

He continued. "I had hoped we could spend some time together."

"Do you want to come in and have a drink?" I asked cheerfully.

"Sophie, drink some water," Poppy ordered.

Literally, stuck in a love triangle with Taj and Jacques, drinking more seemed like the perfect solution. At least if I was smashed, I couldn't answer any more questions or listen to any more pleas.

"One moment." Jacques held up a finger and walked around the corner and into the bar, getting the attention of every woman as he approached our table.

"No more room, Jacques." Taj spoke his first words since sitting down next to me.

"Will you accompany me to my annual party, Sophia?" Jacques asked me, ignoring Taj.

When Jacques called me Sophia, my name sounded so foreign, so cultured, coming from his lips. And I did it. I knew I shouldn't have, but I met those frightening and delicious eyes with my own. As soon as I did, I became a fly in a spider's web.

"Okay," I responded automatically.

"So you will spend your final night with a man you barely know," Taj said, touching my hand with his.

The contact broke Jacques' hold on me. My brain became addled for a moment. I had to concentrate on Taj's lips to understand what he was saying. "Sophie, I know you. We can work things out. Do not do this to us."

"*Ma chérie*, you do not have to stay here. It is your choice." Jacques continued to hold my other hand. "Just come with me to the party and I will chaperone you for the night."

"No," Taj challenged.

I made eye contact with Jacques and immediately grew weak, held captive.

"It's okay, Taj," I said softly. "I would like to go."

"Come, *chérie*," Jacques said.

I eyed each of my hands, held by two different men, and thought of Gabriel's messages. *Baby, the mighty hand of God will reach down from the heavens and pluck you from the clutches of Death*! And that first time we'd met in the park, his message told me to *take this hand* and I wouldn't be alone anymore. Thinking of those messages was the only push I needed.

I stood, releasing Taj's hand.

"Sophie! Don't!" Poppy interjected.

Taj stood so quickly that his chair fell to the floor with a loud crack. "I think you should leave!" He stared Jacques down.

"Not without Sophia, friend," Jacques said crisply, releasing my hand and stepping into the space between me and Taj.

Taj pushed Jacques hard in the chest, but Jacques proved immovable.

"Hey, you two!" the bartender shouted. "Not in my bar."

Taj pushed Jacques again, without effect. Then Jacques, in one swift, fluid movement, pushed Taj back, throwing him up against the bar. Before Taj could stand up, Jacques was right next to him.

"That's it," the bartender said, snapping his fingers at a big guy near the door. "Al! We got a problem here!" Al, the bouncer, rushed toward Taj and Jacques.

Meanwhile, Jacques yanked Taj to his feet as if he weighed nothing, holding him a foot above the ground.

I wanted to yell, "Stop! Don't hurt him!" But I couldn't find my voice. Wooziness set in from having too many drinks, so I steadied myself on the chair back.

Taj swung hard with a right hook. He connected with Jacques' jaw.

"Break it up!" Al pushed the two apart.

Finally, Jacques dropped Taj.

"Both of you. Out!" Al shoved a thumb over his shoulder, indicating the door.

Jacques raised his hands in surrender, backing away, but when Al had his back turned, Taj launched himself at Jacques' midsection and managed to take him down to the ground. Jacques threw him off again and Taj fell into a table, knocking it over.

"I'm calling the cops," the bartender shouted, holding his cell in the air.

"No need," Jacques instructed. "He's done."

Taj groaned, attempted to stand, and fell back again. I wanted to run to him, but if I did, this whole charade would have been for nothing. So I had to ignore him to complete the lie. To protect those I loved.

Poppy ran over to help Taj. I remained stoic, not even acknowledging Taj, while I screamed with rage on the inside. *God, why did I have to make this choice*?

Jacques stood calmly, straightened his jacket, and approached the bar. "I am truly sorry for any inconvenience," he told the bartender, whose face turned from a scowl to a frown as soon as he made eye contact with Jacques.

"Sophie!" Poppy surveyed me from her spot on the floor next to Taj. "What is wrong with you?"

Taj struggled to his knees, cringing.

Keeping my metaphoric mask on, I slung my handbag over my slumped shoulder and decided to leave the whole mess behind me. I'd just leave tomorrow and then everybody could forget me.

Jacques walked over to Taj and pulled him to his feet with one hand, then brushed the wrinkles from Taj's shirt. "I just do not like to see a lady threatened."

Taj seethed, "I would never—" Then he shouted to me, "Sophie!"

I was already at the door, fighting back the tears. As I exited, I heard Taj threaten Jacques, "Stay away from her."

A dull thud had begun in my head. I held my hand to my temple. Just then, my heel caught on a cobblestone. Right before I went down, Jacques caught me in his capable, quick arms.

I offered an awkward, "Thanks."

He smiled and lifted me to my feet.

"Sophie!" Taj shouted, his voice bouncing off the buildings in Pirate's Alley.

Over my shoulder, I could see him struggling to reach me through the dense crowd. But I turned away, slipped my hand in Jacques', pinched my eyes closed, and allowed Jacques to lead me away. *It's the right thing to do*, I tried to convince myself.

"Sophie!" Taj called frantically. And then I couldn't hear his voice anymore.

"Welcome to the Second Chance Mardi Gras Party," the big band singer announced as we stepped onto the dance floor at Jacques' party. "This is the absolute best place to be for a night of debauchery, and in a few minutes, when the clock strikes midnight, we'll start the year all over again with the lights off and a Second Chance kiss."

Jacques had been very kind since we'd gotten to the party, rehydrating me, getting me to eat so my hangover wouldn't be quite so awful. The effects of the pink and purple drinks were wearing off and in their wake was a dull thud in my head and a churning in my stomach.

Jacques pulled me to him as the band struck up a slow dance. I settled my cheek on his shoulder. Being with him was like living in a dream. He was so beautiful, yet so unattainable. Those inconsistencies kept me at bay, but in a strange way, I actually enjoyed being with him. He brought me some strange kind of comfort.

"So you'll leave tomorrow," Jacques whispered into my ear.

I nodded and immediately thought of Taj. A tear slipped down my cheek and onto Jacques' tux.

"I love him," I said plaintively. More tears fell, and I didn't try to stop them.

Jacques inhaled quickly. I raised my head from his shoulder to face him.

"I'm sorry, but I love Taj," I said once more. Neither of us spoke for a good minute. "Am I upsetting you?" It was the most direct conversation we'd ever had.

He chuckled a little. "It's your world, *ma chérie*, I'm just living in it."

"Have you been in love?" I was surprised by my own boldness. Maybe it was because I had nothing left to lose.

"Once." His voice sounded far away, and he seemed to be staring into nothingness. "Love always disappears. Like everything." He searched my eyes and finally said, "Like you."

"I'm not disappearing. Just moving." I leaned my head back on his shoulder. "Do you believe love can overcome anything?"

"When you have nothing and no one, you believe in nothing and no one." An edge had crept into his voice. "You exist, but you do not live. You certainly do not love. You begin to understand that life is fragile and easy to take away."

Jacques' words sent a chill through my body. They were so hopeless. The final notes of the song faded and our slow dance came to a close. Suddenly the dynamic between us shifted. Before, I'd felt comfortable, in some kind of dream state, but now the tangible feeling of doom crawled on my skin.

The singer's voice chimed in again. "Now it's time for our countdown to a new start."

Servers fluttered around the guests with trays of bubbling champagne in tall flutes. Jacques took one for himself and handed one to me, barely noticing the waiter.

The lights dimmed and the crowd counted down. "Sixty, fifty-nine, fifty-eight . . ."

Jacques' face turned dark. "You think you can just mess with peoples' minds?"

"What?" My eyes widened.

"You toy with peoples' lives." He clipped each word. He grabbed my free hand at the wrist, pinching, not letting go no matter how much I wriggled.

The crowd counted down, paying no attention to us. ". . . thirty, twenty-nine, twenty-eight . . ."

"You mean the voodoo shop?" I asked, trying to twist out of his grasp. He was too strong. My breathing quickened. I looked to others for help, but everyone was too drunk to notice. I kept talking, trying to steady my voice. "I know. It's ridiculous that people buy into all the hocus-pocus."

"You know what I'm talking about, *ma chérie*." His voice dropped. "Not gator claws and voodoo dolls. You had your chance to run, but you would not take it. I gave you so many chances and you refused to heed my warnings."

My mind flashed back to the night at the LaLaurie Mansion. Something deep inside of me always knew it was Jacques. He *was* the one threatening me.

"You should have listened," he pleaded.

Startled by my growing realization that he had attacked me that night at the LaLaurie Mansion, I searched his steel gray eyes to be sure. His face softened and his eyebrows went up. His voice cracked. "Why did you not listen?"

". . . three, two, one!" The lights went out and the room turned pitch black. I felt lost in a nightmare now, not believing Jacques' damning words and the hard, physical grip clamping down on me. Death's grip.

Jacques yanked me close to his body.

"I am your angel of death," he growled.

A champagne glass dropped near my feet, shards hitting my boots. He grabbed my neck, holding my jaw with his thumb and guided my face toward his, kissing me wildly. He wrapped his arms around me, resting a hand on the small of my back. The rawness of his emotions terrified me. Moments stretched out, and I felt my lifeline pulled tight, the Fates poised to clip it. Next, a stabbing pain in my neck. He shushed me.

"Don't struggle," he whispered into my ear. His final words made me think of the butterfly in the voodoo shop lying down in the mortar, readying itself for death. It did not struggle, just sacrificed itself for the greater good. Then, he released me and I fell to the floor in slow motion, spreading my hands wide to catch myself. I got the wind knocked out of me when I hit.

"Jacques?" I choked, reaching out as if to touch a ghost. Then I held my hand to my throbbing, stinging neck where I found a strange object sticking out of it. The lights blazed back on. He was gone. I pulled the object from my neck. A syringe with fresh, shining blood on it. My blood. Thoughts sped through my head. The death threats on pretty ivory paper. The careful calligraphy. I remembered Jacques' business card with the words *My Voodoo Butterfly* scrawled in the same beautiful writing.

Jacques' words, "I am your angel of death," echoed in my ears, followed by Father Malachi's words, "Hope exists. God exists. All you have to do is believe." And, finally, Gabriel's message, "Ask for God's help!" My heart beat slowed.

Please, God, I believe. I believe! But I still could not catch my breath. I mouthed the words silently. Still nothing. Finally, I gathered all the strength I had. With my last breath I yelled, "Please, God, help me!"

Suddenly, there was a flutter of activity all around me. Shouting. Screams. Arms and hands. Then everything went black.

Chapter 26
Break on Through to the Other Side

"Help!" I sputtered, trying to keep my head above water. "Help me!"

The freezing air turned my breath to vapor.

The dark water choked me. Held me under its weight.

Icy claws clamped around my ankles. Tiny goblin hands tore at my clothes.

Night conquered the sky. Darkness permeated the water.

I chose to stop fighting.

Instead, I submitted. Slipped below the surface.

The greedy fingers dragged me down farther and farther.

I held my breath, only for so long, preparing to give up.

One last despairing glance at the water's surface.

Lightning streaked across the sky.

And!

A hand broke through, shattering the water into a thousand pieces.

Gabe's voice echoed in my ears. "You won't make it, child, unless you reach for the hand that saves."

The saving hand grabbed my wrist and yanked me up. The grasping goblin hands scratched my legs, refusing to let go. I kicked at them.

"Don't struggle," a woman's voice assured me.

Despite burning lungs, I stilled myself.

My heart pounded.

My insides screamed for oxygen.

Almost there. My lips parting . . . *Almost* . . .

I broke the surface. Took a giant breath. Sputtered.

The hand dragged me onto the shore, freeing me from the dangerous water.

"Thank you," I repeated over and over, clutching the savior's hand.

Then I blacked out.

"Through many dangers, toils, and snares," I heard a woman singing, "I have already come . . ."

Still in a state of lucid dreaming, I imagined that I was in Heaven.

"Am I dead?" I mumbled, waking and then feeling my face with my hands. "Nope. Definitely still alive."

The woman sang on, "'Tis grace that brought me safe thus far and grace will lead me home . . ."

I felt the edges of a quilt pulled under my chin. Peeking out from under the blanket, I scanned the moonlit room.

The stranger continued to hum "Amazing Grace" and my eyes barely made out the horizontal lines of log walls. *A cabin. Somewhere.*

Outside, in harmony with the woman's voice, I could hear the chirping of tree frogs and crickets and birds. My mind grappled with all of these sensory details before it took another step back.

How'd I end up in the river?

Fear should've had me sneaking out a window and running far, far away, but a curious, inexplicable bliss forced me to throw the quilt aside and tiptoe toward the front door. I felt like a kid sneaking a peek at Santa Claus on Christmas Eve, all optimism and exhilaration.

I peeked through the nearest window and searched through cupped hands for my savior, but before my eyes could adjust to the moonlight, the woman's voice stopped. Then I smelled that familiar, comforting scent of pipe tobacco. Checking for my grandmother's apparition, I glanced over each shoulder.

If Grandma Seraphina has my back, it's all good.

The stranger on the porch called out, "You must be feeling better."

Shit.

"Well, c'mon out, *petite*. Let me look atcha."

What else could I do? I eased the door open and walked through. As my eyes adjusted to the starlight, I could see the outline of the woman sitting on a porch swing. We were on a quiet river bend, somewhere in the bayou it seemed. *Maybe I drank more than I thought.* I held my hand to my head, but there was no trace of a hangover. I still couldn't bring myself to believe that Jacques had harmed me intentionally, but I clearly remembered hitting the floor. *He just let me fall.*

"Come, *ma petite*," the woman said, patting the seat next to her.

Timidly, I walked nearer and she struck a match, momentarily illuminating her profile. The strange woman gazed at the water, puffed on her pipe a few times, and waved the match out.

Well, that explains the tobacco smell, I thought. *So not Grandma Seraphina after all.* My heart fell. As I inched toward the stranger, my mind puzzled, *Is this woman for real? Am I just passed out at Jacques' party and this is some kind of hallucination?* I observed the calm water and shuddered, thinking that, perhaps, the drowning part had been real.

The shadow woman spoke again. "I enjoy a smoke at night."

I inched toward the porch swing. Like a honeybee to a wildflower, my body gravitated toward her. So I sat. The woman continued to look out over the water. Neither of us spoke, and I searched the water, too.

Eventually I asked, "Where am I?" My voice felt small and unsure, the voice of a toddler.

"In-Between," she answered resolutely.

"Between where?"

She took another drag on her pipe before continuing. "*My* In-Between. My Other Side, *petite*."

"Other Side?" I tested the strange words on my tongue, but instead of panic, I still felt that strange surge of blissfulness. "But—" I couldn't finish my thought because it just didn't make sense. My brain was still computing, I was still breathing, my heart was still pumping. I turned to her, hoping for a better explanation for what was happening.

"You're neither living nor dead, child. You're in the In-Between."

"How?"

"Ever heard of a near-death experience? Well, *petite*, you're having one."

I lifted my hand to my neck, recalled the sharp pain and the syringe at Jacques' party, but there was nothing on my neck. No scab, no soreness, no blood.

"You do remember, then," the woman said gravely. "It was Jacques who tried to kill you. Your *anj* of death."

"Why?" I asked, still feeling incomprehensibly happy, despite being dead, but also utterly confused. "I thought he . . ." I whispered.

The woman replied, "He meant to shepherd you to the Other Side and—"

"Why?" A toddler's favorite question.

She ignored my question and puffed smoke into the air.

"So I'm not dead?" I clarified.

"Well look at that! A complete question. Now we're getting somewhere." The woman chuckled and took another drag on her pipe. "No. Not completely. Just in a coma."

"Coma," I said, finally taking a shock to the system. Astonished, I settled back into the swing. "But I feel fine. Wonderful, actually."

The strange woman's body shook with laughter.

"I guess this experience will snap you right out of that atheism, huh?" She turned to me, her face still obscured by the dark. "We all have our doubts."

Awe swept through me as I remembered Gabe's prophecy. *You won't make it, child, unless you reach for the hand that saves.*

"You're the hand that saves," I said, awestruck.

She chuckled again. "Gracious! I like the sound of that." She gazed at the water. "Now then," she said matter-of-factly, "we must use this opportunity to get you trained up as a Mind Changer."

"How—?"

"You never mind that." She reassured me, "You're safe here."

But I realized I *could* die and that would mean—

"Taj!" With his name on my lips, my consciousness flew across space and time, leaving the strange woman on her porch swing.

Chapter 27
Near Death

I was being yanked upward. Blasting through the sky. Past the moon and stars.

Then blackness.

Spinning through a prism of light. Love's warmth filled me.

Emptiness.

The warmth returned. Static electricity on my fingertips. A vortex of energy swallowed me.

Then nothingness.

Next an awareness of people. Seated around a hospital bed. I was in the bed.

Taj is there.

Taj.

Relief coursed through me.

Poppy looked up at me—*this* floating me, not the one in the bed. She wore a black cross smudged on her forehead.

Ash Wednesday, I realized.

Yanked upward again. Through the many floors of the hospital.

Into the black night.

Nothing.

Then I was sitting back on the porch swing with the strange woman. As I fully entered my body on the Other Side, my breath caught in my throat. On the journey back,

I'd picked up a load of emotions and they bubbled, like fizz, to the surface and I began to cry.

The woman shushed me and I melted into her mother-like arms.

"It'll be all right. Grandma Seraphina's here now."

Just as abruptly as I started, I stopped crying. I searched her face, making my eyes adjust to the dim light. She took a long drag on her pipe and the tobacco burned brightly, revealing my grandmother's face.

"It *is* you," I whispered, expecting the dream to evaporate if I spoke too loud.

"Mmm," she affirmed.

Exhausted from my excursion to the real world and back, I settled my head onto her shoulder. She leaned her head on mine.

"But you already knew that," she said and laid her corncob pipe on the armrest so she could brush her fingers through my hair. With each caress, the layers of emotional armor fell away. I wept and she talked softly to me in the sweet grandmother's voice that I'd always yearned for. "I'm here, *ma petite*." She patted my hand, where it rested between us, and enveloped mine in hers. We sat like that until my tears dried.

Eventually she picked up her pipe and lit it, leaning back and wrapping her free arm around me.

"You love him," she said. "This Taj." I nodded and snuggled into her. "We can use that." I looked up at her not understanding. She chuckled and kissed my head. "Marie always said I pushed too much." She squeezed me and said, "Cling to that love, Sophia. Use it. Love will power your spells." We rocked for a bit before she continued. "I've seen the two of you together. He can give you the love you need. Your mother and I could never get love right. We didn't love each other like we should've and we certainly didn't love the right men."

It dawned on me that I could get real answers about my mom. A question made an 'O' on my lips, but I couldn't quite decide which one to ask. There were so many that I wanted to ask them all at once.

"You must forgive her, *petite*," she stated simply.

I averted my eyes, because she'd struck right to the root of all of my problems. My mommy issues. From them stemmed a lifetime of fear, anger, and mistrust of others.

"Don't turn your back on love," Grandma Seraphina said. "I'm just giving you what you asked for." I searched her face. "Don't you remember? At my funeral, you lit a candle and asked to, 'find someone you were meant to love.' I believe those were your words. Well, I found him and you are just gonna what? Up and leave him? Move back to Saint Louis?" She clicked her tongue at me. "What are you afraid of, *ma petite*?"

I did what I did best when a conversation didn't suit me. I stonewalled.

"Don't you start that with me, girl. You're kin and you gonna let me in."

I took a deep breath. I was in some other dimension, for God's sake, so I didn't have to keep the walls up.

"You're right," I admitted.

"Course I'm right. Grandma Seraphina's always right."

The five-year-old afraid of the dark emerged and I admitted, "I'm scared... and now... I could die." I searched her face for an answer.

"You *will* wake up," she resolved. "But you have to decide if your love will live or die."

Just thinking about Taj brought a smile to my face. All the long talks we'd had during our time in the shop, all our adventures seeing the sights and eating the food of New Orleans. I missed him already. My smile faded when I realized how terrible I'd been to him at Night Creatures. Even if I was doing it to protect him.

"I don't know if I can love him the way he loves me," I whispered.

"You don't have to. Just let him love you."

I thought back to the day I'd learned the love potion from Poppy. I'd inspected the jar of oak leaf powder, smelled the earthy goodness of the oak leaf powder as soon as I'd opened the jar. That goodness had never left me. It would be forever linked with the love I had for Taj. He was the embodiment of strength and stability that the oak stood for in the spell.

She smoothed my hair with her hand, continuing, "You're a strong woman and you will make an extraordinary Mind Changer." My heart jumped. A tiny smile crept into the corners of my mouth. "We'll both learn from your mom's experience."

Grandma Seraphina hadn't said "failure" with regards to my mother's running away, and she didn't seem to view it that way. Instead, her tone was loving—understanding, even—and I wondered how things had ended with my mother and grandmother when they were still alive.

"I pushed too hard." Grandma nodded and took another drag on her pipe. "I'm taking responsibility for that."

"Why did she keep the truth from me?" I whispered. "Why did she keep *you* from me?"

"I haven't felt her on this plane, so I can't speak for her," she replied. "When it's time for your heart to understand, you'll know."

"I can't get the spell to work," I said simply.

"Two things I've noticed with you." She raised her pointer and middle fingers in a peace sign. "One. You have to forgive your mother."

I took a deep breath.

"She's not even alive anymore, *petite*, and you let her run every facet of your life. Non-forgiveness holds us back and keeps us from our true power."

"You're right," I said. And I meant it. I would've

never admitted that in the real world, but here, the truth just came right out.

"Of course I'm right." She nodded and a chuckle rumbled in her belly.

"And the second?" I asked.

"Fear is blocking you. Your fear of the dark specifically. That's a deep-seated one for many people. But to banish the shadows, you simply . . ." Grandma Seraphina struck a match. " . . . shine your light." She puffed on her pipe to spark a new wad of tobacco and then waved her hand to extinguish the match.

"But I'm not afraid here," I admitted.

"That's the light of truth shining in your heart. Look at this place." Grandma Seraphina waved at the stars and her eyes glittered in the moonlight. "People spend their lives afraid of the unknown, but just see how stunning the sky is at night. The darker it is, the more beautiful the stars." She pointed her pipe's stem to the sky. "Everyone wants to understand what's 'out there.'" She pointed the pipe at her heart. "But they'll ignore what's in here." She returned the pipe to her lips, the sparkling, fiery tobacco making her face glow as she puffed. She turned back to the water and rested her hand on mine. "That's enough for now, *petite*."

I knew she was right.

"Near-death can really wear a girl out," I quipped.

She laughed. "Why don't you go on up to bed." From the tone in her voice, I knew there was no arguing with Grandma Seraphina, and I was tired anyway, so I stood to go. "There's fresh sheets on the beds upstairs."

I leaned down to hug her and wondered if Heaven could get any better.

Chapter 28
Metamorphosis

The smell of sweet fried batter drifted up to the loft, where I slumbered underneath a cozy quilt. The sun streamed in through a tiny square window in each gable. I raised my hands above my head, stretching, yawning, smiling.

"So this is what it feels like to wake up at Grandma's house," I whispered to myself. Excitement bubbling up in me, I threw the quilt off and shimmied down the ladder into the warm glow of the kitchen.

"Beignets and coffee, *petite*?" Grandma Seraphina, *my* grandma, spoke over her shoulder as she scooped the angular donuts from a deep cast-iron pan.

"Community Coffee?" I asked, sniffing at the old-fashioned percolator on the stovetop.

"Is there any other kind? Get yourself some beignets there"—she pointed to a heaping plateful on the counter next to her—"The powdered sugar's on the table."

I grabbed a couple and sat down.

"It seems like we could be alive right now," I said through a mouthful of beignet. But I was well aware that we were both in Grandma's Heaven, and I had no idea when, or if, I would return to life. After polishing off both beignets, I took a sip of my coffee.

"Why does it feel so . . ." I shrugged and searched for the right word. " . . . normal?"

"This place supplies everything you need to create your personal Heaven." She laughed a little to herself. "In my past life I never liked cleaning up the kitchen. I just loved the cooking. So now I just leave my dishes in the sink and go about my business for the day. Magically, the kitchen cleans itself. Spick and span."

She slid a fresh beignet on my plate and I noticed the brilliant, though not entirely normal, sunrise outside the kitchen window. Unlike sunlight that made you squint, I could gaze directly into the sun, its rays sparkling with a rainbow of colors, and see that at its core was a tunnel swirling away and away.

"What's that?" I nodded out the window.

"All That Is," she said. "The place where all things come from and where all things go."

"Oh." I drew the word out, having no idea what she was talking about.

"It's our doorway," she simplified. "It leads me to you and you to me."

"Does it go away at night?"

She dropped the final bits of dough into the fryer and the oil popped.

"No," she said. "I'm just not ready to give up the habits of daily life yet; I want the sun to still rise and set. The All That Is always is. More coffee?"

"Yes, please."

She walked over to me, percolator in hand, and filled my cup before returning it to the stove. I loved how she was taking care of me.

"So what are we doing today?" I asked, an ear-to-ear grin of anticipation on my face.

She opened the cabinet next to the sink and grabbed a coffee can, setting it on the table in front of me with a dull thud.

"Start with understanding ritual," she said. "Ritual concentrates a conjure. You pair the power of the mind with the power of your heart. All the spiritual masters across space and time know this."

"Isn't it more important to follow the directions?" I asked. "I always thought the spells were like recipes." I blew on my coffee to cool it down.

"No, *petite*, that's what I'm telling you," Grandma Seraphina huffed. She studied the ceiling for a moment and took a deep breath. "Here," she said, snatching the coffee can from the table and I could see how my mom and her would've butted heads. A lot.

I raised my eyebrows and mouthed, "Oh-kay."

"Let me show you," she said sharply and then softened her tone. "Now, pay attention."

This was her in Heaven? Grandma must've been really tough in real life.

She grabbed a generous pinch of black grounds, leaned over, and began sprinkling them onto the floor tiles.

"Wha—?" I asked, but she put her palm up to stop me.

"Just," she said, impatience creeping into her voice.

I slumped back into my seat and crossed my arms on my chest. She ignored me, leaned forward, and continued her work. Sprinkling and sprinkling, she formed a picture. First, a cross with equal-length arms then, grabbing another handful of coffee, she drew small circles at each end of the cross' arms. Finally, she put little crosses in the center of each circle and within the four intersecting angles at the center of the main cross.

She sat back and spoke. "You can harness the universal energy using physical ingredients, like coffee or cornmeal or whatever you can sprinkle on the ground but it needs to be something that can be brushed away, so it doesn't open a permanent doorway to the Other Side." She took a sip of her own coffee.

"Oh!" I sat up because it struck me that I'd seen Poppy making one of these designs in the shop. "It's a verver." I tried out the word with the best Creole accent I could conjure.

Grandma Seraphina smiled and cooed, "Very good."

"Poppy told me it makes something like a three-dimensional hologram?"

She leaned over once more and carefully formed a perfect circle next to the image she just made.

"A simple circle," she said, "can provide protection against dark forces."

"Like a force field," I jeered, raising an eyebrow.

"Yeah, we just gonna ignore that healthy skepticism." She paused. "As soon as you leave the circle, you'll be unprotected, so it's a limited device. Still, it's useful in a pinch."

I pointed to her first drawing, the more elaborate one.

"What's this design?"

"It honors Papa Legba, the guardian between the worlds of the living and the dead."

I pointed to it. "So, if I make it back to the world of the living, I should use this to come back here and see you."

"You can come in your dreams, too, but your journey will be more predictable through a doorway." She put her hands on her knees and pushed herself up, grabbing a few items from a nearby cabinet. "You should do a couple of things to help you transition." She showed me a cigar first then conspiratorially held up a bottle of rum, uncapping it. "Papa Legba loves to have a good time, now, doesn't he? Here, take a few puffs on a cigar . . ." She lit the stogy with a match and demonstrated, waving smoke away from her face. "*His* favorite way to smoke, not mine." Shrugging, she said, "We all have our vices."

"Yep," I agreed, staring at the rum bottle and thinking of Mom.

Grandma handed the lit cigar to me and I puffed on it a couple of times, which started me hacking up a lung.

"Not a smoker, huh?" she asked.

Still coughing, I shook my head and placed the cigar on the ash tray, waving the smoke out of my face.

"A shot of rum," she said, pouring the clear liquid slowly into a shot glass. She held it out to me.

I stared, refusing to take it.

"You know that's what got me here in the first place," I reminded her.

She smiled.

"Jacques was just doing his job," she said kindly.

"What does that even mean?" I asked.

She shrugged off the question and offered the shot glass to me again.

"Oh, all right." I accepted the tiny glass and slammed it back, choking down the burning sensation.

"Now," Grandma instructed. "Place the lit cigar and rum bottle within the verver as an offering to Papa Legba." She set it at the center of the design. "When you step through the smoke, you'll walk through the doorway."

I began to feel lightheaded.

"Stand up with me, *petite*."

She helped me to my feet. The room spun. I held my hand to my head.

"It was just one shot," I remarked. "Why am I so dizzy?"

"It's the spirits. They go to your head sometimes." Grandma put an arm around my waist.

"What kind of rum was that?"

"Not *those* kind of spirits. The loa." Abruptly, she shouted out, "Saint Peter, Saint Peter, open up the door! I'm calling to you, come to me! Papa Legba, Papa Legba, open up the gate for me! On my way back, I shall thank you for this favor."

"Why Saint Peter?" I asked, guessing there was some kind of Catholic-voodoo connection. Asking a question made me feel like I had some control and was trying to stay sharp even though my head was getting all fuddled.

"They're both gatekeepers."

I nodded, making a mental note, but I didn't know that it would stick because my head was really swimming now. "Do you have—?"

"Here." Grandma Seraphina handed me a notebook and pen before I could even get the words out.

I jotted down the information, then placed my notes on the table.

"Now repeat after me, *ma petite*." She gripped my waist strongly, supporting me, as we repeated the invocation and a holographic image slowly rose from the ground. Framed in the flickering image I saw my comatose body. It was surreal to see my body in the land of the living, and yet, here I stood in the land of the dead. The hologram widened and I could see Poppy, Taj, and Father Malachi perched around my hospital bed.

"Taj," I whispered reflexively.

As soon as I spoke, all three figures turned their heads in my direction. They squinted in confusion, not seeing me. Then Poppy smiled knowingly and nodded to this invisible me.

"They can feel our presence right now, *petite*," Grandma spoke quietly. "We could enter the doorway right now, but only as spirits."

"That's how you were able to come to me?" I remembered the haunting in Grandma Seraphina's room my first night in New Orleans when she turned on all the lights. She nodded and then swiped the verver with her foot, smearing the design and the holographic image shrunk, instantly, disappearing into the ground.

"We mustn't leave inter-dimensional doorways open for too long, because dark forces can sneak through."

"But look at this place," I said, not believing anything dangerous could live in Grandma Seraphina's Heaven. "It's so beautiful and peaceful. There couldn't possibly be anything evil here."

"There are lower dimensions with unspeakable . . . things." The word 'things' soured her face, "A verver acts like a beacon. All sort of paranormal entities could descend to earth through one."

"Should I even make ververs then?"

She patted my cheek gently. "Sometimes it's necessary, *petite*. You just need to have a healthy respect for your power. When you open a doorway, be as quick as you can."

"You said I can just come to the Other Side in my dreams. So wouldn't that be better?"

"Dreaming doesn't follow our will, so use ververs when you need them. They're also good tools for remote viewing your mind-changing targets."

I must've looked really worried because she rubbed my arm.

"Don't worry, *petite*." She smiled broadly. "Sometimes you just have to let go and let God."

She pulled me into a hug and I laid my head on her shoulder. I knew I'd have to let go of my inner control freak, but it still made me uncomfortable. Even in Heaven.

"Poppy and Father Malachi dreamed that you told them 'Sophie is coming,'" I said.

"I did. You need family, sugar. You can't do everything yourself. Malachi can be your father. Poppy's your sister."

If they could take a leap of faith and trust in a dream, then I shouldn't just dismiss mine.

"You're right," I admitted.

"Of course I am. Grandma Seraphina's always right," she said, smiling broadly.

"What else?" I asked, eager to learn more secrets of the Mind Changer.

"Practice speaking to the Other Side, whether it's me, your mother, whoever's passed. The ancestors guide you, but only if you listen." She held her finger up. "Bad things happen to people when they don't listen to their hearts."

"Or ghosts," I added, remembering she'd whispered to me in the cemetery and in my bedroom. "If I could just get to the point where the voices didn't scare the hell out of me."

She laughed. "I know Poppy told you about the importance of honoring the ancestors, but our relationship with them is even more important, with the magic that we cast. When you pray to the ancestors, especially *our* family's long line of Mind Changers, you draw on the power of everyone who came before you. All of humanity. Everyone has a family if you honor the ancestors."

I smiled. If that was the case, I would never be alone.

"And for heaven's sake, wear my shawl! Don't just throw it on the floor like it's nothin'!"

I thought of my frantic packing on Mardi Gras and studied the floor, "Sorry."

"It can connect you to me." She sniffed. "Plus, New Orleans gets cold at night."

"Thank you." I leaned into her and thought to ask, "Why didn't my first two mind-changing attempts work?"

"Because they were your first two mind-changing attempts," she said and clicked her tongue. "You did very well, but your lack of faith would've spoiled the spell no matter how hard you tried. I will say again that if you do not *believe* that a true transformation is possible, then you cannot make it happen. Plus"—she raised her hand to emphasize—"having other people around confuses the energy." She scowled. "Poppy should never have gone with you. That was extremely dangerous. Never do that again."

"I didn't know," I said, raising my voice, irked that she was coming down so hard on me.

She took a deep breath and put her palm to her head. "I can't do this. Not like Marie." She looked at me with humble eyes, then down at the floor, toeing the coffee grounds.

"I *will* be better," she resolved, pressing her lips together.

I knew she meant it, but I also knew that her spunky nature would show itself again.

She raised her eyebrows and said, "Anyway, the first attempt was on Jacques and there's something . . ." She knitted her eyebrows together. " . . . off about him."

Just the thought of coming in contact with him again made me shudder.

"Will Jacques come for me again?" I asked.

"No."

"How do you know?"

"How does a fish know to stay in water?" She grabbed her pipe, lit some tobacco, and blew smoke into the air. "Jacques really isn't the terrible monster you think him to be," she said mysteriously. "Anyhow, without the monsters, there'd be no need to exercise courage."

"If I could just get the spell to work." I shook my fist dramatically in the air.

A deep laugh rumbled up from her belly.

"There you go. Get riled up, *petite*." She stood and said, "Now tell me about that young man we saw through the verver. Tell me about your Taj."

Grinning like a love-struck teen, I nodded, but my smile faded.

"I was really terrible to him the last time I saw him," I confided.

"Well, clearly he loves you, *petite*, or he wouldn't be holding vigil at your bedside."

"I want to be with him but it's impossible. Even if I do make it back to the real world, that doesn't mean he'll take me back. Then there's the whole problem that started this chain of events. My job intrinsically puts him in danger. It always will," I explained. I cleared my throat and fought back tears. This was the first time I'd gotten sad in Heaven.

"My goodness, *petite*." She petted my hair and said, "This *is* a strong love. It's nearly impossible to feel negative emotion in this place unless it's coming from a place of deep, deep love."

"I won't put him in danger," I said, gritting my teeth and swatting at a stray tear on my cheek.

She braided my hair loosely and said candidly, "He's a big boy. He can make his own choices."

"But there's no way that I can tell him what I do for a living. Ever."

"Nonsense. I told Malachi."

"I guess," I said, a tiny spark of hope igniting inside of me.

"When the time's right for *him* to know, *you'll* know. Don't slam the door on your destiny so easily. Put it in God's hands."

I clenched my jaw, still not knowing what to do. Maybe Grandma was right, and I could have both a purposeful life and the love of a lifetime.

She asked softly, "You want some more coffee?"

"No thanks," I said, biting my lip, trying to come up with a solution by myself because I didn't know how to "let go and let God."

After breakfast, Grandma led me outside. She left the counters messy, the sink piled with dishes, and the coffee grounds on the floor just like she said she could in her Heaven.

Crisp green grass crinkled under our toes, reminding me of how Mom loved to walk barefoot.

Which made me ask Grandma Seraphina, "If you could communicate with me so soon after you died, how come Mom hasn't tried to contact me?"

"Time doesn't exist here, *ma petite*. Hours, minutes, years, it's all the same. She must not be in the right place, metaphorically speaking."

"Have *you* seen her?" My eyes searched hers. "I guess I want to know she's okay."

She wrapped a stout arm around my shoulder.

"Not here, *ma petite*. I haven't seen her here."

We walked on. Grandma Seraphina's Heaven was on a river bend where twisted cypress trees lounged in the water, with knees bent to their chests and monarch butterflies in their green, leafy hair.

"Here we are," she said, with deep satisfaction in her voice.

Shaded by the cypress trees, were several tall, clear boxes stacked like bee hives amidst tall grasses and wildflowers. As we neared the boxes, I saw that they were filled with butterflies at different stages in their metamorphosis: hanging as a chrysalis, emerging from the cocoon, drying and opening wrinkled, new wings.

My eyes widened.

"Wow . . ." I dragged out the word, deeply feeling the wonder of my inner five-year-old surge up. Several Blue Morphos swirled playfully around my hair and I laughed, completely enchanted by the dancing butterflies. "This is wild."

Grandma smiled widely, pleased with my response.

"Remember the butterflies at my funeral?" She cocked her head to the side. "They were for you."

"For me?"

"For you." Grandma slid open a drawer of one of the clear hives and checked the chrysalides inside and then carefully slid the tray back into place. "To help you find what you needed most. Faith." She explained, "If you could see something like that, then maybe you could believe in that which you *cannot* see."

"They certainly caught my attention. They swarmed me."

"They swarmed you to show you that you were not in harmony with All That Is." She cooed to the butterflies, "Transforming so nicely, my little darlings." She turned her attention back to me. "Obviously you weren't paying attention because it took you this long to notice my messages." She put her hand on her hip and cocked her head to the side.

"Oh, boy. Here we go," I said under my breath.

"Lord, I tried everything." She ticked the items on her fingertips. "A plague of butterflies, footsteps, apparitions, turning your bedroom lights on. Nothing. You tried to explain it all away, *petite*. But *I* will not be explained away. Nothing in this dimension can." Her eyes shone. She busied herself with another drawer and confessed, "I was stupid, you know. When I was alive." She bowed her head. "Now I know why Marie left, why she stayed away." Reaching down into the tall grasses, Grandma plucked a plant with broad green leaves. "Milkweed."

"Why?" Even in a near-death experience, I didn't understand why Mom kept me from my grandmother and my birthright.

Grandma Seraphina began picking off the milkweed's leaves and made a pile on the top of a hive. Wherever she tore it, the plant oozed milk-white.

"Isn't it obvious?" She posed the question.

I racked my brain, but came up with nothing.

"She did it to protect you."

"Protect me?" I thought about the years of rage that I'd bottled up, but in this dimension, anger could not exist, so a deep desire to understand and forgive filled me.

"Marie always feared voodoo. She refused to learn. I'm sure she never told you about me because she knew if you became a Mind Changer, you'd be put in harm's way. It's just the nature of the job, *ma petite*." Seraphina shrugged and slid open a drawer of caterpillars.

"But there is a little monarch," she said, sprinkling in the milkweed leaves.

I tilted my head to the side as Grandma held her hand up and a monarch flew from a cypress branch above and landed on her knuckles. "Monarchs were always Marie's favorite."

I remembered the monarch butterfly that had been coming around me since I came to New Orleans.

"I think I've been seeing the same butterfly," I said, realizing that Mom could've been trying to help me—protect me from Jacques, even—this whole time.

"Have you?" she said, not sounding a bit surprised.

A tear came to my eye and the tiny monarch fluttered from Grandma Seraphina's hand to my shoulder. As it landed, I cupped my hand to my mouth, remembering that a monarch had perpetually fluttered at my window in Saint Louis, too. And I understood that, even when I thought I was all alone in the world, my mother had watched over me. The tear slid down my cheek.

Grandma Seraphina nodded.

"See the black outline?" She pointed to the butterfly's wings. "It's female. They have the darker veins, you see?"

"Yeah," I said.

"It makes a nicer contrast, I think." The monarch lifted, disappearing into the treetops. "Why don't you just relax while I finish up here?"

I settled onto the soft grass, leaned up against a tree, and felt grounded. The trees whispered above and I pulled a long piece of grass from the ground and nibbled its end, tasting its earthy freshness. Upriver, a flock of snowy white egrets rose and flew past the sun. Grandma Seraphina's Heaven subtly thrummed with a soft energy, pulsing softly, like the sound of a mother's heartbeat. The place lulled me as if I were a baby. I dissolved completely into the moment, piece by piece, into the stillness of my heart, where time and space were suspended, stretching into infinity. My eyes focused on nothing and I listened to the quiet longings of my heart.

The security of the place surrounded me and transported me to places that I'd shut away in a dysfunctional childhood. For all those years, I'd convinced myself that Mom was nothing but a drunk and a terrible parent. The walls protected my heart from her, but it also imprisoned me in a lie, the lie that was the constructed story of who *I* thought she was. I'd forgotten there were good times, too. Picnics at Forest Park, backyard water fights, impromptu dance parties around the living room, jumping on beds, bedtime stories, kisses on scraped knees, hugs and snuggles, hot chocolate and old movies on Saturday nights.

My heart welled with love for her, with pure happiness, when I remembered those things. I hadn't felt anything positive for Mom in such a long time. A smile brightened my face and I put my hand to my heart, cherishing her presence in my life. These positive feelings would have been impossible for me without this safe, otherworldly place. I closed my eyes and took a deep breath and then came the quiet reminder in my heart, *Love powers the spell. Love will protect you both. Believe!* The wind whispered around my hair and then stilled, leaving me only with the echo of its message. Love would protect Taj. I had to believe that.

"*Ma petite?*" Grandma Seraphina asked softly.

I blinked and looked around. She'd been tending the butterflies for I didn't know how long.

"Hmm?" I murmured, waking from my daydream.

"You're not in this dimension, are you?" She chuckled. "I was saying that you can become the most powerful Mind Changer."

I pulled my knees to my chest. "Easy for you to say. You were such a natural."

"I struggled. I was only human." She languidly reached up to the nearest tree branch and snapped off a dry twig. "Every human has doubts."

"You didn't," I said skeptically.

"I'm no saint." She nestled the tree branch into a different caterpillar drawer. "Even Jesus had doubts."

I plucked a blade of grass and slowly peeled it in half lengthwise.

"I just don't get it," I said, picking another blade of grass and doing the same thing. "I just can't make the spell work."

"Sweet Poppy is an excellent mambo, but only a Mind Changer can teach another Mind Changer. You'll be ready." Seraphina looked around, dusted her hands off, and said, "Finished here."

Wrapping my arms around myself, I felt transformed somehow—not perfect, because what was perfect anyway? I did, however, feel like the lifetime of psychological gunk I'd accumulated was wiped clean. That was when I realized I'd successfully performed the most important mind change of my life: my own.

I felt connected to my spirit and purpose. I understood that I could fulfill my paranormal purpose and still be Sophie, the human who makes mistakes. But more than anything else, my heart longed for Taj. I knew that I wanted to love him for the rest of my life. I gazed into the swirling, sparkling All That Is and knew I wanted to go home to him.

Chapter 29
The Wake

Something woke me and I automatically reached across the bed for Taj, finding only empty space.

"Sophie!" Someone shouted my name.

I sat upright in bed and listened until my ears rang. Moonlight streamed into the cabin's loft so that I could see that Grandma Seraphina wasn't in her bed.

"Sophie. . . home. . . now. . ."

I recognized Poppy's voice, cutting in and out, coming from somewhere outside. I jumped out of bed and ran over to the loft's window. Peeking out, I could see the All That Is dimmed for nighttime in Grandma Seraphina's universe.

"Sophie. . . don't. . . us! Wake. . . now!" Poppy's voice urged.

"Sophia!" Grandma Seraphina shouted from the kitchen below, and I peered down through the loft's ladder. She was in her nightgown with a shawl wrapped around her shoulders and her arms crossed. "You have to go." She waved me down. "Now, *petite*, now."

As I scurried down the ladder, she opened the cabin's front door and stepped onto the porch, raising her hands. She walked forward, arms outstretched, focusing on the All That Is.

I grabbed my shoes and followed.

She strode toward the dock, arms still raised, and curled her fingers, drawing her hands to her as if she were tugging a rope. The All That Is blazed brighter than I'd ever seen it, so much so that I shaded my eyes with my hand. The wind whipped up waves on the river, making it lap at its banks.

The current slowed and then, amazingly, changed direction, the powerful current fed into the All That Is at the horizon line. I knew that Grandma Seraphina willed it so.

I hopped on one foot, struggling with my shoe.

"No need for those, *ma petite*," she said sharply, her eyes focused on the All That Is.

Desperately, I searched the blazing ball of light to understand what was happening. I looked to Grandma Seraphina for an explanation.

Is she sad? I wondered. *Disappointed? Relieved I would live*? Because all of those emotions churned inside of me.

"Your door's closing," Grandma said, still gazing into the All That Is. "You're body will die, *petite*. If you don't go now."

The urgency hit me like a punch to the gut. I had to choose life, the life of a Mind Changer with all of its danger and complication, or death and stay here to be with my grandmother in Heaven where I'd finally have family and the love of a mother figure. My heart knew the right answer. I needed Taj. I'd go back, fulfill my destiny, complete a mind change, and this time failure wasn't an option. I lunged forward, hugging Grandma Seraphina tightly.

Two days, I thought. That's all I'd gotten with her. Just two days.

"I don't want to leave you," I said, clinging to her shawl, laying my head on her shoulder and fitting her embrace the way a grandchild should. "I may never see you again."

"I will always be here for you, *petite*. Always and in all ways." She squeezed me and I realized then that parting was just as hard for her as it was for me. "And don't forget that you've got family that's alive, too. Poppy would go to the ends of the earth for you."

I nodded because I knew she was right. Poppy had become my sister and I needed her. Tears ran down my cheek. The sudden rush of emotion let me know that my spirit was reconnecting with my body. Grandma took a step back from me, wrapping her shawl tightly around herself.

"You will change the world, *petite*." She held her hand up, like she hoped to pause this moment in time.

"I love you," I said.

"Love you more."

Turning away from her, I walked down the dock. When I reached the end, I curled my toes over the edge and peered into the deep, dark water. The current was so strong. My cells tried to run the old programming of uncertainty, hopelessness, and inadequacy, resisting the spiritual transformation I'd just undergone. Doubt crawled inside of me like thousands of tiny spiders.

I turned back and yelled, "What do I do?"

"Jump!" she shouted.

"You gotta be kidding me," I said to myself. Those waters had tried to drown me when I came to the Other Side and many, many times in my nightmares. Every particle of my being did not want to jump. The All That Is pulled harder and the wind whisked my hair into a frenzy. I held back my tresses in a ponytail at the nape of my neck, trying to gain the courage to just jump. But my inner cheerleader failed. I searched the opposite river bank for a way out. The cypress trees waved me on. My heart thumped in my chest.

"I can't," I gasped. Backing away from the edge, I turned around again to face Grandma.

"Sophia, you must go now!" she yelled through cupped hands.

Inching my way back out there again, I finally had my toes hanging off the very edge of the planks. I had no idea what lay beneath the calm surface, but I shivered as I remembered the goblin hands dragging me down before. I could still feel their greedy claws scraping my skin.

"Sophia!" Grandma's voice made my heart jump. "Go now, before it's too late! You cannot stay here any longer."

"This is crazy," I whispered, holding my nose. "I don't even know how to swim."

Self-doubt, that oh-so-familiar leech of a demon, crawled from the remote corners of my mind.

Now! my heart urged, my spirit holding the doubt at bay. Without another thought I turned my back to the water, held my arms out, and fell backward.

My body hit the water.

The river enveloped me.

I sank.

And waited for the greedy goblin hands.

But . . .

Nothing pulled me down.

Instead, the All That Is breathed holiness into the river. The water turned crystal clear, revealed a thriving stream with fish, plants, and even trees rooted deep into the riverbed. The All That Is showed me the flash of one of my earliest memories that I had forgotten long ago.

When I was about five or so, I'd gone to the local swimming pool with Mom. She looked happy, her face round with health and her skin glowing that beautiful warm shade that Grandma Seraphina had. Mom sported stylish sunglasses and a floppy hat. To me, she was the most beautiful woman in the world.

"Sophia," Mom cautioned. "Not too far."

While she sat at the edge, sunbathing, I crept closer and closer to the deep end, wanting to play with the big kids. As I inched toward the safety rope, the slope of the pool's bottom made the water rise and lap at my chin. On tippy toes, I closed my mouth until the water reached my upper lip. My foot slipped a little and water went up my nose, and, instead of keeping calm, I flailed and fought the water. If I would have just stood up, I would have been able to tiptoe back to safety. Instead, I panicked, and would have drowned. But then I was suddenly safe in my mother's arms.

"Sophia," Mom said reassuringly. I gripped her tightly, choking and sobbing. "Shhh," she whispered into my ear, "I told you not to go so far, you little daredevil."

When I calmed down, Mom held me at arm's length. At first, I clutched at her and panic set in.

"Sophia." Then she laughed and that got me laughing, too. "Calm down. I'm right here. I'll never let anything happen to you. Okay?"

She swirled us slowly around and I settled down.

"Now try kicking your feet. I've got you," she encouraged me.

I put my chin into the water and held on tight to Mom's safe arms and kicked. She turned circles again and I slowly loosened my grip. Eventually, I barely held onto her with the very tips of my tiny fingers.

"Hold your breath if the water comes up to your nose," she said.

Over the course of that summer, Mom taught me to swim. She watched over me until I could do it on my own. She supported me and we were happy. So happy.

"Don't struggle."

I heard Mom's voice again, this time in Grandma Seraphina's Heaven. A complete love and acceptance of myself, on a deep-soul level, regardless of the things that had occurred in my life, filled me. The waters of the All That Is enveloped me in their sacredness, provided me with the wellspring of positivity that I needed. Forgiveness swept through me.

My body remembered what it already knew. Just as Mom had taught me, I kicked my feet and palmed the water with cupped hands. Certainty filled me and I calmly leaned back and dipped my hair in the water, floating and then, playfully, doing the backstroke. My heart shone with faith. I'd beaten the dark and, at last, I was free.

"Sophia!" Grandma Seraphina shouted, hurrying along the bank to keep up with me. "Be who you're meant to be."

Filled with pure bliss, I kicked my legs and dipped my arms into and out of the mystical waters.

Grandma continued to tick off instructions. "Be strong, *ma petite*. Use your power for good. Let the magic guide you. Forgive! Love!"

I felt swept up in a benevolent force that led me directly toward the sparkling light of the All That Is. Bathed in the celestial glow, I could feel my spirit returning to earth and my senses deadened as I transitioned.

"*Ma petite!*" Grandma shouted from the embankment.

I treaded water.

"Yeah?" I yelled back.

Her face shone with pride.

"Now wake up!"

The dazzling colors of the Other Side went black. The smell of fresh air turned sterile. The soft wind blowing through the trees faded, as did the delicate splashes of my backstrokes. All sounds of the bayou disappeared: bull frogs stopped croaking; cicadas ceased buzzing; water no longer lapped at the grassy river bank. Everything faded to tinny, white noise that sounded like nothing at all.

On my return journey from the In-Between, my mind's eye saw the flash of a man's face. His brow set. An absence in his eyes made them bottomless black pits. I knew his darkness would be the first monster I would face after emerging from the light.

The man's features imprinted in my brain with its lined

forehead, downturned mouth, clenched jaw. Despite his inner darkness, burning candles surrounded his physical body. The image of him standing among the tiny lights didn't make sense at first, but then my mind's eye scanned the area, giving me a wider view, and I recognized the interior of Saint Louis Cathedral. People filled the pews and lined the walls. I focused on the four-foot-tall pillar candle that had just been lit in a special ceremony.

Easter Vigil, I realized.

I zeroed in on a woman with dark hair wearing a red trench coat—my coat, I realized—and I recognized myself stationed below the statue of Saint Joan of Arc. I was having a prophetic vision.

Suddenly, the me in the vision rushed out of the cathedral doors and into Jackson Square. The man with dark eyes followed me. My spirit eyes steadily watched him stalk me through the darkened streets of the French Quarter. With each passing block, he crept closer. I hesitated under a street light, illuminated.

He glanced over each shoulder and approached cautiously while I rifled through my purse.

He reached into his jacket pocket, moving closer and closer until he was right behind me.

Abruptly, I turned to face him before he could pull the gun. My move surprised him, but I remained completely calm. He pointed the pistol in my face as an afterthought. The man and I exchanged words as he continually pointed the weapon at me. He reached toward me with his other hand.

Suddenly, a shockwave of bright white light burst outward from us.

My premonition ended as abruptly as it had begun and, though I didn't get to see how it ended, I knew this was a revelation of my first real mind change.

The remaining traces of my spirit left the Other Side and the light of the All That Is dimmed, but I heard the echo of my grandmother singing "Amazing Grace." Her voice lulled me back into my body. Then other voices spoke. I didn't know if they were from the living or the dead. After a few moments, I finally recognized them.

Taj and Poppy.

A stranger said, "She probably won't wake up." He sighed. "Even if she did, there's no guarantee she'll have normal brain function."

"No," Taj and Poppy barked in unison.

"The medical expenses will become," the man grasped for the right words, "financially crippling. Do you—?"

"No!" Poppy interrupted, her voice hoarse.

The man cleared his throat and tried again. "Do you know if she has an advance directive?"

Now I could feel the familiar touch of Taj's palm on my left hand and a small, slender hand—I guessed Poppy's—on my right. Traces of tobacco smoke in the air let me know that Grandma Seraphina's spirit hovered around me.

Why can't I open my eyes? I wondered.

An annoying beeping inserted itself into my growing awareness. A short pause. Then another beep. I lay at a forty-five degree angle under crisp sheets that rubbed against my legs and feet. I willed myself to move. Grasp Taj's hand, sit up, scream, wiggle my toes. Anything. But I just couldn't.

"The answer's no," Poppy said with finality.

The stranger, my doctor I assumed, walked across the room and a moment later the door clicked shut.

"I'll continue the healing spells," Poppy told Taj. "The socyete can start a prayer chain."

Taj sniffed and let go of my hand and I could hear soft paper sliding out of a cardboard box at my bedside. He blew his nose and then the tissue fell with a crinkle against the trash bag by the side table.

Suddenly, I was all in.

I gasped, shot up straight in bed, and then slouched back from lack of muscle control. Poppy screamed and Taj yelled my name. I lay completely still for a few seconds, with my eyes closed.

Taj asked incredulously, "Is she awake? Is this some kind of reflex?"

I could feel his face inches from mine, but I couldn't get my eyes to open.

"Get the nurse," he ordered Poppy.

"You get the nurse," Poppy, her usual sassy self, replied. "I want to be here if she wakes up. Here." She leaned over my body and pushed the nurse button attached to my bed.

"Sophie," Taj said softly. He nuzzled my ear and whispered, "Woman."

Woman. Oh, how I'd missed hearing him call me that.

He said softly but urgently, "Wake up."

I want to. Hope swelled within me. I could feel each facial muscle click into place and I smiled, my eyes fluttering open. Then my eyes clamped shut against the glaring overhead lights.

"Turn off the lights," Taj ordered.

Poppy released my hand and rushed across the room to flip the switch.

"Sophie, we're here," Poppy said.

Taj's wonderful voice said, "I'm here. It's—it's Taj."

Cautiously, I opened one eye and then the other to see the silhouettes of Poppy and Taj, holding vigil at my bedside.

"Sophie, the nurse is coming." Poppy took my hand again in both of hers.

My eyes finally focused and I slowly turned my head to see Poppy's face. Happiness surged inside of me and she squeezed my hand excitedly. Then I slowly turned my head to look at Taj and my heart filled with love. He held my hand to his lips.

"I'm . . ." I tried to speak.

Alive, I couldn't say the word with my sandpaper throat. My entire being was filled with relief, though, that I'd actually made it back to my body in time.

"Water," I said. Despite the chain-smoker rasp, I felt completely energized after that crazy swim back from the afterlife.

Did I just do that? Oh, yes I did. I smiled again, my mouth feeling funny after not working for—*how long had I been out of body*?

Taj propped a pillow behind me and Poppy held a glass of water to my lips.

"Take your time," she said.

After a few sips, I sank back on the pillows.

"Sophie," Taj said. "We almost, we didn't know if . . ."

"You would wake up," Poppy finished his sentence.

"I know," I said hoarsely. "I heard."

Taj and Poppy both averted their eyes. It's uncomfortable to take someone else's life in your hands, but I knew they were on my side.

"It's okay," I said.

"That's pretty amazing that you could hear us," Poppy said excitedly.

"We didn't know how aware you were," Taj said.

Glancing down at my hand, I saw the IV stuck in my arm and I really, really, *really* wanted it out. But I couldn't move my arms yet. I huffed. My heart lurched in my chest as the old worrywart in me tried to settle in. Type-A Sophie ran through a quick list of the worst-case scenarios for my immediate and long-term future. Months—no, years—of therapy, pain, medication, paralysis? I fought the panic back, giving "Type-A Sophie" the evil eye, and she backed off.

That's right, sister. I'd been through too much to resume

a life of what-ifs. Fear couldn't have me. Ever again. I'd journeyed to the one place that people shouldn't return from, and even more miraculously, I'd shed all of the heavy emotional armor that I'd outfitted myself with during a dysfunctional childhood.

Gone, I thought and closed my eyes and laid my head back on the pillow. *All gone*. Relief surged through me and I felt light. Opening my eyes again, I looked up at Taj, my Indian knight in shining armor. Just drinking him in helped me return to that feeling of bliss I'd enjoyed on the Other Side.

He's the key to powering your spell, Grandma had said.

Taj reached for the nurse button and pressed it several times in rapid succession.

"Doesn't this thing work?" he asked, giving me a smile mixed with equal parts relief and concern. I knew that on the inside he was crazy with worry, but he was showing me his game face. "Don't worry. They're coming," he said, brushing my hair back from my eyes with his fingertips.

I wanted to kiss each and every one of those beautiful fingers. Wanted him to wrap his arms around me. I tried to wiggle my fingers. Still nothing. Frustration fizzed inside of me, and then a tiny monarch butterfly floated down from some mystical place and settled itself onto my hand.

"It's been in the room the entire time," Poppy told me, patting my shoulder.

"We tried to let it outside," Taj said. "But it keeps making its way back somehow."

I smiled. Mom was not only here for me now, but she'd been there to comfort Taj and Poppy as they faithfully waited for my return to life. That little butterfly, combined with the leap of faith that had gotten me back to my body in the first place, invigorated my spirit once more. Focusing my eyes on Taj's hand holding mine, I tried to move my fingers.

"Sophie?" He ran his fingers through my hair, but I maintained focus on our hands. He held his breath.

"Wha—?" Poppy asked.

Taj shushed her.

I concentrated with everything I had in me. After what seemed like an eternity, my pointer finger moved ever so slightly. Utter triumph filled me. I gasped and smiled.

"Sophie!" Poppy clapped her hands together, holding them in prayer position in front of her mouth, waiting to see what would happen next.

I moved my concentration to my arms and legs. Sweat dampened my hairline, but I lifted each arm and leg at least a centimeter off my bed. I wiggled my fingers and toes with less and less effort, until finally, my body listened completely to my brain's signals. I lifted my hands in front of me. It was like I was made new, seeing my hands for the first time. I touched my face and neck and arms, checking to see that I truly existed back on Earth. I held my fingers to my face, feeling my smiling cheeks.

The nurse strode into my room, flipping through a handful of paperwork.

"How can I help you, my dears?" she asked kindly, not bothering to look up from the chart she was reading.

"Hello," I chirped.

That got her attention. She promptly dropped her entire pile of papers on the floor.

"Sweet baby Jesus," she said, holding her hand to her mouth. She rushed toward the door and shouted over her shoulder, "You hold on right there, Sophie. I'll go get the doctor." She hurried out of the room, forgetting the paperwork scattered across the floor.

Awe filled me. I swung my legs over the edge of the bed, preparing to walk.

"Oh no you don't." Taj carefully lifted my feet back on the bed, lifted my hand to his lips, smiled with those devastatingly beautiful brown eyes. In an instant, the sensation from the love spell filled me. I felt limitless, all endless blue sky and vast sparkling ocean. Just like on that first day at the shop, I felt complete freedom, expansion, and timelessness, the feelings that only true love can give you.

I'm just giving you what you asked for, Grandma had said.

I searched Taj's eyes.

"Sophie," Taj said softly, "We didn't know—I—"

Tears gathered at his lashes, but he fought them back, averting his eyes. I held my hand to his face. My Taj, the man who brought me into the light, the one who taught me to love. I'd never seen him cry before. Hell, I'd never even seen him have a bad day. And even after I'd been a monster, pushing him away . . . hurting him . . . he stood vigil at my bedside not knowing if I would live or die. He had fought to keep me.

The door blasted open.

"Is she still coherent?" a doctor demanded and, upon seeing me, shouted to the two nurses following him, "Check her vitals! We need to make sure she remains stable."

The doctor concentrated on evaluating my condition, barely looking me in the eyes. I sat quietly, feeling my body surge with more and more energy with each heartbeat. He shined a light in each of my eyes.

"How do you feel, Sophie?" the doctor asked, his kind eyes finally finding mine.

I took it as a sign that he finally knew what I already knew. I was alive and 100 percent fine.

I nodded at him.

Taj started to help me sit up.

"I'm fine," I said, wanting to show the doctor that I could sit up unassisted. But the remark was just enough to wound Taj and he stepped back as if I'd just smacked him. I couldn't blame him. The last time we'd seen each other, I'd chosen Jacques over him, walked off—completely drunk—on Jacques' arm to some party. I'd turned my back on Taj. After what I'd done, I was determined to make things right between us.

The doctor put his stethoscope on my heart, asked me to breathe in and out, listened to my abdomen and back, too, then draped the tool around his neck.

"Sit on the edge of the bed here," the doctor said, pulling a reflex hammer from the pocket of his white coat.

I swung my legs over the side of the bed and sat up straight.

He tapped gently underneath my kneecap and my foot jumped. He asked me to bend and straighten my arms and legs, flex my hands and feet, wiggle my fingers and toes. All of which I could do with absolutely no problem.

"Very good," he said. "Let me check one more thing." He flipped through the papers in my chart and paused for a bit to read the top page.

"You are very lucky to have come out of your coma. Or whatever it was exactly."

"'Whatever it was?'" I asked.

"It wasn't a traditional coma. You could breathe on your own and you never needed a feeding tube or catheter. Nothing. You just couldn't wake up." The doctor patted my knee. "Like Sleeping Beauty." The doctor looked at Poppy and Taj before admitting to me, "We had nearly given up hope that you would come out of it."

He shook his head and chuckled.

"An Easter miracle," he said, throwing his hands up.

"Easter?" I asked, doing a quick mental calculation, realizing I'd been out of body since Mardi Gras. I bit my lower lip. *But it only felt like two days.*

"Tomorrow's Easter Sunday," the doctor confirmed.

Poppy interjected, "And now a miraculous resurrection."

I raised my eyebrow at Poppy, my lovely drama queen, but knew she was absolutely right. I'd cheated death.

"Some comatose patients never regain consciousness," the doctor said, sending a shiver down my spine. "Most that do, don't recover this quickly."

My body had lost forty days, but with each passing moment, it grew stronger. A hunger rose up inside of me, but not for food. I wanted a mind change. Bells at the cathedral tolled the hour and I glanced out the window, knowing the man from my premonition needed me. The sun sank and the pale outline of a full moon rose to replace it. I needed to get powdered up and head to the cathedral.

"Well . . ." The doctor rubbed his chin. "I'd like to keep you for twenty-four hours. For observation."

My eyes widened and caught him off guard.

"Don't have any plans, do you?" The doctor chuckled again and flipped my chart shut.

"Sounds good," I said, giving my best 'good patient' smile.

"Try and get some rest." He walked out of the room, with both nurses following and as the door closed behind them, I turned to Poppy.

"I have to get out of here," I whispered. "Like. Now."

"What?" Taj interjected. "No way. How could—? Poppy," he pleaded. "Tell her."

"I know how to do it," I encoded the message, hoping she would understand and Taj wouldn't ask questions.

Poppy remained silent, never taking her eyes off of mine, as if trying to assess the situation. I could tell that she was struggling to figure out the best course of action. Help me get out of here, or make sure I stay in a safe place to recover. I also understood that she couldn't talk about mind changing in front of Taj, so I spoke carefully.

"She taught me all I needed to know," I said cryptically.

"Okay," she conceded.

"Who told you what?" Taj asked cautiously. "What are you two talking about?"

I held Poppy's gaze, but could see Taj's dropped jaw in my peripheral vision.

Don't look, I steeled myself. *Focus, Sophie.*

"You better not," he warned. "Or I'm going to—I'll call the doctor and make him sedate you." He pointed at me and then at Poppy. "Both of you."

Neither of us replied.

"I have to do it," I said to Poppy. "To-night."

Taj put his hands to his temples. "Are you both crazy? Sophie is in no condition to be walking out of this hospital tonight."

I swallowed, pinching my eyes closed. What could I say to him to make him understand? Finally, I looked him in the eye.

"Taj," I said, "I can't tell you what's happening right now. You're just . . ." I balled my hands into fists. I wanted to tell him *everything*. About mind changing, about magic being real, about my time on the Other Side. I wanted him to forgive me. I wanted to tell him I loved him. I wanted my happily-ever-after.

Hope surged in my chest and I clung to my new belief that love could conquer all. We could work things out and I would be able to tell him who I really was. The feeling of weightlessness, that had rushed through me when I handled the love potion on my first day at the shop, surged through me again forming a tidal wave of optimism. That magic had been real. That spell had opened the door for Taj to step into my life.

He was *the one*. I'd envisioned him for the love spell. He would understand all of my secrets, the whole heaping hot mess of them. I sighed, knowing that unless I completed this mind change, there was not even a need to tell my secrets, because we couldn't be in a relationship. In order for us to be together, I needed to know that I had my full power. That I could protect him. In case Jacques came back. Or any other voodoo evildoers tried to hurt him.

"Taj," I appealed, putting my fist on my heart. "You're just going to have to trust me."

He wouldn't budge. He was trying to protect me and it made my heart swell that he cared for me so much. I had to try another approach.

"I feel fine," I told Taj, jumping out of bed and doing a goofy dance to demonstrate my health. "See."

Taj eyed the door.

While his head was still turned, I mouthed to Poppy, "Help! Me!"

"I'm! Thinking!" she mouthed back.

I pointed to an invisible watch on my wrist, then glanced out the window to see the sun dip below the tree line. If I didn't hurry, Easter Vigil would be over and I would miss my chance.

Taj threw his hands up. "I'm guessing this has something to do with the shop. But whatever it is, it can wait until you are well. Poppy and I have things under control. Even Avi and the boys have been helping out, so the business is covered for as long as it takes." He held my hand gently and looked deep into my eyes.

How could he completely unravel me with just one look? My intuition urged me, *Go now*! It was time. I was poised to do what I was born to do. *Only one thing will convince him*, I realized.

I grabbed Taj's hands in mine and kissed them. For a few moments, I searched my heart for the words that would make him understand.

"Taj," I began again. "I care for you. Deeply." I searched his eyes for understanding. "There have been things going on in my life that I haven't told you about and they caused me to . . . I hurt you." Tears collected at my lashes and I leaned forward, my voice becoming urgent. "I need you. Everything in me needs you. You may not understand it now, but I have to do this one thing. And if I don't do it tonight, I'll have to leave New Orleans. Forever." One chance. That was it. And if I didn't succeed, I'd lose everything.

His posture stiffened and he said sharply, "So you want me to put your life in danger by letting you leave the hospital?

What if you relapse?"

"I won't," I said, desperate to make him understand.

"You cannot know that."

"It's hard to explain . . ." I remembered the voice from the Other Side: *Love powers the spell. Love will protect you both.* "I just know," I said resolutely.

"You're not a superhero, Sophie," Taj said.

I closed my eyes and sighed at the irony of that statement. *Well, actually* . . . In a final gesture of faith, I stepped close to him, placing each of my hands on either side of his face. His five o' clock shadow felt rough on my fingers and it hit me that he'd been through so much as he waited for me to awaken. If I died mind changing, then Taj's heart would surely break.

Searching his eyes, I knew the magic words I needed to say. The magic words that would make him understand. The magic words that would give me the power to become the Mind Changer and be who I was destined to be.

"I love you," I said from the purest place in my heart. My eyes glanced down at his mouth and then back up into his soft eyes. We said nothing. And understood everything. My body moved naturally into his. My mouth found his. Our lips searched gently, tentatively at first, as if we were starting over. But very quickly, I felt Taj's strong and kind presence infiltrate my senses. The peace and humility at the very core of his being, the very qualities that gave me strength, meshed with the truth of me. Our kiss escalated. My passion fueled my desire to let him know that I needed him. I was completely his . . . across all space and time . . . stretching out to forever.

Poppy cleared her throat, bringing us back to the present moment.

We stopped kissing and I leaned my forehead against his. We both blushed and then giggled like two tweens.

God, this feels good. He feels good. I wanted to just stay with him and never even think again about being apart. But I had to go. Like Joan of Arc, I'd be the woman warrior, but unlike my patron saint, I could return from the battlefield to my gentle man's loving arms. He would be my sword and my shield, protecting my heart while at the same time fueling my spell.

"I need your help," I said to him.

He sighed and looked toward the door.

"Please, Taj. Help me stay," I said.

He exhaled and let his head drop back. Then he raised his head and his eyes burned into mine. He kissed me again.

"Crazy woman," he said, his lips hovering over mine.

Poppy hurried over to the door and peeked out.

"The nurses are changing shifts," Poppy said. "Put those on." She pointed to a pile of clothes on a chair.

I raised an eyebrow.

"What?" She shrugged. "I had a feeling you'd need them today."

I pulled the T-shirt over my head and slid into the jeans.

"Shoes?" I asked.

She grabbed my sneakers from the cabinet.

"We could always make a run for it." I snickered. "At least I think I can run." My body felt stronger with each passing moment. No pain. No weakness.

Taj checked the door as I tied my laces.

"The coast still clear?" I asked.

"Two nurses, but I'll create a diversion." He raised his eyebrows. "Bollywood style."

I hugged him one last time, burying my face into his neck. After a few moments of being in his arms, I gave him yet another longer than necessary kiss.

"I love you," he said.

"Love you too," I replied.

Then excitement spread across his face. "Here it goes," he said and then exited the room. He hurried over to the nurses' station where I heard the feigned panic in his voice, "She wanted to go for a walk and fell. Over here."

Peeking through the door, I saw both nurses hurry after Taj as he led them around the corner and on a wild goose chase.

Chapter 30
Easter Vigilant

"Well that was easy," I said as we hurried through the hospital's front door.

"Most coma patients don't usually try to escape," Poppy quipped, hailing a cab. "So what's the plan?" Poppy asked as the driver stepped on the gas and slung us back in our seats.

"No plan," I said.

"Well, there's no way you're going out without your mind-changing powder on." She cocked her head to the side and pulled on her sassy pants. "That's what got you dead in the first place."

"For your information, I was planning on wearing it." Since I'd seen the Other Side with my own eyes, I was the skeptic no more. "Tonight's going to be different," I assured her.

The conviction in my voice must've caught her off guard, because she stared down her nose at me.

"What changed your mind?" she asked.

"I did."

We spun through the apartment like two hurricanes. I grabbed my purse and dumped its contents on the bed then dug through my dresser and found one of Grandma Seraphina's sachets of mind-changing powder. It was the only thing I placed in my purse. Just like in my vision.

"Here," Poppy said, holding up a makeup brush and a compact of mind-changing powder.

I threw my coat off, along with my shirt and jeans. Sitting in nothing but my skivvies, Poppy powdered every bit of my skin. In the mirror, I could see that the mind-changing powder gave my skin an iridescent glow. Like a buzzing light bulb, I felt like I was the container for an enormous amount of energy.

"Ever since I came back from the dead . . ." I paused but reassured myself that if anyone understood, it would be Poppy.

"Mmm-hmm." She dusted between each finger.

"It's like my body has a new . . . intelligence . . . or something. It's like—It's like it knows what to do without me even trying."

Poppy didn't skip a beat and said matter-of-factly, "You carry the Mind Changer DNA going back, um, let's see"—she tapped her lip with the brush's handle—"Ten generations." She finished dusting my feet. "Of course your body knows what to do. Just let it."

Mind changing was a natural part of me, and now, I knew it would come out if I would just allow it.

"There," she said. "That should do it."

I stood and we both looked at my image in the mirror. My skin literally shone, emitting a sparkling aura like pictures I'd seen of Our Lady of Guadalupe.

"Wow," Poppy said, awestruck. "Never saw it do that before."

After a few moments, the shining dulled, which was fortunate because glowing in the dark would definitely be a problem. I didn't need to attract *that* much attention to myself.

The bells at the cathedral tolled.

"That's my cue." I shimmied back into my clothes and reached for Grandma Seraphina's shawl, but hesitated.

"What's wrong?" Poppy asked.

Remembering my premonition, I grabbed my red trench coat instead.

"This is the way it has to be," I said, slipping the coat over my shoulders.

"Bright red should definitely get your target's attention," Poppy quipped.

"Exactly." I would lure him in, let him think he was in charge, and then confront him. Just as it had been shown. "Okay," I said and hurried toward the door.

"Wait," Poppy said.

"I have to go," I said. "Or I'll miss my chance."

She grabbed my hands in hers, bowed her head, and quickly recited the Prayer to Saint Michael aloud. I bowed my head and joined in. When we finished, she pulled me into a quick hug and stood me back up straight.

"I still think it's too dangerous for you to go alone." She bit her lip. "Maybe Taj was right. What if you relapse?"

I shook my head.

"Seraphina told me I have to do this on my own," I said. "That's why it never worked before."

"Fine," Poppy conceded, handing me my can of pepper spray.

"I don't need it."

"You sure?" Poppy sounded genuinely surprised that I was going to give up my blessed pepper spray.

"The spell will work."

"Okay." She held up her hands.

I slung my purse, containing the sachet of mind-changing potion, over my shoulder. Then Poppy, like some fairy godmother, threw one more sprinkling of mind-changing powder over me.

"You be careful, girl," she told me. "Love you."

Stepping into the twilight, I tugged my coat collar up around my ears and shoved my hands into my pockets. Several blocks away, the cathedral's spire rose into a starless sky. My senses prickled with a new sensitivity, but instead of feeling fear, the way I would have before my sojourn to the Other Side, I felt stronger and better prepared to do my job. Up ahead, the sharp notes of a harmonica floated into my awareness and I saw Gabe sitting against a brick wall, rainbow suspenders and all. He stopped playing as I approached.

"He's coming for you, you know," he said, not looking up, the harmonica at his lips.

"I know," I said resolutely.

"Death," he clarified.

"I've already faced that."

A dark rumble, akin to laugher, issued from his throat. He finally raised his face from the harmonica and a triumphant smile spread across his face.

"You shall overcome," he said. "Go forth, *petite*," he whispered.

Considering that his blessing, I turned on my heel and pushed forward with sure and determined steps. For true love, I would face down death. Again. And again. And again.

The day of Grandma Seraphina's funeral I'd been a lost girl, fighting my way through a plague, but now I walked with certainty and peace. No bugs. No storm. The sun finally fell and light left the world. Tonight was the night I would reinvent myself in the dark. But instead of fearing it, I felt attuned to my surroundings. When I entered Jackson Square, I felt at home in the city's hustle and bustle, instead of disoriented and scared like I had been on my first day in New Orleans. The usual bunch of sinners and saints filled the area, including tourists, hawkers, pilgrims, and—

"Hey there, sweetie." Nico's familiar schmoozey voice seemed right on cue.

"Hey, Nico." I greeted him with an actual smile on my face. His reading had been almost completely wrong, but he had prophesied that I'd go to Malaysia one day. Who knew if Taj and I would visit his home country together. Maybe it had been a lucky guess, but Nico had pulled the Malaysia rabbit out of thin air.

"How about a reading on this fine evening?"

I shook my head and nodded to the cathedral.

"Just here for Mass," I said.

"You know where to find me," he said, shooting me the double finger gun and went back to his table, hawking his psychic wares as he went.

Well that was easy, I thought. *So far so good.*

As I neared the cathedral doors, a crowd gathered around the priest who was standing next to a small fire pit. Glancing in the direction of the river, I noticed an enormous bonfire on the opposite shore. The strange man with alligator boots had told me that was Madame LaLaurie, a ghost, living in the swamps a century after committing her terrible crimes. Maybe I'd have to deal with her evil one day. I shivered and focused on the task at hand.

"The Easter Vigil liturgy begins here . . ." The priest spoke loudly, with arms raised. " . . . outside of church, to mark the official start of Easter." He blessed and lit the four-foot-tall paschal candle.

I noticed a subtle prickling on the palms of my hands. As discreetly as I could, I examined them. Nothing.

A man lifted the lit candle and processed with a handful of servers and the priest. They marched down the center aisle, the church dark except for the paschal candle's light, and the rest of us filed in behind them.

While walking up the aisle, the man chanted, "*Lumen Christi*."

Light of Christ, I remembered from my Catholic upbringing.

The parishioners responded, "*Deo gratias*."

Thanks be to God.

The man processed a bit more, then stopped, and repeated the sacred words. The crowd responded in turn.

A swirling feeling enveloped my hands, as if I was washing them under warm water. I rubbed them together, trying to dispel the sensation, but they continued to heat up.

The man walked forward once more with the candle and chanted, "*Lumen Christi.*"

The crowd responded, "*Deo gratias.*"

Finally, the candle was placed at the altar, while the congregation passed around small taper candles. Then I remembered the many candles around my target in the premonition, and knew this was my moment, even though I still hadn't laid eyes on the man.

The priest said, "May the light of Christ, rising in glory, dispel the darkness of our hearts and minds."

The warmth in my hands increased nearly to the point of burning before it leveled out. I wiggled my fingers and squeezed my hands into fists, shaking them out a bit. Glancing down, I noticed the same soft glow, that we'd seen at the apartment, emanating from them.

Damn! I shoved my hands in my pockets and slipped to the back of the church. Facing the wall, I cupped my hands in front of me and saw them shimmering like pixie dust.

Oh, that's subtle, I thought.

There was no way I could hide illuminated skin from all of these people. A lady offered me a candle. I grinned. The woman nodded for me to take it.

"Go on," she whispered, smiling sweetly.

Smiling back, I momentarily thought of the panic that would ensue when she saw my Tinker Bell hands. I took a deep breath, looked up at the Joan of Arc statue, and was completely aware of the irony of this moment. Joan's visions ended in heresy and fire and now, here I was, following my own vision. Would I get burned too? Wincing a little, I reached out and took the candle from the woman. She steadied my hand with hers and, gently, touched her lit candle to mine.

Pointing to the paper drip protector around the candle, she whispered, "Not like the old days when you could get burned." She winked and turned her attention back to the service. Didn't even bat an eye. I glanced over each shoulder to see if anybody else noticed my glowing hands, but everyone was focused on the Mass.

Only I can see it, I realized. *Hmm. Why didn't Grandma tell me about that?*

I focused on what I needed to do. Find my target. The organ above me bellowed and people sang with candles held to their hearts. The lights of the world. Peace filled me and Gabe's message nudged me. *Go forth*!

The premonition had me leaving the church, so I handed my candle to a latecomer. Once outside, I walked toward Pirate's Alley and slowed to be sure the target was following me. A few seconds later, he emerged from the church, and when he noticed me, I hurried into the alley. With each step, an almost superhuman strength welled up inside of me. My legs felt a shock of electricity every time my feet hit the pavement. Before this night, I'd feared the dark, but no more. My heart pumped steadily. Resolve settled into my bones.

Though I was by myself, I knew I was not alone. Beneath the surface of my reality, existed other beings in other dimensions and I could feel them all around me. Ghosts, the loa, angels, demons, monsters for which I had no name. They orbited me, and even though I couldn't see them, they asserted themselves into my world, pushing into the thin veil between mine and theirs.

The man's hard-soled shoes struck sharply against the cobblestones and the *click-click* brought me back to the night at the LaLaurie mansion. Back then, Jacques' footsteps had made me panic.

But not tonight, I resolved. Vitality swept through me. The material of my red trench coat brushed against my bare arms, but I knew the powder had become one with me. A strange new instinct thrummed within me, catapulting me forward. The night air, cold and damp, crept into my clothes. My eyes adjusted to the dim light and I could see the sharp lines of buildings rising above on either side of me. I walked swiftly down a small side street.

Slow down. Let him catch up, my intuition urged.

Eventually I heard the *click-click* of his shoes again.

"Good," I said under my breath.

Rounding the corner and walking into a completely deserted street, I stopped beneath a streetlamp. The silvery light settled around my shoulders and fell to my toes, illuminating me completely.

"This is it," I said, knowing the location was exactly like in my vision.

Pretending to check my purse, I waited for the man to come closer. And, just like in my premonition, when he was within arm's reach, I would face him.

He snuck closer and since I couldn't hear his footfalls anymore, I had to feel out the situation.

Now, my intuition commanded. So I spun, catching him off guard.

"No!" I scolded like a teacher to a bully. "Stop!"

Eyes wide with fear, he pulled the gun too late to take me by surprise. He raised his chin and steadied the pistol, regaining his composure.

"Your purse," he grunted. He checked over each shoulder. "Now!"

"Yes," I said, my voice steady, but I made no move to give him the handbag.

"I'm not kidding, lady!" He accentuated his demand with the gun.

Slowly, ever so calmly, I held the purse out to my attacker. Then, a monarch butterfly flitted around me and landed on my outstretched hand.

"Open it!" the man commanded, thrusting the weapon in my face. "Slowly!"

As I slowly unzipped it, a fog began to gather at ground level. It reminded me of Madame LaLaurie's fire and the strange fog that had snaked its way toward me and that terrible man in the alligator boots. I knew I couldn't let fear take hold of me, so I opened myself more to the energy within. It surged and kept worry-prone Sophie at bay. I opened my handbag.

The mugger relaxed his stance a bit, seeing that there was no room for a weapon in it.

"What is that?" he asked after seeing that I had nothing but the sachet in my bag.

"This?" I held the sachet by its strings. "This can change your life."

"What is it? Drugs?"

Closing my eyes, I called on the ancestors like Grandma Seraphina had told me.

"What are you doing?" the man demanded. "Open your eyes!"

When I opened my eyes, ghosts surrounded us. They filled the road, lining the sidewalks and spilling into the side streets and alleyways, but the target was blind to it all. The fog retreated, moving toward the river, avoiding the greenish ghouls. A charge filled the air like lightning ready to strike. A hand settled on my shoulder and I sensed Grandma Seraphina's spirit.

She whispered into my ear, "When you pray to the ancestors, you draw on the power of everyone who came before you."

Breaking eye contact with my target, I peeked over my shoulder. There stood Grandma with her mother behind her and her mother's mother. Even a phantom projection of Margaret and Yolanda stood behind me. I remembered them working on a juju that day I delivered the package and knew that they'd used a verver to come to support me on this mind change, too. I looked at them, their images flickering like a tube TV going in and out, Margaret waved to me, and Yolanda nodded with puckered lips. The faces went on and on and on. I didn't recognize any of the others, but I knew they were my ancestors and probably angels or spirits working for good, too.

"Do it, *petite*," Grandma whispered.

Clarity of purpose buzzed inside of me. Still holding my purse in the air between us, I cried out, startling the man:

> "Butterfly wings mixed with bone dust
> Take these innocent lives we must.
> The sacrifice is great to evade harm's way.
> God change your mind from night to day."

The man grabbed my purse. Clutched it to his chest. Still pointing the firearm in my face. His arm began to shake. A gust of wind blasted through the street. I maintained eye contact with the target. Thousands upon thousands of phantom butterflies flew on the wind, sparkling phosphorescent green and shining like the sun.

"What the—?" the man yelled, swatting wildly at the air around him. He sensed the butterflies, but was blind to them.

The swarm surrounded me, too, but I was attuned to them. Protected by them, even. I focused on my love for Taj, saw his face in my mind's eye. The butterflies glowed brighter green. A bright light surrounded me; a fire that didn't burn.

The man began screaming, finally seeing. I continued to fuel the supernatural power with the love in my heart. He swatted at the bugs, his gun waving violently. I just had to trust in my vision that he wouldn't hurt me and this mind change would be a success. His screams saturated the air with fear, but the fear didn't touch me. A green-tinted aura swirled all around him. Engulfed him in loving power.

I repeated the spell.

He held the pistol out in the air between us. Shielded his eyes with his arm. Prepared to shoot.

My arm warmed from the inside out and my hand shook.

Now! the ancestors whispered in unison.

He pulled the trigger. Simultaneously, energy burst from my hand with the light of a thousand stars.

Time slowed. I moved quickly and easily while my target stood frozen in time. Glancing down, I saw the bullet suspended in front of my torso. My hand still pointed at the target, I stepped out of the bullet's trajectory. The purest white light poured from my heart. Down my arm. Into my hand. And struck the man in the chest. The same shimmering light filled his entire body and aura.

Success. I knew intuitively when the transformation was complete.

The ghosts offered hushed congratulations all around me.

"Wonderful!"

"Splendid, Sophia!"

"Well done!" they whispered.

The light slowly dimmed in my body, the remaining energy going out of my hand. But it still glowed brilliantly within the man. I lowered my arm, my heart full of pride, my body surprisingly energized. I felt whole and complete instead of depleted. The ghosts and butterflies spun around me, until I was standing in the center of a vortex. Grandma Seraphina stepped through the swirling phantoms and embraced me.

"I love you, *ma petite*," she said.

I wanted to hug her back, but she was no longer of this world. The phantoms spun into the sky. And, in a snap, they were gone. She was gone.

Time surged forward. My target and I were in the moment when he had pulled the trigger. The stray bullet finished its trajectory into a nearby brick wall.

The man shook his head, still pointing the gun where I had stood before. Then, as if for the first time, the man noticed the pistol in his hand. He pinched it between his thumb and forefinger like it was a piece of trash. Not even noticing I was watching him, he turned his nose up in disgust at the weapon and threw it into the nearest storm drain. He glanced around his feet at the sparkling jade haze that still lingered.

I took a deep breath, inhaling the freshness of the air, like a spring breeze had swept the place clean, leaving behind the very essence of newness.

The target scratched his head, started to leave and then, finally, noticed me standing there.

"Oh my God!" He started, clutching his chest. "I didn't see you there."

He was telling the truth. His new eyes had never seen me. Because before, his state of mind had clouded his judgment and wouldn't let him see anything but darkness, hatred, despair.

I held out my hand, the same hand that had just changed him, but he would never know.

"I'm Sophie."

He took it.

"Tom." His brow no longer weary. His eyes no longer bottomless pits. Tom was a clean slate and no longer a threat to me. He pointed to the general area where we stood and his eyes filled with the wonder of a child.

"You know," he said. "I'm not exactly sure how I got here . . ." He laughed, a natural joy welling up in him, "But I feel great."

"I'm glad," I said. Then I beamed at the fact that I was officially the Wonder Woman of voodoo.

"I haven't felt like this in a long, loooong time," he confided, and spread his arms to the sky, with an enthusiastic whoop. His joy filled me, too. He stopped suddenly and checked his watch.

"You shouldn't be out here, miss. Would you like me to walk you home?"

"Sure," I said.

I noticed there was no trace left of the lingering fog or the phantoms. *Boo yeah*. I stood tall, a proud and strong warrior woman.

"So tell me about yourself, Tom," I started a new conversation.

"Well," he said, "I've been having one hell of a year."

Chapter 31
Transforming Love

"So-phie," Tom welcomed me brightly when Taj and I stepped into Transformation Tattoos, Tom's shop on Bourbon Street.

"This is Taj," I said.

Taj stepped forward and shook Tom's hand.

"We come bearing gifts," I said.

Taj lifted a bag containing a muffaletta sandwich and a bottle of sparkling grape juice. No wine. Tom's drinking was one of the things we'd talked about when he walked me home the previous night.

"An Easter feast," he said. "You didn't have to do that."

"No problem," I said cheerfully.

Tom held his hand to his heart and bobbed his head, "Thank you." He took the food from Taj, who gave me a sideways glance wondering why this man with skull tattoo sleeves was being so sunny.

"It's not just the sandwich," I said as if that explained everything.

"I won't ask," Taj replied.

"Well this is it," Tom said proudly, setting the bag behind the counter. "My dream."

"Good location, here on Bourbon Street," I said. "For all those late night drunken bad ideas."

"We don't try to encourage those kinds of tattoos." Tom laughed. "Unfortunately, drunk people can be pretty insistent."

I nodded, remembering my bad behavior the night of Jacques' party.

"Well, I know what I want," I said. "I've been thinking about getting one for a long time, just haven't really had the right opportunity, I guess."

Taj pulled a picture from his back pocket of a monarch butterfly in flight that I'd printed off the Internet. He handed it to Tom.

"I want it right here," I said, pointing to the web of skin between my forefinger and thumb.

"Awe-some," Tom lilted. "And this one's on the house, Sophie."

I opened my mouth to object, but he raised a hand.

"I won't accept your money," he teased, but then his gaze turned serious. He stared at the floor and said, "If I hadn't met you last night . . ." He shook his head.

We both knew he could've ended up dead or in jail.

"Last night?" Taj asked.

"I had to go out and do that thing, remember?" I said, waving away the question. "And I bumped into Tom. He walked me home." I raised my eyebrows and smiled brightly, hoping Taj would accept that explanation.

"Woman," Taj said, examining me down the bridge of his nose.

"It's fine," I said, kissing him quickly before settling in the tattoo chair. I couldn't tell him about what happened, but he didn't say anything else, so he trusted me enough to let it go. *Thank. God.*

"Right or left hand?" Tom asked.

"Right." I wiggled my fingers in bibbidi-bobbidi-boo fashion. "It's my magic hand." Plus, I'd learned from Poppy that legitimate voodoo magic is practiced with the right hand. She'd pointed out that only black magic was performed left-handed.

"Why this one?" Tom asked as he sized it properly for my hand.

The butterfly tattoo would remind me of many things: to believe in the powerful and unknowable forces of the universe; that I had family on Earth and on the Other Side watching over me; and that I had true love in my life. I looked up at Taj and my heart leapt with joy because nothing stood in the way of our love anymore.

"Transformation," I said. "I've completely changed for the better."

While Tom meticulously traced the design onto my hand, I leaned over to watch him work and Taj's fingers found their way to the small of my back. Having Taj so close, just being there for me, felt so sexy. So right.

"This is forever," Taj reminded me.

"Yes it is," I said, confident that our love would last forever, too.

"You're sure?" Taj asked.

"Absolutely." Wrapping my free hand around his neck, I drew him down to my level and kissed him.

"All right," he said.

And I knew that, with him, everything would be all right.

Tom finished transferring the design on my skin and leaned in close, examining his work. He made a few small revisions and then looked at me.

"Okay?" Tom asked for my approval.

I squeezed Taj's hand for support and my heart beat hard. No more second-guessing myself. I knew what I wanted.

"It's perfect," I said, my hand shaking because it was really gonna hurt. I took a deep, quick breath to calm my nerves.

"You don't have to do this," Taj said, laughing.

"We could try another day," Tom suggested. "Really, it's totally cool."

You are a voodoo superhero, I steeled myself. *Act like one.*

Sitting up straight in the chair, I decided. "Do it. Final answer."

"Here we go," Tom said. He took my hand, like a sculptor holding new clay, and his relaxed persona calmed me.

Taj took my other hand and said, "You can squeeze as hard as you want."

The tattoo gun buzzed to life.

"This will feel like a constant bee sting," Tom warned.

I thought about the pistol last night and Tom's intention to harm me. He carefully positioned the tattoo gun, his tool for artistic expression.

Tom murmured, "Try to relax, okay?"

As he touched the implement to my skin, the hot sharpness of the needle carved the pattern into me. Out of the blank canvas of my hand, a monarch butterfly taking flight emerged.

Taj rubbed my other hand and I squeezed tight when the pain got really intense. He laughed nervously and wriggled his fingers. "You're very strong, woman." To distract me from the pain, Taj whispered into my ear, "It's your little voodoo butterfly."

Jacques' face flitted into my mind and I blushed when I thought that he was a part of the reason that I'd chosen this tattoo. He'd called me his voodoo butterfly. As frightening as he was, Jacques was a piece of the transformation I'd made since inheriting the shop and becoming a Mind Changer. Goosebumps ran up and down my entire body.

And he was still out there somewhere.

Without the monsters, there'd be no need to exercise courage, Grandma Seraphina had told me on the Other Side.

Taj leaned down and put his lips to my temple. He completely undid me with his kiss and I loved it. The endorphins finally kicked in and took the edge off the pain.

My voodoo butterfly would remind me of my mom because I knew now, after talking with Grandma Seraphina on the Other Side, that Mom had been with me many times after her death in the form of a monarch. And I felt a deep satisfaction that Mom's cigar box of cryptic items made sense now. The items helped keep Mom connected to her sense of purpose and her loved ones even though she didn't feel safe returning to New Orleans.

I admired Tom's skills and said, "This tattoo will remind me that all my ancestors are with me."

"Ancestor's, huh?" Tom said, rubbing my skin with a paper towel as blood seeped up from the black and orange patterns.

"It's important to the work I do," I said.

"Oh really, what's that?" Tom made eye contact.

"I own a shop here, too. Seraphina's House of Voodoo?"

Tom brightened. "I know that one. Cool." He sat up from his work for a moment and raised his eyebrows. "Know any spells?"

"Lots. Actually, we have some prosperity charms if you're interested," I said.

"Does that stuff actually work?" Tom asked skeptically.

And I totally got it. Up until I saw the Other Side with my own eyes, I'd been the doubting Thomas, too.

I glanced up at Taj, who tilted his head to the side waiting for my answer. Since I'd manifested him with my love spell, Taj was my most convincing evidence that magic worked.

"For believers, it works," I said with a conviction that surprised even me.

"Hmm." Tom sounded more optimistic, like he could at least accept the possibility. He sat back and eyed his work. "I think we're all done here, Sophie. What do you think?"

I held my hand in front of me and stretched my fingers long to admire the masterpiece. Taj nestled into my neck and kissed me in that spot, *oh yes*, that lovely spot that made my knees turn to gelatin.

"Do you like it?" Taj asked.

Since coming to New Orleans, I'd survived an otherworldly plague, escaped supernatural fog, survived death, and, oh yeah, gotten everything I ever wanted.

"It's perfect," I said.

Tom smoothed some ointment on the fresh tattoo and started to place gauze on top of it.

"Could I put that on later?" I asked. "I want to show it off first."

Taj and I stepped into the kitchen and the smell of comfort food greeted us.

"Happy Easter," Father Malachi said, slicing the ham.

"Smells delicious," Taj complimented.

"Mmm-hmm," I agreed and walked over to Poppy where she stirred beans and rice at the stove.

"Where you two been?" she asked, not looking up.

"Oh, nowhere," I said, flaunting my tattooed hand next to her head and wiggling my fingers to get her attention.

Poppy's eyes widened to the size of saucers and then she grabbed my hand to check it out. "No. Way!"

"Careful," I said. "It stings."

"You got it," Poppy said, her mouth agape. "I can't believe you got it."

"She was very brave," Taj said.

"Well now," Father Malachi said. "Let's see." He adjusted his glasses on his nose and held my hand at arm's length. "A monarch," he said, pleased, because he knew that was Mom's calling card.

Poppy gushed, "I love it! It's so you."

I beamed.

"Tom did it for me, actually," I said.

Poppy and Father both nodded, but didn't say a word.

Last night, after the mind change, Father Malachi and Poppy had met Tom when he delivered me to my doorstep. After he'd dropped me off, I'd explained his situation. Tom's business was going under, he'd had too much to drink last night and went out looking for a fight. But as he walked me home, he came up with a plan for getting himself and his business back on track.

Poppy crinkled her nose. "Did it hurt?"

"Just like a needle stabbing into my skin a million times a second."

"Eww," she said.

I knew her phobia with needles.

"You should get one," I teased.

Taj kissed my forehead. "Where are your gauze?"

"In my coat pocket."

As soon as he left the kitchen, Father Malachi whispered, "How is Tom feeling today?"

"Really good," I whispered back, wanting to do a crazy, celebratory dance across the kitchen floor, but I kept myself in check.

"The time was just right for your first mind change," Poppy chirped and added some okra to the gumbo.

"Seraphina would be proud of you, my dear," Father Malachi said. He cleared his throat and held onto the chair back for support, grief crossing his face. It was still difficult for him to say Grandma's name. I rubbed his shoulder and rested my hand there for a moment, before grabbing an apron from the pantry.

"Go relax, my dear," Father Malachi said, taking the apron from me. "I can help Poppy."

"Yeah, it's not like you didn't just wake up from a coma," she said sarcastically. "We got this."

"Go visit with Taj," Father said, shooing me out of the kitchen.

I reached out for Taj's hand and he wrapped his fingers in mine. We stepped out to the balcony overlooking Chartres Street.

"Give me your hand, woman," Taj said. Tenderly, he taped the gauze over my tattoo.

"Thanks," I said.

Taj slid his fingers through my long, brown hair and held the bright purple extension I'd borrowed from Poppy.

"What's this?" he asked.

"That's my wild streak," I teased. I shuffled out of the high heel shoes I'd borrowed from Poppy, too. "And I decided to get rid of all the clothes that Jacques has given me," I confessed. "I know who I am and it's not his dress-up doll."

Taj brushed my cheek with the back of his hand.

"I know who you are," he said.

Nodding, I noticed the soft notes of a harmonica drift up to the balcony from across the street. As soon as I spotted Gabriel, he stopped playing and raised a hand to wave. Even though he couldn't see me, I smiled. Behind Gabriel, a dark shape passed and the smile immediately left my face. The signature black clothes, especially the black wool coat on a sunny day, stood out against the crowds of people in Easter pastels. Jacques stared back at me, the edges of his mouth curling upward.

A bus zoomed in front of Jacques and Gabriel, blocking them from view. Then they were gone. Goosebumps skittered up my arms and the hair on the back of my neck bristled.

Taj stepped behind me and wrapped his arms around my waist, nuzzling into my neck.

"Love you, woman," he said, bringing me back to the moment.

I knew that I couldn't live in fear of Jacques. For better or worse, my messenger angel and my angel of death would be a part of my new supernatural life.

*And maybe...*The slightest flutter of hope tickled my rib cage. Now that I had a handle on my power, maybe I could change Jacques. If I was ever confronted by him again.

Even if I never saw him again, I had to trust that my power and my purpose would protect me and those I loved against the dark forces at work in our universe. Because the alternative—living a boring, unfulfilling life back in Missouri—would be far worse than this exciting, love-filled voodoo life.

I turned to face Taj and nuzzled his nose with mine. He kissed me, and I sighed in pure bliss.

"Time to eat, you two love birds," Krishna said, popping his head out the door.

"Hey!" Taj scolded Krishna.

Not missing a beat, I gave Taj another big PDA-worthy kiss and Krishna ducked back inside.

We followed to find Avi unwrapping tandoori chicken, vegetable korma, and naan.

"Let's pray," Poppy said as everyone stood around the table. We clasped our hands in front of us, while Poppy recited a simple prayer, "Thank you, God, for our food and our family and our friends." She looked at me with a conspiratorial arch of her eyebrow and said, "But especially for changing our minds for the better."

I sat down at the table and realized that, since coming to New Orleans, I'd unexpectedly fulfilled the most important to-do list. The one of my heart. There's no way that magic didn't exist because, in the enchanted city of New Orleans, I'd found everything.

Epilogue

Twilight settled into the city's bones as I walked through the quiet streets not knowing who or *what* I'd encounter. Stopping under a streetlight, I pulled my iPod from my pocket.

"Let's see," I said, vapor emerging from my lips with each word. I scrolled through my playlist, the diamond butterfly ring on my right hand catching the light. I kept the ring as a reminder of how close I had come to death, but the truth was, if Jacques hadn't sent me to the Other Side, I would have retreated to Saint Louis and my completely uninspired quarterlife crisis.

"Perfect," I said, pressing 'play' and sliding the iPod into my pocket. The sounds of a creaking door and a howling wolf filled my ears, followed by the rising music of Michael Jackson's "Thriller." The irony of my song choice made me giggle. Taj had downloaded the album for me and I closed my eyes for a moment to think of him. Immediately, my body filled with the warmth and confidence that I felt when I was around him.

"My Taj," I said with a huge grin on my face. My heart beat steadily. "Well, come on!" I called into the vacant street, striding forward, chin raised. Daring the dark. "Come out, come out, wherever you are," I said under my breath.

And they did. Dense otherworldly shadows crept around corners of buildings and perched on the shingled roofs. These were the dark creatures that infected human minds taking various forms like doubt, loneliness, despair.

But *I* could actually change the world. It was my life's purpose to do so. I advanced into the night, illuminated by my purpose. I called out to the shadow people, "I am a protector! I am a warrior! I am a Mind Changer!"

CPSIA information can be obtained
at www.ICGtesting.com
Printed in the USA
LVHW081205230620
658775LV00010B/570